THE
FIFTH
RING

MITCHELL GRAHAM

An Imprint of HarperCollinsPublishers

EOS
An Imprint of HarperCollins*Publishers*
10 East 53rd Street
New York, New York 10022-5299

Copyright © 2003 by Mitchell Graham
Cartography by Elizabeth M. Glover
ISBN: 0-06-050651-2
www.eosbooks.com

First Eos paperback printing: February 2003

Eos Trademark Reg. U.S. Pat. Off. And in Other Countries, Marca Registrada, Hecho en U.S.A.
HarperCollins® is a trademark of HarperCollins Publishers Inc.

Printed in the U.S.A.

10 9 8 7 6 5 4 3 2 1

For Jane, who is all my reasons

ACKNOWLEDGMENTS

It is often said that writing is a unitary profession. That may be so; however, the description falls far short of being accurate when it comes to publishing a novel. I have come to learn, as most writers inevitably do, that producing a book suitable for public consumption is nothing short of a collaborative effort on the part of many people. Some of them were eager volunteers and others grudgingly conscripted, but who, nevertheless, gave generously of their time and advice. Thus, with humility and gratitude, I wish to express my thanks to the following:

Jane Vernikoff Schlachter, Doug Gross, Devi Pillai, Diana Gill, Jason Schlachter, Christine Cohen, David Schlachter, Thomas E. Fuller, Dara Schlachter, Chris Hinkle, Steve Stone, Deborah Gross, Thomas Egner, and my wonderful agent and muse, Linn Prentis.

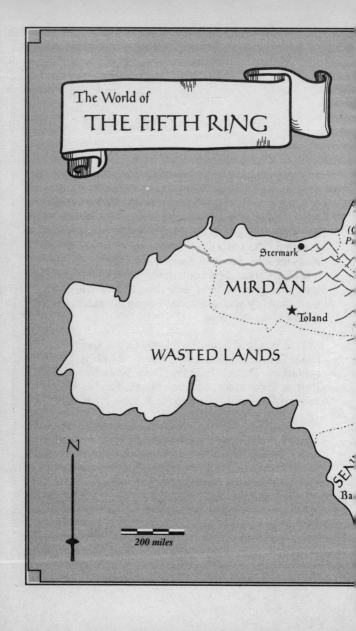

THE
FIFTH
RING

1

Alor Satar

KARAS DUREN STRODE DOWN THE HALLS OF HIS PALACE, passing servants and guards alike. The servants shrank back into the shadows, and the soldiers who lined the polished granite hallways kept their eyes straight ahead. If the king was in a bad mood, the less attention drawn to oneself, the better.

Duren moved with the energy of a much younger man, his body still hard and slender at the age of sixty. His hair was dark, almost black, and straight, with streaks of gray throughout, held at the back of his neck by a leather thong. He swept through a large rotunda, across a floor of white marble past the dusty portraits of his ancestors, then entered the new wing of his palace, still under construction after three years. A serving girl coming out of his wife's quarters was so surprised by the king's sudden appearance that she dropped the tray she was carrying. She immediately fell to her knees. Duren showed no reaction other than to turn a pair of dark, hooded eyes in her direction as he strode past. Two dour-faced soldiers stationed on either side of the entranceway snapped to attention when they saw him coming, smartly bringing their right arms across their chests in salute.

Duren descended a wide marble staircase to an elaborately tiled courtyard bordered by hedges more than twice the height of a man and so dense it was impossible to see through them. A squad of soldiers, one positioned every fifty feet around the perimeter of the garden, came to attention when they caught sight of him. At the far end of the courtyard, an opening cut into one of the hedges revealed two solid-looking wooden doors. They were recessed and easy to miss, unless one were looking straight at them. Without being asked, an officer with prominent angular features and a trim beard opened one of the doors and held it for the king. Duren stared at him for a second and gave the briefest of nods before walking through.

Beyond the doorway was a narrow corridor and a staircase lit by oil lamps. The stairs eventually led down to a much larger room, reinforced by numerous wooden beams and scaffolding. This was where the excavation had originally begun. At one end, a portion of the wall had been carefully removed to reveal a large octagonal column of clear crystal. The column rose from below the level of the floor and disappeared into the ceiling, eventually surfacing twenty feet aboveground, on the other side of the hedge. Initially, the crystal had been so covered with vines and earth that five men labored nearly a week to remove it all. Duren paused briefly, watching the spectrum of rainbow colors refracted by sunlight passing through it. They seemed to move with a life of their own on the opposite wall.

The stairs had been discovered shortly after construction for the new section of the palace had begun. Normally, the discovery of old ruins would not have elicited much excitement—such events had happened before. But this time there was something different. The master builder duly reported finding the staircase to the king, along with the fact that it was made of neither stone nor wood, but seemed to be constructed of a metal no one had ever seen before. Duren had immediately recognized the find's significance. Thirty workers then spent three months clearing away all the rubble and debris. For his part, Duren regretted having to kill them all. Good workmen were notoriously hard to find.

They found the first room shortly after the staircase. Empty, containing neither furniture nor any artifacts, the only interesting thing about it was the crystal, which was revealed when part of the west wall collapsed. Karas

Duren guessed that nobody had seen the place in more than three millennia.

Duren had found the second room, containing the remains of the old library, by accident. At first, most of the books with their archaic words made little sense to him, but little by little he began to decipher and understand them. They were written in the language of the Ancients.

Translating the texts was painstaking and laborious. Though much of the information and references were oblique, he learned, to his amazement, that men once flew in machines and could move from place to place by virtue of their thoughts alone—facts so staggering that they left him breathless.

Only a god can do such things, he thought.

The books told of the ancient war and the destruction that followed; of weapons that laid waste to whole areas of the planet. The weapons in particular fascinated him, and he was saddened to think such marvelous technology might be lost forever. But still . . . one never knew. A lot of books, for instance, *had* survived. But late one evening while wandering through a largely undamaged section of the main library, Duren came upon a startling example of the technology he'd been reading about when he entered a side room he'd not yet explored. As he did, the entire room was bathed in a brilliant white light. It was unlike any light he had ever seen before or that an oil lamp could produce.

Duren instantly dropped to a crouch and drew his knife. Not moving a muscle, he waited, watching the shadows in the corners for any sign of an attack. The dazzling lights went off and the minutes ticked by and nothing happened. Alone in the dark, he called out, challenging whoever was in the room with him to show themselves, but no one answered. He listened carefully and could detect no sound other than the passage of air through the strange grill-like vents high in the corners of the room. Eventually he relaxed and stood up. When he did, the white lights came on once more. Not startled this time, Duren identified the source as coming from a series of long glass tubes in the ceiling high above him. Another tentative experiment convinced him the tubes were some type of lamp, reacting to his presence.

Astounding, he concluded. *Simply astounding.*

More impressive still was the fact that anything three thousand years old could still be working. He wanted to share this miracle with someone else, but the risk was too great. *Light!* No burning torches or oil lamps. Brilliant white light—without the necessity of fire. The concept was incredible. His instincts told him that this discovery was for him alone.

Even more excited after this incident, Duren poured through volume after volume, insatiable for knowledge. Some books crumbled to dust the second he touched them, but thankfully, others survived intact.

The weeks passed, and he read and learned, spending virtually every waking hour in the library. Duren lost all track of time. His family worried about him, and there were whispers at court about what he might be doing for so many long hours in the room, but no one dared approach him, not even Octavia, his wife of thirty years. Guards were positioned outside, and no one other than himself was ever allowed in.

Duren came to learn that the Ancients could do many things with their minds alone. Traveling was just one of them. He raced to unlock their secrets, creating journals of notes in the process. If the Ancients were gods, he could be one too. This single thought occupied his every waking hour. He would create things with a mere wave of his hand, and nations would bow down before him. His enemies would prostrate themselves at his feet, for he alone in all the world would hold the power as he believed he was destined to do.

His mind eventually turned to his enemies, as it did frequently. Thirty years ago, the nations of the West had beaten him, thanks in large part to the failure of his Sibuyan allies to hold the flank during the final battle. *Cowards!* For thirty years they had penned him up within his own borders, but all that was about to change.

He decided that *they would be his first order of business*.

One night, while reading an ancient text, he came across an obscure reference to the crystals. Until then he had assumed the large crystal in the outer room was merely some form of decoration, or artwork—now he was not so sure. Most important, he learned that the crystals did not operate by themselves. They were activated by a special ring of rose gold, which enabled a wearer to link to them. At one time, according to the books, thousands of rings existed in the world. Each adult was given one when they reached their twentieth birthday. But then the Ancients began to destroy the very miracles they created—with the exception of eight special rings.

It made no sense at all.

Reference after reference talked about the eight. Convinced that rose gold still remained in the world, Duren sent agents far and wide in search of it and the rings, but they returned time and again empty-handed. The crystal remained dark, and Duren sank into black despair.

Over the next year, excavations continued with painstaking care on the outer courtyard. Various objects were recovered, most of which meant nothing to him. Some had been so damaged over time that no one could tell what they were. Then one afternoon, late in the day, when the shadows were long and the sun cast a reddish glow across the sky, a lone workman stumbled across a metal box buried deep in the ground and brought it to the king.

"My lord, this was found while we were digging by the fountain," the man said, holding out the box.

Duren looked up from the book he was reading, annoyed at the interruption.

"You said to bring you anything we found at once, my lord," the man prompted.

Duren looked at the box and then at the workman. "Have you looked inside?" he asked.

"Yes, my lord," the man said simply. "There are four metal rings of a strange color. The inside of the bands bear some kind of writing that I have never seen before."

Duren's hands started to shake, and he was forced to grip the table to keep it from showing. "Who else saw you recover this?"

"No one, sire. I swear it. Those were your instructions."

"You are sure?" Duren said quietly.

"No one," he repeated.

Duren got up from the desk, rising to his full height. Despite his age, he was still a tall, imposing figure, and it pleased him to have people look up when speaking to him.

"I do not tolerate deception in anyone who serves me," he said, bringing his face close to the workman's.

"Sire, I do not deceive you. I am speaking the truth. I swear it."

Duren searched the man's face, seeking some sign of disloyalty. Finding none, he relaxed, smiled, and put his arm around the man's shoulders.

"You have done well—very well. What is your name?"

"Roland, my lord."

"Yes . . . Roland, of course. Yours will be an honored name above all others." Duren's fingertips lightly touched the other man's face. "Yes . . . yes . . . an honest face . . . a loyal face. I know where loyalty is to be found, Roland. You know that, don't you?"

"Your people love you, my lord."

"I know," Duren replied absently, looking at the box.

He cupped the worker's face in both of his hands and stared intently into his eyes. Roland was at a complete loss as to what he was supposed to do, so he just stood there. Over the years, he had learned that where lords and ladies were concerned, the best thing was to say as little as possible.

"Yes, I can see it in you. You are an honest man—trusting and honest. Come with me, Roland."

Duren put his arm around the man's shoulders and led him over to the crystal.

"Have you any idea what this is?" he asked.

Roland shook his head.

"No . . . no . . . of course you don't." Duren chuckled under his breath. "This was the source of the Ancients' powers. They were like gods, Roland. They could do anything, using only their minds," he whispered in the man's ear.

Roland's eyes grew wider and he stared at the crystal in wonder.

"Do you have any idea what this box contains?" Duren asked.

"Rings, my lord?"

"They are the links to this very crystal," Duren explained patiently, as if speaking to a child. "Attend." Without hesitation, Duren opened the box and slipped a ring onto his finger. He closed his eyes for a moment, then fixed his attention on a chair standing nearby.

"Rise," he commanded.

The chair remained where it was.

"Rise," Duren repeated again, with greater force than before.

Roland looked at the chair expectantly, then looked at the floor, wishing with all his heart that he were someplace else at that particular moment.

In annoyance, Duren tried again, using the second and the third rings, with the same results. He was positive that he was correct. These rings *were* the links. They had to be. When he took the fourth ring from the box and placed it on his finger, his face had begun to darken. This imbecile had brought him trash, he thought. Perhaps he *wanted* him to look foolish. Anger began to seethe deep inside Duren's chest. He could see that the man was pretending to look at his feet, all the while laughing silently at him. Slowly, Karas Duren's hand crept toward the jeweled dagger in his belt.

What happened next didn't occur immediately, but an odd tingling sensation began emanating from the ring and coursed through his arm.

Duren's eyes widened in surprise.

The sudden explosion of the chair shocked them both. One minute it was there, and the next it was a pile of splinters. Roland's mouth fell open and he backed away, flattening himself against the wall. It took virtually all of

Duren's considerable willpower to regain his own composure. After a moment, when his breathing returned to normal, he ran his hands deliberately through his long hair and made an elaborate show of adjusting his black velvet cloak as if nothing out of the ordinary had occurred. Roland stood gaping as Duren casually flicked a few tiny pieces of wood from his sleeve. Though the king was exultant, he deliberately kept his face serene. There was still the problem of Roland.

He walked up to the frightened workman and placed both of his hands on the man's shoulders affectionately.

"Do not be afraid, my friend. You have served me well."

"Thank you, my lord," the man stammered. "May I go now?"

Duren blinked. "Go? How rude of me. You must accept my apologies. Of course, you may go."

Roland got as far as the stairway before a sharp, piercing pain caused him to gasp out loud. He reeled backward against the wall as the pain struck again, and tossed his head from side to side, trying to rid himself of it. Roland pressed his knuckles against his temples. After a second, his mouth opened to scream, but no sound came out.

Fascinated, Duren watched the man slowly sink to his knees, his eyes bulging. A trickle of blood began to flow from Roland's ears. When he saw the blood, Duren averted his eyes. Since the time when he was a young boy and his father cut animals open to show him what was inside, forcing him to watch, the sight of blood had never appealed to him. It brought back memories of childhood nightmares—fierce faces of the dead animals with angry red eyes and mutilated bodies glaring at him in the dark. Often he had woken up screaming as a child. Occasionally, the nightmares followed him into adulthood. In his own way, he tried to atone for the bloodletting by setting aside vast parklands as wildlife preserves all around the country. People scratched their heads in confusion at his actions, eventually attributing it to the vagaries of royalty.

When Duren did finally look back at Roland, he saw the man lying on the ground on his side, legs kicking wildly. Roland's hands opened and closed convulsively for a while, then his whole body stiffened and he was dead.

Later, carefully stepping across the body so as not to get any blood on his cloak, Duren sat down next to Roland and explained his future plans to him; why it had been necessary for him to die. He patted Roland on the chest like an old friend and whispered in the dead man's ear that he would of course have an appropriate arrangement of flowers sent to his wife.

When he was through talking, nearly two hours later, he sent for the morticians to make burial arrangements. The king's artisans, under his personal direction, built a small shrine in Roland's honor in the very room where he had died, and placed his head, now encased completely in silver, on a marble pedestal in front of it.

Duren thought Roland would be pleased.

Elgaria, Town of Devondale

FIVE HUNDRED MILES TO THE SOUTH, IN THE COUNTRY of Elgaria, Bran Lewin came to a halt where the forest road forked.

"All right, I'll see you at the church after I've delivered this cord of wood to Helen Stiles," he said to his son.

"Are you sure you won't need my help?" Mathew asked.

"Oh, I think we'll be able to manage. You need to get to town. You've got a big day ahead. Besides, Obert is generally there in the mornings to help Helen with the chores. I'll meet you at the square as soon as we're finished."

Bran and Mathew hugged briefly before separating; Bran proceeded down the left fork while Mathew took the right.

Mathew Lewin was a skinny-looking young man, only a few weeks shy of his seventeenth birthday, his adolescent proportions accentuated by thin legs and a pair of boots that seemed too large for the rest of his body. He was dressed more for the country than the town, wearing brown breeches and a sturdy woolen shirt. He started over the small bridge that led into Devondale and paused for a moment to watch his father before continuing.

The ancient wooden boards creaked under the weight of his boots as he crossed to the other side. The bridge had been there so long no one could remember who built it, or even when it was built. Beneath it, a rapidly running stream bubbled noisily over the rocks. Popular rumor went that more than five hundred years earlier, during the second Orlock War, a battle had been fought near the village. A neighbor had told him that both the bridge and stream were named for Martin Westry, the man who commanded the force that defended the town. The battle was a story passed down by word of mouth over subsequent generations, and no one really knew for certain whether it was even true.

At the end of the bridge Mathew turned left and broke into a jog along the dirt path that would eventually widen and become Devondale's main street.

It was a cool, pleasant day in late winter, and the first signs of spring were beginning to appear. The branches of many trees already contained tiny buds, and with the exception of a few scattered clouds, the sky above was a sharp blue. The morning air had a fine crisp feel, rich with the scent of pine needles covering the ground.

That morning, Mathew's mind was on other things, specifically the conversation he'd just had with his father and the fact that he was already late for the warm-up practice Father Thomas wanted to hold before the fencing tournament that afternoon. After listening to Mathew ask him for months and months, Bran had finally given in and agreed it was time for Mathew to have a sword of his own. He could hardly believe his ears when his father casually brought the subject up as they walked toward town. Now, so buoyant were his spirits, and so preoccupied was he with how he was going to fence that day, that he completely failed to notice the two dark-robed figures who stepped out of the trees directly in front of him. Their sudden appearance was such a surprise that he took two steps back, nearly falling.

Both men were dressed like Cincar traders, the cowls of their robes pulled down low so it was impossible to get a good look at their faces. Mathew swallowed and took a deep breath, trying to get his heartbeat to return to normal.

"Your pardon, young man. We didn't mean to startle you," the taller of the two men said. "We're looking for the South Road and a merchant named Harol Longworth. We were told he would be coming this way."

"Harol?" Mathew replied. "We just passed him about fifteen minutes ago."

He tilted his head to the side to get a better look at the man's face, and the stranger turned his head away.

"This is the South Road then?" his companion asked.

"Yes."

"We thank you for your help," the first man said. "Please don't let us detain you further."

Strangers were a common enough occurrence during Spring Week, when the population of Devondale swelled to nearly three times its normal size. The man's voice, however, sounded more mocking than grateful as he and his friend stepped aside to allow Mathew to pass. For no reason Mathew could name just then, a vague feeling of discomfort began in the pit of his stomach, which increased as he walked by the strangers. He could almost feel their eyes watching him. Out of caution more than anything else, Mathew moved his cloak slightly to one side with his elbow as he passed, giving him better access to his belt dagger.

Nothing happened, other than encountering the smell of a strong cologne as he passed. Mathew put about fifty feet between himself and the strangers before turning to look over his shoulder, and was surprised to find they were already gone. He frowned and searched the shadows, but saw nothing. After a few more seconds he shook his head, chiding himself for having an overactive imagination, and resumed his jog along the path.

Whatever misgivings Mathew had were all but forgotten by the time he reached the town square in the center of Devondale proper. The square contained several large old shade trees and a few wooden benches, as well as a white, octagonal-shaped gazebo with a wooden shingle roof and latticework around its base. Two separate paths ran from one side of it to the other, and a walkway framed the entire perimeter. It was one of his favorite places.

Mathew abruptly slowed down to a walk, self-conscious about drawing unnecessary attention to himself. Had he not done so, someone would certainly have stopped him to ask what his hurry was. That was Devondale. Everybody knew everybody.

The town council always took special pride in keeping the grass in the square neat and trim, and some of the local women took it upon themselves to see that flowers were planted around the base of the trees in spring and autumn. Since it was still a little early in the year, the beds were all bare, except for a few green sprouts that had begun to push their way up through the soil. Sunlight filtered through the branches of the trees, making a spiderweb of shadows on the ground. At the far end of the square an elderly white-haired man was busy with a saw, trimming the lower branches of a maple tree. They both saw each other and waved at the same time.

Mathew noticed the colorful banners hung across the street in preparation for the Spring Week Festival. The festival always promised to be exciting; though to him, it had seemed to grow a little less so in recent years.

Spring Week in Werth Province was a time everyone looked forward to. There would be jugglers, fireworks, contests, and dancing. Harol and the other merchants would set up stands to show the latest goods from their travels.

It might be a good idea to get a new pair of boots, Mathew thought.

Although his present ones were well broken in and had good wear left, they *were* getting a little snug. And his father had commented over dinner a few weeks ago that he thought Mathew had grown another inch or two. For his part, Mathew didn't feel any different. But he decided, somewhat pragmatically, it was just as well his feet were keeping pace with the rest of his body.

The first gentle sounds of a flute and violin reached him before he got to the end of the square. Unfortunately, since Mathew was effectively tone deaf, the music was just so much noise to him, and after seventeen years he had no need to see who was playing. Though he could distinguish a violin from a flute as having a thinner sound, that was about the extent of it. Sometime before old Father Haloran died, the priest and his mother had made a number of abortive attempts to increase Mathew's appreciation for music. Ultimately, he suggested that Mathew direct his efforts toward the study of math.

Every Sixth Day, Akin and his brother Fergus, silversmiths by trade, sat in front of the council building under the old oak, playing for anyone who cared to listen. They had been doing that for as long as Mathew could remember, and to his mind it wouldn't be a Sixth Day afternoon without them. Privately he suspected that even if no one were to show up, the brothers would probably continue to play to an empty square.

Devondale itself wasn't a large place, and he knew just about everyone who lived there, so it came as a surprise to see three soldiers walking down the street just ahead of him, wearing the dark brown cloaks of Lord Kraelin's men. Of course, Mathew had seen soldiers before, but their presence *was* a bit unusual. The town was not exactly in the center of the realm.

With his long legs, Mathew quickly caught up to them and nodded respectfully when they glanced in his direction. The leader, a plain-faced man with somewhat high cheekbones, wore an officer's silver leaf insignia on his left breast. He eyed Mathew briefly and returned a curt nod before resuming his conversation. The word "Orlocks" caught his ear as he walked by, almost causing him to miss a step.

Orlocks? Why in the world are they talking about Orlocks? he thought.

Before he could give the matter any further consideration, he heard his name called from across the street. "Ho, Mat."

A sandy-haired boy emerged from the doorway of Margaret Grimly's cloth shop and trotted over to join him. Mathew's face broke into a smile as they shook hands. Collin and he had been best friends since they were children. Also seventeen, Collin was just above middle height, and though shorter than Mathew, was broader in the chest and shoulders. His eyes were a warm brown that always seemed to carry a hint of mischief in them, and for reasons Mathew was at a loss to explain, most of the girls in town seemed to find it attractive.

"What were you doing in there—buying a dress?" Mathew joked.

Collin shrugged. "Margaret needed help unloading some new bolts of cloth, and my dad volunteered me for the job."

"What's the matter with Albert?"

His friend looked around to make sure no one was watching and mimed a small drinking motion with his hand.

"Really?"

"Albert's a good man and all, but my dad and I had to help him home twice last week," Collin said.

"Twice? What did Margaret say?"

"Nothing you'd want to hear," Collin said, keeping his voice down.

Mathew shook his head sadly.

"Hey, did you know there are soldiers in town?" Collin asked.

"Just passed them," Mathew said, indicating with his head.

Collin began to turn out of reflex.

"Stop that," Mathew hissed.

"Huh? Why?"

"Because they'll see you."

"So? Who cares if they see me? I'm not breaking any law."

"Neither am I. I just think it's better if we keep to ourselves." Mathew by nature was an observer with a precise eye for detail. He also tended to be a good deal more cautious than his friend.

Collin shrugged and turned back. "What do you think they're doing here, Mat?" he asked. "Nobody ever comes to Devondale."

"There's trouble at the border again," Mathew said. "My father and I met Harol Longworth on the way in and he told us about it."

Suddenly full of interest, Collin asked, "What sort of trouble?"

"Fighting."

"Fighting? Who's fighting?"

"Soldiers from Alor Satar and Kraelin's troops. Harol said he was in Sturga and heard the news there."

Collin let out a low whistle. "Duren again, huh? Do you think we'll go to war with them?"

"I don't know. I certainly hope not. From what he said, it sounded more like a skirmish, but even that can't be good. By the way, weren't we supposed to meet Daniel here? Where is he?"

"He went ahead with Lara and Carly after I had to stay and help Margaret," Collin replied. "We're both late now."

At the mention of Carly Coombs, the corners of Mathew's mouth turned down. It wasn't that Carly was a bad sort, just annoying to be around. He stood too close to you when he spoke, and he tended to rattle on and on about the most senseless things. Or at least they seemed senseless to Mathew. In truth, he'd always felt a little guilty about avoiding Carly, and once even tried to include him in their circle of friends, but nearly everyone agreed that Carly was too irritating to take for any extended period of time. Mathew supposed that he couldn't help being irritating. His parents were much the same way—they got right in your face when they talked.

Maybe his children will turn out normal, Mathew mused.

Like many of the other young men in town, Carly regularly showed up for Father Thomas's fencing classes. Unfortunately, Carly never improved much. Year after year he did the same thing, and year after year he fell for the same tactics. He had a tendency to overreact with his chest parry, swinging his blade far too wide to the outside of his body, which left a small area of his flank exposed just below his sword arm. Virtually everyone in the province who fenced eventually picked up on his weakness. After parrying the attack, they would cut back under Carly's blade and hit him on the hipbone. It absolutely drove him to distraction, and he would stomp off the fencing strip when the bout was over, his face beet red, complaining about what a "lucky shot" it was.

Once, during a competition with a team from a neighboring town, after Carly's third loss in a row, Mathew's friend Daniel pulled Carly aside and tried to tell him what he was doing wrong. The information just seemed to pass over his head. Completely oblivious, Carly replied, "I can't believe he got in a touch like that. Did you ever see such luck?" Daniel had rolled his eyes and went to get a drink of water.

By the time the boys caught sight of the little gray church, Mathew had rehearsed at least five different scenarios regarding the tournament in his mind and his pulse was beating more quickly. For the past month he had been able to think of little else, and his stomach was turning now that the time was approaching.

At one time the church had been a light brown or tan, but the passing years now rendered the stones a dull gray. A stained-glass window, the pride of the congregation, had recently been added above the double doors. Just to the right of the church was Father Thomas's rectory, and on the other side there were two more houses and the beginning of the North Loop Road, which led away from Devondale toward Gravenhage.

"Uh-oh," Collin said, "I think church is over."

Mathew muttered a curse under his breath when he saw people filing out. He hated disappointing Father Thomas. Not that the priest would say anything, but you'd know it all the same. Both boys picked up their pace. Fortunately, a few people were still standing around in groups chatting, as was the custom after Sixth Day services.

While he was trying to think of what to say to Father

Thomas, a movement well back in the trees caught his attention. Mathew frowned and stopped, staring at the woods to get a better look.

"What are you doing, Mat? We're late for the practice already," Collin said.

"I . . . thought I saw something moving in the trees by Silas Alman's house."

"Where?"

"Over there to the left," Mathew replied, pointing.

"I don't see anything," Collin said. "What was it?"

"I'm not sure . . . something. . . ."

"It's probably just Silas. It is his house. C'mon," Collin said, pulling Mathew by the elbow.

"Maybe you're right."

"Hey . . . are you sure you're okay?"

"I'm fine," he replied, shaking his head. "The competition probably has me a little on edge, that's all."

"Just relax, Mat. You'll do swell."

Mathew started to say something, but abruptly stopped when something white moved in the woods again.

Maybe Collin's right, he thought. *It probably is Silas*.

Still staring at the woods, he continued walking toward the church.

3

City of Sturga, on the Elgarian border

WITH THE POSSIBLE EXCEPTION OF QUINTON SOAMES, most of the people who lived in northern Elgaria were preoccupied with the violent storm that had broken over their country. Soames was a thin, slightly built man in his mid-fifties, with a large Adam's apple and quick, nervous hands. Depending upon the circumstances, his occupation tended to vary between soldier and thief. Tonight he was the latter.

Two full days of lashing rain and wind had slowly died down about an hour earlier as the storm moved out to sea. Since then the temperature had dropped, resulting in a gray fog that floated wraithlike through the town. From the window of the home he'd just broken into, Soames cautiously moved the curtain back an inch or two and peered into the street. Fortunately for him, whoever lived in the house was away. He wiped the perspiration from his face, took a deep breath, and waited for his heart rate to return to normal. He had just run almost ten blocks.

A few more seconds one way or the other, he thought. The important thing was that he was safe and there was nothing to indicate that he was being followed.

Directly across the street from the house, a row of shops were shut down for the evening. Soames peered suspiciously at the shadows in the doorways, his nose twitching speculatively. He waited another three minutes until he was satisfied, then slipped quietly out the front door. Given the late hour, it was not surprising the street was deserted.

All the decent citizens are probably in bed, he thought.

Out of long practice, Soames kept close to the buildings as he walked toward the harbor.

Not too fast and not too slow, he told himself. *Just one of the locals out for the evening.*

The night air was cool and damp, filled with a watery haze that was getting thicker by the minute. Diffuse yellow light from street lamps spilled onto the wet bricks beneath them. He could almost taste the salt in the air from the ocean.

Soames smiled to himself and fingered the gold in his coin purse as he walked. He was a lucky man. If the merchants were willing to pay good money for the artifacts he'd been smuggling out of the palace ruins, it made no difference to him whether they were from Elgaria, Alor Satar, or Sennia. Money was money. After three months of successful pilfering, no one was any the wiser.

At least until tonight.

Soames knew that bringing a third party into the scheme would increase his risk, but it couldn't be avoided. When the king had heightened security around the excavations, he needed help to get the job done.

Wilson's loose tongue had almost gotten them both killed earlier. Neither of them had seen the ambush until it was too late.

Stupid, he thought, *just plain stupid*. With two arrows in his chest, Wilson was probably dead. He'd warned the fool to keep his mouth shut. *Well . . . too bad for Wilson.* Due to some quick thinking, he had managed to get away clean before he was identified. Certainly whoever had tried to kill him was still out there, but they were probably blocks away now. *The fools.* He would just have to lay low for a while, till things calmed down.

Every once in a while he checked back over his shoulder for any sign of pursuit, all the while keeping well back into the shadows. With a little more luck, he would make the fifteen-mile ride back and slip into the palace unnoticed. It was wonderful.

Sturga was an old city—one of the oldest in the North Country. Once an active commercial center, it had the misfortune of being located directly on the border between Elgaria and Alor Satar. When the war concluded, the city had been virtually divided down the middle by the two nations, and was now governed by two separate counsels, each with its own mayor. Its streets were narrow, twisting, and uneven, worn down from centuries of use. Though most of the homes he passed were neat and tidy with wood shingle roofs, he noticed that a few had the new red tiles that were becoming so popular over the last few years. Most of the homes were made predominantly of either brick or gray stone. Some had heavy wooden beams set in faded yellow plaster, parts of which had fallen away over the years, revealing the foundation material underneath. It would be a perfectly pleasant neighborhood when the sun was out, Soames decided. Just the kind he would live in one day.

Quinton Soames was a trusted officer in Karas Duren's personal bodyguard. He had been a soldier ever since he was twenty years old, and it was all he really knew, except for thieving. When construction on the new palace wing in nearby Rocoi began almost a year earlier and the ruins were discovered, he was the one they entrusted the task of cataloging the artifacts. Most of it was junk, of course—combs, brushes, pieces of glass, and some pots. Still, if people were willing to part with good money for that kind of rubbish, who was he to argue? A few of the pieces were even valuable, like the odd ring he sold earlier that evening for six gold crowns.

Must have been its color, he decided.

They had also found parts of old machines the Ancients might have used at one time or another. But no one at the palace had any idea what they did. Whatever the machines were, it was obvious the king had an interest in them—an obsessive interest, in Soames's opinion. Rumors had been flying around the palace for weeks about what Karas Duren was doing day after day in the ancient library they unearthed. And there were other rumors too. Terrifying rumors that Duren was dealing with Orlocks.

Soames gave an involuntary shudder and checked over his shoulder again. After being gone for almost thirty years, the talk was, the Orlocks had suddenly reappeared. Even seasoned veterans who had fought alongside them in the last war would only speak about the creatures in whispers. To make matters worse, they were said to be cannibals. Soames had seen them once, many years before, during the Battle of Ritiba, with their pasty white skin and disheveled yellow hair. He had no desire ever to see them again. What the Orlocks had done to the people there still made his skin crawl. Every so often the images would return to his mind or find their way into his dreams. If the rumors were true, the king had to be out of his mind to even consider dealing with the creatures, and Duren was no fool. In fact—

Soames froze as a boot scraped against the cobblestones behind him. He quickly backed into a darkened doorway, his hand going to the hilt of his sword. He kept very still and listened.

A minute passed, then another. Try as he might, he could hear nothing save the sound of his own breathing. Vapor from his breath drifted into the chill night air. Nothing moved on the street, but then, the fog made it difficult to see.

Just as well, he thought, *because it will hide me too.*

While he waited, a scrawny cat wandered out of an alley. They looked at each other for a moment before the cat turned and silently padded down the block, disappearing into the fog.

Soames shook his head. *This town is beginning to get to me.*

He let out a breath and stepped out of the doorway. The marketplace was no more than five blocks away, along with the stables where his horse was waiting for him.

Before he reached the end of the block, he heard the

faint scuffling sounds again, only now they seemed to come from both sides of the street.

Soames forgot about appearances and began walking more rapidly, his own boots sounding unnaturally loud as they struck the pavement. After fifty feet he stopped and spun around. There was whispering behind him. His heart pounded harder and sweat beaded on his forehead despite the temperature. He swallowed hard and broke into a trot.

He heard the noise again when he turned the corner—more scuffling and whispers, but much closer than before. At the end of the street, across a wide square, he could see the shops and stalls of the market.

Quinton Soames started running.

The stables were at the opposite end of the quay, alongside the harbor. At that moment he would have been happy to see anyone, no matter who they were, but given the time of night, he knew it was unlikely. Childhood fears of monsters and demons began to nip at the corners of his consciousness as the fog closed in around him.

Something moved in a shop window to his left. A moment later there was another movement on the opposite side of the street, and for a split second Soames could have sworn he saw an iridescent pair of eyes looking at him from shadows. He stopped so abruptly he almost fell on the wet cobblestones, then regained his balance and veered sharply down a side street. His heart was beating so fast now it almost hurt.

The street wound its way past old houses with tiny courtyards and eventually turned back onto the main thoroughfare. Fifty yards in front of him he could see the faded green shutters of the stableman's house.

His luck was still holding.

Moving quickly from doorway to doorway, Soames paused long enough at each to make certain he had shaken off the pursuers. He stopped in front of the stableman's house and glanced through the windows.

No lights on. So far, so good.

He plucked the dagger from his belt and, with deft fingers, quickly slipped the latch on the door and went in.

It took a full minute for his breathing to return to normal as his eyes adjusted to the dark. He was in a kitchen. A copper kettle sat on the stove, and a small table with two chairs stood in the far corner of the room. The limestone floor wouldn't creak when he walked on it. In the center of the room was a solid-looking butcher block table with a bowl of peaches on it. Soames absently picked one up and took a bite, then wandered over to the window and looked out. He congratulated himself on eluding the patrol once again, but their persistence was becoming annoying. He was far too clever for their clumsy efforts.

Once he was certain they were gone, he'd let himself out, get to his horse, and be back at the palace before the guard changed. For the first time in several minutes Soames let himself relax and examined his surroundings. Even in the dark he could tell it was a pleasant little room. Exactly the kind he was going to have one day. He fingered his gold coins lovingly and thought about what it would be like—away from the army, away from the king with his unpredictable moods. Just a quiet, peaceful life—

Soames never got the chance to complete his thought. The kitchen window burst open, showering him with glass, and a powerful arm gripped him around the throat and lifted him off his feet, pulling him backward. Soames fought wildly, trying to break the grip. Panic seized him and his legs kicked out. He tried reaching his dagger, but as soon as he did, his arms were also pinned. In the struggle, his coin purse broke loose and the gold crowns clattered out onto the floor. The arms that held him were immensely strong, almost completely white, and hairless. The grip around his throat never slackened, and soon his struggles grew weaker. Terror took hold as he fought to remain conscious, still trying to pry the arm loose from his throat.

Through a haze of pain he watched the kitchen door slowly open. There was just enough light from a nearby street lamp to see by. He tried to scream, but there wasn't enough air left in his lungs to do so.

A slender figure wrapped in a gray cloak stepped into the room. Like the creature holding him, its skin was parchment white and disheveled yellow hair hung down almost to its shoulders. The Orlock glanced around the room for a moment without speaking, then slowly walked up to him.

"The ring," it said, holding out its hand.

"What?" Soames gasped.

"I don't wish to ask again, human."

Soames's ferretlike eyes narrowed as his mind raced to find a way out of the situation. "I don't know what you're talking about. I just came to town to visit a friend and maybe have a drink or two. That's all. If Duren finds out you've attacked one of his officers, you're going to be in deep trouble."

The Orlock stared at him without blinking for a moment, then glanced at his companion, who was holding Soames.

"We know about the last ring that was found this morning, and we know you took it. You've been stealing artifacts from the palace and reselling them here in Sturga for several months now. Since you're an officer, I'll assume you possess some degree of intelligence. So, let us make a deal. Hand over the ring to us and we'll tell Lord Duren you escaped. You can keep the rest of your plunder and your life. I assure you it's a far better bargain than Karas Duren would extend.

Soames shuddered at the thought, but his eyes again narrowed shrewdly. "Why so interested in the ring?" he asked.

"We're not—Duren is."

"Then we're both out of luck," Soames said. "I sold it to an Elgarian merchant named Harol Longworth. By now he's already on his way to Devondale for their Spring Festival. But he's coming back in three days. I can get it for you then. I swear."

The Orlock looked at Soames for several seconds, then

reached out and took him by the chin, turning his head one way and then the other. Very slowly the creature leaned forward and brought its lips close to Soames's ear.

"What a pity," it whispered.

In the month that followed Roland's death, Karas Duren learned more about the rings. While he came to increase his abilities significantly, he also found the results were not always predictable. Sometimes things exploded, melted, or just disappeared without his intending them to do so, which proved very annoying.

Try as he might, he was never able to learn why the Ancients wanted to destroy the very things that gave them virtually unlimited power. Such incongruities baffled him. Certainly an exercise in poor judgment, he concluded. In the end only eight rings remained. He possessed four of them, which left four others unaccounted for. One was stolen earlier, leaving three loose in the world. Duren had instructed his agents to redouble their efforts to recover them. This was the subject of today's meeting. The two men with him were his sons, Armand and Eric.

After the soldier closed the door behind them, Duren raised his hand, and the lamps around the room blazed, revealing a large manlike creature in the corner. Its skin was pasty white, and disheveled strands of yellow-white hair hung down just past a pair of slender shoulders. Its face was large and misshapen, with a flat nose and wide nostrils. Both of his sons immediately drew their weapons, but Duren restrained them, reaching out to place a gentle hand on each of their arms.

"It's quite all right, Hrang is a friend. I am so grateful you came," he said to the Orlock. As Duren spoke, a large chair scraped across the room to him, and he sat down. Armand and Eric glanced at each other. The Orlock displayed no reaction.

Ever so slowly, Duren's sons released the grips on their weapons. Only then did the Orlock appear to relax, lowering the axe he was carrying. His black eyes, however, continued to move between all three of them, watching and alert. The creature was dressed in black from head to foot and wore a hardened leather jerkin designed more as a piece of armor than for comfort.

"Have you found what we spoke of?" Duren asked.

"We found it, Duren," it replied in a low tone of voice, not much louder than a whisper.

Armand, the older of Duren's sons, started to react when the Orlock failed to use his father's title, but Duren shook his head, unfazed.

"Excellent," he said. "Give it to me."

The Orlock hesitated before continuing. "We were too late. The ring was sold to a human, an Elgarian merchant, by one of your *ex-soldiers* shortly before we got there."

"Ex-soldier?" Armand asked.

The Orlock laughed once to himself, but didn't respond to the question.

A small tic appeared under Duren's left eye, and he seemed to be containing himself only with effort. "You disappoint me. I do not like to be disappointed," he said, emphasizing each word.

The creature immediately backed up against the wall, putting his hands to his throat, and began to gasp for air.

The tic under Duren's eye became more pronounced.

Confused, his sons looked from their father to the Orlock and then back again. Duren watched impassively as the creature went to its knees, choking. Seconds passed before he released it.

"I want those rings—*all of them.* Do you understand me, Hrang? Nothing else matters—nothing. Plans have been made. Events set in motion that cannot be stopped. I would not like to be disappointed again."

The Orlock, whose expression was unreadable, nodded, rose slowly and started walking toward the darkened library. When he got to the door, he stopped, looked at each of the three men in turn, laughed again under his breath, and was gone.

Armand was a big man with large hands, broad shoulders, and a full beard. He was dressed in the same black and silver uniform as his soldiers. As soon as the Orlock disappeared, he spun around on his father and snapped, "Have you lost your mind?"

Duren raised his eyebrows and considered his son's question. "I don't think so," he said eventually.

"But, Father, Orlocks?" Eric said. "This is insanity. What have we to do with Orlocks?"

"What has anyone to do with Orlocks for that matter?" Armand added.

Eric was shorter than his brother and considerably less wide, closer in physique to his father. Sharp features and intense brown eyes immediately gave the impression of intelligence. Unlike Armand, he was dressed in green and black silks. Where his elder sibling was blunt in manner and speech, Eric was far more reserved and polished. Though he lacked Armand's physical prowess in battle, he was acknowledged by both of them to be the superior tactician.

Duren regarded each of his sons, a faint smile playing on his lips. "One world, one rule," he said eventually.

The message was clear at once. They had seen the very same words carved at the base of their great-grandfather's statue in the palace rotunda almost every day of their lives. Large, forbidding, and possessed of an uncanny ability to discern the weakness of his enemies, Oridan had nearly achieved his goal on two different occasions. Almost single-handedly he had carved the nation of Alor Satar out of the bloody succession wars nearly 160 years before, to become the most powerful and feared country in the eastern world. Oridan's goal became his son's, and though less successful than his father, Gabrel Duren had managed to nearly double the size of Alor Satar in the fifty-three years he ruled. Gabrel was their grandfather.

Eric had not yet reached his ninth birthday when his father's campaign against the West had collapsed, thanks in large part to the weaknesses of their allies. He remembered the events in vivid detail. Armand and he had spoken of it to each other on numerous occasions, reviewing the things that went wrong. Their father never did.

"How will this time be any different, Father?" Eric asked.

Duren walked across the room and stood next to the odd crystal column rising out of the floor. His fingers ran lightly over the smooth surface almost like a caress, barely touching it.

While he did so, his eyes became distant and unfocused, but he spoke not a word. Armand and Eric looked at each other, puzzled by their father's odd behavior, and waited.

After a moment Duren turned back to them and sat down to explain.

4

Devondale

MATHEW SAW LARA AND DANIEL WAITING FOR THEM BY the entrance to the garden next to Father Thomas's house.

"Hello, Mathew," Lara said, smiling as she saw him walk up.

He returned both her smile and greeting as he shook Daniel's hand.

With wide cheekbones and expressive brown eyes, almost hazel in color, Lara would have been considered beautiful by any standard. Her face was framed by a mass of thick chestnut hair that hung loosely about her shoulders. A year or two earlier, her figure had lost most of its angular features, rounding out nicely. Mathew noticed she was wearing her hair back that day, which made her look older. He wasn't sure how he felt about it, but decided that making no comment would be best as Collin greeted the others.

"Hey, did you hear about the soldiers in town?" Daniel asked.

"Yep," Collin answered. "Mat and I passed a group of them on the way here."

"I wonder what they're doing here in Devondale."

"Didn't you listen to Father Thomas's sermon at all?" Lara asked. "They want volunteers to go to Sturga and fight the Bajani. They've been raiding the border towns."

"Well, they can ask till their hearts are content," Collin replied. "I'm not going off to fight anyone. I've never even seen a Bajani."

"Collin Miller, you couldn't go if you wanted to," Lara said. "You're not old enough,"

"I could *too* go. Rory Osman went just last summer, and he's only four months older than me."

"Rory Osman is *a year* older than you—*and good riddance*," she said emphatically. "He was nothing but a braggart, a troublemaker, *and* he lied about his age."

"The soldiers looked like they were headed in this direction," Collin said, changing the subject, and looking somewhat unnecessarily down the street. "Mat overheard them talking about Orlocks."

Daniel and Lara both blinked in surprise and turned toward Mathew.

"I said I *thought* I heard one of them say something about Orlocks, but I'm not certain. I was just passing by and I wasn't trying to overhear their conversation." He gave Collin a sour look.

"No one in Devondale would even know what an Orlock looks like," Lara said, lowering her voice. "My father says they haven't been seen since long before we were all born. I thought all of the filthy things were destroyed in the war."

"I suppose they were," Mathew replied cautiously. The mention of Orlocks made him grimace. If there *were* any Orlocks still left in the world, he wanted nothing to do with them.

While his friends were talking, Mathew glanced around Father Thomas's garden—it looked oddly empty. Usually there were at least eight to ten others there by now, and today there were only the four of them.

"What are you looking so confused about, Mathew?" Lara asked.

"I thought there would be more people here for the practice, that's all," he replied.

Lara took a deep breath and smiled. "Mathew Lewin, I swear, if your head wasn't fixed to your shoulders you'd leave it at home. Father Thomas told us last week that services would be short today because of the tournament. Practice ended a half hour ago. Everyone's already left for the square. I had Garon take your equipment down there for you," she added, affectionately brushing a rebellious lock of hair off his forehead.

Mathew's eyes widened in surprise and he glanced at Collin, who just shrugged.

"Goddamn it! We were so blasted busy at the farm it must have slipped my mind. Oh hell, I hope he's not angry . . ."

He was about to add something stronger, but seeing Lara's eyebrows arch and the smile disappear from her face, he decided against it. Ever since she made the transition from tomboy to young woman about a year earlier, Lara had begun to show an increasing dislike for strong language in public, even though she could curse as well as any man he'd ever met if she wanted to.

"Uh . . . sorry, I . . ."

For an answer to his mumbled apology, he got a lifted chin and a disdainful "Hmph," before she turned and walked out of the garden gate.

Daniel watched her leave and shook his head. "I wonder where they learn that look?" he said.

"I think their mothers teach them secretly when no one's around," Collin replied, pushing Daniel toward the gate. "Let's get moving."

As they emerged from the garden and were starting down the street, Mathew's arm was gripped by a set of strong fingers. Turning, he looked back at the broad, smiling face of Ella Emson. Her husband, Lucas, the town's blacksmith, was with her. Lucas was a wide man, thickly muscled, with a full beard, short brown hair, and an amiable expression. His wife nearly matched him in both height and girth.

"Why, Mathew Lewin, just look at you!" Ella exclaimed. "I swear you've grown another six inches since I saw you last. How have you been? And how is that father of yours?"

"Thank you, ma'am. I've been just fine. My father's well too. But if you'll excuse me, I have to get—"

"Oh, I just can't believe it. Can you, Lucas? I remember when he was born. Don't you, dear?"

"Yes, Ella. Of course I remember. I was there, wasn't I?" Lucas replied patiently. "Missed you in church, Mat. Will Bran be here today?"

Collin and Daniel discreetly separated themselves from Mathew and kept walking. They looked over their shoulders sympathetically and wiggled their fingers goodbye.

"Yes, sir. I'm sure he will," Mathew replied. "If you'll excuse—"

"You know, Mathew," Ella said, leaning forward in a conspiratorial manner, "your father is still a fine-looking man." She mumbled something else, partly to herself, that Mathew couldn't quite catch except for the words "good provider," but he decided it would be best not to ask her what she'd said and encourage her further.

As Ella mentally tallied Bran's qualities, she absently brushed back the same lock of hair off his forehead that Lara had a moment earlier.

Mathew had gotten used to women doing that. For reasons he was never able to fathom, they simply couldn't abide something out of place. He couldn't imagine another man doing it, or even caring if his hair went in five different directions at the same time. Rather than try and hold back the tide, he put up with the occasional adjustments and held his tongue.

Apparently satisfied with whatever calculations she was making, Ella noticed Mathew was still standing before her. "Do you know," she said, picking up where she'd left off, "a woman's touch around your house would be a welcome thing after all this time."

Feeling trapped, Mathew tried to think of some polite way to separate himself from Ella without hurting her feelings. "Yes, ma'am . . . I mean, I don't know exactly. I guess you'd have to speak with my father. But right now, I really have to—"

Completely undeterred, Ella sailed on. "Mathew, I have a *wonderful* idea. I can't imagine why I didn't think of this sooner. Why don't you and Bran come for dinner tomorrow? My sister and her daughter, Brenna, are visiting for several days, and I'm sure Chantelle would *love* to see your father again. You do remember them, don't you? From Rockingham?"

As a matter of fact, Mathew *did* remember them. He also recalled his father comparing Chantelle's face to their horse Tilda, so he didn't think Bran would be overjoyed at the prospect of having dinner with them. To make matters worse, Brenna seemed to favor her mother a great deal. The chances for a quick disengagement appeared to be fading as Ella gathered momentum. Suddenly, help came from an unexpected quarter.

"Ella, let the boy go," Lucas said, stepping in between them. "He needs to be at the square right now for the tournament. We can discuss all this later." He gave Mathew a private wink and added, with more concern than might have been strictly necessary, "I think you'd better get a move on, lad, or like as not, they'll start without you."

"Father Thomas is certainly not going to start without him," Ella said to her husband. "But I suppose Lucas is right. You shouldn't be standing here gabbing the day away when you need to be somewhere." Ella wagged a plump finger at him for emphasis. "There'll be time enough to chat after your fencing thing is done with. Honestly, I think these tournaments are just an excuse for you men to get out of work."

Lucas rolled his eyes to heaven, but with the wisdom of a man married many years, he wisely said nothing. Realizing that his own mouth was open, Mathew closed it with a snap and bid them a hasty goodbye before hurrying down the street.

By the time he reached the square, there was a flurry of activity going on. The teams from Gravenhage and Mechlen had arrived and were taking their packs down from the horses. Though Mathew recognized a number of boys by sight from previous competitions, his shyness had prevented him from making many friends. He did recognize Berke Ramsey, and looked away.

Almost twenty, two years older than many of the other boys, Berke was brawny and good-looking, and for some reason known only to himself, had taken a dislike toward Mathew. He seemed to have a special talent for picking out and preying on the weaknesses of others. In Mathew, that turned out to be shyness and lack of confidence. Several times in competitions over the years, when the boys would get together at the conclusion of the meet to socialize, Berke made a habit of mimicking Mathew's mannerisms and speech. The result turned Mathew's adolescent self-consciousness into active misery, so he made a point of avoiding Berke whenever possible.

It took Mathew only a moment to locate Daniel and Collin in the crowd. Carly Coombs and Garon Lang were there as well. While he was shaking hands with Garon, he overheard Carly chattering on about something or other to Collin, whom he suspected was only half listening.

Lara joined them a few minutes later. She had changed into men's clothes, indicating she was going to fence as well. Mathew had gotten used to seeing her in dresses recently and thought the breeches looked a little odd, but conceded that they allowed for greater freedom of movement, even though they tended to accentuate her hips and bottom. He was still looking when she turned around and their eyes met. Flustered, Mathew cleared his throat and occupied himself with making sure the handle of his blade was sufficiently tight. Lara raised one eyebrow and made a point of deliberately brushing past him. He did his best to keep a straight face.

Lara was the only girl in Devondale interested in fencing, and she was quite good enough to compete with the boys. In the beginning, the other teams had complained it wasn't fair having to compete against a girl, but she silenced the protests after winning matches in several different competitions. She wasn't as strong physically as her male counterparts, but as Father Thomas had told them many times, speed, agility, and, above all, intelligence, were far more important. A good fencer, if he or she was careful, could use their opponent's strength against them, and Lara was good.

Mathew saw Father Thomas talking with two men. The gray-haired individual was none other than Jerrel Rozon, who coached the Gravenhage team, and the other one was Thom Calthorpe, who taught the Mechlen team. Mathew knew from conversations with his father that Rozon was a former general in the Elgarian military. If living a quiet life since retirement had softened him in any way, it wasn't apparent.

His father had told him that Rozon's men began referring to him as the "Anvil" after the Battle of Tyron Fel, though never to his face. The nickname stuck after he held his ground against three successive Sibuyan charges, without so much as taking a step backward.

The other man, Thom Calthorpe, was big and had an honest face and a straightforward manner. Mathew had met him at a number of different competitions over the years and liked him from the very beginning. Calthorpe was a keen a tactician and an excellent teacher, but unlike Rozon, he was willing to share his thoughts or offer advice, even with fencers on the other teams.

Mathew thought Father Thomas fell somewhere between the two coaches in philosophy. Though he concealed it well, Father Thomas *definitely* did not like to lose. Several years before, when everyone had gone home, Mathew watched him practicing with his father. They were about the same age and both had served together in the army. Father Thomas was tall, slender, and as quick as a cat. They went at each other for the better part of an hour and seemed evenly matched. Fascinated, Mathew sat in the corner absorbing it all, hoping to be as good one day. It was the first time he remembered thinking that Siward Thomas wasn't a typical priest—an opinion shared by a number of women in the village as well. When relatives with eligible daughters happened to visit, he never seemed to be at a loss for dinner invitations.

"Attention everyone . . . attention," Father Thomas

called out, standing on the lip of the fountain in the center of the square. "If you will be kind enough to gather to me for a moment, we will begin shortly."

All the competitors on the Devondale, Gravenhage, and Mechlen teams crowded around him in a semicircle.

"First, a warm welcome to all of you. We know that some of you have traveled far to join us, and we are most pleased to have you as our guests. It looks like the Creator has favored us with a fine, clear day for a competition."

Heads bowed in unison as Father Thomas raised his right arm in benediction. "May His grace shine on each of you, and . . . ah . . . may He make your blades accurate and legs strong."

Jerrel Rozon glanced up, raising a speculative eyebrow.

"A bit of help from above is always welcome, Jerrel," Father Thomas whispered in an aside. Other than a hint of a smile that touched the corners of Rozon's mouth, and an imperceptible nod of the head, his expression didn't change.

"A welcome also to Lieutenant Darnel Herne and his men, who have graciously agreed to serve as our judges today."

Everyone turned to follow the priest's gaze to the west side of the square, where the soldiers were standing. Mathew counted twelve of them, and immediately picked out Darnel Herne as the officer he had passed earlier. The competitors applauded politely while Lieutenant Herne raised his hand in acknowledgment, adding a salute to Jerrel Rozon, who accepted the courtesy with a nod of his head.

"Today, we will have a meet within a meet. Not only will each of the teams compete for the first prize, the six men—"

"Or women," Lara called out.

"Or women," Father Thomas added, with a deferential nod in Lara's direction. "The *competitors* with the best record will fence in a round robin to determine our champion. Lieutenant Herne, Bran Lewin, and I will make up the committee on rules in the event of a dispute."

Mathew blinked and looked around, surprised that his father had already arrived. *He must have nearly killed Obert to get that entire cord of wood unloaded,* he thought.

Bran caught his son's eye and winked.

"In the team event, you will each fence three bouts. The first team that reaches ten victories against their opponent shall be declared the winner. We will use the long boards as our field of combat.

"You must stay on the strip at all times," Father Thomas told them. "Should you step off the end with both feet, a hit will be awarded against you. Are there any questions from the competitors?"

"When do we eat, Father?" a brash voice called out. Mathew immediately identified the speaker as Giles Arlen Naismith, from Gravenhage. Jerrel Rozon turned a hard glare in the boy's direction. After a moment, Giles lowered his eyes, concentrating his attention on examining his boots, but the grin never left his face. A stocky teammate standing to his right bumped him with his shoulder, and Giles bumped him back in return.

Mathew had had trouble with Giles the last few times they'd competed. Giles was nearly his own height and seemed to be made of all confidence and swagger. Although certain that he was technically a better fencer, Mathew had lost to Giles the last three times they met, which frustrated him no end. Giles's attacks were unorthodox as well as fast, and they came from the oddest angles.

"An excellent question, my young friend," Father Thomas answered. "Master Naismith, isn't it? You will be pleased to learn that the good ladies of Devondale, having you in their thoughts, have prepared a fine table to fill your empty belly . . . and head."

That brought a roar of laughter from everyone there, and even Giles shook his head, smiling good-naturedly.

"Ready yourselves. We will begin in ten minutes. Good luck to all."

* * *

While people turned their attention to last minute checks of their practice weapons and equipment, Mathew walked quickly to the rear of the town council hall. His stomach never cooperated before a competition, and it would have been unthinkable for him to allow anyone to see him get sick in public. Of course, the butterflies were there again, and he felt the familiar constriction in his throat just before his stomach began to heave.

From past experience, he knew he would be fine once the tournament actually began, but having this sort of thing happen was still embarrassing. On several different occasions he had started to talk with his father about it, but shame prevented him and the conversation never took place. When his stomach settled down after a minute, Mathew took a sip of water from the bottle he was carrying, wiped his mouth, and started to make his way around to the front of the building.

Abruptly, he became aware that he wasn't alone. Standing at the end of the building were two of the boys from Gravenhage, staring at him in disbelief. The larger of the two was Berke Ramsey, and the other was a teammate of his whom Mathew didn't know.

"Are you okay?" the teammate asked.

"Oh, ah . . . yes, I'm fine. It's just my stomach sometimes gets the better of me at these things."

Mathew was not prepared for what happened next. Both boys stared at him a moment longer before bursting into laughter and hurrying off.

Wonderful. he thought. *This is all I need.*

Once he rounded the building his worst fears were confirmed. Berke and his friend were standing with Jerrel Rozon and Giles Naismith, obviously relating what had just happened. Berke saw him and pointed in his direction, convulsing in laughter.

Mathew felt his ears go red and walked stiffly past them with as much dignity as he could salvage. It was small satisfaction that whatever they were saying did not appear to amuse Jerrel Rozon. Mathew couldn't hear the words, but at least the smiles quickly disappeared as Rozon shoved them back toward the rest of their team. Giles eyed him solemnly, his expression unreadable.

Jerrel Rozon watched the gangly young man go by. Seventeen-year-olds were strange things at best, but there was something about this one that pricked his attention. His face might have been a bit pasty, and he looked none too steady on his feet, but Rozon could see the bright blue eyes taking in everything. *Bran Lewin's boy*, he thought, and made a mental note to himself about him.

Based on the draw, the first match was between Mechlen and Devondale. Two benches were set up parallel to the fencing strip on either side of a scorer's table so that team members could sit and observe the action. Mathew quietly took his place next to Daniel. "Who goes first?" he asked.

"Collin and that fellow over there," Daniel answered, indicating a dark-haired boy with a serious expression. Mathew nodded. "You're second, followed by me, Lara, Daniel, Garon, then Carly."

"Second?"

Fencing in second position meant he would have two bouts in the first half of the match, which surprised him. In his estimation, Collin was the stronger fencer, and he was puzzled by Father Thomas's selection.

"Mm-hmm," Daniel replied. "Father Thomas thinks we might be able to win early if we get off to a strong start."

Unfortunately, no one bothered to tell Mechlen about it, and the match turned out to be much closer than anyone thought. More than two hours had passed since they started fencing. Mathew's nausea was long gone, replaced by nervous energy. When the third and final round was called, Devondale was down by three bouts and in danger of being eliminated.

Father Thomas walked over with the pairing sheet and crouched down before his team. He told them that

Mechlen's coach, Thom Calthorpe, had already made his choices, so it was just a matter of matching up who would fence whom. Mathew watched the priest position himself to block anyone from observing their deliberations. He showed the first name on the list to Collin.

"No problem, Father. I can beat him." Collin made the statement so matter-of-factly, Mathew felt a twinge of jealousy at his friend's confidence.

"Lara?"

Lara looked at the next name on the list and shook her head. "I'm not sure, Father."

She glanced at Mathew, who nodded reassuringly before looking back at Father Thomas. The priest searched her face for a moment, then patted her on the knee and turned to Daniel.

"Understood. Daniel?"

His friend stared at the name and then at a boy sitting on the opposite bench. "I think so—yes," he said softly.

Neither Carly nor Garon seemed certain about their chances with the third name. Father Thomas looked thoughtfully at each of them before taking a deep breath. "Well, Carly, you *have* been coming to church regularly, so let us hope the Creator enjoys this sport. You will fence third."

Garon didn't know if the Creator took any interest in fencing or not, but he appeared pleased that Father Thomas had picked Carly. This left Mathew in the fourth position, with their number one fencer. Having already worked out the order, Mathew half expected Father Thomas to say something to him, and was mildly surprised when the priest simply squeezed his shoulder and said, "Let's get ready."

After making some quick mental calculations, Mathew thought it was more likely than not that the final and deciding bout would fall to him. He couldn't begin to guess at Father Thomas's reasoning and fervently wished he were someplace else, not in the center of everyone's attention. A sizable crowd had gathered to watch the conclusion of the match. Mathew thought about it for a moment, and became angry with himself for his own attitude, eventually deciding that whatever happened, he would make the best of it.

True to his word, Collin beat his opponent handily. Daniel also managed a win. Devondale was down only by two bouts with two to go when Carly took his place on the strip. Considering how Carly generally fared in such matters, Mathew didn't hold out much hope for his team.

Just as Lieutenant Herne was about to give the command to fence, Mathew saw Father Thomas exchange a look with Collin, who abruptly stood up and signaled for the lieutenant's attention.

"Excuse me, sir, but I believe his boot lace is becoming undone," he said, pointing at Carly's right foot. "Here, let me help you with that." Before Carly or Herne could say anything, Collin quickly stepped over, knelt down with his back to the lieutenant, somewhat theatrically, and made a show of retying the lace. During his brief ministrations, Mathew could see Collin's lips moving, but he couldn't make out anything he was saying. Lara and Daniel saw the same thing and exchanged puzzled glances. From where Mathew was sitting, it appeared that Carly was about to say something, then changed his mind.

"Gentlemen, if you are *quite* finished?" Lieutenant Herne asked.

"Oh . . . of course. Thank you, sir. Just wanted to be safe," Collin said, returning to his seat. The lieutenant eyed him skeptically, then cleared his throat, turned his attention back to the competitors and gave the command to begin. The look on Collin's face was pure innocence.

"What was that all about?" Mathew asked under his breath.

Collin's attention remained fixed on the bout and his expression didn't change as he replied, "I told him that everyone in Werth Province knows that they can hit him on the hip because he always overreacts with his stupid chest parry."

"Oh," Mathew said.

"I also told him to keep his blasted elbow glued to his right side during the bout or I would personally drown him in the well," Collin added, continuing to smile.

"Oh," Mathew repeated. "I hope Father Thomas didn't hear—"

"Mat!" Collin said, shocked.

Mathew frowned and glanced at Father Thomas, who was watching the proceedings with a beatific expression on his face. He returned Mathew's look with a pleasant nod.

Whatever Collin had said to Carly, it seemed to work. Three times Carly attacked, and three times he was parried, but his opponent's riposte kept missing when Carly deflected it with his elbow, which he immediately returned to cover his exposed hip. To his credit, Carly took advantage of each miss and scored on the counter riposte. Clearly confused by what was happening, the other boy looked at his coach, who responded with a shrug. The balance of the bout went very much the same way it began, and Carly eventually got the win.

When the last hit was scored, he was so beside himself with excitement, he jumped straight up in the air yelling like a madman, and almost forgot to shake the other boy's hand. Lara leaned over and gave him a kiss on the cheek when he returned to the bench, still beaming. Mathew couldn't remember seeing anyone turn that red before, but he was very happy for Carly.

His own bout was less dramatic, despite his earlier trepidations. He had observed his opponent, Wayne Jackson, carefully in each of his previous bouts. Though he was a tough competitor, Wayne was also a good head shorter than Mathew, and had less reach. Conscious that everyone on both the Gravenhage and Mechlen teams were watching, Mathew took the strip, a plan already formed in his mind. He shut out the catcalls and derisive laughter from Berke Ramsey and his teammates and concentrated on the task before him.

Instead of maintaining a normal fencing distance of about six feet, Mathew lengthened their contact by an additional half step, placing himself just out of the boy's range. One after another of Wayne's attacks fell short, which only caused him to press harder as he attempted to close the distance. The result was disastrous, and he wound up both overextended and off balance, making him a very vulnerable target. By the time the last hit was called, he was so desperate to get to Mathew that he completely telegraphed his intentions. The moment Lieutenant Herne gave the command to fence, Wayne started down the strip with one rapid advance after another while Mathew retreated. With time running out and his opponent drifting farther and farther away, the boy threw an all out effort into his lunge—and fell short. Mathew saw it coming and stepped back, using his longer reach to hit him on the shoulder. The Devondale supporters erupted in a cheer.

The victory was now secure and Devondale was declared the winner. Thom Calthorpe generously came over to shake hands and offer his congratulations, while Father Thomas gathered everyone from his team in a circle and raised a cheer for Mechlen, as was the custom.

Mathew should have been happy and pleased with himself, but he wasn't. When they were done, he separated himself from the group and walked alone across the square to the old stone well. Tight-lipped, he kept his eyes mostly on the ground, avoiding those glances that followed him.

He was painfully aware, at least in his own mind, what people were whispering, and suspected that some of those comments would probably reach his father. The win, elegant though it had been, was of no consequence to him. He had gotten sick in public, and everyone was going to assume he'd been afraid. It would only be a matter of time before the story fully circulated, and the prospect made him miserable. Though few people would even give a second thought to such things, it assumed a place of primary importance in the mind of an awkward seventeen-year-old.

* * *

He brought the bucket up from the well and took the tin ladle off its hook. He was just finishing his third cup when he heard footsteps behind him and turned to see two people approaching.

"How have you been, Mat?" Giles asked mildly.

"Fine, Giles, and you?" he replied.

Mathew recognized the other man as one of the soldiers he had seen earlier. He appeared about the same height as Giles but was built more solidly and was clearly several years older. Except for a prominent scar above his left eye, he had the same coloring and facial features as Giles. Several times in the past, Mathew had overheard different Devondale girls commenting about Giles's curly brown hair and good looks. Though he knew it may have been a little small-minded, Mathew wrote it off to a lack of discrimination on their part.

"Oh, sorry. This is my brother, Terren," Giles said, introducing them.

Unsure what to expect, Mathew kept his expression neutral as he and Terren shook hands. He tossed the remaining water in the cup on the ground and refilled it from the bucket, offering it to Giles, who, oddly, didn't take it right away. Instead he searched Mathew's face for a moment before finally accepting the cup, gulping down the contents in a single swallow. His brother waved it away.

"That was a good bout you fenced at the end," Giles said. Terren nodded in agreement.

"Thank you," Mathew replied.

The compliment came as a surprise, but also made him wary.

"It looked like you beat him with your head, I think. Yes?" Terren said, his comment more statement than question.

"I was lucky," Mathew replied guardedly.

"Lucky?" The soldier's brows came together and he appeared to think about what Mathew had said for a second.

"No," he said, shaking his head slowly. "I suspect luck had very little to do with it. Rozon didn't think so either. Actually, he pulled me aside just to watch it."

Rozon? Mathew wondered just how many people had been watching the bout. The whole thing had seemed pretty elementary to him. It was just a matter of carrying out his plan.

"Well, I would wish you luck, but I believe you are fencing my brother next. So," he said, clapping them both on the back at the same time, "I will say only that it was nice to meet you, young man." He turned to Giles, ruffling his hair good-naturedly, and added, "And you, I'll see later." Terren started back to the square and called over his shoulder, "Both of you have a good match."

Surprisingly, it sounded to Mathew as though he meant it.

"*Young man!* He's only four years older than us," Giles snorted when his brother was gone.

"He seems nice," Mathew offered.

"Oh, he is. I mean he's my brother and all, but sometimes he gets a little full of himself. He helped raise my sister and me after my father died, so he always tries to act like he's older than he is."

Mathew didn't know that Giles had a sister, or that his father was dead. He felt a twinge of guilt because he had been doing his best to dislike Giles, and here he was acting in a perfectly pleasant manner.

"I see. I'm very sorry."

Giles waved away the politeness. "It's really not as bad as all that. You should meet my sister, Lea. She's two years younger than me and fussier than my mother ever was," he said, shaking his head.

"Was?"

"Yeah, both my mother and father were killed when I was about nine."

Mathew stared at him. He had no idea that both of Giles's parents were dead.

"They were coming back from Tyron Fel, where my aunt Shela lives. She'd just had a baby, and my mother thought it would be a good idea to stay with her for a week until she got back on her feet."

Mathew thought he should say something, but was at a complete loss for words.

"They never made it there. They ran into a band of brigands. My uncle and some other men found them three days later. Throats were cut and they'd been robbed."

"Giles, I—"

"Kind of stupid, isn't it, robbing someone with no money? They were carrying food and baby clothes."

All Mathew could think of was to dumbly repeat, "Giles, I'm really sorry. I had no idea."

He had been prepared to lump Giles together with the rest of his team, but found himself beginning to like him instead. Despite the brashness he'd displayed earlier, Giles actually seemed a genuine and straightforward individual.

After taking another drink, the other boy shook his head, clearing away the memories. "That wasn't what I came over here to say. I don't even know what made me bring it up, to be honest."

"My mother died when I was nine." Mathew felt silly almost as soon as the words were out of his mouth.

Giles looked at him for a moment, then said, "Damn, the world's an odd place."

They stood staring at each other for a moment, and then a strange thing happened—they started laughing.

"Well, I guess it is at that," Mathew agreed.

"Look, Mat, I know you saw those two muttonheads telling Jerrel Rozon and me what happened a while ago."

The smile faded from Mathew's face and he retreated to his habitual wariness.

"Well, forget it, would you? It doesn't mean a thing. They're fools. You know what Jerrel told them?" Giles asked.

"No," Mathew replied cautiously.

"He told them that *he* got sick to his stomach just before every battle he ever fought. Can you imagine that—Jerrel Rozon."

In fact, Mathew couldn't imagine it. Jerrel Rozon looked to be about as soft as granite. And he was considered one of the most brilliant commanders in Elgaria. *Jerrel Rozon getting sick before a fight?*

"On my honor, Mat. That's just what he said, and some other choice things too that . . . uh . . . polite company prevents me from repeating."

Mathew looked at Giles closely but could find no hint of mockery or sarcasm. In fact, it seemed quite the contrary. Suddenly, he found the whole incident funny, something that was highly unusual for such a reticent young man. Both of the boys began laughing again, although neither was certain exactly at what.

"Let's get back before they come looking for us," Giles said, clapping Mathew on the back.

Mathew reached out and squeezed Giles's shoulder in return, and they walked back across the square together.

The world certainly was a strange place.

5

Alor Satar, Karas Duren's palace in Rocoi

ERIC DUREN BENT DOWN AND GRASPED THE MIDDLE OF
the statue, grunted and lifted with all his might. His father, standing next to him, lifted at the same time. Sweat
broke out on Eric's forehead, but slowly, after three failed
attempts, they succeeded in raising it to about chest
height.

When it was about halfway up, Eric leaned backward
sharply, pulled, while Karas Duren pushed as hard as he
could. Eventually they managed to stand it upright, then
both of them collapsed to the ground.

"Next time make the servants do it," Eric gasped, trying to regain his breath. "That's one of the advantages
about being the king."

Duren chuckled and rolled over onto his back, looking up at the sky. "Some things are worth working for,"
he said.

"I don't see why we need another statue. The garden's
already full of them."

"It's a gift from our Bajani friends," Duren explained.
"The Kalifar of the Five Tribes is coming to visit next
week. It seems they have reconsidered our proposal for an
alliance."

Eric Duren propped himself up on one elbow and
looked at his father. "The Elgarians closed the ports?"

"They're an extremely predictable people. Those raids
you've been staging along their northern border turned
out to be the final straw."

Eric shook his head and laughed softly, and Duren

shared in the moment, patting him on the leg. "Don't you think the Bajani will eventually find out it was us?"

"By that time I imagine the war will be over."

"What about Cincar?" Eric asked. "We're going to need them too."

"Cincar is not a problem. With Elgaria out of the way, they'll have a free run at the shipping lanes in the Southern Sea. They'd like that almost as much as seeing King Malach in his grave," Duren said. "He was the one who froze them out of the western markets, and Naydim Kyat's father has never forgotten that."

"We'll need to be certain," Eric said. "Their navy could be a huge factor if they decide not to join us."

"We signed the treaty yesterday, before you returned from your visit to our western neighbor."

"What about the men I took? Armand is going to have a fit if he finds out any more of his soldiers have . . . ah . . . suddenly deserted, shall we say."

Duren rolled over, looked at his son and shrugged. "The casualties of war, I'm afraid."

His father said this so blandly, it sent a chill down Eric's spine. At the bottom of the hill, just before the garden path disappeared into the trees, there was a large blackened area of ground. Several workmen were busy with rakes and shovels, trying to smooth a mound of earth in the center that reminded him of a large grave. He was certain it hadn't been there before he left.

"Did we have a fire while I was gone?" he asked.

"Not really," Duren answered, pushing himself up to his feet and dusting off his shirt. "Some of my experiments don't always go as smoothly as I would like."

Another shudder ran down Eric's spine. "Have the Orlocks had any success in finding the other ring yet?"

A brief look that might have been annoyance appeared briefly on Duren's face, but vanished as quickly as it came. He stared off at the horizon toward the south and said absently, "They're in a place called Devondale at the moment, following the merchant that traitor sold it to. We should have it soon . . . very soon."

"Where's Devondale? I've never heard of it."

"It's a small town in Elgaria, about four hundred miles south of Anderon. The nearest city is Gravenhage."

"What in the world are they doing there?" Eric asked.

"The merchant who Soames sold the ring to apparently goes there every year for their Spring Festival to sell his pots and pans. Hopefully, with all the crowds, the Orlocks can slip in and get it quickly."

"But, can they be trusted?"

Duren shrugged. "I suspect so. We've reached an understanding with each other, so to speak. The ring actually has no value to them. When the Ancients created the last eight, they made each of them unique; able to work only with one person. It's actually something of a miracle mine functions at all. Perhaps it's a sign from God our time is at hand, wouldn't you say?"

"I wouldn't know," Eric said. "I'm more comfortable relying on myself than waiting for divine messages."

Karas Duren looked at his son and smiled. "So am I, Eric."

"Father, I know what you've told me about the ring, and I've seen some of the things you can do, but are you certain we're taking the right path? The West is not simply going to disappear."

"Disappear?" Duren repeated.

"Yes, Father, that's what I said. They are not . . ."

Eric's voice trailed off when he realized his father was not looking at him. A servant girl was walking toward them, carrying a pitcher of water and glasses on a silver tray. He had seen her around the palace a number of times before, a pretty young thing with dark brown hair and large hazel eyes, though her name escaped him at the moment. His mother had probably sent her with drinks for them.

The girl stopped in her tracks as a loud, high-pitched whine came out of nowhere. It didn't seem to emanate from anywhere in particular, but was all around them.

Several of the servants working at the burnt area also looked up.

The whine continued to increase in volume, but his father stood there, not moving.

A second later the girl dropped the tray she was carrying. The pitcher and glass crashed to the ground as a brilliant white light enveloped her. The light formed itself into the shape of a column, became opaque, then shrank, compacting itself into a ball before it winked out of existence. Only the echo of a distant chime remained.

In shock, Eric jumped to his feet. The girl was gone—vanished, as if she had never been there. On the ground lay the silver tray with shards of broken glass around it.

Eric heard his father take a deep breath and say, "One never knows, do they?"

6

Devondale

TOWARD THE END OF DEVONDALE'S MATCH WITH Mechlen, Collin Miller watched the gray clouds roll in from the west. The temperature had dropped, and if the treetops were any indication, the wind also seemed to be freshening. They would have to hurry to get the competition over, he concluded. At most there were only two hours of good light remaining. Father Thomas apparently had similar thoughts and called for the match with Gravenhage to begin.

Across the square, Mat and Giles Naismith were walking with each other, talking and smiling. Although Collin didn't care for Giles, he conceded that wouldn't be a bad thing if he managed to get his friend to ease up on himself a little. In the last half hour, at least two people had told him that Mat threw up behind the town council building. One of them, Gene Warren, who lived in Mechlen, also said that Berke Ramsey was spreading the story around. At least Gene had the decency to ask if Mat was all right rather than gloat as that pea brain Berke did, Collin thought.

Collin watched Mat and Giles shake hands as they separated. "What was that about?" he asked as Mathew walked up.

"Nothing really. He was just telling me not to be so hard on myself."

"Good advice," Collin agreed. "Father Thomas gave us the bout order while you were over there. You're up first, followed by Lara, Daniel, me, Carly, and Garon."

"Who do I fence?" Mathew asked, lowering himself to the ground. Once he was in a sitting position, he spread his legs as wide apart as possible and reached toward his toes, limbering up.

"I think Berke Ramsey is first for them."

Mathew paused in mid-stretch. "Really?" he said, looking up at Collin. "That's interesting."

Collin frowned. Personally, he couldn't see anything interesting about it at all. Mathew's face had a distant, preoccupied look, but Collin decided not to say anything for the moment.

Father Thomas stood on one of the small benches and called for everyone's attention. "Gentlemen . . . and lady," he added quickly, with a brief nod to Lara, who inclined her head. "The first match will begin in two minutes. If you would be kind enough to take your places."

Both teams went to their respective benches, and Mathew took his position on the fencing strip. Though his friend appeared calm, in fact almost nonchalant, Collin could see that Mathew's eyes were fixed on Berke, who sauntered onto the strip with an idiotic grin on his face. He also noticed the fingers of Mathew's left hand tapping rapidly against his thigh.

"Make sure he doesn't get sick on you, Berke," one of his teammate's called out, just loud enough for everyone to hear, which brought a burst of laughter from the Gravenhage team. Collin's temper flared and he started to get to his feet, but a surprisingly firm grip on his shoulder restrained him. He hadn't even heard Father Thomas come up behind him. Giving in to the pressure, he sat back down and fumed. While the laughter slowly abated, Collin noticed that neither Jerrel Rozon nor Giles had taken part in it.

Well, there's a point for them, he thought.

The faint smile on Mathew's face also faded away.

"You would be wiser to demonstrate your skill with a weapon, as opposed to your tongue," Lieutenant Herne snapped. "Are you ready?"

Both boys nodded, and he gave the command to begin.

I hope Mat wipes that stupid grin off his big ugly face, Collin thought.

Playing to the audience, Berke adopted a menacing look, took a quick advance toward Mathew with his arms spread wide, and jutting his head forward, suddenly said, "Boo!"

If Berke expected Mathew to jump or faint, he was sorely mistaken. From a seemingly casual on guard position, his blade virtually trailing on the ground, Mathew suddenly snapped out a tremendously powerful lunge. Caught completely by surprise, Berke took its full force directly in the chest and went down like a bag of sand. Mathew stood over him for a moment, shrugged, and calmly walked back to his line, where he appeared more concerned with flicking lint from his sleeve than he was with his opponent. Half the population of Devondale, who had turned out for the competition, erupted in a cheer. A few laughs could also be heard from some of the other competitors. Carly Coombs jumped out of his seat, pumped his fist in the air, and shouted "Yes!" but a stern look from Lieutenant Herne quickly returned him to his place.

"Are you all right?" the lieutenant asked.

Berke scrambled back to his feet but didn't answer. He stood there with his chest heaving, glaring at Mathew, who in contrast seemed unconcerned with what had just happened. Instead, he stared directly back at Berke, which was the equivalent of waving a red flag in front of a bull.

"I asked if you were all right?" Lieutenant Herne repeated.

"Fine," Berke snapped. "Let's get this over."

"Very well, then. Begin!"

Both boys advanced to close ground. It was plain to Collin that Berke wanted to engage and try to control Mathew's blade in the four line, or chest side, as fencers called it. After allowing their blades to cross just at midpoint, Mathew returned the slightest pressure with his fingers in opposition. Berke overreacted. Mathew saw as much, feinted straight forward, then drove a perfect disengagement to the opposite line, hitting him cleanly on the shoulder.

Lieutenant Herne awarded the hit, and Berke, incredulous, looked all but ready to chew nails. The third and fourth hits went in much the same way, with one scoring to Berke's high line and the other to his low line. After each touch, Mathew shrugged as if it were no big deal, shook his head, and strolled back to his line.

Collin pulled his eyes away from the bout for a moment to glance at Lara. She was beaming with pride, both of her fists were clenched so tightly, her knuckles were showing white.

On the fourth hit, Mathew even started back for his on guard line *before* Lieutenant Herne made his award, as if the decision was a foregone conclusion. This only appeared to infuriate Berke further. Now down four to nothing, with only one chance remaining to him, when the command was given Berke charged down the strip, swinging his blade wildly from side to side in an attempt to score on Mathew's flank. With their bodies in close proximity, both blades became tangled. And while each competitor was struggling to get his weapon clear, Berke abruptly raised his forearm and struck Mathew under the chin, snapping his head backward.

"Halt! *That* was a deliberate foul, and you are warned," Lieutenant Herne said. "Repeat this conduct again and both you *and* your team will be disqualified. Do you understand me?"

The lieutenant was clearly upset. Lara took a wet cloth to Mathew, whose lip was split and bleeding. After holding it in place for a moment, she said something to him that caused Mathew to look at her sharply before she returned to her seat. Fouls happened all the time in competition, and everyone more or less expected them, but few were ever committed intentionally. This one was about as serious as you could get. Collin glanced over at Jerrel Rozon. The former general did not appear pleased.

The moment the bout resumed, Berke again charged down the strip at Mathew. This time, instead of making a chest parry as he had before, Mathew reversed himself and swept the line in the opposite direction, using a counter parry. He caught Berke's blade cleanly, but rather than going straight in, executed two quick disengagements. Berke fought madly to recover and defend himself, but to no avail. The fifth hit landed, and Mathew scored the victory. Lieutenant Herne didn't even bother to announce the call. He simply shrugged and pointed to Mathew, who stood waiting to shake his opponent's hand. The only sign belying Mathew's apparent outward calm was the continued tapping of the fingers of his left hand against his leg.

For a moment it looked to Collin that Berke was either about to start a fight or stalk off the strip, but with everyone watching, he grudgingly accepted Mathew's proffered hand.

As soon as Mathew got back to the bench, he was the center of attention, being hugged from all directions by his teammates.

"That was just amazing!" Collin said when they finally sat down. "I'm telling you it was just . . . hey, are you okay?"

Looking closely, Collin saw that Mathew was rigid and tight-lipped. Though his face was impassive, it appeared that he might get sick again. Inching closer to him, Collin said in a low voice between clenched teeth, "Mat, if you give them the satisfaction of throwing up, I swear I'll kill you myself."

Collin continued to smile and nod and was about to add something even stronger when it struck him that Mathew's casual behavior during the bout had been an act. Collin had always known his friend was intelligent— but this was better! Devious, even. Maybe Mat had possibilities after all.

On Mathew's opposite side, Lara slid closer to him, kissed him demurely on the cheek and whispered something in his ear that returned the color to Mathew's face. He responded by clearing his throat while she looked primly ahead.

Lara didn't fare as well in her bout. Despite putting up a good fight, she lost. So did Daniel, followed by Carly, whose enthusiasm still appeared undiminished. For the next hour the score swung back and forth between the two teams. The second round was a repeat of the first, as was the third, and once again the outcome of the meet rested on the last bout, which, as luck would have it, fell to Mathew and Giles.

After both boys took the strip, Mathew glanced over at his father, who was standing next to Jerrel Rozon and Thom Calthorpe. Bran gave him a quick smile. Not only were the competitors from both teams on their feet to watch the bout, but just about everyone in Devondale was also there.

"Gentlemen, are you ready?" Lieutenant Herne asked formally.

"Ready," they both answered.

"Begin!"

Giles immediately advanced, as did Mathew. Each began to probe the other's defenses with a series of feints and small attacks. Father Thomas was fond of telling his students that fencing was much like playing a physical game of chess at lightning speed, and this bout was proving an excellent example of that concept.

Giles was the first to score with an attack to Mathew's flank. Mathew responded by winning the next two hits. After that, the tempo of the bout began to slow, and neither was able to gain an advantage. Much later, Mathew would tell Collin that he had no idea how long they had been fencing. His mouth felt dry as dust and he'd wondered if Giles was feeling the same thing. Seconds later, Giles attacked again, evening the score at two hits each, and then went ahead to lead by a single hit when Mathew's counterattack missed.

Mathew went back to his on guard line, seemingly frustrated, Collin thought, because at the last moment Giles contorted his body to avoid his riposte. On the next hit, Mathew drew even once more, but now, his leg muscles must have been burning and his weapon would have felt a good deal heavier. Like him, Giles appeared to be breathing harder. Perhaps buoyed by the observation, Mathew pressed his advantage and launched a long attack straight at Giles's chest, only to miss when his opponent twisted and ducked. It resulted in another score against Mathew.

Mathew went red with embarrassment, and Collin guessed he was berating himself. He was now behind four to three, and the winner would need five hits. Collin and Garon called out some words of encouragement, but Mathew didn't seem to hear them, so intent was his concentration.

Mathew's father had told him a good fencer needed confidence in equal measure to his talent to achieve success. He'd told Collin as much. Unfortunately, at the moment Mathew seemed consumed by embarrassment at missing an opportunity to prevent an ungainly maneuver. He was still one hit away from leveling the score, but he was also one hit away from losing if Giles landed first.

When they resumed, Giles closed the distance and Mathew seemed to see his opening—Giles was keeping his arm too far to the inside, exposing his flank. Mathew seized the opportunity and lunged with everything he had. The attack caught Giles by surprise. It looked certain Mathew had the hit, until at the last moment Giles somehow managed to make the parry. Mathew barely avoided the riposte, and redoubled his attack, only to be parried again a split second before his point landed. A furious exchange followed. Abruptly, Giles crouched down and sprang forward, attacking from an unusual angle to Mathew's high, inside line. Try as he might, Mathew was unable to deflect the blade, and Giles scored the final hit, winning the bout.

There was a stunned silence from the Devondale team and spectators. Eventually someone remembered their manners and began to applaud. Both boys shook hands, and Giles grabbed Mathew around the neck, hugging him. Mathew shook his head, smiled, and returned the hug.

When he sat back down, Collin tossed him a towel and patted him on the back. Whatever else Mathew was feeling at the moment, there was no indication of it on his face.

"My friends, if you will please give me your attention, I would like to make the awards," Father Thomas announced. "This has been a wonderful competition, and we have seen young men . . . ah . . . and young women, with fine talent. I know that your teachers are proud of you all.

"For the victorious team, I present this banner made by our own Margaret Grimly, to Jerrel Rozon of Gravenhage." Rozon came forward and shook hands with Father Thomas, while the members of the Gravenhage team cheered enthusiastically and the Devondale spectators applauded politely. After he accepted the banner, Rozon raised it aloft, acknowledging the spectators. It had five gold stars in a circle on a field of dark blue, representing the five provinces of Elgaria, with the name "Devondale" stitched in gold at the bottom.

"Now, if Masters Naismith, Lewin, and Miller will kindly step forward, I will make the final awards. For the individual winners, I have three fine prizes, courtesy of Harol Longworth," Father Thomas said, pointing to a table that had hurriedly been set up. On it were a belt knife, a large blue and white porcelain bowl, and a thick ring of reddish-yellow metal.

"As our champion this day, the honor falls to Giles Naismith to select first."

Giles walked up to the table, looked at the prizes, and after a moment's reflection, selected the ring. He smiled, tossed it in the air, and caught it again. Mathew went next and took the knife, leaving the bowl to Collin. Each of the boys stood together holding up the prizes for the crowd to see, as both onlookers and teams cheered.

Collin watched two men removing the fencing strips and planting torches in the ground as they hurriedly set up tables. Several of the town's ladies brought out trays of food and drink, just as Father Thomas had promised. The pungent smell of roasting meat in the air reminded him that he was famished. After shaking hands with everyone he was supposed to, he stepped away to gather up his equipment and look for a place to change into a fresh shirt.

Lara was already there, talking to Beckie Enders, another girl from Devondale. Her things were tied in a neat bundle. She had somehow managed to change into a dark green dress and comb her hair, which impressed him since he didn't see how she'd had the time to do it. On top of everything else, she was wearing rouge on her lips. It was the first time he could recall her doing that.

"May I see your bowl, please?" Beckie asked as he joined them. She was about a year younger than he was, a pretty girl with big brown eyes and curly blond hair that fell to her shoulders. Her father ran the mill just outside of town. At the last Winterfest, Collin had danced with her and even toyed with the idea of stealing a kiss or two behind the barn.

"Sure," he said, handing it to her.

"It's really lovely. Congratulations, by the way. You did so well today."

"Really?" He was surprised and slightly embarrassed by her comment, because it didn't seem like a great accomplishment to him.

"Of course. You were wonderful," she said, hugging him.

"Oh . . . well that's nice."

She didn't break away immediately, and when the hug lasted marginally longer than it might have, Collin felt his face begin to feel warm. Beckie certainly smelled nice, he thought.

"My father told me Harol got it from some fellow near Sturga. What are you going to do with it?"

"What?"

"The bowl, silly."

The corners of Collin's mouth turned down as he examined the bowl she held in her hands. The inside contained a garden scene, with some type of tree he'd never seen before at the bottom. The sides were also decorated with vines and flowers. As far as bowls went, he supposed it was all right. "I guess I'll give it to my mother," he said. "She likes things like this."

Beckie's face lost some of its earlier warmth. "Oh, I see," she said, handing it back to him. "Yes, I'm sure she'll like it very much. Well, I'd better be running along now. Are you coming, Lara?"

"You go on, Beckie. I'll be there in a moment."

Collin watched her go, baffled by her sudden change of mood. He was more confused still when Lara gave him a kiss on the cheek.

"What's that for?"

"If you gave that simpering idiot your bowl, I'd have broken it over your head."

"Give her my bowl? Why would I . . . ?" It took a second for Lara's meaning to dawn on him. "Oh . . . Did I look very silly?"

Lara affectionately grabbed a handful of his hair. "No more than normal."

He grinned. "Well, I guess that's something."

"Have you talked to Mathew yet?" Lara asked.

"Sure I talked to him . . . why?" Seeing the serious look on her face, he asked, "What's the matter?"

"I think he blames himself for our losing."

"God, that's so stupid!" Collin said angrily. "Everybody lost. He didn't lose all ten bouts, did he?" He quickly glanced around the area and spotted Mathew walking alone by the town council building.

"I tried to tell him the same thing," Lara said, "but he's

just so . . . so . . . oh, I don't know." She made an exasperated sound.

"Maybe I should give *you* this bowl to break over his head."

Lara looked in Mathew's direction and shook her head sadly. "He always thinks everything is his fault. You'll talk to him?"

"Sure."

"Good. I'll see you at the dance in just a little while," she said, giving him a quick hug.

"Dance? I thought we were going to eat. I'm starving."

"Don't worry. You'll be able to eat all you want, but there's going to be dancing too," she said brightly. "Fergus, Akin, and some others are going to play music. Isn't it wonderful?"

The last words were said over her shoulder.

Lara lifted her skirt slightly and hurried across the grass, slowing to a more ladylike pace when she got closer to the tables. Collin watched her go and shook his head. Women never ceased to amaze him. In the last year, the tomboy who could climb a tree as well as any of his male friends had undergone a metamorphosis. From the way in which she had begun to dress and carry herself lately, and the furtive glances she cast in Mathew's direction, Collin was certain that she was aware of the change. He assumed Mathew would eventually get the message.

It was almost dark and torches were already lit. Fortunately, the temperature seemed to be holding. Someone even put candles in jars around the perimeter of the square, creating a long string of lights, which he thought looked nice. He ducked behind a building, quickly pulled off his wet shirt and put on a dry one. When he came out, Mathew was still there, walking alone, his hands clasped behind his back. Collin put down the bowl with his things and trotted across the square, falling in step alongside his friend. Both boys walked along in silence for a while before Mathew spoke.

"I'm sorry, Collin, I tried my best. I really did."

This is so typical, Collin thought, wishing he'd remembered to bring the bowl with him to bounce off his friend's head.

"Look, it's no use blaming yourself," he said. "Anybody might have had to fence that last bout—me, Daniel, Garon . . . anybody. It's just rotten luck it fell to you. But that's the way things go sometimes. Near as I can figure you lost one bout all day long, right?"

"Well yes, but this one was so important . . ."

"They were *all* important. You could have lost the first or the second instead of the last. The result would have been the same. We all dropped bouts. That's why it's called a *team* competition. Get it?"

"Sure, but . . ."

"No buts about it. Let me see that knife you won."

Mathew glanced at Collin, hesitated for a moment, then handed him the knife. It was about seven inches long, with a fine carved bone handle. The metal of the blade was a grayish-black, with wavy lines going through it that reminded Collin of wood grain.

Collin whistled. "I've never seen any steel like this. It looks sharp enough to shave with." He tentatively tested the edge with his thumb, and pulled it back quickly. "It's sharp, all right. I bet it's worth a bunch. Want to trade? I have the most attractive bowl. I'm sure you'd just love it."

In spite of himself, Mathew smiled.

"I guess we had better get over there before all the food is gone," Mathew said.

Daniel and Lara were seated together, already eating, but they had saved places for Collin and Mathew. After they sat down, Collin returned Lara's speculative look with a nod and a quick wink. He leaned over to whisper something in her ear but didn't get the opportunity to do so when Elona Marshal brought a large plate of food over and put it down in front of him with a shy smile.

"I thought you might be a little hungry after all that hard work," she said. She put a hand gently on his shoulder and added, "We're all so proud of you—all of you."

"Thanks. I just did my part. We all did," Collin said, motioning to the others at the table.

"Oh, of course. That's what I meant. Are you going to stay for the dance?"

"You know me, I wouldn't miss a dance for anything. Maybe you'll save one for me." He grinned at her.

Elona's smile broadened. "I'd love to," she said quietly.

"Mmm . . . this is great," Collin said, taking a bite of the meat. "I was starving." He was about to take another bite when he noticed Elona staring at him oddly. He raised his eyebrows. "Is something wrong?" he asked.

"Oh, no," she answered quickly, with a small giggle. "Beckie said you have big shoulders. I was just looking at them. I guess I'd better run back in case anyone else needs me. Eat your dinner before it gets cold. See you all later."

Collin watched her walk away, observing the little sway of her hips. He was imagining what it would be like dancing a lively jig with a pretty girl like Elona when a high-pitched voice interrupted his thoughts.

"Oh, you have such big shoulders," Daniel said, fluttering his eyelashes.

Collin's ears went red and he spun around, only to find three blank expressions looking back at him.

"Fine bunch of friends you are. It's getting so a fellow can't even pass a few innocent words with a nice girl before you all jump on him."

Mathew and Lara were trying their best to keep their faces straight, then Daniel added in a nasal falsetto voice, "Would you save me a dance too, you . . . big . . . strong . . . man?"

He only just managed to duck as Collin threw a roll at his head. Lara, Daniel, and Mathew immediately burst into one of those uncontrollable bouts of laughter that sometimes happens to people in public places. A moment later, despite his best attempts at looking annoyed, Collin started to laugh as well.

A few tables away, Bran Lewin and Siward Thomas

watched the four of them convulsing in hysterics, although at what, neither had the faintest idea. They exchanged glances with each other, shaking their heads in bemusement.

It took Collin little time to finish his food, and he sat back contentedly sipping on a mug of good, cold berry wine and enjoying the evening. Mathew and Lara had moved to the end of the table and were talking with each other, their heads close together, and Daniel was talking to Sue Anderson at the next table.

Beckie Enders came by then to refill Collin's plate. He was so pleasantly full at that moment, the last thing he wanted was more food, but he thanked her nevertheless. She responded by giving him an unreadable smile, which only served to increase his discomfort. While she was walking away, he noticed that she and Elona said something to each other as they passed. He wished he knew what it was. A little voice in his head told him that he had better make sure and dance with both girls before the night was over.

Anyway, that won't be such a bad thing, he thought. *There is nothing like a good jig to get a fellow's blood going.*

While he was wondering how to discreetly get rid of the extra food without offending Beckie, the music started up. His problem was solved in the form of Daniel's dog, Goldie, who was seated nearby waiting for an opportunity to help with any leftovers.

Dogs are always hungry, aren't they?

Looking surreptitiously around to make sure no one was watching, Collin whistled softly and quickly placed the plate of food under the table. Goldie scampered over and wasted no time clearing the plate off. It was gone so fast, Collin made a mental note to speak with Daniel about feeding his dog more often.

People soon began leaving the tables and drifting toward the music. The brothers, Akin and Fergus, were playing a lively tune called "Tarrydown Lass," and several couples were dancing already.

Off to the side, Ella Emson had finally succeeded in cornering Bran, and was talking to him about something or other. One thing was certain—the folk of Devondale loved a celebration. More and more people joined in, forming a circle and clapping their hands in time to the music. A group of four men and women took the middle, locked elbows and alternated crossing back and forth with each other's partner. When they were finished, others replaced them, as the music got faster and faster. Collin joined the larger circle and began clapping in time along with the rest. Verna Darcy and Ben Fenton, who were engaged to be married that summer, also joined in, along with Marla Farolain and, of all people, Lieutenant Herne.

He was about to check and see what Mathew was up to when Lara scampered up with him in tow. She grabbed Collin's hand, pulling the both of them into the circle where Elona was waiting to become his partner. Two boys from Mechlen joined them with two of the local Devondale girls.

It took an effort for Collin not to look amused at the sight of Mathew's face, a study in concentration as he struggled to make some sense of the song. Lara, of course, knew Mathew was tone deaf and covered for him nicely.

Just as they were supposed to, the boys split off, forming a line on one side, and the girls threaded in and out between them, hands on their hips, as the dance continued. Collin noticed that Mathew succeeded in navigating himself somewhat awkwardly around the dance floor and got through the song with only minimal damage to a few toes. When it was over, everyone smiled and clapped. It was a beautiful night, and Collin couldn't have been in better spirits.

Mathew opted out of the next dance to go for a walk with Lara, while Collin and Elona went for punch.

Thankfully, Beckie was dancing with Giles Naismith and seemed to be enjoying herself. Nobody seemed to mind the faint chill, and there was even a hint of jasmine in the air.

When they got to the punch bowl, Collin noticed loud-mouth Berke Ramsey and two of his friends off to one side, drinking from a small flagon. He didn't have to guess what they were drinking. Dismissing them from his thoughts, he handed Elona her drink.

"Collin Miller, you certainly surprise me. I didn't know you could dance like that. That was just wonderful."

"Well, there are a lot of things about me you don't know."

"Really? Like what?" she asked, wide-eyed.

"Oh . . . just a lot of things." He wasn't serious when he said it, but it sounded charming and mysterious. Unfortunately, now he didn't know what else to say. *That was the trouble with trying to be clever with a girl*, he thought. *It doesn't always work out the way a fellow expects.*

An interval passed before she said anything.

"Hmm, I wonder." Elona tilted her head to one side and looked at him more intently. The torches at the dance floor back-lit her long brown hair. "Collin, have you ever thought about what you're going to do when you're older?" she asked.

"What'd you mean?"

"I mean your father has a farm, and your oldest brother has a nice farm near where we live. Do you think you'll do farming as well?"

"I can't stand farming," Collin said emphatically. "Nope. Not for me. What I'd like is to travel and see some of the world. I might even join the army . . . I don't know."

"Oh," she said softly, and turned away to watch the dancing. Neither of them spoke, and after a few minutes the silence began to feel awkward. He knew it wasn't what she wanted to hear, but he couldn't just mislead her, or worse lie outright. Anyway, what was so wrong about wanting to see the world? Devondale was boring. Nothing ever happened in it. Elona was sweet, but he was only seventeen, and there were a lot of pretty young girls in the world.

He was trying to think of something more moderate to say when she spoke first. "How long does a person have to stay in the army, Collin?" she asked.

"Stay? I don't know really. I guess it just depends."

"I imagine anyone as good with a sword as you are would probably be an officer, wouldn't they?"

He shrugged. "I'm really not all that good with it, you know. Mat's much better than I am. Now, if they let me use my long staff, that would be something."

"Are you good with that too?"

"Sure am. I can already beat my dad—at least most of the time. And he wins the competition each year."

"But isn't a sword better to use?"

"A man who knows how to use a good long staff can hold his own against anyone. At least, that's what my dad always says. C'mon, let me show you."

Grateful for the change of subject, Collin took her hand and led her to where he'd left his things. He picked up his staff and proceeded to demonstrate what he hoped was an impressive series of spins, blocks, and strikes against an imaginary opponent. Elona watched with apparent fascination. When he finished, she clapped delightedly.

"Here, you try."

"Me? I couldn't possibly. I wouldn't know what to do."

"C'mon, it's easy. I'll show you." Getting behind her, he put the staff in her hands—and his arms around her at the same time. "This is the first position. You see?"

"Yes, I see," she said, looking back at him.

"Uh . . . actually it's a little better if you pretend there's a person in front of you," he prompted.

"All right," she said, snuggling her shoulders backward against his chest. "What do I do now?"

For the next few minutes Collin showed her some simple moves, and she told him how impressed she was, even though he wasn't sure she was paying that much attention. He was trying to teach her a block and cross strike when a he heard a slurred voice.

"You should use a man's weapon, not a toothpick, if you want to fight someone."

Collin turned to see Berke Ramsey and his teammate, Evert Sindri, standing a few feet away. From the grins on their faces and the way they were swaying, he guessed that they were more than just a little drunk. Uninvited, the two approached.

"This is good enough," Collin said.

"Collin's teaching me how to defend myself," Elona said brightly.

"Well, I'm sure he's doing a wonderful job, and I bet *you* won't even throw up if you get scared," Berke said.

Impressed by his witticism, Berke and Evert burst into laughter.

"Excuse me?" Elona said.

"Didn't Collin tell you? His friend Mathew was so scared at the competition, he threw up."

To her credit, Elona lifted her chin. "I'm sure if Mathew threw up, he had a very good reason for it. And I seem to recall him beating you, didn't he?"

Berke made a dismissive gesture with his hand. "Playing with little practice blades is one thing, nobody gets hurt, but I'll wager a silver elgar that he'll run like a scared rabbit at the first sign of trouble. Cowards usually do."

Berke and his friend nearly doubled over with laughter again.

Collin was about to tell them what idiots they were when he noticed that Berke was standing directly over his staff, straddling it. A quick flick of his wrist brought it up with a snap, and Berke's eyes bulged as he doubled over, grabbing himself. With a groan, he slowly sank to his knees, then toppled over onto his side. Evert started for him, and Collin swung the butt end of the staff around in a quick arc, catching him just behind the ear. Evert hit the ground next to Berke.

Elona gasped and put a hand to her mouth.

Both boys were lying there groaning when Father Thomas happened by, saw them, and rushed over. "My lord, what's happened here?" he asked, crouching over the boys and looking at Collin for an explanation.

"Father, curse me for a thick-handed fool. They were just telling me what a coward Mat is, and I was showing Elona here how to use my staff, and . . . well . . . I guess I just wasn't paying enough attention."

Father Thomas blinked and looked from Collin to Elona, who nodded in agreement.

"They said that Mathew is a coward?"

Both nodded again, vigorously.

"Indeed?"

Still rocking back and forth on the ground and holding his private parts, Berke let out another groan. Father Thomas considered the scene a moment longer, took a deep breath, patted Berke sympathetically on the shoulder and stood up.

"Well . . . breathe deeply, my son . . . breathe deeply," he said, then stepped over Berke's body and hurried back to the dance.

7

Devondale

COLLIN AND ELONA FOLLOWED FATHER THOMAS'S EX-
ample and hastily made their way back to the dance,
where they found Mathew and Lara just returning from
their walk, holding hands and laughing. Neither mentioned the incident that had just occurred. The music was
still playing, and everyone seemed to be enjoying themselves. Mathew was about to ask Collin where he had
been when he spied Ella Emson waving and making her
way through the crowd toward him. He thought to escape
but saw that it was too late.

"Yoo-hoo, Mathew Lewin, have you seen your father
around? I was talking to him a moment ago, and he just
seemed to disappear."

"No, ma'am," Mathew replied politely. "I was out for a
walk myself and only just returned. I haven't seen him."

In fact, he could see Bran standing off to one side, talking with Jerrel Rozon, Thom Calthorpe, and Father
Thomas, who apparently made an effective shield, but he
kept that to himself.

Ella made a vexed sound, then sighed and scanned the
area once more for her prey.

"I think he might have gone for a walk over by the council building," Mathew offered, pointing in the opposite direction from where Bran and the others were conversing.

"Oh, well then, I'll just see if I . . ."

Ella's expression froze as her voice trailed off and her
mouth fell open in shock. She was staring over his shoulder, and as he turned to see what she was looking at, the

music abruptly stopped and someone screamed. Next to him, Lara put her hands to her mouth and gasped.

Thad Layton stood in the middle of the dance floor, cradling his son Billy in his arms. The little boy was covered in blood and his head hung back limply. Mathew was in as much shock as everyone else at the appalling sight. Even from where he stood, he could tell that the boy was dead. Somebody in the crowd yelled to call the doctor, and everyone began talking at once, asking questions, as people crowded forward. Thad, unsteady on his feet, looked dumbly around him for a moment, then dropped to his knees, still holding his child. He was wearing the clothes he farmed in, and the sleeves of his vest and woolen shirt were stained dark with the child's blood.

Father Thomas and Bran pushed their way forward, followed quickly by Jerrel Rozon and Thom Calthorpe. "My God," Father Thomas said under his breath. "What happened, Thad?"

With Bran's help, they gently took the boy from his father's arms, laying him on the ground. Jerrel Rozon cast a speculative look at Thad Layton, then knelt down on one knee, examining the little boy's body. Even from where he stood, Mathew could see that something about the boy's arms and legs didn't seem right. They were twisted and bent at impossible angles.

"Thad," Father Thomas repeated. "Thad, you've got to tell us what happened."

Thad blinked and looked around, his salt and pepper hair in disarray. It seemed he didn't know where he was.

"Thad, look at me, man," Father Thomas said, taking him by the shoulders. "What happened to your boy?"

For a moment Thad's lips worked, trying to form words, but nothing came out.

"Tell us, Thad," Bran said, kneeling down at eye level with the man.

"Boars," he said slowly. "He was out playing in the north pasture with Stefn Darcy. When they were late for dinner, Stel sent me to fetch them back. I found him lying there, Father . . . like this. There was nothing I could do . . . nothing," he repeated, as tears welled up in his eyes.

Thad's farm was nearly ten miles outside of town, Mathew thought. He'd carried his son the entire way.

Father Thomas reached forward and gently closed the boy's eyes before putting an arm around Thad, helping him rise. "It's all right, my son, we know . . . we know."

Abruptly, Jerrel Rozon stood up and spat on the ground. "No boar did this," he said, backing away from the body. The vehemence in his voice turned every head in his direction. "See for yourselves," he said, looking at Bran, then at Thom Calthorpe.

Both men exchanged glances and bent down for a closer look at the body. Rozon looked around and found Orin Kirk, one of the older boys on the Gravenhage team. "Collect your things, and get the others together," he said. "We're leaving."

A moment later Thom Calthorpe stood up, shaking his head. "I don't know, Jerrel. It could be."

Mathew wanted to ask his father what he'd seen about the boy's body that had upset Jerrel Rozon, but the grim expression on Bran's face stopped him.

With a small motion of his fingers, Bran signaled Father Thomas over and whispered something in his ear, then they both moved off with Jerrel Rozon and Thom Calthorpe, talking intently. After a while, Rozon looked at the hushed gathering and asked, "Is that young Herne still here?"

"Here, sir."

"How many men have you?" It may have been a question, but it sounded more like an order.

"Twelve, sir."

Rozon's mouth tightened, but he went on quickly, "I want you to find the mayor and the rest of the town council at once. Get them out of bed if you have to, and have them meet us at the inn in half an hour—no more. Do you understand me?"

"Yes, sir, I do," Herne answered. He turned and began

issuing orders to his men, who saluted and melted away into the crowd.

Meanwhile, Lucas Emson had spread a cloak over the little boy, then he and Akin Gibb picked the child up and carried him away. Mathew thought it odd that they were heading in the direction of the inn rather than the church.

With the conversation between them concluded, the group around his father dispersed. Rozon headed toward the Rose and Crown with Thom Calthorpe, and Father Thomas walked quickly toward the church. Bran caught Mathew's eye and motioned to him.

"Father, I don't—"

"Later," Bran said, forestalling any questions. "The rest of you will need to stay close," he added to the others. "Get whatever things you have and meet us at the inn as soon as you can."

"Maybe I should be going home," Elona said hesitantly. "My mother might start to worry."

"No," Bran replied sharply. "Do as you're told and get yourselves to the inn." It was a tone that brooked no argument.

Elona and Lara curtsied and hurried off to gather their belongings.

"I'll make sure they get there," Collin said, grabbing Daniel by the elbow.

"See that you do, boy," Bran said, clapping him on the back and adding a gentle push to get him started. "Oh, and if your dad's about, tell him I need to speak with him."

"Right," Collin called over his shoulder.

"Come with me," Bran said to his son.

"Where are we going?" Mathew asked.

"To Randal Wain's shop."

Mathew stopped abruptly and looked at his father. They were in the middle of the street. "I think you'd better tell me what's wrong," he said seriously.

Bran stared back at him for a moment, then sighed and rubbed the bridge of his nose. "You're right, lad, but we can talk while we're walking."

Mathew nodded, and fell into place again beside his father.

"You may not have seen the marks on the little Layton boy, but Jerrel was right. No boar could do damage like that. The bite marks on the back of the boy's legs were from a rounded mouth, not a pointed one, and the teeth were square, not sharp. Calthorpe's not sure, but I am. I don't think he wants to believe it. That child was killed by an Orlock."

Mathew nearly missed a step. "What? How can you be certain?" he asked.

"The bites were only part of it. There was a smell too. It's been a very long time, but I'm not likely to forget anything like that. The wounds had it about them, and nothing else I know carries the same stench. Siward—Father Thomas—agrees with me. And I think Calthorpe knows it as well."

"I understand," Mathew said slowly. He had known right away that something was very wrong, but this . . . His father's mention of the Orlock's smell brought to mind his meeting on the road that morning with the two strangers and their strong cologne. "I think they were here earlier," he said.

Bran stopped walking and looked sharply at his son, who stopped too. Mathew told him about the cowled men he'd met at Westrey Bridge earlier. When he finished his father nodded.

"Orlocks have been known to travel in disguise before," Bran said. "Some actually managed to get into our camps during the war. They're cleverer than you think. Fortunately, when you get close their game is up. But you say they asked about Harol Longworth?"

"Right."

"That makes no sense. He's just a merchant. What could they want with Harol?"

Mathew shook his head as they both started walking again. "What do you think we should do?" he asked.

"First, we're going to get you that sword we talked about. Then we'll let the town council know what's happened. Likely, they'll send as many men as we can muster out to Thad's place in the morning."

"The morning? But didn't Thad say that his son was playing with Stefn Darcy? There's another boy still out there. I think we should go now—right away."

"I don't want to say this, lad, but if the boys were together when the Orlocks found them, there's nothing we can do for Stefn." Bran looked up at the sky and frowned. "And with the weather closing in, it would be suicide to take men out at night." He sighed. "I feel like you do, Mat, but the advantage would be on the Orlock side, and they can see in the dark where we can't. What's more, we don't know their numbers. All we'd do is get more people killed."

Mathew knew that what his father was saying made sense, but he was still sick at the thought of the Darcy boy at the mercy of Orlocks.

Randal Wain was waiting for them in front of his shop. A thin, wiry man who walked with a pronounced limp that caused him to favor his right side, he had retired from the army, like Bran, and come to Devondale to live. He was an accomplished bladesmith. The consensus was that Randal knew more about blade and arrowhead making than anyone in the province. Men came from as far as Anderon to trade with him.

"Siward Thomas sent word you needed to see me," he said, without any preliminaries.

Bran nodded as they shook hands. "Thanks for coming, Randal. We'd like to look at some of your work, if you wouldn't mind. It's time Mathew had a sword of his own."

"Well, of course I wouldn't mind. It's how I make my living, isn't it? For this young fellow, you say?" He turned to Mathew and looked him over as they shook hands. "Grown another head taller since the last time I saw you, boy."

"Yes, sir, I guess." Mathew was surprised when Randal didn't release his grip. Instead, he took Mathew's forearm with his other hand, and then his upper arm at the bicep, squeezing each of them in turn.

"He'll do," he said. "Let's get out of this chill."

Once inside, he lit a lamp, gesturing for them to look around. Mathew had only been in Randal's shop once, years before, when Bran brought him there to replace a blade that had broken. Weapons of every type lined the walls and cases—halberds, rapiers, broad swords, pikes, knives, and spearheads. He had never seen so many weapons in one place. While Randal was rummaging around the clutter, looking for a match to light another lamp, Mathew noticed an odd-looking sword and picked it up. It had a curved blade that ended in separate points and was unlike any weapon he'd ever seen. Despite its length, the sword was surprisingly light, with an intricate scrollwork pattern etched from the handle to about halfway down the blade.

"Bajani," Randal said from across the room. "They're an odd bunch, but they know how to make a blade . . . Ah, here's what I'm looking for."

Pulling a sword from a pile of other weapons, he walked over to Mathew, rested it against a table, and then gripped him by the shoulders.

"Let your arms hang natural by your sides, son."

Mathew put down the weapon he was holding and looked at the sword Randal had brought over while the swordsmith stepped back, continuing his assessment of him. The sword appeared nondescript at first glance, and the blade dull. Puzzled, Mathew glanced at Bran, who shrugged. When he looked at the sword again, he realized that his first impression had been wrong. The blade's finish wasn't dull at all, but a flat gray metal, with wavy lines running from its tip to the hilt. It was the most unusual steel he'd ever seen. Noticing his interest, Randal picked it up and handed the weapon to him.

The fit and balance were remarkable. Mathew examined it more closely and decided the fine-grained pattern was actually integrated into the metal itself.

"Kayseri steel—it'll never rust and'll cut through just about anything," For emphasis, Randal took the blade

from Mathew's hand and brought it down on an old
dented helmet lying on the table, splitting it neatly in two.

A low whistle escaped Mathew's lips as he stared
wide-eyed at the helmet. Bran put down the bow he was
examining and came over to look too. Randal handed him
the weapon, and he hefted it a few times testing its feel.
Eventually they stepped aside to discuss the price, while
Mathew discreetly looked at some arrowheads in a case
at the opposite end of the room.

After a little old-fashioned haggling, the transaction
was concluded, with Randal throwing in a scabbard and
belt to match.

"That's a fine present your father's bought you," he
said to Mathew.

"Yes, sir, I know."

"See you do it proud."

"I will, sir."

They said their goodbyes and were at the door when
Randal called Mathew back. "Weren't sure you could beat
that Naismith boy, were you?" he said.

"No, sir, I guess I wasn't. I didn't know you were
watching."

"I was. You have to believe you can win. If you don't,
you're as good as finished before you start. Do you know
the best way to deal with a flank attack, son?"

"Well, I haven't really thought—"

"You drive for the center. Ask your father or Siward
Thomas about that sometime."

Mathew would have preferred to skip the conversation,
but he thanked Randal for his advice, and he and Bran,
left the shop. A light snow had begun falling.

"What did he mean by that?" Mathew asked.

"It's not important, lad. We can talk about it later if you
wish."

The Rose and Crown was just a short distance from the
square on the opposite end of town. While they walked,
Mathew pulled his cloak more tightly around him to keep

out the chill. As Bran had said, the weather was closing in, and the temperature continued to drop. In the light from the street lamps he could see the swirling flakes of snow. If it didn't let up soon, it looked like they would be in for an early spring storm.

By the time they reached the inn, a good-size crowd had already gathered. One by one, the five members of the town council hurriedly arrived. Lieutenant Herne, seated off to the side with several of his men, nodded to them as they entered.

The common room wasn't large by the standard of most inns, but it was well-decorated with polished floors of dark oak and a large stone fireplace that dominated its center. Most of the tables were occupied with men and women talking quietly among themselves. Mathew recognized Jerrel Rozon and Thom Calthorpe. Thad Layton was also there. Collin, Daniel, and Lara were standing next to the stairs, and he separated from his father to join them. Bran went over to have a few words with Collin's father.

"What's everyone waiting for?" Mathew asked his friends, keeping his voice down.

"Father Thomas," Daniel answered.

Just then Father Thomas came in, causing a buzz. For the first time that Mathew could recall, he was not wearing his black clothes. Instead, he was dressed in dark brown breeches, with tan boots folded over at his mid-calf, and a green shirt and cloak. He was also carrying a sword.

Truemen Palmer, the town's mayor, got to his feet as soon as the priest entered and held his hands up for quiet. He was a heavy man, with a shock of pure white hair and a weathered, ruddy face. The conversations immediately ceased and everyone turned their attention to him. Even the serving maids carrying drinks stopped to listen.

"My friends, by now most of you already have an idea why we're here tonight. We've had a tragedy—a terrible tragedy. Thad and Stel Layton have lost their little boy."

A few heads turned sympathetically toward Thad, who sat grim-faced and silent. Wila Burmack, standing just behind him, gently placed a comforting hand on his shoulder.

"I'm sorry to say this is not the worst of it," the mayor went on. "Jerrel Rozon and Bran Lewin have looked at the boy's wounds and they believe the child was killed by an Orlock."

Everyone was on their feet at once, talking and shouting. Marla Farolain gasped, covered her mouth with her hand and looked about to faint. One of the serving girls dropped the pitcher she was carrying; it shattered to pieces on the floor. Mathew, however, was watching Thad Layton, who slowly got to his feet. His face looked like it was made of stone, and his fists were clenched so hard, his arms were shaking.

It took a full two minutes for Truemen Palmer and Father Thomas to quiet the room again. Finally, someone had the sense to ask what they were going to do. The mayor ran one hand through his hair and massaged the back of his neck.

"We'll be going out after them at first light," he said. "Bran Lewin will lead one group, starting from the south side of town, and Jerrel Rozon will lead the other, from the north end. If all goes well, it should take us a little over a half hour to converge on Thad's farm. That's the most likely spot to begin. From there, Jerrel and his young men will split off and head back to Gravenhage to their families. I know many of you haven't seen battle before, but I can tell you—"

Before he could say another word, Thad Layton, who was standing nearby, stepped in front of him. His chest rose and fell heavily, and he was flexing his hands, clenching and unclenching them into fists.

"Thad?"

Palmer reached out to touch him, but to his surprise, and the surprise of everyone else in the room, Thad knocked his arm away and bounded to the front door, shouldering two men aside as he ran out.

"Stop that fool!" Rozon snapped. "He's going to get himself killed!"

Father Thomas and two of Lieutenant Herne's men went after Thad, calling his name. Three minutes later, they returned—alone. Father Thomas looked at Rozon and shook his head slightly. On the side of the room Mathew felt Lara slip her hand into his, and he squeezed back gently. The buzz of conversation gradually died down enough for Palmer to resume speaking. He had only just begun, however, when a flurry of activity by the window interrupted him again. Marla Farolain and Sara Lang had pulled both Bran and Thom Calthorpe aside and were talking to them. Mathew couldn't hear what they were saying, but the conversation was obviously urgent. Sara had hold of Bran's shirt and Marla was waving her arms excitedly and pointing at the door. Then Bran disengaged himself and turned to Palmer.

"Truemen, I think we have another problem. Sara's son, Garon, and Lee Farolain went out after the Darcy boy about fifteen minutes ago."

Palmer stared at him in disbelief, then abruptly turned to confer with the rest of the council, signaling Bran to join them. A minute later they called for Jerrel Rozon, Thom Calthorpe, and Lieutenant Herne. The discussion was becoming more heated. All of them were on their feet, including Silas Alman, one of the older council members, who was vehemently shaking his head no. Thom Calthorpe apparently shared his sentiments. Some minutes went by before a decision was reached, and from the look on Silas's face it was clear that he wasn't happy with it.

"You men, get your horses and weapons," Palmer announced. "We'll meet at the stables within the hour. We're leaving immediately."

People wasted no time filing out of the room. In the corner, Bran was talking to Collin's father, Askel Miller. He was about Bran's height and age, with the same sandy brown hair as his son. He was generally considered the best hunter and marksman in Devondale. Collin, who it seemed had inherited many of Askel's abilities with a bow, often said that his father could track a rabbit over bare rock if he set his mind to it.

"I'll be right back," Mathew said, letting go of Lara's hand. "Stay here."

Bran and Askel had just finished shaking hands as Mathew walked up. Askel gave him a quick smile and grabbed Mathew's arm as he walked by, but then stopped and looked him sharply up and down.

"Good lord, Bran, what are you feeding this boy?" Askel called over his shoulder.

Despite the gravity of the situation, Bran and Mathew grinned. He and Collin had slept at and eaten dinner at each other's houses so many times over the years they knew the other's home as well as their own. Collin's mother Adele often affectionately referred to Mathew as her third child.

"At least he thinks you feed me," Mathew said.

Bran gave him a sour look and guided him toward the door.

"Where did Askel go?" Mathew asked.

"To get his bow and an extra sword for Collin."

Mathew's pulse quickened. "We're going with you, then?"

"I'd rather you didn't, you can believe that. But you're both old enough now, and we're going to need every pair of eyes we have."

"Do you think there'll be fighting?"

"It's possible, lad. If there is, you, Collin, and your friends, are to stay well back. Do you understand me?"

Mathew's face turned serious. "I understand. But why am I going, if I'm not to do anything?"

"I didn't say that. You're a fair shot with a bow, which may be important before this evening's over. Orlocks don't travel by themselves. And where there's one, there's usually more. I just can't understand what's brought them back after all these years."

"Excuse me for a second," Mathew said, and hurried across the room to Lara, pulling her aside.

"I have to go out with the other men," he said quietly. "I want you to stay here until we get back or send word that things are safe."

As a heated conversation began to develop between Mathew and Lara, Bran discreetly looked the other way. After a few moments, their whispers got loud enough to be heard across the room. It ended with Mathew spinning on his heel and starting for the door. He only got a few steps before Lara caught him. She grabbed him by the shoulders, turned him around, and kissed him full on the lips, then pushed him toward his father. A few glances were exchanged but no one made any comments.

"What did she say?" Bran asked as they stepped out into the street.

"Nothing that you'd want to hear," Mathew replied glumly.

Bran chuckled. "I imagine it's the same kind of thing your mother used to say to me."

"Something like that," Mathew replied.

While they walked to the stable, Bran Lewin snuck a sideways glance at his son and shook his head. Mathew was at least three inches taller than he was.

They grow up so fast, he thought. *Where does the time go?*

Mathew looked down at his own footprints in the snow. There was better than two inches on the ground already. A snowfall this late in the winter was unusual, and conditions looked like they were going to get worse before the night was over. Mathew tried to put the conversation with Lara out of his mind as he pulled his hood up, drawing the strings tighter around his neck. As if things weren't difficult enough, the wind was also picking up, which was going to make visibility a problem.

"How are we getting to Thad's farm?" he asked.

"I sent word to have Tilda saddled for you. Askel's bringing his bay for me to ride," Bran replied.

* * *

People soon began arriving in twos and threes. Most were
carrying long bows, but some had swords as well.
Mathew was a little surprised to see Silas there, considering his earlier attitude. He was wearing a rusty old helmet
that was too big for him, and carrying a long pike. It occurred to him as he glanced around that he knew every
face there. The atmosphere was a somber one, and few
people were talking. Some nodded when they saw him,
and he nodded back. Mathew rested a hand casually on
his sword hilt, hoping its addition would make him look
older. He also found that walking with a scabbard took
some concentration. Twice in the last hour it had gotten
tangled with his legs, nearly causing him to fall. The last
thing he wanted to do was to kill an Orlock by making it
laugh itself to death.

Jerrel Rozon arrived a few minutes later, with the rest
of the Gravenhage team, followed by Lieutenant Herne
and his men. The boys from Mechlen, Father Thomas,
and the rest of the town council were the last to arrive.
Outside of a few people whose farms lay near the outskirts of the town, it appeared that the entire male population of Devondale was represented. A good number of
women were also present. Many were insisting on going
along and had to be persuaded, not without some difficulty, to stay in the town. To his surprise, Lara was there
too. People in Devondale didn't take well to being told
what to do, and this seemed to go doubly for the women.
When Mathew approached her to explain it was the sensible thing to do, she nearly snapped his head off. Fortunately for him, the stableman chose that moment to bring
Tilda out, which gave him an excuse to check her saddle
and get out of Lara's glare.

She is one stubborn girl, Mathew thought, but he was
proud of her for wanting to go all the same.

People began to mount their horses as the mayor called
out the names of those who would go with Bran and
those who would go with Rozon. Finally, two groups to-
taling forty men each were ready to depart.

Mathew wasn't sure when it dawned on him, but it seemed logical that if everyone were to leave, there'd be no one left to defend the town. It was such an elementary concept, it seemed silly, but no one had thought of it.

"Excuse me, Mayor?"

"Yes, Mat," Palmer said, turning his horse around.

"I know it's not my place, but, uh . . . shouldn't we leave someone here to defend the town while we're gone?"

The mayor's eyebrows lifted and he sat back in his saddle, then he looked at the other members of the council. Seeing four embarrassed faces, he turned to Rozon and Bran, who both shrugged slightly and looked abashed. A conference was quickly convened on horseback. While they were considering what to do, the sound of snickering and laughter from the Gravenhage team attracted Mathew's attention.

In a voice just loud enough for everyone in the immediate area to hear, Berke Ramsey said, "I told you he'd find a way not to go."

Mathew's face went red. That was not at all what he'd intended. The conversations around him died quickly and a number of heads turned in his direction. Until that moment, he had been toying with the idea of trying to talk to Berke privately and see if they could mend fences, but his last comment changed all that in an instant. Berke was a fool of course, but now he'd left him no choice. A torrent of thoughts swept through Mathew's mind. More glances were being darted at him as the meaning of Berke's words became clear to everyone there. Being called a coward was not something Mathew could simply ignore. His mind weighed all the pros and cons before reaching his decision.

Slowly, Mathew dismounted and walked over to Berke. "Get down off your horse."

The other boy looked surprised, for a moment, but it was quickly replaced by arrogance as he dismounted. Several of the men around them began to back away.

Thom Calthorpe, who was near enough to have heard the comment, understood what was happening and interceded quickly.

"Come, come, I'm sure that was not what he meant. Tensions are high, and the wit was not. Perhaps you should tell this young man that was not what you intended," he said, addressing Berke.

Berke was two years older than Mathew and nearly as tall, but considerably heavier and built like a boxer. He stood there belligerently with his hands on his hips.

"Master Ramsey," Calthorpe prompted again, more forcefully than before, "surely you didn't mean to imply—"

Berke glanced at the faces around him and recognized that the situation had become grave.

When Mathew recalled the expression on Berke's face at the end of their match, he knew it would only be a matter of time before there was another incident. People like Berke Ramsey fed on the weakness and misery of others, and the last thing Mathew wanted at that moment was to ride out with men who thought that his courage might be in question.

Berke said, "Well, what I meant was—"

"If he is willing to apologize and admit his error before everyone here, I will accept that," Mathew said.

Berke's temper flared, just as Mathew knew it would.

"*Apologize to the likes of you!* Not bloody likely."

"You see? He leaves me no choice."

If Mathew had let Berke's comment pass as the grumbling of a sore loser, it might have gone unnoticed, but now that he had taken a stand, it was impossible to ignore.

Thom Calthorpe closed his eyes and took a deep breath.

"As the insulted party, I believe I have the choice of weapons, do I not?" Mathew continued.

"Well, uh . . ." Calthorpe said.

Before he could answer, Jerrel Rozon rode up and asked, "What goes on here?"

"I have been insulted, and he refuses to apologize, so I have no choice in the matter," Mathew said calmly, unbuckling his scabbard. "We will use daggers."

Rozon heard the earlier remark along with everyone else, and he was fairly certain the Lewin boy knew exactly what he was doing. *But daggers?* The boy had just soundly beaten Ramsey with a sword only a short while ago, and now he was willing to stand there as calm as a tax collector and give up the advantage. There were looks of surprise and shock on the faces of everyone present. *Ramsey is a fool*, Rozon thought, but at the moment he could ill afford to allow a duel to take place.

"Gentlemen, we can settle this matter when we return," he said. "Right now we have work to do."

"If he thinks I'm going to apologize—" Berke snapped.

"Get . . . on . . . your . . . horse and do not speak another word," Rozon said to Berke, emphasizing every word, his eyes going cold and hard. After a brief pause, the larger boy did as he was directed, and then, turning to Mathew, Rozon added, with a gesture in Tilda's direction, "Master Lewin?"

Mathew opened his mouth to say something, but a slight shake of Rozon's head forestalled him.

They held each other's gaze for a moment before Mathew turned away.

Rozon watched the awkward-looking young man mount his horse, face impassive, and stare straight ahead. He glanced around, caught Bran Lewin's eye, and received an imperceptible nod of approval. Rozon found that his own heart was beating faster, and he took a deep breath.

The boy must have ice water running through his veins, he thought before pulling up on his reins and turning his horse toward the road.

For his part, Mathew never believed for one moment that Berke would apologize. He knew Berke would sooner die than submit to a public humiliation. When he reflected on the fact that he might have been lying dead in the street, it sent a shiver up his spine. Nevertheless, the point was clear. Although everyone knew him as the boy who got sick at the thought of a competition, he was also the same person who could challenge someone to a duel in cold blood when his honor was questioned.

In the end, the council decided that Father Thomas and twenty men would stay behind.

8

Devondale, Layton Farm

THE ANDERON ROAD LED TO ELGARIA'S CAPITAL CITY OF
Anderon. Everyone in Devondale simply referred to it as
North Road. When they reached the outskirts of town,
Bran divided the men into two columns, sending Akin
Gibb and Ben Fenton about a mile ahead, to act as scouts.
Two of the soldiers with them, Ivor and Galdus, brought
up the rear, along with Collin and Mathew. Both men had
the look of seasoned veterans, and Mathew was grateful
they were along.

After another mile, Bran reined in his horse and called
the men together. The wind and snow had increased to the
point where he had to shout to make himself understood.

"In about a half hour, we'll be at Thad's farm," he told
them. "We don't know what we're going to find there, so
you'll have to keep your eyes and ears open. The most
important thing is to locate the little Darcy boy, and get
the others back to safety. Lee Farolain and Garon Lang
are also out here somewhere. So are Thad and Stel Layton. Understand this—our friends come first, the Orlocks
come second—so let's have no heroes.

"Jerrel and his group are taking the South Road, so
we'll reach the farm before they do. If there's to be a
fight, our signal will be three horn blasts. We'll deploy
into two lines, in the same way you're divided now, and
come at them from either side of the farm. Jerrel will
strike straight on, from the head of the valley."

Bran took a moment to go over his instructions again,
making sure they all understood which side of the farm

they were to attack from, if the order was given. He made them repeat the instructions back to him. Ivor and Galdus listened, exchanged glances, and nodded to each other in approval.

"*No one is to move before the order is given.* Is that clear? Now, I know some of you have seen battle before, and some have not. Mark this well—don't engage an Orlock closely if you don't have to. Use your longbow first."

"You've fought the Orlocks before, Bran," Fergus said. "What are they like?"

Bran pulled the horse's reins in tighter and patted her neck to calm her as she stepped nervously in place. The bay's nostrils flared and her head bobbed up and down in agitation.

"You'll know the first time you see one. Most are larger in height and weight than a normal-size man. They're manlike in appearance, for the most part, but their skin is dead white, and their hair hangs down well past their shoulders. You'll almost certainly smell them before you see them. There's a stench they carry you're not likely to forget. Despite what they look like, they're cunning and intelligent, so don't underestimate them."

A few looks were exchanged, but no one asked anything further.

Pulling his hood back over his head, Bran turned his horse and signaled for them to move out. Mathew watched his father's back, wishing that he could possess the same outward calm. He supposed such things came with age—along with a stable stomach. His own had begun to flutter, and he had to struggle to maintain a calm appearance. To his annoyance, Collin appeared relatively unconcerned, given the circumstances. There were plenty of other men around him, but that did little to ease his feelings of isolation as the weather continued to worsen and the temperature fell.

The road began to climb after they left the forest. Thad's farm lay at the end of a long valley, nestled between two ridges. Mathew knew the area well and was thankful there would still be a fair number of trees around to provide cover for them until the last minute. The snow was already ankle deep on the horses, which would make the descent down the ridge difficult, if not treacherous. To complicate things, a fog was beginning to roll in. Mathew glanced over his shoulder and could see it creeping around the base of the trees they had just emerged from, moving silently over the ground, covering it.

Once on top of the ridge, the trees began to thin. From that point on, the hard-packed dirt road flattened, rising now and then to follow the contours of the land. Without the shelter of the denser trees, the wind also picked up, whistling at them and whipping their cloaks around. No one seemed to have much of an appetite for conversation, and they rode on in silence for the next fifteen minutes. Several times Mathew thought he could see the valley floor stretching beneath them, but the fog and blowing snow made it impossible to spot Rozon's group. He knew they were getting close to Thad Layton's farm, and closed his eyes in a silent prayer for his friends.

Suddenly, the birds in the trees ahead of them took flight. Akin Gibb came charging out at a full gallop, bent low over his horse's neck, chunks of earth flying from beneath the horse's hooves. Mathew had known Akin all his life, and had no idea the man could ride like that. Bran halted the column as Akin skidded his horse to a stop.

"Dead . . ." He barely got the words out as he tried to catch his breath. "Both dead."

"Slowly, man, slowly," Bran said. "Tell me who's dead."

"Garon and Lee—both dead. God . . . I've never seen anything like that!"

"Where?" Collin's father asked.

"About three minutes," Akin said, pointing in the direction he had just come from. "Oh, God, it was horrible!" he added, covering his face.

"Akin, where's Ben?" Bran asked sharply.

"Back there. He's with them. I came back to get you."

"Were there any signs of a fight?" Askel Miller asked.

"No, nothing."

"Did you see anything else? Smell anything?" Bran asked.

Akin shook his head.

"All right," Bran called out. "Bows at the ready. The first half of you with me. The second half, starting from Lucas on back, will follow in one minute. Let's go."

Mathew watched the first group disappear back down the road, into the glade Akin had ridden out of. When it was time for them to follow, he spurred Tilda forward, urging every bit of speed out of the old mare that he could. The snow stung his eyes as he rode. His father and the other men soon came into sight. He could tell that they had surveyed the area and had now dismounted and were standing in a semicircle, looking up into one of the trees. Mathew reined his horse up and saw what they were staring at.

Twenty feet above his head, the bloody bodies of Lee and Garon hung upside down by ropes. Both boys had been skinned. Mathew's mouth fell open in shock. It felt as if he had just been struck by a blow. His stomach revolted and it took every ounce of his willpower to force himself to breathe. Even a hardened soldier like Ivor let loose a string of oaths as Bran and Askel lowered the bodies to the ground. Ben Fenton sat with his back against the trunk of a tree, staring blankly ahead, not speaking. Fergus Gibb dismounted and put an arm around his younger brother. These were farmers who had never been very far from Devondale, and this was a sight no one could be prepared for.

Akin shook his head and said, "Why would they do something like this?"

"Food," Bran said over his shoulder. "They planned on coming back for them later."

"Dear God," Akin said under his breath, turning away.

Mathew slowly walked to the edge of the ridge to clear his mind. He'd been talking to Garon only a few hours

ago. *What sort of creature could do this to another living
being?* He didn't know how many minutes passed. Instinctively, he began to check for signs on the ground, but
the snow had blanketed whatever was there. He took a
deep breath and looked out across the valley below him.
Most of it was still shrouded in fog. For an instant he
thought he saw something, but it was gone again as the
fog closed back in. A moment later the movement was
back. Yes—there it was! The dark brown cloaks had to be
Lieutenant Herne and his men. They were just over a half
mile away, moving steadily along the South Road.

"C'mon, Mat," Collin called. "We're getting ready to
ride."

Before the fog closed in again, he was able to make out
the rest of the column, winding its way up the road—but
that wasn't the only thing that attracted his attention. At a
point where the road turned into the valley, he saw something else move.

"Mat, we're going."

Mathew crept to the edge of the ridge and lay down, ignoring the biting cold and the snow, and shielding his
eyes from the wind. His heart pounded while he strained
to see what the movement was. A minute ticked by, then
another, and then he saw them—about twenty white
shapes concealed in different places on either side of the
road. Another eight were on the opposite side of the
stream, which ran parallel to the road. Even from this
distance, the axes and pikes they carried were plain
enough. The mathematical part of his mind registered
the sound of his companions leaving, at the same time
calculating how long it would take Rozon and his men to
reach the bend in the road. Somehow he had to warn
them. He dared not call out, and the hill was too steep
and treacherous to take Tilda down, but surely he could
make it.

Impelled by the urgency of the moment, Mathew made
his decision. He swung his feet over the edge, testing for
a foothold, and using his arms for support, began to lower

himself. The snow was achingly cold. He was partway over the edge when someone grabbed his shoulder. Mathew reacted without thinking and thrust himself forward. He fell about six feet down to a small ledge, rolled to his right and came up with an arrow notched.

"Damn . . . what's the matter with you? You nearly scared me to death," an offended Collin protested from just above his head. "Your father sent me back to get you. He needs you to—"

A fierce gesture from Mathew silenced him. "Get down," he whispered.

"What is it?" Collin asked, looking around.

"Down there in the trees, behind the rocks," Mathew said, pointing.

Collin shielded his eyes from the wind and squinted in that direction. "Right, right, I see them," he said after a second. "Where do you think you're going?"

"Rozon, Herne, and the others are coming up the road right now. They should be here in about five minutes. I've got to get down and warn them."

"Wait, I'll come with you," Collin said, unslinging his bow.

"No!" Mathew whispered sharply. "Get to my father and tell him what we saw."

"Mat, what are you doing?"

In truth, Mathew wasn't sure what he was going to do. He just knew that someone had to warn Rozon. "I'll think of something," he said, with a shake of his head.

Collin wanted to argue, but Mathew was already well below him, moving quickly between the snow-covered boulders.

The fog made it difficult for Mathew to keep his bearings, and every sound seemed magnified in the heavy air. Although he was hurrying as fast as he could, the snow, wind, and lack of visibility greatly slowed his progress. The hill was so steep that it was impossible to go straight down, and he was forced to constantly cut sideways. Just how much time had elapsed was impossible to tell, but he knew that Rozon and the men had to be very close. Thirty yards farther down, the ground started to flatten out. Mathew quickly crouched down low behind a good-size boulder and listened. By now he should have heard the sound of horses or men talking. Instead, a fetid odor reached his nostrils, followed by whispers in a language he didn't understand. They were close. He began to ease backward, but froze when something metal scraped against one of the rocks to his left. Somehow he had managed to come down just behind the Orlocks. Seconds ticked by. He tried to make his legs start moving but couldn't.

One hundred yards away, Jerrel Rozon and his party came into view. Mathew knew he needed a signal as he crouched in hiding, filled with self-contempt at his own cowardice. This was something men talked about behind their hands in low voices. In another minute it would be too late. To him, death would be preferable.

Slowly easing two arrows out of his quiver, he cut strips of cloth from his cloak and wrapped them securely around the shafts. With his left hand, he felt around the pocket of his cloak until he located the little tin cylinder that contained his remaining match. He struck it against the side of a rock and held his breath. When it flared, he quickly cupped his hand around the flame, shielding it from the wind. The first arrow caught fire right away, and he used it to light the other. Seventy yards.

Now or never, he thought.

From behind the boulder, Mathew rose and fired the first arrow high into the air directly in front of Rozon's path. He changed his position at once, loosing the second arrow. He heard a surprised chorus of shouts as the Orlocks charged out of the trees. From the corner of his eye he saw Jerrel Rozon throw up his hand, halting the column.

His heart was pounding so rapidly in his chest now that Mathew was certain the Orlocks could hear it. Moving again, he notched another arrow, firing as he ran. An Orlock near him went down, making a loud gurgling sound, the arrow piercing its throat. A large shape loomed up beside him, and he barely had time to duck as an axe buried itself in the tree just where his head had been. He could feel the splinters of wood striking his face from the force of the blow. Mathew fired point-blank into the creature's chest. A pair of dead black eyes stared into his for a moment before they glazed over. There was barely time to get out of the way as it fell forward.

Got to keep moving and firing, he thought.

He intended to take as many of the Orlocks with him as he could, before they downed him. Somewhere in the back of his mind the three blasts of a horn registered. Seconds later the air was alive with the clash of steel and screams, as Jerrel Rozon and Lieutenant Herne led a full-scale charge directly into the Orlocks. At the same time, Bran's group struck from the rear like a thunderbolt, splitting into twin lines, exactly as he had instructed them.

Still moving from tree to tree, firing as he went, Mathew watched with horrific fascination as Galdus and Ivor rode by him yelling like madmen and beheaded two Orlocks. To his right he saw Bran engage a huge Orlock. Mathew's heart nearly stopped as the Orlock swung a double-bladed axe at his father. Bran neatly sidestepped the blow and struck backward at the thing's neck as its momentum carried it forward and past him. Unfortunately, the blow was mistimed, and only caught the Orlock across the back. The leather armor it wore absorbed most of the impact, though a line of red blood erupted from the wound. With a bellow of rage the creature spun and came at Bran again. Mathew drew his bow and took aim.

Too close—they're too close.

He dared not risk a shot. Behind Bran he saw Collin's father, Askel, firing arrow after arrow from his horse. One Orlock went down with an arrow through its eye, and another took one straight into the mouth. Almost directly in front of him, Mathew saw one of them pull Ivor from his horse and plunge a knife into the soldier's throat.

Still trying to make his way to his father, Mathew

nearly tripped over the body of Ben Fenton and gasped in shock. Ben lay there with blood seeping slowly from a huge gash that ran from his shoulder to his hip. His eyes stared straight ahead, sightless.

He couldn't say how long the battle went on, but slowly, outnumbered, the Orlocks were driven back out of the trees and up into the valley. From behind him, above the noise of the fight, Mathew heard Jerrel Rozon call out, "Gravenhage and Devondale, rally to me." A small force of about twenty quickly gathered behind him at the mouth of the valley and charged after the fleeing Orlocks, riding them down one by one. Despite being in retreat, the Orlocks managed to kill four of the closest pursuers with a well-timed volley of spears.

Try as he might, Mathew was only a little closer to his father. He could see Bran continuing to retreat as the Orlocks pressed forward. The sound of snapping branches directly behind him caused him to turn, and he saw twenty more Orlocks pouring out of the trees.

A pitiless white face looked into his and said, "Time to die, boy."

Mathew had no time even to register his surprise. He leaped backward in desperation to avoid the point of a halberd thrust directly at his stomach and managed to save himself. But the Orlock advanced on him, its upper lip drawn back in a snarl, exposing grayish teeth. He knew that any attempt to notch another arrow would end with him being skewered or cut in two.

Have to gain time, he thought.

On the next lunge, he sidestepped as he'd seen his father do, and swung his bow as hard as he could, breaking it across the Orlock's face. It was enough to momentarily stun it. The effect of the blow didn't last long, but it was enough to allow Mathew time to draw his sword. Strangely, the Orlock made no move toward him. Instead it reached up and wiped the blood from its face with the back of its hand, then slowly licked it off, never taking its eyes off Mathew. Almost frozen in place, Mathew watched in horror as the creature raised its weapon above its head and charged forward. He was barely able to deflect the blow, but the shock numbed his whole hand as the Orlock wrapped its arms around him and they careened down the embankment toward the stream. Their faces were so close, he could feel its breath on his face.

Mathew landed on his back, stunned, most of the wind knocked out of him. For some reason, the blow that he expected to end his life never came. Just to his right, the Orlock lay on its side, not moving, with Mathew's sword sticking through its back. Slowly, his senses began to return. They had fallen almost fifteen feet down the bank. Somewhere above him, he could tell the fighting had moved into the valley. He got shakily to his feet and with an effort managed to roll the Orlock over, pulling his sword free. He wiped the blood off on the snow. Even in the rictus of death the creature was frightening to look at.

The stream flowed rapidly to his left. The rushing water, fed by the recent rains and snow, drowned out most of the noise from above. Over the years, it had deeply undercut the banks on either side so that they were well above his head. Yelling for help was out of the question. For the next five minutes Mathew tried to climb his way out, but without success. Each time he managed a foothold, he lost it again on the wet, moss-covered rocks. *Think*, he told himself. Going up wasn't an option, nor was going south, since the stream descended into a canyon on the other side of the valley. With no other choice, he decided to make his way upstream to where the land leveled out and he'd have a better chance of escape.

In minutes the progress became more and more difficult. The rocks along the bank were covered with lichen and snow, and he had to fight just to keep his balance. Each time he slipped, his foot plunged into icy water, and despite his boots, his toes were beginning to lose feeling. Once, he missed his footing and fell—the water was so cold it felt as if his skin was burning. After twenty minutes, exhaustion began to set in. He was cold, wet, tired, and miserable. It was worse when he estimated he had come only a half mile at best, and still saw no way to the top. Although the bank walls protected him from the howling wind above, he could tell the storm was gathering strength. Snow was coming down more heavily. He trudged on for a while longer, and to his relief, the stream bed gradually began to rise to a point high enough for him to try climbing out again.

Just ahead of him he spied an old dead tree that had fallen into the stream.

It might work, he thought.

Mathew tested his weight on the trunk—it seemed sturdy enough. He unbuckled his scabbard and started to climb. From their last dip into the stream, his fingers were still numb, and he had to flex them to get some feeling back. The spiderweb of branches and ice-coated limbs impeded his progress at first, but after one or two failed attempts he succeeded in working his way through them. When he was almost level with the top, the wind nearly caused him to lose his balance. Several times the hilt of his sword became snagged. With no other choice, he unbuckled his scabbard and tossed the sword up onto the bank, so he could use both hands to help him inch forward.

Finally, Mathew found himself standing on the roadside, breathing heavily from his climb. But when he looked for his sword, it was missing. He blinked and scanned the area. A short distance away, three Orlocks stood watching him through the blowing snow. They were dressed in the same white armor he had seen earlier. Given the conditions, it was an effective camouflage. He realized that they must have followed the course of the stream from atop the road, knowing he would exit where he did. The one in the middle had a scar that ran from his ear to his mouth, and was holding Mathew's sword in his hands. Oddly, they made no movement toward him. They just stood watching. The wind around them whipped the yellow hair back off their shoulders, but they seemed not to notice. In desperation, Mathew looked around for some means of escape and saw none.

Then the scar-faced one spoke. "Show us your hands, boy."

My hands? He wasn't sure he'd heard correctly. Maybe they were asking for him to surrender. But remembering what they had done to his friends, he had no intention of giving up without a fight, as futile as that would be.

"Show . . . us . . . your . . . hands," the Orlock repeated.

It took a moment for Mathew to realize that the creature was not looking directly at him, but down at his hands. So were the others, which made no sense at all. All he had was his belt knife, and that was no match for a halberd and two swords. He drew it and stepped back. As soon as he did, the Orlocks spread out and began to advance on him.

Then, from behind the Orlocks, there was a loud shout. Before they could react a rider burst from the trees at full gallop and crashed into them, knocking two of them to the ground. Taking advantage of the momentary confusion, Mathew dove to retrieve his weapon. Giles Naismith brought his horse to a halt, turned and fired an arrow directly into the nearest creature's chest. Its eyes opening wide in shock as it stared at the shaft protruding from its body, the Orlock dropped to its knees and fell face forward. A pool of blood began to form under its body, staining the snow red.

"Mat, to your right!" Giles yelled as Mathew scrambled to his feet.

From the corner of his vision he saw the movement and spun around, getting his blade up in just enough time to parry the blow.

Another inch and it would have been my head.

With the creature off balance, Mathew pivoted to the left and swung his sword, putting all of his weight behind the blow. The blade caught the Orlock at the base of its neck, severing muscle and arteries, blood erupting from the wound. The Orlock let out a terrible scream and ran forward a few paces before collapsing. Everything was happening so fast that Mathew barely had time to think before another sound caught his attention. He turned to see the third Orlock grab the reins of Giles's horse and pull him from the saddle.

"No!" Mathew screamed, dashing toward them.

The thing had Giles by the throat and was shaking him like a rag doll.

Oh God, I'll never make it! his mind screamed. Horrified, Mathew saw the Orlock's dagger go up. With a burst of speed he didn't believe himself capable of, he covered the remaining ground, lowered his shoulder, and drove into the creature at full speed, knocking the Orlock and Giles down. The collision was just enough to deflect the blow. The Orlock let out an oath of some sort and started to get up. It never made it to its feet, as Mathew's sword severed the head from its body.

Giles was lying on his side just a few feet away, one of his legs twitching spasmodically. Mathew quickly went to him, knelt down and gently rolled him over. A dark red stain was slowly spreading across his chest. He tore open Giles's shirt and quickly found the wound. Though he'd deflected the blade, it wasn't enough. The dagger had gone in just below the collarbone, and the wound looked to be a deep one. A small trickle of blood ran from the corner of Giles's mouth. Deliberately, Mathew forced himself to slow down and think about what to do. *First, stop the bleeding and clean the wound,* he thought. He grabbed up a handful of snow and cleansed the area around it.

"Not much of a rescue, was it?" Giles said, looking up at him. His voice sounded weak and hoarse, though he managed to prop himself up on one elbow.

"Stay still, will you? We're going to have to get you back to a doctor, quick. Where is everybody?"

"Your father and a few others are out looking for you. Jerrel went on to Gravenhage with the rest of our people. He didn't want to, you understand, but his family is there. You should have seen him, Mat—he charged right into the middle of them. No hesitation at all."

"I saw."

Giles paused for a second as his face contorted in pain. "That fire arrow—it was you, wasn't it?"

Mathew nodded, cutting a piece of cloth from the bottom of his own shirt and pressing it against Giles's wound. Giles grimaced again.

"I thought so. Collin told me you went down to warn us. If it wasn't for that signal, we'd have been caught from both sides," Giles said, gripping Mathew's arm.

"Stay still," he repeated. "What about the others? Was anyone—"

"You lost five people from your village, I think—don't know their names. Calthorpe also left for Mechlen as soon as it was over."

"Did they find Thad Layton or his wife or Stefn Darcy?"

Giles shook his head and started to cough. "There wasn't any sign of them. The farm was ransacked and burnt to the ground—nothing left. Snow's covering everything. I'm sorry, Mat."

"It's all right," Mathew said. "We did what we could. Let's see about getting you back. Now where's that horse?" He looked around.

Giles tried to get up, but Mathew restrained him. "For the love of God, lay quiet, will you? You're hurt."

Giles nodded weakly and sank back down again. Not seeing the horse, Mathew looked up and down the road in both directions, expecting to spot it a short distance away, but it was still nowhere in sight. After a brief search, he found its tracks heading directly back toward Devondale.

Wonderful.

Despite the cold, his mouth was suddenly dry. The distance to the village was better than five miles, and in this snow . . . A small moan from Giles made up his mind.

Well, it can't be too hard to construct a litter, he thought. He had seen people do it before, and he berated himself for not having paid more attention. He found two saplings and used his sword to cut them to the correct size. A length of creeper vine would be sufficient to lash his cloak to the poles and act as a harness of sorts. He remembered that if you braided several strands of the vine together, it made a solid enough rope. He and Collin had once tied some to the limb of an old tree by the lake and used them to swing out over the water.

With some effort, he managed to transfer Giles on to the litter. Giles tried to assist but lacked the strength to help. Once Mathew had him securely in place, he hoisted the poles onto his shoulders and tentatively tested the rig. It seemed sturdy enough, and so, looping the vines across his chest as a harness, he began to trudge forward.

Though he had on a heavy woolen shirt, he was sweating after only a few hundred yards. The wind began to cut through him. After a half a mile, he was breathing heavily and his shoulders ached from the effort. Every so often, when he took the time to rest, he checked on Giles. What he saw scared him. Something told Mathew it would be best for Giles to remain conscious, so he kept up a steady conversation, though Giles was plainly weakening.

After an hour, Giles stopped speaking or responding to Mathew's questions and his eyes remained closed. The blood near the wound turned black and crusted over, and the skin around it seemed warm to the touch. Another hour later, when Mathew checked again, he noticed a distinct odor coming from it. Even the slightest touch caused Giles to groan.

He couldn't begin to count the times he had been over the South Road. If someone had asked him, he would have told them that it was flat, but each little grade now seemed like a mountain. Toward the early hours of the morning, the snow began to let up and streaks of orange appeared on the eastern horizon as the sun rose. Mathew's vision was swimming by then. He was no longer even aware of the cold, and his shoulders were so numb he couldn't feel them any longer. He knew the sun would be fully up soon, and that would help. It was a grim realization that both their survival depended on his ability to remain alert. Watchful, Mathew peered into the gray shadows and forest around him as he pulled the litter.

He had no idea how long they had been going, and he began to measure their progress by yards and minutes. If he had to drag Giles one step at a time, so be it. Every so often, Mathew tried to fix how far he'd come in his mind, but for some reason the answer kept eluding him. He thought that odd, that Devondale couldn't be so far away. Soon, he played a game with himself, looking at an object in front of him and counting down the distance to it. Fifty yards, forty yards, thirty yards . . . rest . . . try to recover. Despite his tone deafness, he hummed a tune his mother had taught him between gulps of air, though he didn't know why he was reminded of it just then.

Mathew swayed on his feet, steadied himself, and looked back. The trail the litter left in the snow looked like a drunk had been pulling it. Straight was better, he told himself.

Shortest distance between two points, or something like that, he remembered, which struck him as funny. He started to laugh, but something in the back of his mind told him what he was doing was dangerous. With an effort, he gathered his will, fixed on a tree ahead of him, and began all over again. Fifty yards, forty yards . . .

All at once, Giles began to thrash about, nearly unbalancing him. Exhausted, Mathew sunk to his knees, set the litter down as gently as he could, and staggered back. Giles's forehead felt hot to the touch, and he was shivering at the same time. He pulled Giles's cloak tighter around him and put snow on his face to cool him. Giles's lips were moving and he was mumbling something. Mathew bent close to listen but couldn't make any sense out of it.

It's just the fever talking, he told himself.

Slowly, Mathew pushed himself to his feet, steadied himself, and blinked to clear his vision. He knew this section of the woods. They were still at least two miles from the village. *Maybe somebody'll come along to have a picnic and see us.* The thought struck him as so funny, he started to laughing again.

A journey starts one foot at a time. That's what Bran had always told him, but his legs felt so heavy now. It would be nice just to sit down for a while and maybe sleep for a bit, but a part of his mind screamed that it would be fatal to them both. Mathew rubbed his eyes with the knuckles on the back of his hand and shook himself out of his reverie. He refocused on the road once more. When he bent down to pick up the litter, he gave a quick glance over his shoulder to check on Giles and noticed something shiny lying in the snow.

Frowning, Mathew went back to see what it was. He recognized the rose gold ring that Giles had won in the tournament, and bent down to pick it up. It was heavier than it looked.

Must have fallen while he was tossing about.

His own breeches had no pockets, and Giles was lying on his cloak, so he slipped the ring onto his finger for safekeeping. Almost immediately after he put it on he felt a tingling in his hand that ran all the way up his arm and then quickly disappeared. He blinked in surprise and shook his head.

I'll give it to him when he wakes up.

With a deep breath, he hoisted the litter again, leaned forward sharply, and took a step.

Push off with the right foot; now push off with the left.

Fencing and youth had given him strong legs, but each yard was a fight. His next target was a big oak tree about a hundred yards away. He drove his legs backward and started to close ground on his objective.

Only thirty yards to go now, he told himself. *At least Giles is quiet . . . nice dress Lara was wearing at the dance . . . the others are probably worried by now . . .*

A half hour later, using the last reserves of his strength, Mathew tugged the litter to the side of the road and sat down heavily beside it, leaning back against a tree. He closed his eyes and tilted his head back, letting the sun warm his face.

"Just need to rest for a bit," he told Giles. Despite the morning chill, the sun felt wonderful. Perhaps a little sleep would be just what he needed.

Fifteen minutes later Mathew awoke with a start and pushed himself up onto his hands and knees. They had to keep moving. He felt light-headed, and it was difficult to keep his thoughts focused.

"We're not far from the village now," he said patting Giles's hand. "Westrey Bridge is just around the—"

His words froze in mid-sentence as Giles's arm swung to the ground. It took only a glance to tell him his friend was dead. Mathew stared at Giles's face for a moment, then sat down again, leaning wearily against the tree. He looked up through the branches at the sky. The clouds were no longer gray. They were broken and white, with promises of blue between them. Feelings of sadness, grief, and loss began to build so slowly, he was hardly aware of them at first, nor could he have separated one from another as the tears welled up in his eyes.

A short distance away, the stream bubbled noisily over rocks and forest birds called to each other, but he sat there, not hearing or seeing anything or knowing what to do—just letting the tears slowly roll down his face.

He had no idea how long he sat there. And in the days that followed, he could only dimly recall hearing the sounds of horses and of people shouting.

9

Alor Satar

KARAS DUREN SAT BACK IN HIS CHAIR, LISTENING TO HIS son Armand go over the final plans for their invasion of Elgaria. Even with the Sibuyan forces hitting them from the north and Nyngary and Cincar attacking the center, Duren knew the south was still vulnerable. That was why he had contacted King Seth and agreed to employ fifteen thousand Vargoth mercenaries to help him. Armand had objected bitterly, claiming the Vargothans were loyal only to the highest bidder.

It was something that couldn't be helped.

King Seth sent him Abenard Danus, a seasoned soldier who possessed all the warmth of a cobra but whom he knew would get the job done.

Duren had met the man several times, and rather liked him.

Danus was shrewd, intelligent, and utterly ruthless. At the moment, he lounged against the wall, sipping a glass of wine, nodding occasionally as Armand pointed out key passes and routes to him on a map spread across a large table in the middle of the room. The Sibuyan general, Oman Shek, and his Cincar counterpart, Naydim Kyat, stood on the other side of the table. After they took the city of Tyraine, Armand explained, Vargoth's soldiers would secure those passes in order to prevent reinforcements from getting in or out. Tyraine was the most important commercial shipping center in the West, and by closing it down, Elgaria's already shaky economy would collapse in a matter of months. It was a good plan, meticulously thought out, down to the last detail.

Danus and Duren briefly made eye contact with one another, and Danus inclined his head respectfully in acknowledgment.

"Is there something on your mind, Commander?" Duren asked, interrupting his son.

Danus stuck his lower lip out and he slowly shook his head.

"But I sense there is," Duren said.

There was a pause before Danus answered. "We'll do the job we're paid for," he said. "But why do you want us to rename the city Octavium?"

"My wife's name. I thought she might enjoy having a city named after her."

Danus considered that for a moment and shrugged. "You've also told us to destroy anything that bears the name Elgaria on it, correct?"

"Correct."

"I can understand renaming cities. That sort of thing happens in a war. The winner's prerogative, you might say, but why go to all the trouble erasing the name Elgaria? It's a needless waste of time."

Oman Shek and Naydim Kyat looked up from the map to hear the answer.

"Because, my dear commander, when the war is over, I intend to eliminate all trace that Elgaria ever existed from the face of the world. No names . . . no references . . . no whispers in the dark. Nothing."

Karas Duren and Abenard Danus held each other's gaze for a moment before a smile slowly spread across Danus's face and he lifted his glass in salute.

10

Devondale

WHEN MATHEW OPENED HIS EYES, HE WAS LYING IN A bed in a room he didn't recognize. To his surprise, his friend Daniel was seated in a chair by a window tinkering with something, his slender features screwed up in concentration. The spectacles he wore were partway down his nose, and his hair was, as always, almost covering his eyes. Over the years, Mathew had come to associate that expression with Daniel's trying to think about four things at the same time. It took him a minute to look up from the glass lens he was carefully turning back and forth between his finger and thumb, and then he blinked in surprise.

"Mat?"

"I think so."

A grin creased his friend's face. "Welcome back."

"Where am I?"

"You're at Helen Stiles's house," Daniel replied, setting the lens down on the table next to him.

"What? How? I don't—"

Before he could answer, the door swung open and Helen walked in. When she saw him awake, her face lit up in a smile, just as Daniel's had. She was a pretty woman, in her late forties, with a plump figure and a pleasant round face.

"Well, there you are at last. I thought I heard talking in here," she said. "How are you feeling, Mathew?"

Mathew sat up on his elbow, looked down and noticed

he was wearing a white bed shirt. "How long have I been here?"

"Three days," Daniel answered, pushing his glasses back up the bridge of his nose.

"Three days! How on earth did I get here?"

"We found you, just outside of town. You must have walked the whole way from Thad Layton's farm."

"We?" Mathew asked.

"One of the search parties, Mat," Daniel said. "I was in the second one with Lara on the South Road when we heard the signal."

"Oh," Mathew said, as the memories began flooding back.

"I'm very sorry about your friend, dear. His family came for him from Gravenhage yesterday," Helen said softly.

"I . . . tried to—"

"Never mind that now—I'm sure you did everything you could. There'll be time enough to talk about all that later. Right now I'm going downstairs and fix you a bowl of soup and some warm bread. I expect your father will be here soon. He's been nearly beside himself with worry. The poor man's been walking back and forth from your farm twice a day."

Mathew looked at Daniel, who nodded in confirmation.

"I guess I'd better get dressed." Mathew said.

Helen became nearly apoplectic as Mathew started to rise, and immediately pushed him back down. "What you'd better do, young man, is stay right where you are," she said, waving an admonitory finger at him.

Helen wasn't a big woman, and he was surprised how little trouble she had restraining him.

"She's right, Mat. You've been pretty sick," Daniel said seriously.

Mathew gave him a sour look and eased back down into the bed. He did feel surprisingly weak.

"Hmph," Helen said with a nod of satisfaction, straightening a stray strand of blond hair that had fallen across her face. "You just stay where you are, Mathew Lewin. And don't even think about getting out of that bed. I'll be back in a few minutes with something to eat. And you," she said turning to Daniel. "Don't tire him out with a lot of your questions."

"Yes, ma'am," Daniel said.

"Oh, I'm glad to see you opened the window a bit," she said with an approving nod. "It was getting very stuffy in here."

"I didn't open the window," Daniel said. "It was open when I got here."

"It was?" She frowned and tilted her head, trying to recall whether she had actually opened it and then forgotten about it. From somewhere in the back of his mind, Mathew could vaguely remember having a dream about wanting to open a window because he was hot.

"Oh, well," Helen finally said with a small shrug. "By the way, that nightshirt you're wearing used to be Benden's favorite. I hope you like it. I'm afraid it may be a little short."

Mathew opened his mouth to answer, but she swept out of the door before he had the chance.

Daniel watched her go, shook his head, and turned back to Mathew. "How do you feel?" he asked.

"Tired."

Mathew rolled over onto his side and propped himself up on one elbow.

"It's no wonder. You've been out for three days. You were pretty sick too—with a fever and all—and you were talking out of your head."

Mathew rubbed his hands across his face and was surprised to find a thick stubble there.

"You need a shave too," Daniel added.

"Thank you," he said flatly. "Did anything happen in the village? Was anyone hurt?"

"Nothing really happened here at all. We lost five people, though, and Lieutenant Herne lost three of his soldiers. Most everyone got back the following morning.

You and Giles were still out, so a second search party went after you. Like Helen said, they found you not too far from the bridge. Thad Layton's dead, but I guess you know that; so's his wife and Ben Fenton—Garon and Lee too."

Daniel's face turned somber at the last part. "Helen said my father's all right? Before we got separated, I saw him fighting an Orlock."

"Your father's fine," Daniel answered. "He can take care of himself, except he's been worried to death over you. He only goes back to the farm to feed the cows, and then he comes right back here again. Something else happened that was odd, you probably don't know."

"What?"

"We didn't find any Orlock bodies."

"That's impossible," Mathew said. "I killed two myself, and I saw at least three of them go down. Lieutenant Herne's soldiers beheaded two of them not ten feet from where I was standing. I'm pretty sure they didn't just get up and walk away."

"I know," Daniel said, holding up his hand. "Your father told us that's the way Orlocks are. They don't bury their dead—they carry off the bodies and eat them."

The image sent a shudder up Mathew's back. He nodded slowly and looked out of the window. It was light outside, and he guessed it was probably late morning. He'd been in Helen's house before but never in this particular room. It was neat and small, but not objectionably so. Apart from the bed, there was a small dresser and a long rectangular table on the other side stacked with different colored sheets of leather piled on it.

"Mat?"

"Hmm?"

"Collin told us what happened. About how you went to warn Jerrel Rozon's group and the fire arrows and all."

"Right," Mathew said.

"Do you want to talk about what happened after?"

There was something odd about Daniel's tone that

caused Mathew to look at him closely. He searched his friend's gray eyes for a clue but found nothing.

"After I got to the bottom of the hill, I used as many arrows as I could. I think I killed two of them and probably a third. I was trying to set another arrow when about twenty Orlocks came rushing out of the trees. One of them grabbed me, and we went over the embankment together. He landed on my sword and was dead when we hit. I spent the next hour following the stream back toward Devondale, to where I could finally climb out."

"Is that when you met Giles?"

Mathew nodded. "I walked right into the middle of three Orlocks, like a damn fool. If it wasn't for him, I'd have been their breakfast."

"What exactly happened?" Daniel leaned forward, his face suddenly intense.

Mathew frowned, but retold the rest of the story as faithfully as he could. When he finished, he said softly, "He saved my life, and I let him down. He's dead because of me."

Unable to go on, Mathew turned and looked out the window. Once again the feelings of guilt and his belief in his own failure surfaced in his mind.

Daniel leaned back in his chair and blew out a breath in exasperation. "Mathew, sometimes, I swear—"

"It was my fault," Mathew whispered, partly to himself.

Abruptly, Daniel was on his feet, looming over him, his face red. "If you weren't lying there, I swear I'd thump you myself. You have got to be the dumbest—"

"What?"

"You build a litter out of nothing, drag someone bigger than you almost five miles through a snowstorm, nearly die of a fever, and you think *you're responsible* for Giles's death!"

"I should have gotten him back. I failed," Mathew repeated, shaking his head.

"Oh, for the love of heaven," Daniel said, flopping back into the chair again. "Do you have any idea what you were raving about when they found you?"

Mathew didn't reply.

"When they found you, you were saying 'I killed him' over and over again. That idiot Berke Ramsey was there with the search party. He went around telling everybody you murdered Giles. Don't you get it?"

"Murdered? I didn't murder him. What I meant was—"

"Oh, nobody believes you murdered anybody," Daniel said, waving his hand. "But I'm telling you you're going to have trouble with him. You mark me."

"But I thought Jerrel Rozon went back to Gravenhage with their team."

"He did," Daniel said, "but when they couldn't locate Giles or you, Berke and Evert Sindri and Giles's brother stayed behind to help with the search. They were in the first party with your father when they found you."

The point of Daniel's questions suddenly became apparent. "And you weren't sure what happened. Is that why you asked me about it?"

He didn't know whether to be hurt, offended, or angry, but it was just like Daniel—always a skeptic. If you told him it got dark at night, he'd probably ask for proof.

"Look, Mat, we've known each other since we were children. I guess I know you just about as well as anybody, but . . . I don't know. I just wanted to hear you say it. I mean, you're wearing the ring he won at the tournament, and . . . oh, heck, I'm sorry."

Mathew looked down at the gold ring on his finger. Until that moment, he hadn't given it a thought. "It fell out of his cloak," he explained. "I didn't have any pockets and didn't want to lose it, so I put it on to keep for him."

He was about to pull the odd-looking ring off his finger when a small knock at the door interrupted him.

"Mathew?" Lara called. "Is it okay to come in?"

"Sure," he answered, pulling the covers up higher.

The door opened a crack and Lara poked her head in. "Are you decent?"

"I am, but Daniel's not."

Lara opened her mouth to say something, then closed it again and gave him a sour look. "Well, I see you're feeling better," she said, entering the room. "Helen had me bring up this bowl of soup for you. Did I interrupt anything?"

"No. Daniel was just about to tell me what he was doing with that piece of glass he was polishing."

"What? Oh, sure," Daniel said. "I have this idea that if I can shape the glass just right, and put two pieces together in this tube here, a person could use it to see things far away, the same as if they were up close." Daniel held up a thin brass tube about two feet in length to show them. "I had Lucas make it for me."

"Why would you want to see something far away, when you could just go and see it?" Lara asked.

"I mean really far away, like miles away. It would look like it's right in front of you. I think if you made the tube long enough, you could even look at the moon or the stars."

Mathew whistled through his teeth.

"Do you know what else?" Daniel went on excitedly. "If you reverse the curve of the glass pieces—I mean from out to in—and you put them in a small tube, you could even see really tiny things, smaller than you can see with your normal vision."

Lara and Mathew looked at each other and shrugged.

"That's pretty impressive," Mathew said. "What are you going to do with it once you finish? You have at least a dozen inventions lying around your house now."

"Oh, I don't know. I suppose I'll think of something."

"Until something else comes along that interests you more," Lara said.

Daniel smiled self-consciously and looked at the floor, while Lara sat on the edge of the bed and turned her attention to feeding Mathew. Until the first spoonful, Mathew didn't realize how hungry he was. When he had almost finished the bowl, she paused for a moment and ran her fingers over his chin.

"Yuck. You look like a bear. I'll tell your father to bring a razor the next time he comes."

"Yuck?" Mathew said, feeling his chin. It might have been a little scratchy, but he didn't think it was all that bad.

Lara surveyed him closer, shook her head, then leaned over to brush the usual lock of hair back from Mathew's forehead. As she did, Mathew suddenly became aware of how close her breasts were to his face. He also noticed the top two buttons of her dress were undone, revealing some of her cleavage. Unfortunately, Lara chose just that moment to look down, and noticed him noticing.

Mathew neither saw her eyebrows arch nor the faint smile that played at the corners of her mouth. While he continued admiring the fulsome view, unbeknownst to him, Lara's left hand slipped under his bedcovers and crept unobtrusively up between the middle of his legs as she fed him another spoonful of soup.

A second later Mathew's eyes flew open in shock and he almost jumped off the bed with a startled cry.

"What?" Daniel said, dropping the brass tube.

"I'm sorry," Mathew replied, catching his breath. "Just a sudden pain."

"My goodness, are you all right?" Lara asked sweetly.

"Yes," Mathew said, drawing out the word and looking at her.

"You really should be more careful with yourself," she said, her eyes wide.

"Don't worry . . . I will," he promised.

Lara apparently decided it might be a good time to get up, which she did, and quickly stepped back out of his reach.

Daniel saw another look pass between them, but decided not to inquire further.

"By the way, where are my clothes?" Mathew asked, changing the subject.

Lara grimaced. "Helen had to wash them; there was blood on them and everything. But do you know what else? You have new boots! Yours were ruined from the snow, and she made you the loveliest pair to replace them," she said excitedly.

"Really?"

"Mm-hmm."

Lara bent down and picked up a shiny new pair of boots from next to the little table.

Mathew felt his stomach sink when he saw them. They were a dark burgundy with little intricate designs at the toe.

"I just think they're the pretti—I mean, handsomest pair I've ever seen," Lara said. "Don't you?"

All he could manage was a weak smile and a nod. She held them up so Daniel could see them as well.

"Very attractive," Daniel agreed, a bit too readily. Catching Mathew's expression, he stifled a grin, and went back to examining the glass lens again.

"Oh, Helen will be thrilled," she said, handing the boots to him. "She really wasn't sure you'd like them. Be sure to say something nice to her."

"I will," Mathew said. But it sounded less enthusiastic than he hoped.

"Well, make sure you get some rest. Right now, I have to help my mother with some chores, but I'll be back a little later."

Lara left with a bright smile and a little wave.

Daniel, noting Mathew's expression, quickly got up as well, on the pretext of going over to Lucas Emson's shop to discuss making some modifications for his invention. Following closely behind her, he stopped in the doorway and turned to Mathew.

"I may just have to get a pair of boots like that myself," he said, obviously amused at his own wit.

He barely managed to duck as one of the boots hit the door just above his head.

The next morning, unable to sleep, Mathew rose early and sat by the window watching the sky grow lighter. He thought about Giles, and his other friends who had died, and about little Stefn Darcy. Why would the Orlocks pick Devondale, of all places, to attack? he wondered.

He was trying to sort things out in his mind, when he noticed a figure standing by the road watching the house. Momentarily startled, he looked more closely. Berke Ramsey stared back up at him for a minute, then turned and walked down the road toward town.

11

Devondale

TWO DAYS LATER HELEN PRONOUNCED HIS HEALTH suitably restored to allow him out of bed. Lara stopped by, as she had on each of the previous days, to check on his progress. She told Mathew that his father would be by later to take him home, which suited him just fine. All of the mothering was getting on his nerves. After delivering the message, she made a point of staying long enough to make certain that he shaved. He grudgingly gave in, putting aside his idea of growing a beard for the moment.

True to his word, Bran arrived about an hour later. His face broke into a broad smile when he saw his son, and they hugged before a word was spoken.

"Looks like Helen's cooking agrees with you, boy," he said, grabbing Mathew by the shoulders.

Mathew couldn't remember ever being happier to see his father. After saying their goodbyes, Mathew tossed his sword and bow in back of the cart and they started walking down the road, leading Tilda.

To his surprise, when they came to Westrey Bridge, instead of turning right, they continued straight ahead.

"We're going into town?" Mathew asked.

"There are one or two things we need to attend to."

His tone left Mathew curious. "Such as?"

Bran's face took on a serious aspect. "There's a constable come from Anderon who we need to talk to."

"A constable? Why?"

"Palmer rode out to the farm this morning and spoke

with me. It seems that Berke Ramsey boy made a complaint against you over the one who died."

Mathew's temper flared. "Look, if anyone—"

Bran held up a hand, cutting him off. "No one doubts your word, lad—at least nobody from Devondale. He hasn't gotten many people to listen to him over the last three days, but there's also no denying the accusation is serious. That's why the constable is here."

"Daniel was right. I should have finished my business with him before we left," Mathew said hotly.

"Perhaps . . . but you'll do nothing now. You're to keep your temper and answer just what is asked of you. Do you understand me?" Bran was leaving no room for argument.

Mathew fumed inside but kept on walking. They crossed the bridge in silence and entered the square. It was still the same town, and all the sights were familiar, but many of the barricades erected the night they left were still up, giving things an odd appearance.

In front of the council building several men stood waiting for them. Trueman Palmer was there. So were Berke Ramsey, Silas Alman, Father Thomas, and two other members of the council. Mathew assumed that the slender, well-dressed man in dark blue was the constable, and the two men standing off to one side, similarly attired, were with him. When Berke saw them approaching, he pointed in their direction and apparently said something to the others because the entire group turned at the same time.

"Steady, lad," Bran said quietly, sensing Mathew tighten.

After tethering Tilda to a nearby post, Bran walked up to them and said, "We're here," without preamble.

"Thank you for coming, Bran . . . Mathew," the mayor replied, nodding to each of them. "This is Jeram Quinn from Anderon. You already know that Jeram is the king's constable. And these are his men," he added, indicating the other two.

Mathew followed his father's directions and ignored Berke's sullen expression. He acknowledged Quinn and his companions with a nod. He noticed they were all carrying swords, and from their look, they knew how to use them.

Quinn stepped forward and offered Bran his hand. "I know your mayor has told you why we're here. You don't remember me, do you? We served with Lord Kraelin's regiment against the Sibuyan, more years ago than I care to recall."

Bran frowned at him for a moment, before his expression softened. "I remember you. It's been a long time," he said, shaking the constable's hand. "You've fared well."

Quinn shrugged elaborately. "A bit older and grayer, I'm afraid. Mathew, I'm Jeram Quinn," he said, extending his hand.

Mathew stepped forward and took it. "Yes, sir."

"Tall boy," he said, looking Mathew up and down. "What have you been feeding him?"

For all his pleasantry, the constable's grip was firm, and his gaze was clear and searching.

"Not enough," Bran answered flatly.

"Why don't we go inside so we can all sit and talk?" Palmer suggested.

Before Bran could answer, Quinn said, "Do you know, we passed a fine-looking inn as we entered your village. I've been constable these past fourteen years, and I do believe this is my first visit here. I took the liberty of asking the innkeeper if he would allow us to use one of his private rooms where we can chat for a while."

Mathew thought "chat" was an odd word to use, since the constable's dour-faced men didn't look particularly chatty.

"We can say what we need to right here," Bran replied.

"Come come, man, it's been a long journey for us and we're not here to arrest anyone—only to inquire and learn what happened. A serious charge has been made. I know you can appreciate that. Since my arrival, I've had an opportunity to talk with your good Father Thomas as well as your mayor, and after hearing them, I have questions of

my own. I would prefer to ask those questions in a relaxed atmosphere."

Berke started to speak, but a sharp look from the constable forestalled him. He shut his mouth, apparently
content to sneer at Mathew instead.

Bran's face, however, was devoid of reaction. He considered the constable who returned the gaze with a frank
expression and waited. An almost audible sigh could be
heard from the mayor and his councilmen when Bran finally made up his mind with a curt nod. Without another
word, everyone turned and walked down the street toward the Rose and Crown. Both of Quinn's men took up
a position at the rear, a fact that was not lost on Mathew.

When they reached the inn, he was surprised to see
that Collin, Daniel, and Lara were waiting for them. In
addition, Lieutenant Herne was there, standing beneath a
painted sign that bore a rose and crown on it. Mathew
started to walk toward his friends, but a small shake of
Collin's head stopped him.

Cyril Tanner, the inn's balding proprietor, met them at
the door, sunlight reflecting off his shaven scalp. He was
a heavy man, with a considerable stomach and a beard as
round as his head. He wore his usual spotless apron and a
wide, amiable smile.

"Welcome, gentlemen," he said, and led them across
the common room.

At that time of day there were only a few patrons seated
around the fireplace or in the booths that lined the sides of
the room. Since it was mild out, the fire remained unlit
and their passage attracted no particular notice.

The private room contained a long oak table with four
chairs behind it and another one positioned at its end. A
number of benches, three to a side, were arranged in
rows, facing the table. The room itself was about thirty
feet square and paneled in the same light-colored wood
as the rest of the inn. The floors consisted of wide, rough-
hewn wooden planks. Two shuttered windows on opposite ends of the wall behind the table framed a tapestry

depicting a hunting scene that hung in between. On the wall to their right was a pair of crossed swords set over a shield bearing a crest Mathew had never seen before.

"It's an honor to have you here, Constable," the innkeeper said. "I've set the room for you as you asked. I trust you will find everything in order."

"Thank you, Master Tanner." Quinn replied, pressing a silver elgar into the man's palm. "Perhaps something to drink and a bit of lunch would be in order."

"Of course, of course . . . I'll see to it at once," the innkeeper said, hurrying away.

"Excellent."

Quinn walked around the table and took the center chair. "Master Palmer, if you and your council members would be kind enough to join me over here, perhaps we can get started."

With no instruction from him, the constable's men stationed themselves on either side of the door.

"What is this?" Bran asked.

Mathew recognized his father's tone and put a hand on his arm. "It's all right," he said.

Bran looked at him, then turned back to Quinn. "I asked you a question," he repeated slowly.

"Be at ease," the constable said, holding up a placating hand. "This is an inquiry only, as I have told you—not a trial. I am here merely to find out what happened. They are here to assist me."

"I don't like men with weapons standing at my back."

"You have my word . . . they will take no action except upon my order."

Bran grumbled something and sat down.

"Young man," Quinn said, addressing Mathew, "you know why I am here, and what this is about, do you not?"

"Yes, sir. I suppose so."

"Fine. Then let me tell you this. You need not speak to me, or say any word at all, if you don't want to."

"I have nothing I want to hide," Mathew said seriously.

"Very well. Would you take a seat here?" Quinn indicated the chair at the end of the table.

Mathew could feel his pulse pounding in his ears, but he walked deliberately to the chair, kept his face devoid of expression, and sat down. Everyone else in the room also found places and seated themselves.

"Mathew, would you tell me what happened four nights past, and how Giles Arlen Naismith came to die?" Quinn asked.

Mathew slowly recounted the details of the story once again. He looked directly at the constable as he spoke. It took him considerably longer than he thought to tell it. Every so often the constable would nod his head slightly, but other than that, he gave no indication as to what he was thinking.

"So you say it was an Orlock blade that killed him?"

Mathew looked out the window for the first time and paused a long while before answering. "If I had been stronger . . . I would've gotten him back in time, and he might still be alive."

"And then again, he might not," Quinn mused to himself.

"The responsibility was mine and I failed him."

Seated next to Bran, Father Thomas smiled slightly and looked down at his feet. Mathew didn't know how long he had been talking, but he was more than grateful when the innkeeper returned carrying the refreshments. Unlike others in the room, the constable refused any wine. Instead he drank down a full mug of cold water, then leaned back in his chair and rubbed his face with both hands.

With the small break concluded, he asked Mathew to be seated next to his father, and signaled to one of the men at the door, who nodded and stepped outside. A minute later Lieutenant Herne strode briskly in, saluted, and stood at attention in front of the constable.

"Pray, be at ease, Lieutenant. You may have a seat over here."

Herne made a small bow and sat stiffly upright in the chair the constable indicated.

"You are Darnel Herne, Lieutenant, in the service of Lord Kraelin, here in Werth Province?"

"I am."

"And as I understand it, you found yourself in this village four days ago, did you not?"

"I did, Constable."

"Would you tell me, in your own words, what occurred at that time—and for heaven's sake, *relax* young man."

The corners of Herne's mouth turned down, but he did ease his posture, if only a fraction. "We were seeking volunteers for the army," he began, "when news of the Orlock attack came. A decision was made to form a rescue party for the little boy—Darcy, I believe his name was—and the farmer—Layton, the man whose son was killed. Two separate groups were formed. Bran Lewin led one party, and I deferred to General Rozon, who led the other."

Quinn nodded and scratched some notes on a piece of parchment.

"The weather was difficult, with the storm bringing not only snow and wind, but fog as well. We were no more than one hundred yards from the Layton farm when a fire arrow halted us. A second arrow followed it almost immediately. We understood it to be a signal of some sort, though none had been specifically arranged. Just after the second arrow was fired, we saw a band of Orlocks break from the trees. General Rozon immediately ordered a charge. If not for this boy's warning, we'd have ridden straight into a trap and been cut to pieces."

"Did you actually see this young man there?"

"I did, Constable. When we engaged the Orlocks, I saw him moving through the trees firing arrows at them."

The mayor exchanged glances with two of the men on the council, and gave a curt nod of satisfaction as Herne continued.

"I attempted to reach him, but was cut off by the creatures. The last thing I saw was one of them grabbing him. They both went over into the stream and I feared he was dead, either from the fall down the hill or from the Orlock."

"How steep was the drop?" the constable asked.

"Perhaps fifteen feet. As I said, I did not think he would survive it. When the fight concluded we came back to look for him, but there was no sign to be found."

"Nothing?"

"Nothing. But considering the snowfall, it was not surprising we failed to locate any tracks. If the truth be known, Constable, I prayed that he was dead rather than taken by the creatures."

"And was that when you organized a search party?"

"It was. His father would not accept the fact that his son was dead and insisted on it. I would have done the same if it were my son."

"If you please, Lieutenant, stick only to what you actually saw and observed," Quinn admonished.

Herne cleared his throat, paused for a moment, and accepted a mug of water that Quinn pushed toward him.

"Rozon and most of his young men continued on to Gravenhage, as was agreed earlier," he continued. "Some, including Giles Naismith, decided to stay with the people from Devondale and aid in the search. We were separated when the storm worsened."

"Tell me, Lieutenant," Quinn asked, "were you present when they found Mathew and Giles?"

"No, I was not."

"I see. Is there anything else that you would like to say?"

Herne frowned and considered the question before shaking his head. "I can think of nothing else."

"Let me pose a question then—to you. There was, I believe, a fencing meet on the day the Orlocks attacked, was there not?"

"Yes, Constable."

"And you presided as an official at this meet?"

"Correct."

"Am I also correct that the two young men we have been talking about met as contestants in that competition?"

"That is also true, Constable," Herne replied.

"Lieutenant, did you have an opportunity to see and observe them during the course of the day?"

"I did."

"Would you say there was any animosity between Mathew Lewin and Giles Naismith?"

"No, sir, I would not. They conducted themselves as gentlemen and acquitted themselves honorably."

"You are certain of this?"

"Certain."

"Would the same thing be true for Masters Lewin and Ramsey?"

Herne paused for a moment before answering, then shook his head slowly. "Regretfully, I could not make such a statement where Master Ramsey is concerned."

"Just Master Ramsey?"

"Yes, Constable. He could have acquitted himself better."

"Thank you, Lieutenant. I said one question, and I believe I asked eight. My apologies," Quinn said. He turned back to his notes and consulted them briefly. "Would you be good enough to ask Collin Miller to come in?"

Collin entered the room and in a clear succinct manner retold what had happened. His version closely matched that of Lieutenant Herne. But as he was about to leave, Quinn stopped him and asked one further question.

"You've said that you were there when Mathew and Giles were found. Is this correct?"

"Yes, sir."

"Do you recall any conversations that may have taken place at the time?"

"No," Collin answered.

"No one said anything at all?"

"Well, Giles was unconscious, you see."

"What about your friend, Mathew?"

"No."

"Not a word?"

"I didn't hear anything," Collin repeated slowly.

"Interesting," Quinn said, and put down a few more notes. "I thank you, young man."

Collin was almost at the door when he stopped and turned back. His face was flushed. "I do have something more to say."

The constable raised his eyebrows and looked up from his notes.

"Mat didn't kill Giles. He was trying to save his life, and anyone who says different is a stone fool and a liar."

"Thank you," Quinn replied. "I shall do my best to remember that. Would you be kind enough to send in the young lady?"

Mathew couldn't imagine what Lara could possibly say that would be of interest to the constable. He glanced at Father Thomas, who appeared as puzzled as he was.

Quinn and the other men rose as Lara entered the room. He made a small bow to her, and she replied with a curtsey. Mathew noticed she was wearing the same conservative yellow dress she had worn to Helen's house the other day. *At least she had the good sense to see that all the buttons were done properly*, he thought. Although why such a thing would pop into his head at that moment, he had no idea. After she was seated, the constable offered her a beverage, which she politely declined.

"You are Mistress Lara . . . ah . . . just a moment while I glance at my notes."

"Palmer . . . Lara Palmer," she prompted helpfully.

"Palmer?" The constable's brows came together and he turned to his right. "Are you related to—"

"My uncle. Hello, Uncle Truemen."

"Lara." Truemen Palmer nodded.

"You didn't tell me you were related to this girl," the constable said, addressing the mayor.

"You never asked."

A general chuckling broke out around the room. Quinn looked like he was about to say something, but then thought better of it, now certain that a joke had been made at his expense. To his credit, he shook his head and smiled along with everyone else.

"Well, Mistress *Palmer*," he said, returning to Lara, "I would like to ask you one or two questions, if I may."

"Of course," she said, inclining her head, with only a slight exaggeration of affect.

"As I understand it, you were among those who found Mathew and Giles. Is this correct?"

"No. I was in the second search party. We came as soon as we heard the horn."

"I see. We have been told that Giles Naismith was already dead when you arrived—this is also true?"

"Yes, he was," she said sadly.

"It would be reasonable, then, to assume that no conversation took place with him. What I would like to know, mistress, is whether you heard Mathew Lewin speak any words at all. I charge you to answer this on your oath."

Mathew saw Lara's eyes flash, which was always a dangerous sign, but they were calm again a second later. "I've given you no oath," she said coolly, "but I'll answer your question truthfully. Yes, Mathew did speak—he said he killed Giles, but you have to understand—"

"Thank you, Mistress Palmer," Quinn said, holding up his hand. "I do not mean to be abrupt, but it is not your opinion that I seek, only what you observed and heard."

The color in her face heightened and she opened her mouth, but the constable cut her off again.

"Thank you, young lady. You are excused."

Halfway out of her chair, Lara halted when another voice spoke up.

"In what condition was Mat Lewin when you found him?" Silas Alman asked from his seat at the table.

"Condition?"

"Yes, yes, condition," he demanded impatiently. "What condition was he in? Was he conscious, awake, alert, sleeping—or what?"

"Mathew was conscious, but he was very ill and taken with a fever," Lara replied.

"Did you exchange pleasantries or good mornings when you rode up?" Silas asked, rising to his feet and planting both hands on his bony hips.

"Oh, no. He didn't even know who we were or where he was. He was just babbling."

"Hmph," Silas said, with a triumphant nod toward the constable, and returned to his seat.

Quinn smiled wryly, nodded back to Silas, and placed another entry in his notes.

"Mistress Palmer, one last question—who else was present with you when you found them?"

Lara frowned and looked up at the ceiling, making a quick mental tally. Mathew could see her lips moving silently while she counted. It was a habit he had always teased her about when they were children.

"Well, Bran Lewin was there, Askel and Collin Miller, Fergus Gibb, Father Thomas, Collin, Daniel, myself, and him," she added, with a dismissive gesture at Berke Ramsey. "There was also another boy from Gravenhage, but I don't know his name."

A derisive snort from Berke caused a few people to look in his direction before they returned their attention to Lara.

"I assume you were aware that I would be asking you questions today regarding what occurred then. Have you discussed what you were going to say with anyone else?"

"That's two questions," Silas pointed out from down the table.

"An occupational prerogative I occasionally claim," the constable responded dryly, never taking his eyes off Lara.

"Collin and I discussed what you might ask. The best thing is always to tell the truth, then you never have to remember what you said," Lara replied seriously.

"An excellent answer. Thank you, young lady. You may stay if you wish."

Lara curtsied again, and seated herself in the back of the room next to Collin. For the next hour the constable heard from Fergus Gibb, Askel Miller, Berke Ramsey, and Evert Sindri, Berke's teammate. When Evert's testimony was concluded, Quinn looked down at his notes, leaned back in his chair, and announced an adjournment for fifteen minutes.

The suggestion was fine with Mathew—he needed a break. When the constable got up, so did he, and left the room to go for a walk. He wanted to be alone for a few minutes.

For all of Evert's efforts to be loyal to Berke, he did more to confirm what everyone else had said than to refute it. When Berke told his side of the story, however, he managed to twist things as much as he could, looking contemptuously at Mathew all the while. He had seen Mathew white with fear, throwing up; he heard Mathew suggest that some people be left behind to guard the town, and implied that his intent was to avoid going in the first place; and Mathew had challenged him to a fight. The damnable thing was that Berke was a smooth talker and made all of it sound plausible.

Mathew walked rapidly across the street to where his father had tied up their horse. He wondered how things had gotten this far, grateful for a few minutes of peace. The humiliation of his own failure was still fresh in his mind, and it wouldn't be long before everyone knew that Giles's death was a result of that. Maybe if he talked to Berke—explained to him that he had done his best, that he'd tried as hard as he could—he might make him understand.

Mathew weighed the possibilities, then decided against it. Berke hated him. That much was obvious. But *why* he did was a mystery. He had spent his entire life growing up in Devondale without encountering anything similar.

While he thought about what to do, something Father Thomas had once said in a sermon came back to him. He told them that both love and hate existed in the world. It was as if they had a life force of their own. Some people enjoyed the society of their neighbors, and others were filled with anger. For them, hatred was its own end. With a maturity beyond his years, Mathew admitted to himself that he probably detested Berke Ramsey as much as Berke detested him. It was all terribly sad.

Out of the corner of his eye he saw Collin signaling. Mathew took a deep breath and walked back. As it turned out, he and Berke were the last to enter the room, and he stepped aside, allowing him to go in first. Berke walked by without saying a word, his upper lip curled back in disgust. Father Thomas's words hadn't meant that much to him—until then.

Mathew was curious when the constable beckoned to the men at the door. After a short conversation, they both left and Daniel appeared in the doorway. He pushed his glasses back up and looked at the people assembled there, assessing the situation. He quickly located Mathew and the others, then proceeded up to the constable's table.

"Ah, there you are, young man," the constable said. "I am sorry that you had to wait so long. Would you be kind enough to take that seat over there."

Daniel nodded and sat down.

"I take it you are Daniel Warren?"

"Yes."

"There is a point or two that I would like to clear up before I conclude my business here. We have listened to your friend's account of what occurred, as well as having heard from a number of others, and now I would like to ask you some questions."

"Fine."

"Mistress Palmer has told us that you were among those who found Mathew Lewin and Giles Naismith after the battle at the . . . ah . . . Layton farm," Quinn said, reading from his notes.

"Right."

"We have also been told that Mathew Lewin said he killed Giles Naismith."

"He was raving and barely conscious," Daniel snapped angrily, coming to his feet.

The constable held up his hand. "We were told this as well."

"Oh," Daniel said, a little abashed.

"Pray be seated and we shall continue. As I understand it, you were one of the competitors who participated in the fencing match four days ago."

"Yes, I was," Daniel replied, sitting down again. "Sorry."

"Quite all right. Loyal friends are notoriously hard to come by. I take it you consider yourself Mathew Lewin's friend."

"Yes, I do," he said in a serious tone, then looked at Mathew and smiled.

"Young man, have you ever lied for your friend before?"

"What?" Daniel said, surprised at the directness of the question.

Father Thomas and Bran looked at each, puzzled at the direction the constable's questions had taken.

"My question is quite simple. Let me repeat it for you. Have you ever lied for your friend before?"

Daniel's color deepened by several shades and his chest rose and fell noticeably. A long time seemed to pass before he responded.

"Yes . . . I have," he finally said.

There was a general stir from around the room and people exchanged glances. The noise quickly died down when the constable tapped his mug on the table several times.

"We were about eight or nine, or something like that," Daniel explained, "and we—that's Collin, Mat, and me— had the bright idea to let loose a couple of frogs we caught in church. I guess we thought it would be fun to see the girls scream. We did . . . and they did. Father Thomas wasn't all that pleased, if I remember right."

Father Thomas slowly turned and looked at Mathew, who shifted uncomfortably in his seat but studiously elected to keep his attention fixed on Daniel.

"Mat's dad cornered me later that week and asked if Mat or I had anything to do with what happened. I told him no."

Quinn nodded his head and indicated for Daniel to continue.

"There was also a time that Mat and Garon Lang made

a bet. Garon said Mat couldn't climb a tree to pick an apple, which was way up on the top branch. I think Mat got the apple, but he also wound up with a broken arm. About halfway down, he fell. I told his dad he tripped over a rock down by the lake."

In response to the constable's raised eyebrows, Daniel added, "The tree was on Rune Berryman's property and we were in enough trouble already."

After finishing his explanation, Daniel sat back and waited. Both his color and breathing had returned to normal.

"My thanks for your candor, young man," Quinn said. "However, I am constrained to ask, if you have lied for him previously, how am I to know you are speaking the truth now?"

"I'm not eight years old anymore," Daniel said simply.

The constable inclined his head and poured himself another mug of water from the pitcher. "So you are not," Quinn agreed. "Let us go back to the competition we were discussing a moment ago, shall we? Did you likewise compete against Master Ramsey?"

"Mm-hmm."

"And how did you fare in your bouts with him?"

"We only fenced once. I lost," Daniel replied.

"I see. Can you tell me how Master Ramsey conducted himself in that bout?"

"He was all right," Daniel said with a small shrug.

"Did he behave in any way differently from any of the other fencers?"

"No. Like I said, he was fine."

"Now, Daniel, did you have an opportunity to see Berke Ramsey's bout with Mathew Lewin?"

Daniel nodded.

"May I take it that means that you did?"

"Yes, sir."

"Fine. Now, based only upon what you actually saw, and nothing else, can you tell us what occurred?"

Daniel proceeded to recite the details of the bout between Mathew and Berke in the same dispassionate, matter-of-fact way he discussed his inventions. When he described Berke's actions at the beginning of the bout along with the foul, Quinn looked up from the notes he was making. He glanced at Berke, who only shook his head in an exaggerated show of disbelief.

"Have you anything else to add, young man?" he asked, when Daniel concluded.

"No, sir."

"Very well, then, you may be seated with your friends, if you wish, while the council members and I discuss this matter privately."

Just as Daniel got up to leave, Quinn said, "Actually, I do have one more question, I would like to—"

A collective groan from nearly everyone in the room interrupted him. The constable put his hand over his heart, and feigned a look of wounded sensibilities.

"—*ask*," he concluded, emphasizing the word slightly. "There were, I believe, certain prizes awarded to the winners of the competition, were there not?"

"Yes, sir, I believe so."

"And do you recall what those prizes were, and to whom they were awarded?"

The constable pointedly ignored Silas Alman, who mouthed "two questions" in his direction and held up a pair of matching fingers for him to see.

"Well, Collin got a bowl. He gave it to his mother, I think. Mat got a knife, and Giles got a gold ring."

"Would that be the same gold ring that Master Lewin is presently wearing?"

Every head in the room turned to Mathew, who slowly stood up.

"Master Lewin, have you something you wish to say?" the constable asked.

"No pockets," Mathew replied simply.

"I beg your pardon?"

"My breeches have no pockets," Mathew answered, walking over to the table. He removed the ring and set it down. Quinn picked it up, examining it.

"I asked Mat the same question," Daniel said. "And that's what he told me. He said he saw it on the ground and picked it up for safekeeping. He couldn't put it in his cloak—"

"Because Master Naismith was using it for a litter," the constable finished. "And," he said, turning to Mathew, "your intention with respect to this ring was . . ."

"To return it to Giles' family as soon as I was able, but—"

"But you are only this day out of your sickbed," Quinn finished once again, nodding. He sat back, searching Mathew's face for what seemed a full minute, then pushed the ring back across the table to him.

"I will leave you to finish your task, young man," he said, not unkindly. Then, in a louder voice for the entire room, he added, "We are concluded here."

Quinn got up, stretched, and rubbed the small of his back.

"Allow me to talk with the council and I will meet you all outside."

Berke stood up with a mixture of disbelief and rage on his face. He turned and stalked out of the room, but not before casting a look of unconcealed hatred in Mathew's direction. He also said something to Evert that Mathew couldn't quite hear.

It was already late in the afternoon when they emerged from the inn. The sun was a red ball just over the tops of the houses that lined the street. Of the storm that had visited them three days before, there was virtually no sign, other than some grimy bits of snow at the base of the building and under a few trees. The breeze felt good on Mathew's face as he stepped into the warm light of a late winter's day. Bran squeezed his neck affectionately, and Lara gave him an impromptu hug. When she did, he was acutely aware of the pressure of her body through her dress and fervently hoped that nothing showed on his face.

They didn't have long to wait. Quinn was the first one out, followed by the mayor, Silas Alman, and the rest of the council. To Mathew's mind, it came as no surprise when the constable strode up to him and extended his hand. He had already observed Quinn's assistants bringing their horses to the front of the inn.

"Well, young man, it has been a pleasure to meet you. I thank you for your cooperation. I would stay longer and enjoy your village, but my men and I have pressing business in Anderon. It's best we get started as soon as possible."

"Is this the end of it?" Father Thomas asked.

"Indeed, Father. In my judgment, this is something that never should have begun in the first place. Unfortunately, the accusation of a murder is a serious thing. I trust you will all understand."

"I understand, sir," Mathew replied.

"I know you do, lad," the constable replied. Turning to Bran and offering his hand, he said, "It has been good to see you again after all these years."

"Just two former soldiers," Bran said, shaking his head ruefully. "I'm a farmer now, and you're the constable."

"Small advancement," Quinn smiled. "There was a time—"

Lara's scream froze the constable in mid-sentence. Mathew lunged just in time to catch Bran as he started to fall backward, with an arrow sticking from his chest. There was blood everywhere. In shock, he lowered his father to the ground as gently as he could. Father Thomas, reacting more quickly, spun around.

"There!" he said, pointing.

Mathew looked up to see Berke Ramsey standing at the corner of the inn, holding a crossbow. His shock changed to rage. Mathew slowly got to his feet and began to walk toward Berke. He saw one of the constable's men start toward Ramsey at the same time. A part of his mind registered Quinn shouting, "Seize that man," and another part saw Berke working the pulleys of the crossbow as he started to fit another shaft into place to finish the job he had begun.

Mathew broke into a full run, covering the distance in

seconds as Berke was bringing the weapon to bear. He and the constable's man both reached Berke at the same time. Mathew lowered his shoulder and drove forward with all his weight, slamming Berke backward against the inn.

Though bigger and heavier, Berke bounced off the wall with a thud, the crossbow falling from his hands. It took only a second for him to recover. He drew his sword and advanced on Mathew. The constable's deputy, knocked to the ground in the collision, started to scramble to his feet. Mathew reached down and pulled the man's sword from his scabbard, spinning just in time to parry Berke's lunge.

He had been taught all his life to present only his side to an opponent, giving the smallest target possible. Facing Berke full on and using both hands on the hilt of the sword, he struck backward, knocking Berke's blade aside, all of the fencing lessons forgotten. He parried Berke's next thrust in the same manner, almost disarming him in the process. A red haze seemed to settle before Mathew's eyes. In a fury, he smashed his blade again and again into Berke's. After a few seconds, the larger boy began to give ground as Mathew counterattacked with a ferocity he didn't know he possessed. Berke backed away from the onslaught, raising the sword above his head to protect himself. Mathew hammered him with blow after blow, driving Berke to his knees. Carried away by the tide of his own emotions, Mathew never once thought about the subtleties of fencing technique.

He didn't hear Father Thomas scream "No!" when he knocked Berke's blade from his hand and seized him by the throat, forcing him onto his back. The constable's men, like everyone else, watched in frozen disbelief as Mathew's fingers continued to tighten on Berke's throat. Panic took hold of Berke and he kicked wildly, and then less, by a degree and eventually not at all.

Mathew knelt there with his chest heaving, staring down at the dead boy. The constable's men, who had tried in vain to pry his fingers from Berke's throat, released their hold and stood back, staring at him. Mathew also stood up. The heat in his face began to drain away, leaving him with an empty, spent feeling in the pit of his stomach.

He forgot the lamentable creature at his feet and stumbled toward his father. The constable was down on one knee, holding a handkerchief to the wound in Bran's chest. It was completely soaked with blood. Father Thomas had his ear close to Bran's mouth. Mathew could see his father's lips moving, saying something while Father Thomas nodded. To one side, Truemen Palmer had his arm around Lara's shoulders. She was crying. For some reason, he couldn't remember ever having seen Lara cry.

Seconds later Bran's lips stopped moving.

The constable looked up at Mathew and shook his head slowly. A small crowd had gathered, and gasps of disbelief came from everywhere. A number of women began to cry. Hands of friends and acquaintances reached out to touch Mathew on the arm or shoulder, but he never felt them. The enormity of what had just happened began to dawn on him, and he looked around dumbly at faces he had known all his life.

Collin was there by his side and put an arm around his shoulders. So was Daniel. Their faces looked pale and stricken. Father Thomas finally rose after saying a prayer for Bran's soul and also went to Mathew.

"C'mon, Mat," Collin said, "let's walk over here for a bit."

But Mathew just stood where he was, not moving or responding to his friend's urging, staring down at his father.

"Mat," Daniel said, "there's nothing you can do now—nothing anyone can do. Please, just come with us for a bit."

Mathew pushed them away and dropped to his knees. He lifted his father's head and cradled it in his arms. Still not quite comprehending, he looked around him for help, but all he could see were expressions of pain and sympathy.

Collin knelt down next to him and began to pull a cloak up over Bran's face.

"No," Mathew said, seizing his wrist.

"Mat," Collin said gently.

"No," he repeated again.

Collin looked around helplessly for Father Thomas, but he was off to one side talking quietly to Fergus Gibb. Father Thomas saw him as well, and raised his hand slightly, signaling for Collin to wait. Once their conversation was finished, Fergus left, and Father Thomas immediately came to them.

"Mathew," he said softly, "listen to me, my son. You must come with me now. I will see that your father is taken care of."

Mathew started to shake his head again, but something in Father Thomas's tone stopped him. The priest's soft brown eyes were intense, and the expression on his face was urgent. Not fully understanding, Mathew gently lowered Bran's head to the ground. He took the cloak from Collin and covered his father. Father Thomas whispered something in Collin's ear, and he promptly departed, as Fergus had, taking Daniel along with him.

12

Devondale

BRAN LEWIN'S FUNERAL WAS HELD THE NEXT DAY.
When Mathew reflected on it—and he did many times
over the years—he recalled that almost everyone he knew
in Devondale was there, along with a number of people he
had never met before. Thom Calthorpe and his wife even
came from Mechlen, although how they learned of the
news, he had no idea.

Mathew seemed to be moving through a fog, hearing
only bits and pieces of conversations. He felt isolated and
very much alone. He stayed the night at Lara's home, and
during that time she never left his side. They didn't talk—
couldn't talk. Well into the early hours of the morning,
she sat by him, holding his hand, watching the sky turn
gray, then blue. And when he broke down and cried, she
held his head against her chest and stroked his hair, rocking both back and forth, back and forth.

Throughout the services, Mathew remembered both
women and men crying in the church while Father
Thomas spoke. The priest tried to offer words of comfort
and talk about a situation that defied any sensible explanation. If someone had asked, Mathew would not have been
able to repeat a single word spoken that morning. He just
sat in the first row, staring numbly ahead, overwhelmed
and disconnected.

When the service was over, people with red-rimmed
eyes and puffy faces slowly filed out of the church and
stood talking quietly among themselves. Bran's body was
laid to rest in the little cemetery.

They had only taken a few steps away from the gravesite when Jeram Quinn approached them, his face somber and he was still in shock like everyone else.

"Mathew," he said, "I just want to tell you that I am so terribly sorry about your father. He was a good man. If there was something I could have done, some way I could have foreseen—"

"Thank you," Mathew replied, shaking the constable's hand. Once again he found himself struggling to hold back tears that were trying to form in his eyes, but his own reticence would not allow him to weep in public. Mourning would come later.

"Thank you," Father Thomas echoed. "If you'll excuse us, Jeram, I'd like to talk with Mathew privately for a moment."

Quinn nodded. "Father, I know this is not the best time to say this . . ." The constable seemed to be searching for the right words. "But you understand the boy will have to come with me. Counsel with him certainly, but afterward he will need to accompany us back to Anderon."

Truemen Palmer, standing nearby, heard the comments and spoke up. "Anderon? What are you talking about, Quinn? The boy's father has just been killed."

"I am aware of that," the constable said quietly. "If there were some other way. But I have no choice, he will have to come with me to face charges."

"Face charges?" the mayor snapped. "Are you insane? His father has just been killed. What's the matter with you?"

"I wish it were not so—truly I do. I like this not at all, but I have a duty to perform."

Through the dull fog of his emotions, Mathew began to realize what Jeram Quinn was talking about. He watched, uncaring, as the constable's men approached.

"You have lost your mind, Quinn," Palmer said angrily. "This is a case of self-defense. You were there. You saw what happened."

Quinn shook his head slowly. "It stopped being self-defense when he knocked the sword from Ramsey's hand

and choked him to death. I might have done the same thing myself were I in his place, but it doesn't change anything."

His voice sounded weary and drained.

"Go inside and talk to your priest, lad," he said, addressing Mathew. "We'll be here when you are finished."

"This is ridiculous," Palmer said. "I will not allow you to take this boy with you."

This sentiment was immediately taken up by the people who had gathered. They pressed forward, and the constable's men looked around uneasily. Mathew noticed that their hands were on their sword hilts.

"I wish it were not so," Quinn repeated slowly. "If you choose to believe nothing else, you may believe that." And then, for the benefit of those within earshot, he pitched his voice louder. "My authority comes from King Malach himself, and I have no choice but to do my duty. Perhaps it would be better if you come with me now, son," he said, laying a hand on Mathew's shoulder.

"Take your hand off the boy," Father Thomas said, emphasizing each word. There was a dangerous note in his tone that Mathew had never heard before.

Quinn turned to him, his face suddenly serious. "Do not interfere in the king's business, Father. You, above all people, should know this."

"I said . . . take your hand from the boy," Father Thomas repeated.

The constable's men started forward, but he halted them. "Do not compound one crime with another, I beg you," Quinn said. "Think of what you are doing, man."

"I *am* thinking," Father Thomas replied, "and I have no desire to hand this boy over to Malach's justice."

"You are leaving me no choice—take him," Quinn said over his shoulder.

"*Don't!*" someone said sharply from behind them.

Mathew recognized Collin's voice. He was standing off to the side with a longbow fully drawn, pointing an arrow directly at one of the deputies.

"Uh-uh, the same goes for you," Daniel said, speaking

to the other deputy from the opposite side. "Take your hand away from your sword."

Like Collin, he also had an arrow aimed squarely at the man. The deputy halted but did not move his hand. Quinn pulled back his cloak, leaving his sword arm free.

"I'm not as good a shot as they are," Lara said, "but even I'm not likely to miss at this distance."

Mathew turned quickly to see Lara step out of the crowd, which very wisely moved away. Cradled in her arms was a crossbow, and she was pointing it at the constable. Mathew hadn't noticed when she left him, and he couldn't imagine where she'd gotten a crossbow.

A look of exasperation passed over Quinn's slender face but disappeared quickly as he regained his exposure. He took a deep breath, then let it out.

"Considering all the circumstances, I know what you are thinking," he said to Father Thomas. "I give you my word . . . he *will* receive a fair trial."

"With all due respect, Constable, you have no idea what I am thinking," Father Thomas replied dryly. "Considering all the circumstances."

Quinn turned toward Mathew, addressing him directly. "I know you are an intelligent lad, but you must consider what you are doing. This will no longer just involve you, but your friends as well. I ask you plainly, will you not come with me?"

Mathew hesitated. He looked from Father Thomas to the constable, and then to Collin, Daniel, and Lara. He was balanced on a precipice, and a good many people were watching him.

Throughout the previous night, he had weighed and reweighed his recent actions. He felt no guilt over Berke's death, but the analytical part of his mind knew there would be consequences. In the end, he decided to take whatever came, and was on the verge of telling the constable that he would go with him when something his father once said came back to him. *If anything should ever happen to me, you're to go to Father Thomas. Trust him and listen to him.*

"I'll stay with Father Thomas, sir," Mathew finally replied.

Both of the constable's men started to move again, but Quinn shook his head. "No," he said. "Enough blood has been shed here, I think. You understand that I will come after you?"

"You are free to try," Father Thomas replied.

The crowd parted as the five of them backed away from the constable and his men. Mathew glanced over his shoulder, surprised to see Akin Gibb and Lucas Emson standing in front of the stables across from the inn. They were holding the reins of six horses.

All the while, Quinn continued to watch them, saying nothing.

When they reached the stables, Lara quickly ducked inside and changed out of her black dress. She reemerged wearing breeches and clothes for riding.

"What do you think you're doing?" he asked, seeing how she was dressed.

"Going with you."

"That's crazy," he said hotly. "There'll be no place for you. *I* don't even know where we're going, or what I'm going to do now."

"In case you hadn't noticed, I just threatened to shoot the king's constable," she explained patiently. "What do you suppose will happen to me when he finds out I've also had his horses turned loose?"

"You what?"

Mathew looked at Lucas, but the big smith only shrugged in reply.

"But—But—" he sputtered in frustration. "Look, you just can't come. For one, you're not old enough, and for another well . . . you're a girl."

"Why you big, thick-headed . . . my mother was a year younger than me when she rode all the way from Broken Hill by herself. Besides, I can ride a horse as well as you can, or anyone else here, for that matter. What's more, you . . . you . . . I don't need your permission to go anywhere. Father Thomas said I could go," she added.

"Father Thomas?"

Lara was already up in her saddle, and from the look on her face, Mathew knew he would have as much chance of convincing the barn door to be reasonable. Father Thomas returned a minute later, having changed out of his black robe into the same high boots and dark greens he had worn several nights ago. After placing his sword in the holder on his saddle, he climbed up and signaled for the others to do so.

Mathew was past the point of being surprised when Akin Gibb also mounted his horse.

"Let's go," Father Thomas said, and started off down the North Road that led away from Devondale.

The last thing Mathew saw as he looked back at his village was Jeram Quinn watching him ride away.

13

Alor Satar, Palace at Rocoi

RA'ID AL MOULI LEANED FORWARD IN HIS CHAIR AND considered his next move. His flank was in danger—under attack by Duren's white hawk—and his fortress was pinned to his queen by the dark hawk. Generally, he enjoyed playing kesherit, with its endless challenges and combinations. The game was an ancient one—*"sheka"* in his country and "kesherit" in Duren's. It had other names in other places. He did not particularly enjoy playing it with Duren, however.

Despite the lavish surroundings of Duren's palace, al Mouli would have much preferred to be in his own home, reading poetry in the confines of his tent and surrounded by his wives and children. Being this close to Duren, or any of the other barbarians, was a necessary sacrifice. Politics, he knew, made strange bedfellows. Al Mouli's own father, the previous Kalifar of the five Bajani tribes, had told him as much when he was only a boy. Now, forty-eight years later, the wisdom of those words rang true.

When the messenger brought him the invitation from Duren, he had been skeptical. Even as the man placed jars of scented oils and gifts at his feet, his first inclination was to send him away, but prudence had prevailed. It was better to be the ally of a lion than to have one at your back. His country's lack of sufficient natural resources, worsened by a three-year drought and Malach's closure of Elgarian ports to Bajan, sealed his decision to make the alliance.

Duren's own people feared him, Ra'id al Mouli noted.
But he did not. Duren needed the Bajani as much as they
needed him, and out of such needs, partnerships were
sometimes born. He might have wished for a better, more
secure alliance, because he placed little trust in the man.
Though doubtlessly intelligent, Duren was brooding and
unpredictable and al Mouli thought him not entirely sane.
But his choices seemed depressingly limited.

The Sibuyan, to the north, were dogs that could not be
counted on, and the Nyngaryns to the south were not
much better. They had been fighting with each other so
long, he doubted they could cease their squabbles long
enough to band together into one worthwhile army.

Ra'id al Mouli stroked the heavy mustaches on both
sides of his chin and concentrated on the game. He was a
large man, with dark intense eyes. Like the rest of his
countrymen, he had an olive complexion. His brown-
belted tunic was made of the finest cashmere, as befitted
the leader of his people. A white silk headdress, which
ended in a scarf over his left shoulder, could be used as a
veil in times of battle.

The solution was simple. He had not seen it until this
moment, but that was the beauty of kesherit. The board's
sixty-four squares offered an endless range of possibilities if one studied the lines carefully enough. Remove the
defender supporting the king, and the king becomes vulnerable. *Not much different from real life*, he thought. So
al Mouli moved his fortress, sacrificing his queen to the
white hawk. The briefest hint of satisfaction played over
Duren's face. On his next move, he advanced his foot soldier to attack the dark hawk and promptly lost his mage
as the hawk took the piece. The movement of al Mouli's
foot soldier and the loss of his mage did two things. First,
it cleared the diagonal that had previously been blocked
by Duren's hawk, and second, it gave al Mouli an open
file to the back row where Duren's king stood. With the
path now cleared, he struck with his fortress from one
side of the board to the other.

The smile slid from Duren's face as he saw the trap

sprung. He sat immobile, searching for some way to
parry the attack. Only his eyes moved. Aware the game
was already over, Ra'id al Mouli looked through the double doors of the balcony at the massive fountain below.
He could hear the sound of water splashing from the marble mouths of those wondrously sculpted horses that rose
out of a rocky landscape in the retaining pond. Alongside
the horses, men with physiques sculpted in incredible detail also rose from the waters and fought to keep the
horses under control. The fountain was an amazing accomplishment, and Ra'id al Mouli had stared in awe the
first day he arrived. He concluded that what made it so
impressive was the combination of movement, sound,
and texture all working together. Duren told him that it
was more than five thousand years old. If its antiquity
was not staggering enough, the sheer beauty was enough
to take one's breath away.

The fountain may have been the central focus of the
garden, but there were also row after row of dark green
ivy hedges in intricate patterns and gravel walking paths
that led a visitor to other statues and stone benches. Some
of the sculptings were women, some were men. All possessed a serene kind of beauty and dignity that touched
Ra'id al Mouli deeply. He thought the garden would be a
wonderful place to study his poetry—providing one
could forget its proximity to the owner.

In contrast to all the beauty within, the garden also
contained something disturbing and frightening. At the
far end lay a flight of stairs, more than thirty feet wide,
hewed out of a gray and black stone. The steps were large
and uneven. Centuries of use had worn their centers so
smooth that they appeared to be slightly bowed in. When
al Mouli had looked at the staircase, he saw that they led
up to another terrace, and out of curiosity, he'd followed
them. At the top of the last step he'd halted and his hand
went for the curved dagger in his belt. There, directly in
front of him, was the yawning mouth of a huge scowling
face carved out of solid rock. The mouth was big enough
for a man to walk through without bending his head, and

it contained two rows of large teeth that looked ready to bite anyone in half who dared to enter. A pair of black holes for eyes stared lifelessly ahead. Instinctively, he'd made a sign with his hand to ward off evil and retreated down the steps, not wishing to look upon the monstrosity any longer.

Now, his attention returning to the game, al Mouli was startled to find that Karas Duren was no longer looking at the board, but staring directly at him. It took an effort to control his reaction, but he managed to return the stare just as levelly. Slowly, from the corner of his vision, he saw Duren's hand move toward the king and topple it over.

"Your game." Duren smiled. To Ra'id al Mouli, it was a cold and chilling smile, more like the relief on a sepulcher, because only Duren's mouth moved.

"I was lucky."

"Were you?"

"Perhaps," Ra'id al Mouli replied with a slight shrug.

There was a knock at the door, and the two men looked in that direction.

"My lord, pardon the interruption, but the Grand Duke Kyne is here to see you," a servant announced.

Duren's mouth turned down. "My brother," he explained to al Mouli. "Very well. Show him in."

Kyne Duren's name was already known to al Mouli, as were the names of every lord and nobleman in Alor Satar, along with the extent of their influence, resources, and loyalties.

One of the guards at the entrance held open an ornately painted door for the grand duke, and Kyne Duren stalked into the room. He was a tall man, about the same size as his younger brother but much broader throughout the chest, and he walked with a noticeable limp that required a cane. His eyes were the same sharp brown, almost black, as Karas Duren's were. Without preamble, the duke unclasped his cloak, threw it over the back of a chair, then sat down heavily.

"Allow me to introduce—" Duren began, but his brother cut him off.

"Have you lost your mind? What in the name of all that's holy do you think you're doing?"

"I was about to introduce you to our guest," Duren went on, unperturbed. "This is Ra'id al Mouli, Kalifar of the Bajani nation. My brother, Kyne . . . the grand duke."

The duke, noticing al Mouli for the first time, nodded brusquely in his direction. Ra'id al Mouli rose, placed an open hand in the center of his chest, and bowed in the manner of his countrymen.

"I asked you a question, Karas," the duke repeated, returning his attention to his brother.

"Actually, you asked me two," Duren replied mildly. "The answer to the first is that I have not lost my mind, and the answer to the second is that I am completing what we started thirty years ago. What our father and his father before his began."

"Then you have most certainly lost your mind," the duke snapped. "How do you think the results will be any different this time? We've been at peace for thirty years."

Ra'id al Mouli heard the question and knew quite well what was different. On the second day after he had arrived in the city of Rocoi, Duren had hosted a dinner in his honor, attended by several of the local nobility. They were all pleasant enough to him, but he noticed that they tended to keep their eye on Duren, constantly watching what he did and to whom he was speaking.

After the dinner, Duren had asked if he would care to walk with him through the estate. He was of course aware that the banquet was a mere preliminary to the inevitable discussion regarding a treaty, since he had not yet given Duren his answer. Being a guest, courtesy dictated that he acquiesce to his host's invitation. While they walked, Duren pointed out several of the sculptures and explained their history in intricate detail. He listened politely. It was clear the man was passionate about his art.

Eventually they emerged from the gardens and came to an open grassy area, a wide avenue that cut through the dense trees running along both sides. Two large stone statutes on pedestals flanking each side of the entrance-way stood about fifty yards from where they stopped.

Duren turned, looked at him, and said, "You are still uncertain of whether an alliance is right for your people."

"You are perceptive, my lord," Ra'id al Mouli had replied, selecting the most deferential response he could think of. "Such decisions are not to be lightly entered into."

"And you wonder whether I have sufficient resources to defeat the West, when I failed to do so before. Is this not also true?"

"I would be a poor leader, and a poorer ally, if I did not consider such things."

"Good. If I can have honesty, then the rest is simple," Duren said.

Ra'id al Mouli looked at Duren and waited patiently.

"In the last year, I have acquired certain . . . abilities, shall we say, that will make victory an easy matter."

"Indeed, my lord?"

Duren's half smile faded from his face as he closed his eyes and held his arm out in front of him. Ra'id al Mouli felt something hot go by his face, followed by a sudden roar. He turned just in time to see a wall of flames, easily twelve feet high, erupt between the statutes.

It was only with the greatest of efforts that he managed to maintain his composure. He looked back in wonder at Duren, who had a cold, intense expression on his face. Before he could speak, Duren tossed the cloak off his shoulder and pointed at one of the statues. A second later it exploded with such violence that it nearly knocked Ra'id al Mouli off his feet. Duren never moved.

Al Mouli had looked at the devastation around him, then back at Duren, who was watching him quietly.

"Only a fool would not be impressed by this, my lord, but I am too old to believe in magic."

Duren began to chuckle, or at least Ra'id al Mouli thought that was what he was doing.

"I do not believe in magic either," Duren finally replied.

"But it is magic of a sort—the kind that has not been seen in this world for the last three thousand years."

Ra'id al Mouli said nothing. His mouth was suddenly quite dry.

"I assure you, Kalifar, what you have seen is no trick. You have just witnessed a portion of the ancient science our ancestors possessed. That was my uncle, by the way," Duren remarked, indicating the remains of the statue. "I never cared for him. Do you wish a further demonstration?"

"That will not be necessary, my lord," Ra'id al Mouli replied. "Am I to understand you possess this *science* and can make it do your bidding?"

"I can." Duren smiled. "With such power at our disposal, how long do you think the armies of the West will stand?"

Ra'id al Mouli *had* thought on it. And while war was not something that he embraced, Malach had left him no choice. His decision might well have been different had he been able to learn who was responsible for the raids on Elgaria's border settlements. The Elgarians accused Bajan—they denied it. When he first heard of the attacks, he sent a delegation to the northern tribes in an effort to find who among his people had done such a thing in violation of his orders. No one there knew anything, and he concluded that the raids were the result of renegades acting independently. He promptly sent a message to Malach explaining the situation. The Elgarians, of course, were not satisfied, and closed the ports in retaliation—the same ports that were vital to the welfare of his country.

As a man given to the study of mathematics, he had concluded the odds in a war were favorable—if Duren could be trusted not to turn on him. On that point, he liked the odds much less. Still, there were few options open to him. Had he known that Eric Duren, acting at his father's direction, along with a group of soldiers disguised as Bajanis, were actually the ones who had conducted those raids—he would never have set foot in Alor Satar—unfortunately he never did.

Last year was a bad year, he thought. The next would probably be worse.

"Not a peace of my making," Duren replied to his brother, pulling al Mouli from his thoughts.

"Karas, I don't intend to get dragged into a war again," the duke said.

"Perhaps it would be better if I withdraw to my quarters and allow you and your brother to speak in private," Ra'id al Mouli offered.

"There's no need for you to leave," Duren said. "You are a trusted ally now. Anything my brother and I wish to speak of, we can say in front of you."

"So," the duke said, "you have formed an alliance with the Bajani without consulting the council?"

"With the Bajani, Cincar, the Nyngaryns, and Sibuyan," Duren answered, staring out of the balcony doors.

"The Bajani have never been involved themselves with either the East or the West," the duke said, turning to al Mouli. "Why now?"

"Unfortunately, the times have changed. I wish it were not so, but necessity dictates that my people can no longer sit idly by—"

"While that fool Malach strangles you by closing off Elgaria's ports, eh?" the duke said, finishing the sentence for him. "Plus an alliance with Alor Satar strengthens you against the ambitions of Cincar from the north."

Ra'id al Mouli bowed slightly in the duke's direction. "Over the years, I have heard the grand duke was a man of perception. Your grasp of the complexities of our position is correct."

"With all due respect, Bajan's problems are not our own," the duke went on. "Ally or no ally. I understand what drives the Kalifar. Without the ability to import food from the West, his people starve. Malach's decision was a stupid one, I grant that. You're forced to buy from them at their prices rather than import. It all comes down to money . . . it always does." He turned to his brother. "But, why are *we* engaging in this madness? Our country is not landlocked."

"Madness?" Duren said softly, looking back from his view of the garden below.

"Yes, Karas . . . *madness*. You heard what I said."

"In one month, we can land 100,000 men at Stermark, Anderon, and Toland, and crush Malach from both sides. Something not even grandfather was able to do," Duren said, looking at the portrait hanging over the fireplace.

"Assuming the council would agree to join with you, it still doesn't answer my question. *Why*?"

"Because, brother, under the rule of one country, we can bring order—"

The duke shook his head in disgust, leaned forward in his chair and began speaking lowered tones, while Ra'id al Mouli, already uncomfortable with the situation, discreetly walked out onto the balcony to allow them to speak.

"Listen to me, Karas," the duke said. "Our father has been in his grave for nearly forty years now. You don't have to prove anything to anybody. It's not necessary. I never cared that he selected you to follow him as king— neither did Jonas. You're a fine ruler in your own right. Alor Satar is the most powerful nation in the eastern world. Leave it alone. None of this is necessary."

"I'm *not* trying to prove anything, despite what you may think," Duren said defensively. "The world is in a state of chaos, Kyne. Cincar is constantly at war with Felize. The Sibuyan and the Mirdites haven't known a moment's peace since before we were born. Travel from one country to another is haphazard at best because the roads are so pathetic, the governments *are* absolutely worthless. They can't even sit down with each other long enough to hammer out a decent trade agreement without a fight breaking out. We could bring order—"

"Order? It's the same thing all over again, isn't it? You haven't changed a bit. Why can't you leave it alone? I would have thought you learned something from your past mistakes."

"You are wrong, brother. I have changed—more than

you could know. Whatever else you believe, you may rely on the fact that I am not the same person I was thirty years ago, or even last year for that matter."

The duke shook his head, heaved himself out of his chair, and started for the doorway.

"I will be no part of this," he said.

"Kyne, I assure you, we will not lose this time," Duren said, standing up. "We cannot."

"For God's sake, how will this time be any different from the last time?" the duke asked wearily.

"This time," Duren explained, taking two steps closer, "I possess such power that no army can stand against us."

"What are you talking about, Karas?"

Duren wanted desperately to convince his older brother of the possibilities that lay before them. Limitless possibilities.

"Listen to me," Duren said excitedly, putting a hand on the duke's arm. "I have discovered secrets the Ancients used in the beginning of the world. Did you know they had machines that could fly? That they could take a heart from one person and put it in another; or create something out of thin air, where nothing existed before? I tell you, Kyne, they were like gods, and we can be as they were!"

Kyne Duren looked at his brother somewhat sadly, Ra'id al Mouli thought as he stepped back into the room.

"Karas," the duke said quietly, "the Ancients destroyed the world with their war. I know nothing of removing hearts or flying through the air, but I do know that what they did was evil. You've been to the Wasted Lands as a child. Do you remember what was there? Nothing! Just sand and the relics of their mighty empires. If they weren't able to control what they created—with all their powers—how can you hope to?"

"You don't understand—"

"I *do* understand. And I know what drives you. You're Karas Duren *not* Gabrel," the duke said, looking at his father's portrait. "Whatever you have found, bury it, or destroy it, before it destroys you. I will have none of this."

"Kyne, I am trying—"

"No more." The duke held up his hand. "I will meet with the council tomorrow morning. There will be no war."

There was a long pause before Duren spoke. "That would not be in your best interests."

"What?"

"I said, that would not be in your best interests," Duren repeated.

"Are you threatening me?" the duke asked.

"No."

When the first pain struck, the Duke's hand clutched his chest, causing him to drop his cane. Duren closed his eyes and formed the mental picture of a human heart in his head. He could almost see it beating in his brother's chest. There were two little valves at the top of the heart: one let blood in, and one let blood out. *What a simple matter, just to close one of those little valves,* he thought.

The duke staggered as a second pain hit him. Duren stood there calmly watching as his brother fought for breath. Ra'id al Mouli came to his feet and started to go to the duke but never got the chance. In the final seconds of his life, Kyne Duren finally understood what was happening. His eyes locked with his brother. With all the strength he had left, he let out a roar and lunged for Duren, his hands reaching for his brother's throat. But it was already too late. Duren stepped backward as the old duke grabbed the lapels of his shirt and slowly collapsed to the floor.

Duren watched impassively, until the last signs of breath had faded from his brother's body, then turned away and looked out of the balcony doors into the garden.

"Well . . . what family doesn't have its little ups and down?" he said to no one in particular.

"You are a monster," Ra'id al Mouli whispered.

Duren brushed a lock of hair from his forehead and replied, "I know."

14

Elgaria, 200 miles south of Devondale

MATHEW LEWIN SAT BY THE RIVERBANK AND LOOKED out over the water. His world had changed. Below him, the Roeselar flowed quietly by. There was just enough moonlight to see the swirling currents as they mixed with the orange of a small campfire burning a short distance away. Far above him in the mild night air the stars flickered against a splendid dark canopy. The constellations were there just as they had always been since the beginning of time, and against the infinite expanse he felt very much alone.

A week ago he lived on a farm in the same village where he had spent his entire life. A week ago his father was alive. Now there was a void in his life, a feeling of emptiness so palpable it threatened to completely overwhelm him. Tears filled his eyes and slowly rolled down his cheeks. Had he stopped—had he controlled himself, he thought once again—none of them would be in the position they were in, deep in a forest, far away from their homes. Remembering made him uncomfortable and he tried to think of something else.

A short distance away he could hear the voices of his friends, talking quietly among themselves. He was thankful for both the darkness and the solitude. A light footfall caused him to turn.

"I'm over here," he said softly.

"Ah, there you are," Father Thomas replied, walking toward him.

Mathew looked away as the priest sat down. He rubbed

his face on his knees, not wishing to let him see the tears on his face.

"It's a lovely night," Father Thomas said.

"Yes," Mathew agreed.

The Roeselar lapped up against its banks, and they both sat listening to its sounds. Far overhead Mathew saw a shooting star flash briefly across the sky. It disappeared above the treeline downstream, where the river turned.

"It goes away," Father Thomas said after a while. "You won't believe this right now, but eventually the pain goes away. Never completely . . . but enough for us to live."

"What kind of God would allow something like this to happen, Father?" Mathew asked, as the bitterness welled up inside him.

There was a pause before Father Thomas answered. "I don't know the answer to that, Mathew. I don't know what kind of God would take your father at so young an age, or little Stefn Darcy, or Thad Layton's son, or any of the others. As a man, I wish I had an answer, but none us can see God's plan—only the Lord himself knows that."

Mathew looked back at the campfire and then at the river again, watching the silver moonlight on the water.

"I've made a pretty big mess of things," he finally said.

"It may seem like that to you right now," Father Thomas said, "but there is a reason things happen the way they do. I believe this with all of my heart. You mustn't blame yourself."

"I've not only ruined my life, but everyone else's."

Father Thomas took a deep breath. "Mathew, listen to me carefully. You did what you had to do. Your friends made their choices freely—just as I made mine. Saying that you've ruined their lives only diminishes those decisions. You are responsible only for your own actions, and not those of anyone else. Do you understand?"

Mathew nodded, not really understanding or believing what Father Thomas was saying. Neither of them spoke. He glanced up at the stars and then out onto the Roeselar once more. After a while he picked up a few pebbles from the ground and pitched them into the river, one by one.

Father Thomas listened to the splashes. A minute passed before Mathew broke the silence.

"We're not going north, are we?"

Father Thomas turned to look at him. In the darkness, only the silhouette of Mathew's face was discernable.

"No," he finally said, "we are not going north. How did you know?"

"After the second day, the sun wasn't on our right any longer. It's been on our left and behind us for the last five."

Father Thomas smiled to himself. He'd forgotten Mathew's eye for details and how quick the boy's mind was.

"You are quite correct. We have changed directions, and for very good reasons. Anderon is to the north, along with our friend the constable and King Malach's courts. It would not be wise to spend any time there right now."

"I see," Mathew replied. "Then where are we going?"

"To Tyraine," Father Thomas replied.

"Tyraine? But it will take us more than two months to get there."

"Quite a bit less if we take this river."

Mathew had heard his father and other men in town talk about Tyraine, but it seemed like the other end of the world to him. He knew it was a city—a very big city. But until then the largest place he'd ever been was Mastrich, and that was only slightly larger than Gravenhage.

"I don't understand, Father. How can we take the river with our horses?"

"There's a small town called Elberton about a day's ride from here. Most of the river traders put in there before proceeding downriver for the crossing to Tyraine and Barcora."

"Crossing? Do you mean across the sea?"

"I do."

Mathew lay back, resting on his elbows, and looked up at the stars. The night was clear enough to pick out the hazy band of light that ran across the evening sky. He had once asked Father Haloran about it when he was very young. The old priest told him that it wasn't haze at all, but the light from billions and billions of stars stretching across the universe. That was the year Father Haloran had died and Father Thomas came to take his place.

"Why are we going to Tyraine?"

"A reasonable question. Actually, we'll only be there a short while. Our final destination is Barcora, which is just on the other side of the border in Sennia. There's an abbey on the outskirts of the city where we'll be safe until we can sort things out."

"Father, can I ask you a question?"

"Certainly."

"In Devondale, before we left, the constable said 'under the circumstances' he knew how you felt. I thought it was an odd way to put it."

Father Thomas didn't respond right away. Instead, the priest pitched a pebble in the river and rested his chin on his knees. Mathew was about to apologize for asking when Father Thomas began speaking.

"The constable had good reason to say what he did. Almost twenty-eight years ago I killed a man."

He could feel Mathew turn toward him in the darkness.

"In those days, your father and I served together in the same regiment with Lord Kraelin's troops. The world was a very different place then, and the Sibuyan War was not a pleasant time. The Sibuyan certainly began things, but Duren controlled them from the beginning. As the fighting intensified, atrocities were committed on both sides. In the second year of the war, Duren somehow managed to convince the Orlocks to side with him.

"For more than a thousand years the Orlocks had stayed away from the world of men, living in their caves deep under the earth. But in the space of a month they began to appear in different battles—particularly those that took place at night.

Our plan was to join forces with General Pandar and General Grazanka at Melfort, and then push on into Sennia. To reach the rendezvous in time, it was necessary to go through the Kohita Pass. The commander of our battalion, a man named Cormac d'Lorien, was determined to make the meeting regardless of its toll on the men, who were utterly exhausted by that time. All of the senior officers urged him to let the troops take a half day's rest, but Cormac refused and ordered the column to advance. He was the son of a baron—an arrogant and pretentious man who listened to no counsel other than his own.

"We walked straight into an ambush.

"The Orlocks hit us in the front, and the Sibuyan from behind. Over half the men—our friends and companions—were killed and butchered. Your father took two arrows that night before we fought our way back across the river."

Mathew swallowed once and tried to make out the expression on Father Thomas's face, but there was not enough light.

"In camp the next morning, we buried the dead while the surgeons stitched the wounded and removed arrowheads from bodies. A young boy—about your age, I would guess—sat some distance away from us staring numbly ahead, unable to move. The older men had been through such things before, but the horror of what had happened was new to him. There can be times, Mathew, when a mind sees too much—more than it can take—and it goes to a place where the battles and killing are far away. So it was with that young man.

"Cormac saw the boy and ordered him to get to his feet—but he did not move. By this time he was incapable of it, you see," Father Thomas said softly.

"A baron's son is not used to repeating himself. When the boy failed to respond for a second time, he struck him across the face and hauled him to his feet, calling him a worthless coward. I could keep my temper no longer. There was a fight. In the end, Cormac d'Lorien was dead, and I went to King Malach's prison for eight years. That is where I met Brother Gregorio and decided to become a priest."

Mathew didn't know what to say. He searched his mind, but no words came to him, so he reached over and put his hand on top of Father Thomas's. "I'm sorry, Father, I didn't mean to—"

"No, no," Father Thomas soothed. "It was a very long time ago, as I told you. So you see . . . one door closes and another door opens. Come," the priest said, affectionately touching Mathew on the head as he got up. "We'd better get back before the others think we've fallen into the river."

"I'll be along in a minute."

He watched Father Thomas make his way back to the camp, a silhouette against the firelight. The fragrance from the first bloom of forest wildflowers drifted up to meet him. Mathew breathed deeply. A week ago there was snow on the ground, and tonight—flowers were growing somewhere in the darkness.

"One door closes and another door opens," he repeated to himself. He stood up and rubbed the small of his back. It wouldn't be dawn for about four hours yet, and sleep suddenly seemed like a good idea.

Collin half opened an eye as Mathew unrolled his blanket and stretched out alongside him.

"Everything all right?" he asked through a yawn.

"Getting there," Mathew answered.

In the flickering firelight, Collin thought he could make out a faint smile on his friend's face before he drifted back to sleep himself.

15

Alor Satar, Rocoi

BEYOND THE MOUNTAIN RANGE THAT SEPARATED El-garia from Alor Satar, Karas Duren walked along the streets of the capital city of Rocoi, giving thought to recent events. His brother was dead. That was a shame, he thought. The man was an excellent general despite his lack of foresight, and he could have used his help. Maybe he *was* competing with his father, as Kyne had said. But so what? Sons did that all the time. What better way to measure one's success? Duren pondered the question for a moment then dismissed it from his mind. Images of his father made him uncomfortable.

There had been no word from the Orlocks about the ring yet, and that scared him. In recent weeks he had begun to believe that his original thoughts about the rings might not have been entirely accurate. Here and there oblique references appeared in the ancient books suggesting that the rings could actually be adjusted to fit a great many people through an alteration of their brain structure. That made it all the more imperative for him to find the ring and find it quickly. Because the books were so badly damaged, he couldn't be certain he was correct. Unfortunately, his experiments on the people his guards brought him usually resulted in the same thing that happened the first time he used the ring on Roland. And there was always so much blood. There had to be a way to get around that, he thought.

* * *

The little boy building a house of sticks turned around when he heard boots scrape against the cobblestones. He looked up and smiled innocently at the tall man standing there, and the man smiled back, but the smile never touched his eyes.

16

Elgaria, 200 miles south of Devondale

THE SMELL OF COOKING WOKE MATHEW. IT WAS AL-
ready light out. He glanced around the camp and saw
Lara by the campfire, turning over what appeared to be
two hens on a spit. She looked back when she heard him
stir and gave him a brief smile.

"Where did you get those?" he asked, bleary-eyed.

"These? Oh, Akin and Collin found them for us this
morning," she said, tearing off a small piece of meat and
tasting it. "Hmm, a little longer, I think."

Found them? Mathew thought.

He got up and began walking down to the river. He
needed to splash some cold water on his face to fully
wake up. A bruise on his shoulder from a tree root he'd
managed to sleep on reminded him to suggest they select
the next campsite more carefully. Hopefully, Elberton, or
whatever Father Thomas called it, had an inn and some
clean beds.

"Don't be long," Lara called. "Breakfast in ten minutes. Tell the others."

Mathew waved in acknowledgment as she turned
away. He continued watching her for a moment, as the
fleeting recollection of a dream he'd had during the night
came back to him . . . a substantial part of which involved
her. *She really does have wonderfully round, slender
hips*, he thought. The barest hint of a smile touched the
corners of his mouth before he shook the thought clear. A
cup of hot tea and a bath would have to do for the time

being, he decided glumly—as soon as one or the other became available.

On the way down to the river he met Collin and Akin, who were on their way back.

"Morning," Mathew said. "Lara said to tell you breakfast is in ten minutes."

"Wonderful," Akin replied. "I'm hungry enough to eat my boot."

"Me too," Collin agreed.

"She also told me you *found* the hens she's cooking."

"Well, 'found' may not be entirely accurate," Akin said, glancing at Collin. "Actually, what we found was a farm, about a mile from here. The farmer was still asleep, and—"

"We didn't want to disturb him," Collin said, finishing the sentence for him.

Mathew's mouth dropped open in surprise. "You stole the hens? What if Father Thomas—"

"'Stole' is a harsh word, Mathew," Akin said, managing to look both hurt and offended at the same time. "As I was *about* to say, we didn't have the luxury of time to negotiate a proper transaction with the man, so we left him three silver elgars."

"Three elgars?" Mathew exclaimed. "Isn't that a little high for two hens?"

"Well, there were the eggs too," Collin said.

"Eggs?"

"Of course there were eggs, Mat. A fine breakfast it would be without eggs."

Mathew looked from Collin to Akin, who nodded at each other in agreement.

"Are you sure you're completely recovered from that fever you had?" Akin asked, searching Mathew's face.

But Mathew's thoughts were still with the hens. "I suppose, as long as you paid for them," he said, "and Father Thomas isn't—By the way, where is Father Thomas?"

"Oh, he and Daniel got up early and rode on ahead to check the trail," Collin said. "You'd better hurry and wash. You know how Lara gets when people are late."

Mathew opened his mouth to say something but then thought better of it. When they turned to leave, he heard Akin ask Collin, "Do you think he's all right? He looks a little confused this morning."

He didn't bother trying to hear Collin's reply, and walked down the small embankment to the Roeselar. He shook his head and thought about Akin Gibb.

Akin was about ten years his senior. He and his brother Fergus were only a year apart, with Fergus the older of the two. Like their father, both brothers also became silversmiths. When he died, they continued his tradition of playing music in Devondale's square every Sixth Day, just as he had done for so many years. Akin was slightly taller than Fergus, with the same slender features, pale skin, and blond hair. If not for the fact that his brother had decided to grow a mustache several years ago, something that virtually everyone in Devondale had applauded, it would have been difficult to tell them apart. Even their laugh and manner of walking were alike.

Mathew had always thought of Akin, who was a deeply religious man, as conservative and quiet, but he was finding out there were other sides to him. For one thing, he could ride a horse like no one he'd ever seen before, and Akin was certainly more comfortable with a blade than Mathew had ever imagined.

He shook his head and reached down to cup some water in his hands.

When Mathew got back to camp a few minutes later, Father Thomas and Daniel had returned. Incredibly, Father Thomas was holding two hens, and the sack Daniel had in his left hand looked suspiciously like it contained eggs.

"That's impossible," Lara was saying to Daniel. "You and Father Thomas found another pair of hens? Next I suppose you're going to tell me the hens are having a meeting here in the woods."

"Uh . . . I'd better see to the horses," Daniel said quickly, not answering her question.

Lara looked at Collin, who smiled innocently and

shrugged. Next she turned to Akin, who seemed overly occupied with examining the edge of his belt knife.

Mathew moved closer, not wanting to miss a word of whatever explanation might be forthcoming.

"Ah, well . . . sometimes the Lord works in mysterious ways, my child," Father Thomas said. "Let us eat before the food grows cold. If you'll excuse me for a moment, I'll just help young Daniel over there and then we can get started."

Lara arched one eyebrow and looked at all of them one by one. When no one returned her glance, she shook her head, took a deep breath and let it out, and decided to let the matter go.

Breakfast tasted particularly good that morning. The sun was already above the treetops, and the sounds of forest birds complemented their meal. While the others rolled up their blankets, Mathew looked out across the Roeselar and thought it would turn out to be a fine day.

It was not possible to make good time going cross-country, but Father Thomas seemed to know his way through the woods well enough. The road they were on couldn't even be called a proper trail. It was hardly wide enough to permit them to ride in anything other than single file. Most of the time they stayed parallel to the Roeselar, but after their midday meal—which consisted mostly of bread, cheese, and, oddly enough, more eggs—they began to move inland. About two hours later the trail ended and they emerged from the heavy forest to find a small road of hard-packed dirt. Apart from being wider than the track they'd just left, Mathew couldn't see much difference.

He did see a difference in Father Thomas, however. The priest was more watchful once they were on the road, frequently scanning both ahead of them and behind. The land they were traveling through began to change over the next two hours. Instead of the low hills and valleys they had seen during the last week, the terrain flattened out and the trees that lined both sides of the road grew less dense. Many of them were of a type Mathew had never seen before. The trunks were large and twisted, with a grayish-green moss hanging from gnarled branches. A few had thick, oddly shaped oblong leaves that measured more than a hand's span in length. Unlike most trees at that time of year, which were either still bare or just beginning to bud, these had apparently remained perfectly green throughout the winter.

Later in the afternoon they finally emerged from the trees and found themselves looking across a broad open field. What they saw there stopped everyone short. At the far right end of the field were the remains of an ancient, elevated roadway stretching off into the distance. Parts were broken, with gaping holes between the sections, but other portions were intact. Mathew had only seen pictures of such things in books before. The road was towering in its majesty and power, yet seemed terribly sad at the same time. They rode by without talking before entering the forest again.

Several times when the road appeared to turn or reached a copse of trees, either Father Thomas or Akin would ride ahead to be sure the way was clear. Mathew thought their behavior overly cautious. If the constable were following them, it seemed reasonable that he would be coming from the opposite direction. From the angle of the sun, he guessed they had turned south again. It was also obvious that the entire party had picked up their pace. But despite this, they encountered no one else on the road.

The day warmed considerably, just as he thought it would, eventually becoming hot enough for him to take off his cloak, which he folded over the front of his saddle. As they rode along, Lara let her horse follow the others' lead and closed her eyes, tilting her face up to the sun. Mathew, riding just behind her, chuckled quietly at the sight of her long hair trailing down behind her.

"Hey," Collin said, falling into place beside him.

"Hey," Mathew answered automatically, shifting his attention to his friend.

"Do you know anything about Elberton?" Collin asked. "Father Thomas told me about it this morning."

"Uh-uh. Never been there. What about you?"

Collin shook his head. "See? That's just what I mean. It's like I told you yesterday. We've never been anywhere, and the first place we get to go is this Elberton."

"What's wrong with Elberton?" Mathew asked.

"Oh, I don't know. But Akin said he was there several years ago and it's a rough sort of town."

"Really? What'd he mean by 'rough.'"

Collin shook his head. "I'm not sure. That's just what he said. I didn't ask him to explain. I didn't want him to think we've never been out of Devondale."

"We haven't. You just said so yourself," Mathew observed. "Did Father Thomas tell you we're going on to Tyraine afterward?"

Collin's face lit up at that. "That's a real city, Mat," he said excitedly. "My dad told me about it once. It's supposed to have a harbor, loads of taverns with dancing, squares, parks, and everything. I spoke to Akin about it and he says—"

"Listen," Mathew said interrupting him, "I never did thank you for what you did back in Devondale, or Daniel either, for that matter."

"Forget it." Collin said, brushing away the remark. "You'd have done the same for me."

"I've gotten us all into a pretty big mess. You can't even go back home now. None of us can."

"So?" Collin shrugged. "There are lots of other places in the world. I couldn't very well let them cart you off to a prison, could I?"

"What about your family?" Mathew insisted.

Collin grimaced, and a few seconds passed before he answered. "My dad knows I'll be all right, and I'll get word to my mom and brothers, somehow. I don't know. I don't have the answers to a lot of things, but I know right from wrong, and what was happening back there was just plain wrong."

"Aren't you going to miss Elona?"

"Sure. She's a fine girl," Collin said. Then lowering his voice, he added, "But there are lots of girls around. You wait and see. Besides, I'm too young to be tied down. Plenty of time for that later. I'd like to see some of the world, wouldn't you?"

Mathew didn't reply right away. They rode along for a while before he spoke.

"Collin, I've been giving this a lot of thought. When we get to Tyraine, I'm going back and give myself up and take my chances in a trial. Constable Quinn said he'll see that things would be fair. I think he was telling the truth. If we keep on like this, it'll just drag the rest of you down."

"I'm not worried about facing charges. Listen, Mat, if you go back, you're certain to go to prison, and for who knows how long. You know what the law says as well as I do. I say we stick with Father Thomas. He'll figure something out."

"But—"

"There are no buts about it. If anyone deserved killing, it was that son of a lizard, Berke Ramsey. I promise you, the world won't miss him for one second." Collin spat on the ground to emphasize his point.

Mathew wasn't so sure about that. The world didn't have to miss Berke Ramsey, only the king's constable, Jeram Quinn. He didn't even know if Berke had any family, though the thought had crossed his mind a number of times in the last few days.

The debate with Collin was abruptly cut short by Akin's return. He threw them a friendly wave and rode over to speak with Father Thomas. As soon as their discussion was concluded, Father Thomas called them together and they formed a semicircle on horseback, facing him. The priest told them he thought it best to continue on for a while longer and then set up camp for the night. If they got an early start in the morning, they could reach

Elberton by midday. Akin also said he had located a good campsite only a short distance down the road.

While Father Thomas was talking, Mathew could see that he was not looking directly at them, but over Collin's shoulder at the road behind him. Collin noticed it as well and started to turn around, but Father Thomas spoke sharply, stopping him.

"Collin, my son, would you oblige me by looking at me for a moment longer, and not looking behind you? Uh . . . uh . . . uh, the same for the rest of you," he admonished, forestalling backward glances by Daniel and Lara.

"What is it, Father?" Lara asked.

"We are being followed."

He said this so matter-of-factly—as if he were discussing the weather—that Collin blinked to make sure he'd heard correctly.

"Are you sure?" Collin asked, letting his hand come to rest causally on the hilt of his sword. "I don't see how the constable could possibly—"

"It isn't Jeram Quinn. We are being followed by Orlocks. Not many, possibly just a raiding party, but where there are few, more will follow."

Mathew heard Lara take a sharp breath.

"Please continue to smile and nod at me, my child." Father Thomas said. "Only two are close, the rest are still a distance from here as of yet."

It was to Lara's credit that she did as he requested. The only hint that anything might be amiss was her sudden pallor.

"Well, then perhaps we had better move on, don't you think, Father?" she said in the most pleasant of voices.

There was genuine affection in Father Thomas's brown eyes when he smiled back at her. He nodded before turning his horse around.

Mathew waited about two minutes, then picked up his pace to bring his horse next to Father Thomas's. Collin followed suit a moment later. The shadows were already beginning to deepen, as the light from the late afternoon sun took on a warm, reddish hue.

Although his pulse had quickened considerably, Mathew deliberately kept his tone neutral. "Father . . . you don't really think the Orlocks are a raiding party, do you?" he asked.

"Why do you ask?" Father Thomas replied, his eyes continuing to scan both sides of the road.

"Because we've been traveling through the backwoods, away from any towns, for over a week now, and it seems to me that there's very little in these woods to raid."

"You're quite correct, my son. I believe they are following us, although for what reason, I cannot say. It is very strange."

"Well, what are we going to do?" Collin asked. "Couldn't we just make a run for it? We'd surely lose them quickly."

Father Thomas stretched in his saddle and put a hand over his mouth as he yawned. "I think the first thing we will do is to make camp," he replied casually.

"Camp?" Collin said. "That's crazy. Just make camp and wait for them to come down on us? Father, I—"

"I said, *make camp*, boy," the priest hissed under his breath. "I didn't say anything about staying in it. We have an hour of daylight at best, and they'll come at night. Akin told me he only saw one scout. Earlier this morning there were two. So I must assume one of them went back to bring their companions. We've been on horseback for several days now, and even though the creatures are on foot, they have been doing a good job keeping up with us. During the war, we found that the Orlocks have considerable endurance. They can stay with a man on horseback for days at a time, and I have no desire to bring them down on Elberton."

Collin grimaced. "I see . . . I think. What are we going to do, Father?"

"When we reach the campsite, Akin will take the horses and tether them a short distance away. There will be a thicket there and a small stream that feeds into the Roeselar, so it will look like they were posted there for the water. Mathew, I would like you and Collin to gather as much brush and kindling as you can. We'll also need some green wood for the fire."

"Green wood? But that will smoke . . . Oh, I see," Mathew said as the reason dawned on him.

"Excellent." Father Thomas smiled. "I'll explain the rest to you when we reach the camp."

They didn't have long to wait. Twenty minutes later Akin pointed out the campsite to them.

A small log home, built on a stone foundation, stood alone about two hundred yards from the road, at the end of a path in a small clearing. It was strange to suddenly come upon a house after seeing only forest for days. The house contained a prominent stone chimney. A wall about three feet high with a wooden gate in the center ran from one end of what must have once been the front yard to the opposite side.. It looked like it was constructed of the same material as the foundation. The gate was badly in a state of disrepair, having fallen off one of its hinges and hanging tenuously from the other.

When they walked their horses in, they could see that only part of the roof still remained. Most of the windows were either broken or long since gone. Mathew noticed that the chimney had an elaborate design of smaller rocks halfway up, which it seemed must have taken someone a long time to do. Off to the right of the house there was a well, fashioned of brick and partially covered with faded yellow mortar. A bucket lay on the ground next to it, the rope nowhere to be seen.

Daniel walked over to the well and peered down into it, then picked up a few pebbles, tossing them in. No sound of a splash came back, only a clatter against other rocks near the bottom.

"Dry," he said.

"I wonder who lived here?" Lara said. "It's such an odd place to make a home—so far away from everything."

"Maybe that's why they left. It looks lonely," Akin said over his shoulder, leading the horses around to the thicket.

Lara surveyed the area around the house and let out a long sigh, then tentatively poked her head into the front doorway. "They didn't even take their stove with them. It's still here. Isn't that strange?"

"What is?" Collin asked, stepping inside the house.

"It doesn't make sense to leave a perfectly good stove behind. You'd think somebody would have come along and put it to use by now." If nothing else, the practical side of Lara's mind strongly disapproved of wastefulness.

Daniel and Mathew joined them a moment later.

"Strange is right," Daniel said.

A large black kettle, covered with dust, still sat on the stove, and a wooden spoon hung from a hook by the fireplace. In the corner of the room were a table and four chairs. One of them lay on its side. They moved quietly through the rooms together, exploring. In one room they found two beds and a small chest of drawers, and in another, an old spinning wheel.

"It almost looks as if the owners just went for a walk," Lara said quietly.

Daniel shook his head. "I don't think anyone's been in here for years. You can see our footprints on the floor."

The floor was indeed covered with dust and leaves that had blown in through the open windows. No one had lived in the house for a very long time.

Everyone suddenly realized they were speaking in hushed tones, when Collin asked, "How come we're all talking so quietly?"

"I don't know," Lara said. "There's something sad about an abandoned home. Don't you think?"

Collin frowned and looked around the room with a puzzled expression. "I guess." He shrugged and headed for the front door. The others followed him.

Once they were outside, Father Thomas called them over and explained the rest of his plan. While he did, he knelt down and finished placing the last of several stones he had gathered for a fire ring, about three feet in diameter. On the other side of the thicket, Mathew could see where Akin had tethered the horses. He also felt a twinge of guilt when he saw that Akin had also unpacked their blanket rolls and set them out while they were in the house.

"Mathew, you and Collin hurry and get the brush and wood we talked about. The rest of you will need to arrange your sleeping rolls on the other side of where the fire will be. As soon as it gets a little darker, I want you to pack the blankets with leaves, branches—anything you can find—so it appears that you're still inside. Do you understand me?"

Everyone nodded, watching the priest closely.

"Because the road bends where it does, the Orlocks will not be able to see us until they are almost on top of the camp. When your blankets are prepared, we will light the fire. Akin, as soon as it is dark, you and Lara will head for Elberton as fast as you both can go."

Lara opened her mouth to protest, but Father Thomas held up a hand, stopping her.

"I know what you are about to say, my child, but please believe me, this is for the best. We do not have much time now, so I ask that you listen carefully and don't speak. I cannot allow you to stay and face these creatures. You must trust me in this."

Lara held his gaze for a moment, then sniffed and nodded.

"If I am correct, there will be perhaps five or six of them," Father Thomas said. "They will expect us to be asleep, not hiding in the woods, when they come."

"And what if you're not correct?" Akin asked softly.

Father Thomas shrugged. "They have proven to be creatures of habit," he replied, not answering his question, "I would be surprised if they have changed their patterns very much."

"Father," Akin said levelly, "I will do as you ask, because you tricked me into giving my promise before I knew what you intended, but I do not like this plan, or leaving you to fight them while we run away."

"I know that, my son," Father Thomas replied gently.

"There's something I don't understand, Father," Daniel said. "What are the Orlocks doing here in the middle of nothing? And why are they following us?"

"The answer is that I don't know, Daniel. Now off with you. The time grows short and we must be ready. Make sure you take your bows with you."

Then, turning back to Lara, he said, "Walk with me, if you will."

It took Lara a few strides to catch up with Father Thomas, who had clasped his hands behind his back and was walking in the direction of the house. But instead of going in as she thought he would, he continued around, going behind it. She followed, and saw a small path that seemed to lead down in the direction of the river. Neither spoke. The trees on either side had grown together over time, forming a kind of archway with their branches. It was a quiet and serene place, and it appealed to Lara. She thought it would look even nicer once all of the leaves returned.

Father Thomas stopped beside an ancient tree whose trunk had gone gray over time. His eyes roamed over the gnarled surface for a few seconds before coming to rest on a particular spot. Reaching out, he brushed away some of the moss and lichen with his fingers, revealing a set of initials carved into the wood.

"I did this on my twelfth birthday," he said absently.

"*You* did this?" Lara exclaimed, her eyes widening in surprise.

Father Thomas smiled. "You were wondering about the house before, weren't you?"

"Yes . . . well . . . but I don't understand, Father. This was your house?"

"It was," Father Thomas said kindly, looking directly at her. "Do not be so surprised, my child, even priests have to live somewhere before they become priests."

"But I always thought you came from Anderon. I remember old Father Haloran saying so."

"I did, but in a somewhat roundabout way. This is

where I grew up. My father built this home," he said, tracing the outline of the initials carved there with his finger.

Lara watched him. Next to the letters S.T. were two more letters, E.T.

"Who does the other set belong to?" she asked quietly.

"They belonged to my sister, Enia," he said.

Father Thomas became quiet for a moment, watching a single leaf slowly fall from the tree to the ground, looking into some distant memory. The use of the word "belonged" was not lost on Lara, but she said nothing, waiting for him to continue.

"She's buried just over here," he said, indicating a willow tree about fifty feet away, sitting by itself in a small hollow near the path.

They walked together down a little grade toward the tree. Lara didn't see the other graves until she was almost on them. She stood staring at the headstones, uncertain what to say, or how to act, as Father Thomas bent down and brushed away some of the leaves and vines from the headstones. The grave on the left was larger that the other two and bore the name "Orlan Thomas." The one next to it read "Irene Thomas," and the last indicated that Enia Thomas lay there. All three graves had the same date of death carved into them.

"May I introduce you to my parents? Mother and Father, I have the honor of presenting Mistress Lara Palmer, late of Devondale Township. And this is my sister," Father Thomas said, turning to the other grave. "Enia . . . Mistress Palmer."

Lara stepped close to the priest and hugged him. "Oh, Father, I'm so sorry," she whispered, starting to cry.

"It's all right," he soothed, stroking her hair. "It's been a very long time, and they are at peace now."

"I don't understand, Father. What happened?"

As soon as she spoke the words, she wanted to take them back, realizing that she might be overstepping herself.

Father Thomas's eyes took on a faraway look. "There was once a town very close to here called Weyburn, perhaps no more than a fifteen-minute walk along the road. It was never very large, I'm afraid, and like Elberton further to the south, much of the traffic on the Roeselar stopped here to trade.

"My mother made dresses and sold them to the ladies who visited Weyburn on the rivercraft. That was her spinning wheel you saw in the house. My father was a stonemason, as his father was before him. He was the one who built the wall and chimney.

"We were at war with the Sibuyan then. Thinking to cut the supply lines to Tyraine and Barcora, Duren attacked both at Elberton and here first. The men of Weyburn fought for two days in the open fields, from behind trees and houses, and in the end, on the docks by the river, before they were wiped out. General Geary and the Southern Army arrived from the southwest in time to drive the enemy from Elberton, but they were too late to save Weyburn. Duren burned the town to the ground and left the women and children to the Orlocks, while he fled north to mountains in Alor Satar.

"When the news reached General Pandar three days later, he sent me home with messages for General Geary. I always felt what he did was a kindness," Father Thomas said. "Bran Lewin and Askel Miller came with me, and we laid my parents and sister to rest here. Askel and I carved the headstones ourselves. Bran had no talent for that," he added, smiling at the memory.

Lara nodded at him, wiping the tears from her eyes but no longer regretting the question she asked.

"The memory of what I found when I returned was burned into my mind forever. I have prayed the Lord to take it from me, because I sometimes wake at night still seeing the same picture in my mind. But I suppose that God has His reasons for the things He does or does not do."

"Oh, Father . . ." Lara said, shaking her head with regret. "This is so sad."

The distant look slowly faded from Father Thomas's eyes and he looked down at Lara with a warm smile on his face. "I know that you are a brave girl, and would stay if given the choice, but you see why I cannot let you do so."

Lara hugged Father Thomas again, and buried her face in his chest.

"Come, it's almost dark now and we must get back," he said softly.

They had only walked a few steps along the path when Lara turned and walked back to the graves. Father Thomas watched while she closed her eyes, thinking that she was saying a prayer.

When she rejoined him, he said quietly, "Thank you, my child. That was very kind. A prayer?"

"I wanted to make sure I would remember their names."

17

Elgaria, 250 Miles south of Devondale

MATHEW AND DANIEL HAD FINISHED STUFFING THE blankets and arranging them by the time Lara and Father Thomas returned. High above them the stars were already beginning to appear in the sky, and crickets called to each other in the woods. They had positioned the blankets between the wall and the house, preventing any direct line of sight from the road. Collin was down on one knee trying to get a fire started and muttering to himself about wasting good matches. On the third try he finally succeeded in getting the kindling to catch, and he bent his head low to the ground, blowing gently, until a small orange flame appeared. In moments the flame grew larger, spreading rapidly to the dry wood. When a gray ash began to form, he added thicker branches, then slowly began placing the green wood on top. In just a short time a thin haze of smoke began to rise from the fire and hung over the camp like a cloud.

Akin stood close by, pretending to watch the fire, but Mathew could tell his attention was fixed at the bend in the road. The light was already getting low, and he guessed the Orlocks would wait until they were settled in for the night before they came. At least, he hoped they would wait. Father Thomas quickly surveyed the campsite and gave a satisfied nod. Mathew absently touched the hilt of his sword and silently thanked Collin once again for remembering to bring it when they left Devondale.

Gradually the sky turned from dark blue to gray, and then to an inky black, as the last glows of red light above the treetops to the west disappeared. One by one, at a signal from Father Thomas, they dropped down behind the wall. Akin made a show of stretching, and yawned a bit too loudly, Mathew thought. By this time there was enough smoke from the fire to make visibility difficult. Anyone watching from the road should have thought they were turning in for the night.

Lara and Akin were on Mathew's right, about fifty feet from him, near the well. Mathew crawled cautiously over to them. Akin saw him and flashed a quick smile. Before either could say anything, a low snap of Father Thomas's fingers caught their attention. Using hand signals, the priest pointed at them, then in the direction of the horses. Akin nodded and immediately started to move, but Lara hung back. In the flickering glow of the fire Mathew could just make out her face. What started as a kiss turned into an embrace, and they clung to one another before Mathew finally whispered, "Go . . . I'll see you in Elberton."

"You see that you do, Mathew Lewin," she whispered back, holding him by the front of his vest. Lara finished the kiss she had begun, reached up and brushed the lock of hair off his forehead, and began to crawl silently after Akin. In less than twenty yards they both disappeared from his sight in the smoke and the darkness.

Mathew closed his eyes tightly for a moment.

God, let them be all right.

Three minutes later another snap and a hand signal from Father Thomas sent Daniel and Collin off to the left of the house and into the trees. Only Mathew and Father Thomas remained now. Mathew realized his hands were shaking, and he took a deep breath to calm himself. The plan was for them to hide and use the trees for cover, until the Orlocks made their initial attack, then catch them in cross fire. An involuntary shudder went up his spine at the memory of his first encounter with the creatures. Whatever they were, there was no question in his mind about their intelligence. That much was obvious from their tactics and planning.

Through the smoke and flickering light of the fire,

Mathew could see Father Thomas's eyes sweeping back and forth across the road. The priest glanced toward the trees that Daniel and Collin had disappeared into moments before. Apparently satisfied they were safely away, he turned back to Mathew and mouthed the word "now," pointing to the opposite side of the house.

Mathew unbuckled his scabbard and dropped to his stomach. With his sword in one hand and his bow and quiver in the other, he and Father Thomas began to crawl across the yard. When they got to the old well, Mathew realized that his mouth had gone dry so he picked up a pebble from the ground and stuck it under his tongue to restore some moisture. At the perimeter of the yard, he rose to a low crouch and ran quickly for the trees. Father Thomas was there ahead of him, already down on one knee, his bow ready. Mathew was able to catch a glimpse of the priest's face. It was cold and hard—an expression he hadn't seen before.

Though his heart was thumping in his chest, he tried emulating Father Thomas, hoping a calm outward appearance would translate itself to how he felt on the inside. Morosely, he thought that Collin probably wouldn't have to work at it at all.

The green wood continued to produce a cloud of smoke covering the camp, but Mathew realized that while it provided excellent cover, it also prevented them from seeing the Orlocks. It was hard enough to hit anything with a bow at night under normal conditions, but it would be doubly hard now that the targets were obscured. He peered at the entrance in the stone wall, then looked down the road, concentrating as hard as he could for the first signs of any approach. Mathew knew he was a reasonable shot with a bow—nothing like Askel Miller, of course, but reasonable. He bit his lip and waited, fervently wishing he could see more clearly.

Then something odd happened to his vision. It was the only way he could describe it later.

Abruptly, the entire campsite and all its surroundings became bathed in an eerie green light. It happened so

quickly, he nearly fell over backward in shock. Mathew
rubbed his eyes, but when he opened them again, the
strange light was still there, illuminating everything. He
looked to Father Thomas, whose attention was still fixed
at the entrance in the wall. Wanting to say something, but
not daring to risk the noise, Mathew blinked several
times, trying to clear his eyesight. It was frightening. He
hadn't the slightest idea what was wrong, but the important thing was that he could still see. In fact, he realized
with a shock, he was able to see quite well—better than
before. The smoke from the campfire was still there, only
now it was no impediment at all. Tentatively, he looked
around, trying to determine what his capabilities were.
What struck him was the fact that he was now seeing
things in far greater detail than he thought possible. The
bark on a tree thirty yards away, shrouded by smoke only
a moment ago, appeared sharp and distinct. He could
even see the rust on the iron cross bar over the well.

Good Lord, what's happening to me? he thought.

A movement, perhaps two hundred yards down the
road in the dark, caught his attention. Deep in the shadows among the trees he saw them advancing slowly, cautiously. There was no mistaking the white faces or the
long yellowish hair. Unbelievably, they looked close
enough to touch.

*This is impossible. Nobody can see things that far
away. It's like . . . looking through those pieces of glass
and the tube Daniel showed me.*

Whatever the cause, he decided he would have to deal
with it later. Living through the night was his main concern at the moment. Mathew gazed back toward the trees
again and caught his breath. There were not five or six
Orlocks, but *twelve*, converging on the house. They were
no more than one hundred yards away now. He desperately needed to get Father Thomas's attention, but the
priest was still watching the wall, trying to peer through
the smoke. The answer came to him in the form of the
tiny pebble he placed under his tongue a few minutes earlier. He took it out and flicked it at Father Thomas, hitting

him on the leg. When the priest looked up, Mathew held up ten fingers, followed by two more. Puzzled, Father Thomas tilted his head to the side. Mathew repeated the signal and pointed in the direction the Orlocks were coming from. Father Thomas finally understood, nodded, and moved silently over to him.

"How do you know?" he whispered.

"I just do, that's all," Mathew whispered back. "There are twelve, Father—I counted."

"Twelve?" the priest said, looking back at the road.

"I swear it."

Mathew could almost hear Father Thomas thinking.

"All right," he finally whispered. "Wait until they're all inside the wall—fire, then change your position. We must make every shot count. I've told Collin and Daniel to hold their fire until they see us shoot first. Can you see how far the Orlocks are now?"

Mathew checked again. "No more than fifty yards, but they're starting to spread out," he whispered.

The corners of Father Thomas's mouth turned down and he looked at the road again. It was apparent all he could see was darkness and smoke.

"Are you ready?"

Mathew nodded.

"Let's go," Father Thomas whispered.

Mathew inched closer to the edge of the trees and saw the first Orlock climb over the wall, followed by another. Two more were coming in through the broken gate at the entrance, while still others were near the far end of the wall, close to where Collin and Daniel were hiding.

He watched as an Orlock hefted a spear in his arm and threw it directly into one of the blankets. More spears followed, striking the other blankets.

To his right, Father Thomas slowly got to his feet and took aim. The twang of the bowstring seemed entirely too loud in the night air. The Orlock closest to them let out a hissing sound and fell forward, trying to reach behind him to grab the arrow that was sticking out of his back. Mathew rose, willing his arms and legs to move, and fired

his own arrow, dropping another Orlock. Surprised and
confused at first, the Orlocks reacted much more quickly
than he thought they would, immediately moving apart.

Remembering Father Thomas's instructions, he
dropped to the ground and crawled rapidly to his right.
From the corner of his eye he saw two more Orlocks go
down, clutching their chests, thanks to Daniel and Collin.
The Orlocks began calling to each other in the peculiar
language Mathew had heard before at Thad Layton's
farm. Nearby, one of them yelled to his companions and
pointed directly at him. A second later the creature
clutched his throat, making a gurgling sound, when
Collin's next shot found its target. There were five of
them in the yard. The one who pointed at him rushed forward, with the rest following.

Father Thomas stepped out from behind a tree, well to
Mathew's left, his bow fully drawn, and called out, "Over
here, you sacrilegious sons of goats."

The Orlocks halted momentarily, and three of them
broke off, running directly at Father Thomas.

Both he and Mathew fired at the same time, dropping
two more. Mathew darted to his left to try and help Father
Thomas but was suddenly confronted by an Orlock crashing toward him wielding a double-bladed axe, its face
twisted in rage. He drew his sword and braced himself as
the creature raised its arms to strike. The timing would
have to be perfect.

What is the best time to attack? his father had asked
him several years ago, just before a competition.

A split second before your opponent does.

Mathew lunged, piercing the creature through the
chest. He immediately recovered and jumped to the side,
pulling his weapon clear. The Orlock screamed in pain as
the axe whistled past Mathew's head, missing him by just
inches. It stumbled forward two more steps, collapsing to
its knees, before it fell forward. Mathew turned to look
for Father Thomas, but the moment he took a step, he felt
something grab his ankle. He began to fall and instinctively threw out his hand. He hit the ground hard and

twisted back around. The Orlock had a hold of him with one hand and was trying to pull a dagger out of its belt with the other. The same sick stench that he remembered so well filled his nostrils, making him want to gag. Unable to break its grip, Mathew struck down with his blade as hard as he could, severing the Orlock's hand from its arm. The creature let out a horrible scream but, incredibly, started to climb to its feet with blood gushing from its wrist. Mathew scrambled to his knees and threw himself forward, ramming his blade into the Orlock's chest, driving it backward. A pair of dead black eyes looked back up at him, filled with hate and pain. Saliva dripped from one corner of its mouth, and even in the last throes of death it raised its head, attempting to bite him. Then it let out a rattling breath and stopped moving.

Mathew got up, backing away from it, fighting to hold down his panic. His feet felt unsteady under him and he was breathing heavily. He searched the area again for Father Thomas, and with a shock realized that the strange green light was gone. There was no need for it just then because the sound of fighting to his right told him exactly where the priest was. Father Thomas was holding his own, but the two Orlocks had separated and were closing on him from opposite sides.

Mathew dashed forward, covering the distance quickly. One of the Orlocks, hearing him, spun around. For a moment Mathew had the distinct impression it said, "There he is," but he had little time to consider it.

The brief distraction was all Father Thomas needed. With a quick feint of his weapon, he smoothly shifted to the opposite line and lunged, killing the Orlock in front of him. Mathew skidded to a halt, coming to an on guard position, readying himself. A smile appeared on the Orlock's white face. Its head almost seemed to be floating above its dark clothing. Some part of Mathew's mind registered the difference in their dress from the last time he had encountered them; the other part was concerned with staying alive for the next few minutes.

The point of the Orlock's sword moved from side to

side in a slow, almost lazy motion as it came closer. The creature kept his eyes fixed on Mathew's chest as opposed to his blade, completely undistracted by any of the small feints Mathew was making. It just kept moving toward him.

A dull thud preceded shock on the Orlock's face as it looked down to see a blade protruding from its chest. It was dead before it hit the ground. Father Thomas placed his foot on the creature's back and pulled his weapon free.

"Are you all right?" he asked, bending over to catch his breath.

"Yes. What about you?"

"I'm getting too old for this," he said, straightening up and wiping the sweat from his face. "Let's find the others."

Most of the smoke around the campfire had already drifted off, as the remaining logs were consumed. With the rising moon, it became easier for them to see. A search of the camp revealed two Orlocks lying dead by the smoldering fire, with arrows sticking from their chests. About ten yards from them Collin lay on the ground beside the well, his head in Daniel's lap.

Daniel saw the expression on Mathew's face and quickly held up his hand. "He's all right, he just got thumped on the head."

Mathew and Father Thomas dropped to their knees beside them. There was a nasty bruise on Collin's cheek.

"What happened?" Father Thomas asked.

"We saw the others go into the woods after you. Those two stayed behind," he said, pointing to the dead Orlocks. "So Collin and I snuck up and shot them. We thought they were both dead, but that handsome-looking fellow on the left wasn't. When Collin got close enough, he bashed him a good one."

Father Thomas sat back and looked at Daniel.

"I told you I wasn't as good a shot as he is," Daniel said. "I'm never going to hear the end of this."

"I don't get it," Mathew said. "How did you—"

"Well, after it knocked Collin down, I shot it . . . twice," Daniel said.

"It would have helped if you shot him sooner," Collin groaned, opening his eyes. "Lord, my head feels like a horse kicked it. Are they dead?"

"I believe so," Father Thomas answered. "It seems I may have underestimated their numbers a bit."

"Umm," Collin said, pushing himself up to his elbow.

"Can you get to your feet? I would like to find a different place to camp for the remainder of the night."

"Fine with me."

Mathew and Daniel helped Collin up, making sure he was steady before they let go.

"I'm all right, stop fussing," Collin said, pushing their hands away. "I've had worse knocks falling out of trees."

"Trees don't hit back," Mathew observed.

Collin gave him a flat look.

"Were you cut anywhere by the Orlock?" Father Thomas asked.

"No. I don't think so, Father. Why?"

"The creatures carry disease with them. That is part of what you smell. A cut from one of their weapons or a bite can kill a man as surely as a sword can."

Collin gave an involuntary shudder at the thought.

"Well . . . if you are not cut and feel well enough, let's retrieve our bows, whatever arrows we can, and be gone from here as quickly as possible."

Mathew's legs felt like lead as the emotions of the last half hour began to drain out of him. He walked in silence with Father Thomas to where his bow was. Only one arrow was worth saving. The other snapped off in the bone and he left it there. Of all the things he had done in his life, he decided pulling an arrow from the body of a dead Orlock had to be the least attractive.

Something was bothering him. The episode with his vision was bad enough, but that wasn't it. The more he thought about it, the more certain he was that he'd heard the Orlock say, "There he is," as if they were specifically looking for him. That made no sense. Until just over a week ago, he had never even seen an Orlock. The only other times he had been near them were at Thad Layton's farm and just before Giles had rescued him.

He remembered the scar-faced Orlock wanting to see his hands, which only added to his confusion. Nothing was making much sense at that moment. Considering the possibilities, he had to admit to himself that those comments might have meant any number of things. Nevertheless, they *were* extremely odd. Mathew thought about discussing it with Father Thomas, but appearing like a panicky fool was not something he was prepared to do right then, so he decided to say nothing and to give it further thought.

18

Elgaria, 20 miles north of Elberton

LARA PALMER PULLED HER CLOAK TIGHTER AROUND her to shut out the night chill and absently brushed some bits of grass from the front of her dress as she and Akin rode toward Elberton. She had always prided herself on having common sense, and riding through the night was plainly not sensible—it was dangerous. Still, few other options seemed available to them at the moment, so she resolved to make the best of it. Lately she had done a number of things that were less than sensible. Where she ever got the nerve to hold a crossbow on the king's constable, she would never know. But letting them take Mathew away was simply out of the question. Her uncle was an honest man who'd have argued and debated with Jeram Quinn, but in the end Mathew would have been on his way to trial in Anderon. As far as she was concerned, Berke Ramsey got exactly what he deserved and a trial was just so much foolishness. Everyone in Devondale knew it.

Her heart gave a tug again at the thought of Bran Lewin, and when she thought about Mathew's loss, the pain was almost more than she could stand. It was all so horribly unfair. He had looked up to his father so much, and they were both so close to each other, which made matters even worse.

Lara didn't remember much about Mathew's mother. She was not quite four years old when Janel died. From the two pictures she had seen, it was obvious that Mathew resembled her a great deal. One was a small charcoal sketch he kept in his room, and the other was an oval-shaped painting a traveling artist had done just after she and Bran were married. Lara guessed that Janel had been twenty or twenty-one in that painting. Out of curiosity several years before, she had asked her mother what Janel was like.

Quiet, reserved, and strong-minded when she had a need to be, her mother told her. The description made sense since children tended to take after their parents.

When Mathew smiled, it was so warm and genuine. Her annoyance over his suggesting that she not come along had vanished several days ago, replaced by a worry for his safety. He could be so insufferable when he was trying to be noble. She was able to take care of herself just fine, thank you. Her mother once pointed out that men could be very annoying, and Lara had to admit that there was a great deal of truth in the statement. On top of everything else, Mathew hadn't even apologized to her yet for suggesting she shouldn't come with them when they left Devondale. It accounted for their lack of conversation recently. He could be stubborn at times, as she well knew.

An owl hooting in a tree close by caused her to jump. Akin looked into the trees and gave her a reassuring smile.

"It's an owl," he said.

"I know. It's just that—"

"I'm worried about them too, but we'd best keep going. Father Thomas said we should reach Elberton in four or five hours. That should put us there before midnight."

Long moments passed before Lara spoke again. "Akin, can I ask you a question?"

"Certainly," he said, turning in his saddle toward her.

"You didn't have to be here, you know. Why did you come?"

"Well . . . Father Thomas is my priest. And when Fergus came and told me that he needed us, it seemed like the right thing to do."

"Just that?"

"That . . . and the fact that I've known Mat—and you, for that matter—since you were both children. What was happening back there wasn't right. I'm no lawyer, but I think I can tell the difference."

"You think Mathew did the right thing, then?" she asked.

Akin didn't answer right away. "I didn't say that. I've thought about it a lot over the last few days, and the truth is I'm not sure. I don't know what I would have done under the circumstances had it been me. Fergus thinks Mat is right . . . but it's not an easy question."

"I know," Lara said. She felt Akin look at her in the darkness and went on. "At the time, everything seemed so clear, but now . . . I've never been a criminal before."

"Neither have I. At least I'm in good company," Akin said, reaching over to squeeze her hand. "Things have a funny way of working out. It helps if you believe that."

"Do you think Mathew will go to jail?" she asked. "You know, he wants to go back and give himself up."

"I know," Akin said. "He spoke to me about it a few days ago. It might not be a bad idea to get it over with. I can't imagine a jury convicting him of murder, but as I said, I'm not a lawyer. Generally, the further away I stay from them, the happier I tend to be. Do you agree with what Mat wants to do?"

Little else had occupied Lara's mind since she learned from Collin that was what Mathew was planning.

"No," she said thoughtfully, "but *something* has to be done. The problem's not simply going to go away by itself, and I don't think Jeram Quinn is about to forget what we did either. I suppose I'll deal with the situation when it comes up. I trust Father Thomas, so I'll wait and see what happens. I don't know if it was a mistake for us to leave or not, but like you said, it seemed like a good idea at the time."

"Along with the fact that you care for Mat?" Akin teased.

Lara felt her color heighten. "Does it show that much?"

"Only in the last year or so when you started wearing dresses instead of your brother's clothes all the time. It's a nice change, though," Akin said, squeezing her hand again.

She put her hand over his and squeezed back. "They'll be all right, won't they?" she said, looking over her shoulder.

"I hope so. Father Thomas is a strange one, but he seems to know what he's doing. He certainly knows more about those creatures and the woods than I do. Now that I think of it, he seems to know about a lot of things," he said, scratching his head. "I suppose if the Lord's going to listen to anybody, he's got a better chance of getting through than most."

Lara smiled in spite of herself.

For the next hour Lara did her best to think of anything other than what might be happening back at the campsite. Under other circumstances she would have thought it a beautiful night, but her heart continued to beat quickly with every step the horse took. After a while she realized she was gripping the reins so tightly that her hands hurt.

Calmly, she told herself. *Calmly.*

"Collin told me that you've been to Elberton before," she said. "Is it very much different from Devondale?"

"Very much indeed," Akin answered with a laugh. "Not at all the sort of place a young lady like you should be alone in."

"I've been to big places, like Gravenhage, you know," she sniffed. "I don't see how this could be much worse."

Akin chuckled again, but catching the lift of her chin out of the corner of his eye, he quickly went on.

"I meant no offense, but Elberton is nothing like Gravenhage. It's a collection of streets, mostly—no proper town square at all. The dock area where the boats going down the Roeselar put in is mostly a place to avoid after dark. They boast the distinction of having not one but three different taverns. The last time I visited, it was easier to get into a fight there than to order a drink. It seemed the cutpurses and thieves outnumbered the citizens."

"Really?" Lara said, taken aback. "Why doesn't their council do something about it? Decent people shouldn't have to put up with things like that."

"The officials were generally more concerned with lining their own pockets than anything else, unless things have changed . . . which I doubt very much. Most of the scum from the river has always seemed to wash up there."

"Well, I hope they have a decent inn. I haven't slept in a bed in eight days, and if I don't get to take a proper bath soon . . . well, I won't be fit to ride with."

"Actually, as I recall, their inn is a fairly nice one. Most of the travelers who come downriver to trade stay there. It's called the Nobody's Inn."

"You're not serious?" Lara said. "What a name."

"I am," Akin answered. "It was kind of a local joke. An outsider would stop someone in town and ask if they could recommend a good place to eat or stay, and people would reply 'Nobody's Inn.' You'd usually get a lot of confused stares."

"Well, I think it's silly. I hope you didn't do such a thing."

"Uh . . . I think we should be there shortly," Akin replied. "If you look ahead, you can actually see the sky is brighter just above the treeline. Most likely, those are the lights from Elberton."

Lara was aware that he had changed the subject without answering her, but she chose not to pursue it. Instead she asked, "What were you doing in a place like Elberton, if it was as bad as all that."

"Believe it or not, there is a guild hall there. I served as an apprentice for a year—as did my brother, and my father too . . . when he was much younger, of course."

"A guild hall, really?"

Akin nodded. "The silversmith hall's over five hundred years old," he told her. "At one time Elberton used to be a lot bigger. When Tyraine came into its own as a commerce port, Elberton began to lose a lot of its trade and fell on hard times, but the silver guild stayed and so did several others. With the prices in Tyraine going up each year, our neighbors in Sennia—who are a most resourceful people, by the way—were only too happy to make the trip across the Southern Sea to trade. They could resell whatever they bought here for a handsome profit back in Barcora."

"I see."

Lara's own father ran a dye and leather shop in Devondale, and having helped run it since she was little, she was no stranger to the commercial practicalities of business.

"I'll feel better once we get there," he said. "I've no liking for being out on this road at night."

"We didn't seem to have much choice," Lara responded glumly.

Though they continued their ride without further conversation, she noticed that Akin tended to watch roadside shadows more carefully than before. Fortunately, they covered the last few miles without incident.

Elberton was very much as Akin had said it would be— just a collection of streets, mostly deserted at that hour of the evening. On the outskirts of town the few people they did see watched them suspiciously and hurried on their way, not wishing to have any contact. Ahead of her and to the east she could see the Roeselar flowing quietly by.

"The docks are at the end of this street." Akin pointed. "You can see some of them from here."

"Yes," Lara answered. She was about to say something else when she stopped in mid-sentence, wrinkling her nose at the air. "My goodness, what is that awful smell?"

Akin sniffed the air and made a face. "I imagine that's the tannery. Their guild is located at the far end of the docks, if I recall correctly. Most days, it isn't so bad. Assuming the wind's blowing downriver, that is. The wool quarter is over here to our left."

A collection of shops, all closed for the night, bore signs that advertised everything from shirts, cloaks, and dresses to pants and blankets. They ran one after another along the narrow cobblestone street opposite them. The street lamps cast warm yellow globes of light on the ground.

Eventually they passed a quaint-looking house with a red light hanging outside it. Two girls, whom Lara guessed were just about her own age, stood outside wearing dresses with bodices cut so low they made her gasp. She thought both would have been very pretty if they weren't wearing so much makeup. One of them, a blonde, smiled pointedly at Akin, looking him up and down him as they rode by.

"Do you know that girl?"

"Oh . . . ah . . . not really," Akin said, blushing a bit.

"Well, she seemed to know you. I've never seen a dress cut so low," Lara told him, dropping her voice. "I don't see how anyone could go out in public like that—and the way she looked at you. What if their parents were to see them?"

"Actually, I don't think their parents live in Elberton," Akin said, glancing back over his shoulder.

"Really?" Lara said, mildly surprised as she mulled over the concept of young ladies living apart from their parents. "Do they belong to one of the guilds?"

"Hmm . . . I wouldn't think so." This time it was Akin's turn to digest a new concept.

They rode along quietly for a few more blocks before Lara asked, "Akin, what kind of house was that?"

"Well, you see, it's, ah . . . a little difficult to explain," he said, not meeting her eyes. "In certain towns it's referred to as a house of—"

"Never mind, Master Gibb. I can guess the rest." Lara sniffed reprovingly.

Akin let out a deep breath and seemed to take a good deal of interest in adjusting his horse's bridle for the next few minutes.

Seven streets later they rode up to the Nobody's Inn. They had barely dismounted when a man came out of the stable directly across the way to take their horses. While

Akin settled on the price, Lara looked up at the building.
It was considerably larger than Devondale's Rose and
Crown, with a double roof and flower boxes on the windows. The roof was made of long rounded red tiles.
Through the large window at the front, composed of separate leaded glass panes in a latticework pattern, Lara
could see quite a number of people seated around the
common room.

No one paid them much attention when they entered the
room. A minstrel was seated on a stool by the fire, strum-
ming a mandolin. He was in the midst of an old familiar
ballad about the deaths of Catrin and Rolan, two young
lovers who threw themselves into the sea. When he concluded, the audience clapped appreciatively and called
for another song.

Lara looked around the room, taking in all the new
sights. Cheerful yellow curtains framed the windows, in
sharp contrast to the dark wood. Flags from Elgaria, Sennia, and another that Lara didn't know, hung above the
fireplace over the minstrel's head. The floor was made of
wide wooden planks covered in sawdust, and there were
paintings of river scenes and boats hanging on the walls.
It gave the impression of comfort without pretense.

"I'll be back in just a moment," Akin said to her. "I left
my violin case in the saddlebag. Wait here for me."

Lara nodded and went over to sit at one of the tables.

In the corner, a well-dressed man and woman glanced
at her briefly and returned to their drinks, not bothering to
acknowledge her smile. Three rough-looking men
dressed like sailors, with tattoos on their arms, turned in
their seats and looked her up and down with something
other than just passing interest. Although their attention
made her uneasy, she resisted the temptation to avert her
eyes and returned their stares before they looked away.

On the opposite side of the room a pretty serving girl,
smartly dressed in a white apron, poured a pitcher of ale
for two men and their lady companions. The green
cloaks and gold braid the men wore marked them as

Duchess Elita's soldiers. One of the women, a plump blonde, smiled and nodded in her direction, but neither of the men even looked her way, for which she was grateful. Akin had told her the duchess's family was closely related to King Malach and had ruled the Berne, Elgaria's most southern province, from Longreath Castle for generations.

The minstrel began to play another song, and heads turned in his direction. Lara was about to turn and watch when she felt a hand on her shoulder. One of the sailors, emboldened by drink and the company of his companions, had taken it on himself to join her at her table. He was a dark-skinned man, with swarthy good looks and jet-black hair, closer to Akin's age than her own. He wore a gold earring in his left ear and tied his hair in a small ponytail at the back of his neck.

"Hello, missy," he said with a smile. "Owen's the name. New in town?"

Before she could say anything, Owen sat down uninvited and put a hand on her forearm.

"Yes, I am," Lara said, "and I don't believe we've been introduced." She started to pull her arm away but stopped when Owen didn't release his grip.

"Introduced? Well . . . we can cure that straight away. Owen Welch at your service. And you would be?"

"Waiting for a friend to return," she replied.

"You mean that blond-haired fellow you came in with? Looks to me like he's shoved off and left you without a proper escort."

"He should be back any moment," Lara said calmly.

Owen glanced around the room with exaggerated affect. "Well . . . all I can say is, you don't capture a prize vessel and then abandon it. If you get my meaning."

God, why me? she thought.

"Look, I really think you should be going," Lara said.

"Going? But I've only just got here. Besides, I'm just about worn-out. You've been running through my mind since you first came in." Owen flashed her a set of white teeth and a broad smile.

"I'm sorry, but I *am* with a friend."

Undeterred, Owen responded by rubbing her forearm and said, "Listen . . . why don't you shift flags to the next table and join my mates and me for a few drinks?"

Seconds later the smile slowly faded from his face when he felt the sharp point from Lara's dagger pressed dangerously at the crotch of his breeches.

"If you don't take your hand off me in the next ten seconds," she whispered, smiling back at him, "you and your friends are going to spend the rest of the evening discussing your shortcomings."

Owen opened his mouth to say something, but didn't. His eyes widened farther and he took in a sharp breath in through his nostrils as the pressure of Lara's dagger increased. His fingers immediately relaxed and he slowly got to his feet, backing away from her. He wasted no time in returning to his own table. When he sat down, his friends said something to him, but he just shook his head, grabbed one of their drinks, and finished it in one gulp.

The minstrel was almost finished with his ballad of the travels of Prince Talbot on the Isle of Calderon by the time Akin returned. Lara slipped the dagger back into the sleeve of her dress and got up to join him.

"Everything fine?" he said.

"Simply wonderful," Lara replied, slipping her arm through his.

19

Elberton, the Nobody's Inn

A HANDSOME-LOOKING WOMAN EMERGED FROM THE kitchen, noticed Akin and Lara standing there, and quickly came forward. She had long dark brown hair, which she wore in a braid over her shoulder. Lara guessed she was in her mid-forties. The woman's eyes were a clear hazel color. She was wearing a well-made vest of green suede that laced up the middle over a dress of dark purple, which showed off her slender figure well, though not obviously.

"Please forgive me," she said, offering her hand to each of them. "I hardly know where my mind has been today." Her grip was firm and dry, with a promise of good strength behind it.

"I'm Ceta Woodall, the owner. How may I help you?"

"Akin Gibb of Ashford, and this is my cousin Lara. We would like to take rooms for the night, and perhaps dinner before we retire."

"Ashford? My goodness, but that's a long way off," she said, looking closely at Akin. "We don't get many visitors from there. Let me show you both to a table, and I'll have one of the girls bring you something right away—or would you rather see your rooms first?"

"Well," Akin said, "the food certainly sounds—"

"I've just been *dreaming* about a hot bath for almost a week," Lara cut in with a shy smile.

Akin's mouth was still in the process of forming the balance of his sentence when he decided to close it.

"Of course, you poor thing. I'll show you up right

away." But then, noticing Akin's crestfallen look, she patted his arm and added, "I'll send Effie along with your food, and some hot towels too."

Mollified, he brightened and followed them toward a staircase at the back of the room. When they passed, Lara smiled sweetly at Owen, who quickly averted his eyes.

"So you're from Ashford," the innkeeper said. "What brings you all the way to Elberton?"

"We're on our way to Barcora to visit my sister. She's just had a baby," Lara answered. "Father wouldn't allow me to travel alone, so he asked cousin Akin to take me. My uncle and his three boys will be joining us here tomorrow."

"Four more?" Ceta stopped and her brows came together for a moment as she rapidly performed some mental calculations. "Yes . . . I suppose we can accommodate them as well, if they won't mind sleeping double."

"Oh, I'm sure they won't, they're a very close family," Lara replied.

Akin glanced at her sideways but kept on walking.

When they reached the top of the landing, the innkeeper turned to her right and opened the second door.

"This will be your room, Master Gibb. I trust you will find it comfortable. I'll send one of the men up with a tub and some hot water for you just as soon as I've settled your young cousin here . . . and the food too, of course," she added, before he could remind her again.

"Oh . . . well, thank you. That will be fine," he said. "Good night."

As soon as he closed the door, the women exchanged a quick smile and proceeded down the hallway.

Lara's room was bigger than she thought it would be. It was certainly larger than Akin's, pleasantly decorated with white curtains on the windows and a chest of drawers. There was also a desk in the corner. A large scrumptious-looking copper tub with raised brass claw feet sat on the floor, in front of what looked to be a most comfortable bed. The window, with its small lead glass panes set in a diamond pattern, was a smaller version of the one she'd seen downstairs in the common room.

Lara looked out and could see reflections of moonlight on the Roeselar, along with a portion of the docks Akin had mentioned. A number of tall masts rocked gently on the river's current, tied up for the night.

"I'm afraid at this time of night all I can offer you is some soup, bread, and tea," the innkeeper apologized. "But the soup is quite good, if I do say so myself. I think we could also manage some apple pie."

"Oh, that would be wonderful," Lara replied, realizing just how hungry she was.

"Have you been traveling a long time, my dear?" she asked as Lara sat on the bed, trying it out.

"Um-hmm, over a week," she answered, and was immediately sorry because she didn't know how far Ashford actually was from Elberton.

"I see. Do you think your . . . *cousin* will want the same thing to eat?"

There was something in Ceta Woodall's tone, a mixture of tact and intelligence, that caused Lara to look at her more closely. The other woman returned the look evenly.

There was a long pause.

"We're not really from Ashford," Lara finally replied. "And Akin isn't my cousin."

The innkeeper's eyebrows rose but her smile remained.

"I didn't think so, dear. In my business it pays to remember faces, and if I'm not mistaken, Master Gibb was an apprentice at the silver guild several years ago. He hasn't changed all that much, a little taller and more mature in the face, but the same person, I would say. If my memory serves me correctly, he was from a small town . . . oh, dear, what was that name?" She frowned, tapping her teeth with a finger.

"Devondale," Lara said. "I'm very sorry we deceived you."

"Devondale," the innkeeper repeated with a satisfied nod. "Quite all right. Actually, you didn't deceive me very much. But thank you anyway for saying it."

"How did you know?" Lara asked, still embarrassed.

"Oh, several things," Ceta Woodall said as she turned down the bed covers. "First, you don't look anything like you're related, and second, neither of you have a northern accent. Almost everyone from that area of the country does. It's quite noticeable really."

"I am sorry," Lara repeated again. "It's just that—"

"I'm quite sure you have very good reasons—particularly for traveling these roads at night. Whatever they are, your confidences are safe with me."

"Yes, ma'am," Lara replied.

"My late husband always told me that tavern owners have to be just like physicians where their patron's privacy is concerned."

"Oh," Lara said, hearing the word "late."

"He died of the plague several years ago on a trip to Verano," Ceta explained, "and I've been running the inn ever since. When Effie comes up with the hot water and your dinner, I'll have her take your clothes and give them a good brushing, if you like. Now turn around and I'll help you undo those buttons. Do you have something else to change into?"

"I have another dress," Lara said, turning around as instructed while the innkeeper began to undo the buttons of her dress.

A tap at the door caused Ceta to pause. "Come in," she called out.

The door opened and a man about ten years older than Lara entered. She recognized him as the same person who had taken the horses when they arrived. He was carrying her pack in one hand and a large steaming pail of hot soapy water in the other.

"Thank you, Will. You can put the clothes on the chest over there, please."

The man nodded and set the pail down. He looked at Lara as he passed with glance that was scarcely less than obvious. After he placed the clothes on the dresser, he made a desultory sort of bow and withdrew, closing the door after him.

The innkeeper watched him go and let out a sigh. "I

may have made a mistake with that one. Watch yourself around him."

In response to Lara's unasked question, she added, "At this time of year, good help is hard to find—you sometimes have to take what washes up on shore. Now if you'll excuse me, I'll go see to your food, and I think we'll let one of the girls bring up the rest of your bathwater."

Fifteen minutes later Lara settled back into the luxury of a hot bath, closed her eyes, and drifted as the tension began to leave her body. She never knew that a bath could feel so good. And she decided, right then and there, to buy a bathtub exactly like the one she was in when she had her own home.

Both she and Ceta had spoken for a little while longer before the innkeeper left. She immediately liked the other woman. Ceta was smart, quick, and independent, with plain speaking qualities Lara admired. While they talked, she did feel the necessity of explaining to her that Akin was not her lover, though she didn't elaborate on the reasons they were traveling together and Ceta didn't press the point. Nevertheless, she wasn't entirely sure Ceta was convinced. For some reason, the idea that someone else might think she was old enough for a lover was . . . well, a bit odd to her. But at seventeen, she had already lost most of her adolescent features. And if the looks she received from Will, Owen, and the other men in the tavern weren't enough, a brief glance at her body while she lay soaking in the tub was sufficient to convince her that she was no longer a child.

A half hour later Lara noticed that her toes and fingers were beginning to take on a pruney look. She climbed out of the bath and wrapped a large towel around her from the pile on the bed. Ceta was thoughtful enough to have put a hot brick between the ones Effie brought up. To Lara's mind there was nothing as luxurious as stepping from a bath into a warm towel.

Effie was her own age and a regular chatterbox. Ceta had told her the girl was trustworthy but warned against sharing anything confidential. As a result, Lara effectively sidestepped Effie's questions with the same story she made up when they arrived. Unlike Ceta, however, Effie was far more direct, asking straight out if she and Akin were a couple. Lara assured her they were not— only relatives, which seemed to stem the inquisition. Effie also made a point to ask if Akin was married or promised to anyone, while she bustled around the room plumping up the pillows, collecting towels, and opening the window to let fresh air in.

By far the most exciting news Lara provided was that four more men would be joining them in the morning, which only led to a further barrage of questions. How old were they? Were they cute? Did any of them like to dance? And . . . oh yes, were any of them married? Thus satisfied, Effie bade her good night and left the room, admonishing her to lock the door.

Lara sat at the desk, sipping her soup and looking out toward the docks. She was daydreaming, imagining what it would be like floating down the river on a boat, when she realized with a start that a man was standing in the shadows across the street, looking up into her room. From the clothes and long hair, she had no problem identifying him. Aware that he was seen, Will stepped out of the shadows, waved, and continued down the street in the direction of the Roeselar. Lara reached across the desk and quickly pulled the curtains closed.

The bed was generous and soft. It felt absolutely delicious when she slipped between the cool set of clean sheets. Once settled, Lara leaned over, blew out the candle, and closed her eyes, waiting for sleep to come.

But come it didn't.

Almost immediately she began to worry about Mathew, Collin, Daniel, and Father Thomas. Fear for their safety gave her an empty queasy feeling in the pit of her stomach. All at once she felt guilty and ashamed to be lying there in a nice bed while they were still out in the forest with who-knew-what. After tossing and turning for the next half hour, she gave up and got out of bed. She found wooden matches in a drawer and used them to light the candle.

Lara slipped into her gray dress, gave a last look in the mirror to make sure that everything was in place and properly buttoned, then opened the door and walked down the hall to Akin's room. She tapped softly, but there was no response. She was about to give up, thinking he was aleep, when she heard the sound of a violin coming from the floor below.

Lara was halfway down the stairs when she saw Akin, seated on a stool by the fireplace, playing his violin next to the minstrel, who accompanied him on a harp. There were fewer people than before, but they all sat there quietly listening to the sweet notes coming from the instruments. Ceta was at a table with a nice-looking gentleman, while Effie and another girl leaned against the kitchen door, their heads resting against the wooden frame. Akin's eyes were closed and he swayed back and forth ever so slightly while he played. Everyone applauded when the song ended, and he and the minstrel shook hands. Seeing Lara standing by the stairs, he motioned her over to a table near the wall. Ceta and her companion glanced up and smiled to her before returning to their own conversation.

"Hello, cousin." Akin grinned, taking a seat across from her.

Lara noticed that he had shaved.

He picked up on her glance and shrugged noncommittally. "I guess the bath wasn't such a bad idea after all," he said.

"It does look nicer," she agreed. There was a pause before she continued. "I just couldn't sleep—I tried, but it wasn't any use."

"I couldn't either," he said. "If they're not here by first light, I'm going back out and look for them."

"And I'm coming with you," Lara said.

"No, you are not."

"Akin . . ."

"What you're going to do is to stay here and keep your

word to Father Thomas. I'll do the looking. He would skin me alive if he found I let you go back out again."

"But why do you get—"

"No," he whispered fiercely. "Absolutely not." His tone gave room for no argument.

"Well, I don't think it's fair at all. Just because you're a man."

Akin looked at her and his expression softened. "I'm as worried as you are, but I can't risk you going, Lara."

He was about to say something else, but stopped abruptly, seeing her eyes fill with tears.

"None of that now . . . none of that," he said gently, pulling a handkerchief out of his pocket and dabbing her eyes. "I spoke to the innkeeper—a nice lady, by the way. She told me there should be a ship going downriver in three or four days. The captain is a friend of hers, and she was agreeable to introducing us."

Lara sniffed and nodded. "How long do you think it'll be to first light?" she eventually asked.

Akin looked out the window before replying. "Five, six hours at most," he said. "You should try to get some sleep in the meantime."

"I can't," she said.

Akin was about to make the suggestion again, but held his tongue due to Effie's sudden appearance, asking if they wanted anything to drink. He didn't, but Lara requested a cup of hot tea.

Effie nodded in acknowledgment but kept her eyes on Akin. "Your cousin didn't tell me you could play so beautifully. Gayle and I was listening at the kitchen. I just loved it."

"Why, thank you," Akin said, looking up at her.

"Wherever did you learn to play like that?"

Lara noticed the wide eyes and slightly breathless speech, but bit her lip.

"My father taught my brother and me when we were both little."

"Was he a famous musician?" she asked, leaning over the table directly between Lara and him.

"Musician? Why no . . . he was a silversmith, as I am," Akin said, leaning backward a bit.

"Really? That's wonderful. You must have very strong hands," she said, taking one of his hands and examining it.

Lara couldn't see anything wonderful about it. In fact the only thing she *could* see at that moment was Effie's ample backside, which she was seriously considering giving a good kick to. Fortunately, they were both spared the experience when Ceta decided to stop by, most opportunely, to inquire if their rooms were comfortable. Effie immediately straightened, curtsied, and hurried to the kitchen, but not before giving Akin a smile that held a good deal of promise.

Ceta introduced the man with her as Dr. Wycroft. A bit shorter than her, he was well-dressed in a long black coat fastened in the front by a gold chain. His hair was mostly gray, neatly trimmed, and he carried himself with an air of confidence. Lara thought he was a very distinguished-looking gentleman.

"Mistress Woodall tells me that you and your cousin hail from Ashford Township," he said, shaking hands with Akin and presenting a slight bow to Lara.

"Yes," Akin replied as casually as he could. "We're on our way to Barcora to visit some relatives. Would you care to sit down?"

"No, no, thank you very much. The hour is late, and I was about to take my leave anyway. Susa Barkley is expecting her first child and I promised to look in on her in the morning."

"Well, perhaps another time," Akin said pleasantly. "We hope to secure passage on a ship in the next few days, but I imagine we'll be passing back through here in a few weeks when we return home."

"To Ashford?" Dr. Wycroft asked, his brows coming together.

"Yes . . . of course," Akin said, looking from the doctor to Lara, then back again.

The doctor's fine features suddenly took on a serious expression and he pulled a chair up to the table. "Then I must assume you have not heard the news?" he asked, sitting down.

"News? We've been on the road for quite some time and have only just arrived."

"My dear young man," the doctor said, putting his hand sympathetically on Akin's forearm and lowering his voice. "I am very sorry to have to tell you this, but ten days ago the Nyngaryns and Sibuyan attacked Stermark, and the Alor Satar and Bajani attacked Toland. If I am not mistaken, Ashford was in the middle of the fighting. The duchess sent troops north to support King Malach at Anderon, which we have heard is also under siege. Of course, much of the news is still incomplete, but the ship's captain who told me is a reliable man, so I think we must give it credence."

Akin stared at him in disbelief. "*War?* I can't believe it."

"I am very sorry," the doctor repeated again, this time looking to Lara. "If there is anything that I can do . . ."

Lara was the first to recover. "No. Thank you, sir," she said. "We are at war, then?"

"That decision is usually something for politicians and the crown, but yes, I would have to say that is exactly what it means."

"This is horrible," Lara said. "Was there any news of Ashford, Doctor?"

"None that I have heard directly, but rest assured, I will certainly inquire. I can understand what a shock this must be to you."

"Yes . . . it is. My relatives and I will have to discuss what to do when they arrive," Lara said.

"Of course, my dear," Dr. Wycroft said. "Ceta told me you are expecting them in the morning. Would that I could have spared you this. We can only pray it will be over quickly. I have no desire to experience a war again. If I can be of any service, please don't hesitate to call upon me."

The doctor rose, shaking Akin's hand once more and giving Ceta Woodall a kiss on the cheek before he said good night and departed.

Ceta watched him go. "He's a good man," she said, and turning back to them, added, "It's time I was off to bed as well. Call on me in the morning. We can walk down to the docks together and I'll introduce you to Captain Donal."

"Thank you, Ceta," Lara said.

The innkeeper gave her a quick wink and then stared at Akin for a second. "He does look better once you clean him up."

But she was gone before Akin could reply.

20

Elberton

THEIR RIDE INTO TOWN WAS QUIET AND UNEVENTFUL. Even after Collin had relieved him to stand guard, Mathew was unable to get any sleep. He'd lain in his blanket and eventually watched the sky turn gray. Painful thoughts of Bran reemerged, and of Giles, and of Berke Ramsey's face as he died. Everything seemed like a jumble to him—his future, Lara, what the Orlock had said. Bran once told him that nighttime always made things seem more serious than they were, and the light of day was far better to put matters in their proper perspective. He wished Bran were there with him now.

In the morning they had a quick cold meal of bread and cheese.

"I used to enjoy cheese," Daniel said, sitting with his back against the trunk of a tree.

"What's wrong with cheese?" Collin asked, taking another bite of his sandwich.

"Nothing, I guess," Daniel replied. "I could just do with a change, that's all. Nine days of cheese in a row may have cured me."

Collin shrugged, took another bite of his sandwich, and got up to tie his pack onto his horse.

"Nothing bothers him," Daniel observed to Mathew. "It's depressing."

They broke camp as quickly as they could and made their way back to the road. After riding several minutes, they passed the ruins of an old town off to their left. The forest

was well on its way to reclaiming the land. The blackened timbers of the few houses and buildings remaining
told them there had been a fire. A few foundations and
chimneys still stood here and there, though most of them
had collapsed or fallen under the weight of downed trees.
Long grass and dried-up shrubs grew everywhere. The
wind blew dust in a cloud along what must have once
been the town's main street. Other than birds chirping angrily at their approach, no sound or sign of life came
from it at all.

"Gosh," Daniel said as they rode by. "I wonder what
place this was."

"Weyburn," Father Thomas answered. "It was called
Weyburn."

He paused his horse for a minute to look at the silent
town, then pulled his reins and continued down the road.
Daniel, Collin, and Mathew exchanged glances and followed him silently.

Elberton was nothing like Mathew expected. The town
didn't seem to have any precise center, or even a beginning point; it just started, one street following another.
The result was somehow unbalanced and awkward. They
had no trouble finding the oddly named Nobody's Inn,
however, which was at the opposite end of Elberton.

On their way, they passed the same house Lara had
asked Akin about, where two sleepy-looking young
ladies were just returning from an evening's work. The
smaller of the two, a pretty brunette with a very attractive
figure, flashed Collin an inviting smile. He slowed his
horse and was about to engage her in conversation when
Father Thomas rode up alongside him and took him by
the elbow.

"Ah . . . come along, my son. Unfortunately, only the
smile is free."

"Oh," Collin said, looking back over his shoulder at
the young lady, who continued to watch him with professional interest.

They had scarcely arrived before Lara bounded out of

the front door and all but launched herself at Father
Thomas, grabbing him in a tremendous hug. Mathew,
Daniel, and Collin received similar greetings. She was
followed by Akin, who elected to simply shake hands.

A sleepy-looking Will, wearing his usual long-
suffering expression, emerged from the stables, took their
horses, and pointed toward the front door of the inn, indicating for them to go in.

Ceta Woodall came out to greet them. She had changed
into a comfortable-looking blue dress with a thin gold
belt that clung well to her trim figure and set off her hair
nicely.

"I was told you were coming, and I'm so pleased to
have you as our guests," she said, looking principally at
Father Thomas. "I take it you must be Uncle Siward, and
these are your boys. Lara's told me so much about you already, I feel as if we're old friends."

Father Thomas opened his mouth, then closed it again
after a glance at Lara and Akin, who smiled back at him.

"I'm very pleased to make your acquaintance as well,"
he said, recovering his composure. "May I introduce my,
uh . . . *boys*, Mathew, Daniel, and Collin."

Despite some puzzled looks, each of them bowed.

"Lara, why didn't you tell me you had such a handsome uncle?" Ceta asked, taking Father Thomas's arm.
"I've put aside two rooms for you. If you'll follow me,
Uncle Siward, I'll show you up. Lara told me you wouldn't
mind doubling. We're a bit full at this time of year."

Father Thomas allowed the innkeeper to lead him
through the common room, which was mostly empty of
guests at that late hour of the morning. Lara, noticing the
priest's discomfort, exchanged a mischievous glance with
Akin, who rolled his eyes. The innkeeper, followed by
Lara, led Akin and Father Thomas to the room she had set
aside for him. Once inside Ceta closed the door and
turned to face the priest.

"Your niece thought it best to keep your plans private,"
she said to him. "I'm sorry, but too many of my people

were around to allow time for an explanation. Several of the duchess's soldiers were also here last night."

Father Thomas listened to her calmly. He wasn't certain, but from the amused twinkle in her eye, she seemed to be enjoying herself. "I see," he said. "Well, perhaps that was for the best after all. Thank you for your discretion."

"Your . . . ah . . ." Ceta frowned at Akin while searching for the right word. Not finding it, she went on, "Well, I'm not sure what your relationship is, but I'm sure Master Gibb will explain to you about the ship and the other news. In the meantime," she added, with a pointed sniff at the air, "I'll have some tubs and water brought up. Midday meal will be in an hour."

Giving Lara a quick wink, she left the room, and a perplexed Father Thomas.

"Remarkable woman," he murmured under his breath.

Akin quickly told them what he and Lara had learned since their arrival. The news of war came as a shock to Father Thomas, but before they had time to discuss it, they were interrupted by a knock. Will and another man came in carrying their things and a tub.

"Where'd you want these?" Will asked.

"The bed will be just fine for the packs," Lara answered, taking charge. "And you can set the tub right there."

When they were finished, Father Thomas fished two copper pennies out of his cloak and gave one to each of the men.

"Thankee, sir," the first man said with a smile and a small bow, before withdrawing.

Will just stuck the penny in the pocket of his vest and said flatly, "She said for me to show you to the other room."

Lara was surprised to find the boys engaged in a quick discussion among themselves. They decided to share one room and let Father Thomas have the other.

They all followed Will out and down the hall to the second room, which was located across from her own.

After helping everyone get settled, Lara went downstairs to talk to Ceta and see if another bed could be brought up.

When the boys were alone, Collin sat on one of the beds and whistled.

"Do you think the news about the war is true?" he asked the others.

Mathew shook his head and stood by the window, looking out at the view, which consisted mostly of rooftops. "I don't know. But if it is, it changes everything. We'll have to go back."

"Go back?" Daniel said. "I thought we've been through all that."

Mathew turned around to face him. "It's not a matter of my going to jail this time," he said. "If we really are at war, then it's up to us to do our duty. I'll just have to deal with the other thing when it comes up."

"And having met Jeram Quinn, how long do you think that will be?" Daniel asked. "I may be going out on a limb with this, but my guess is he didn't take too kindly to our threatening him with bows and arrows."

"I think Mat's right," Collin said from the bed, "We're going to have to go back. Maybe Father Thomas can work something out."

"Father Thomas is as involved in this as we are," Daniel replied. "Look, I'm as keen as you are about doing my duty, but I say let's find out just exactly what the situation is and how bad things are before we make any decisions."

"I don't know," Collin said, stretching out on the bed and looking up at the wooden ceiling. "I guess we need to think about it. Why don't we see what Father and Akin say after lunch? In the meantime, I'd like to see some of this town."

Their discussion was interrupted by the arrival of a third bed and a large tub, brought in by Will and John, as they learned his name was. John seemed harmless enough, but Will went about his business with a sour look on his face, muttering continually to himself. More than once, Mathew caught him looking at his ring. He handed each of them a copper penny, as Father Thomas had done. John left with a smile, but Will just looked at the penny, smirked, and put it in his pocket.

Before the door even closed, Effie and Gayle appeared with a set of fresh bed linens and a pillow for the extra bed. Each girl was carrying a bucket of hot water.

"Here, let me help you with that," Collin said, jumping off the bed and taking the buckets from them.

"Oh, sir, you don't need to do that. It's my job," Effie said. Gayle just giggled and left to fetch another bucket.

Collin poured the water into the tub and handed the bucket back to her with a smile.

"Miss Lara certainly has some handsome cousins," she said, smiling back at him while rearranging a strand of hair from her forehead. "Will you gentlemen be staying with us long?"

"Possibly," Collin said. "It depends how long it will take us to get passage on a boat to Tyraine. We're on our way to visit our aunt. She just had a baby, you know."

"Oh yes, sir. Mistress Woodall told me about it earlier. What did she have?"

"Have?"

"Your aunt, sir," she prompted.

Incredibly, Daniel and Mathew, standing on opposite sides of the room, decided to help by answering "a boy" and "a girl" at the same time.

Bewildered, Effie looked at Collin. "Sir?"

"Ah . . . twins . . . she had twins," he said quickly.

"Oh, I see. That must be why you're all going, then. Although I don't see what use men can be with babies," she teased.

"Yes. Well, the farm needs a lot of work," Mathew said. "Her poor husband is a bit overwhelmed."

"We're very handy," Daniel supplemented.

Effie looked from one to another and gave a small, dismissive shrug. "I'll just be off to fetch the rest of your water. If you gentlemen are interested, there's a tavern down by the docks called the Blue Goose. There'll be dancing and music tonight. Gayle and I'll be there after we're off from work . . . and some other girls too."

"Well, that sounds just wonderful," Collin said, leaning closer and giving her one of his most endearing smiles.

"Won't there be dancing here as well?" Daniel asked.

"Oh yes, sir," Effie replied, "but more the quiet kind, if you know what I mean—for people like your uncle and such."

"He does tend to be the quiet type," Daniel agreed.

"I imagine we'll be able to stop by," Collin said. "After you're done with work, you say?"

"Mm-hmm," Effie said, sounding delighted. She gave them a quick curtsey and left the room.

As soon as she was gone, Collin rounded on them. " 'A boy and a girl!' " he said. "Pathetic. *Simply pathetic*. I swear, neither of you will ever make a good liar."

Mathew began to chuckle, recalling the shocked look on Collin's face. Daniel joined him a moment later. Soon all three of them were laughing uncontrollably.

After almost two weeks on the road, a hot bath felt very nice indeed to Mathew. They had flipped a coin and he lost, so he had to wait for Daniel and then Collin to vacate the tub.

Just as well. It'll give me more time to soak.

He settled back in the water, promising to join them downstairs after he finished cleaning up. With a small mirror balanced on his knees, he lathered his face and enjoyed the sensuous feel of scraping a razor across his chin as he removed two days' growth of beard. The stubble, he noticed, stretching the skin under his throat, seemed to be thicker and darker of late. When he finished, he set the razor and mirror on the stool next to him and lay back to think, weighing the avenues open to him. Each possible scenario ended with his going back—by himself if need be, and striking an agreement with Jeram Quinn that would allow him—and him alone—to bear the consequences of what had happened. If his assessment of Quinn were right, the man would be reasonable. It was just a matter of working out the details. At that moment, however, he didn't know exactly how he was going to manage that.

Mathew dropped his arms into the suds, letting the warm water cover them, and slid backward until the water reached his shoulders. A casual movement of his hand caused the ring to bang against the side of the tub. It made a small clinking sound. Reflexively, he pulled his arm out of the water and examined it. There were markings on the outside, letters worn smooth over time. They were faint and difficult to make out.

Giles's ring.

If nothing else, it *was* unusual. The oddest thing about it, he decided, apart from the words he could not understand, was its color. It was neither yellow nor white, but a kind of rose shade. He had seen lots of jewelry before, but never any gold that looked like it. Not that he had much experience with jewelry, he admitted to himself.

A cool breeze blew in from the window and sent a little shiver up his spine. He sank back down into the warm water and considered whether it was worth getting out of the tub to close it. A second breeze, accompanied by another chill across his wet skin, decided him—the window definitely needed closing.

With a sigh, he reached for the towel and started to get up, only to freeze part of the way as the window slowly slid down, shutting itself. At the same time, the briefest tingling sensation coursed through his arm. The whole thing happened so quickly, it almost felt like a feather touching him but it was definitely there. He recalled experiencing the same sensation in the forest a split second before his vision had changed. He'd put that off then to being nervous at the time.

Stepping out of the tub, he wrapped a towel around his waist, removed the ring from his finger, and set it down on the wooden stool. The tingling did not return. And other than a slight quickening of his pulse, he felt completely normal. On a hunch, he walked over and tried the window. There was no play in the frame, and it certainly was anything but loose—in fact, it took an effort to lift it again.

Experimentally, he looked around the room, then out across the rooftops. His vision appeared the same to him as it had been a moment ago. Mathew picked up the ring, walked over to the light, and turned it over in his hand, carefully examining it. For the first time, he noticed writing on the inside as well, only so small that he could barely make out any of the letters, with the exception of an E and an L that were larger than the others. He gave up and put the ring back on. The tingling came and went so quickly it caused him to question whether it was really there or not. He took the ring off again and lifted it in his palm. It was definitely heavier than it looked, and cold to the touch as well.

He had no idea what any of it meant.

Mathew shook his head, trying to make sense of it. There had to be a logical explanation. If he were a superstitious person, which he was not, he could have attributed recent events to ghosts or evil spirits, but the rational part of his mind rejected such things. He was certain there was an answer, but it lay just beyond his reach.

Mathew dressed and went downstairs, where he met Effie. She told him the others had already finished their meals and had gone down to the docks with Mistress Woodall, to meet a friend of hers. Despite her protests that he needed to eat something, Mathew told her he wasn't hungry and excused himself on the pretext of wanting to go for a walk.

The day was a pleasant one, with only a few light clouds in the sky and a mild breeze from the river. Akin had said that a Dr. Wycroft had told him the disturbing news about the war, and now Mathew looked for a passerby to ask for directions to the doctor's house.

The man he stopped was a skinny fellow, with a large nose and a prominent Adam's apple. He stared at Mathew suspiciously before answering. "You don't look sick," he remarked.

"I'm not, sir. It's for my uncle. We're staying at the inn and he's come down with a fever—can't keep any food down."

The man grimaced and took a half step backward. "Turn left at the end of this street and go four more streets—then turn left again," he said. "You'll see a yellow house halfway down the block. It'll be on your right, as you face the river."

Mathew looked in the direction the man was pointing, nodded, then turned around to thank him, only to find he was already on his way. He shook his head and swore to himself that if he lived to be a hundred, he would never get used to such ill-mannered people. Certainly no one in Devondale would have acted that way. *Well . . . almost no one*, he thought. On principle, he called out, "Thank you, sir," but the only acknowledgment he got was a brief wave over the man's shoulder as he kept walking.

Ten minutes later he located the doctor's house. It was painted yellow and had a wooden shingle roof and bright winter flowers lining either side of a white fence. A simple black metal sign hanging from an iron post read LUCIEN WYCROFT, PHYSICIAN.

Mathew knocked at the front door and was met by the housekeeper, a heavyset woman, who looked at him in the same way the man in the street had just a few minutes before.

"Good morning," he said. "My name is Mathew Lewin. I would like to see the doctor, if I may."

"It's the afternoon, if you haven't noticed," she said. "Does the doctor know you?"

"No, ma'am. He met my cousin last night at the inn with Mistress Woodall. I would just like to ask him a few questions."

"The doctor is a very busy man. He can't be bothered by every—"

"What is it, Forba?" a male voice called out from inside the house.

"It's nothing, Doctor," the housekeeper called back,

planting herself squarely in the doorway, "just some person who—"

Normally the calmest and most circumspect of people, Mathew's temper chose that moment to flair. "Nothing!" he snapped. "Of all the rude, obnoxious . . . I don't know how you people are raised here, but we're taught to have better manners where I'm from, particularly to guests in our town."

In shock, the housekeeper took a step back and opened her mouth to speak, but before she could, a voice said from behind her, "And where might that be, young man?"

Mathew barely caught himself before he could say "Devondale," and instead replied, "Ashford, sir. I believe you met my cousin, Akin Gibb, last night."

"Ah, yes. It's all right, Forba. Do come in."

The housekeeper folded her hands in front of her and snorted as she stepped aside, fixing him with a distinctly disapproving look.

"If you will follow me," said the doctor, leading the way to his study.

The room was nicely appointed with comfortable-looking furniture. After seating himself behind an old wooden desk, he indicated for Mathew to take a chair. It appeared to be made of the same black leather as the desktop.

"I ought to apologize for my behavior a moment ago," Mathew said before the doctor could speak.

Dr. Wycroft waved the apology away. "It's quite all right. Forba can be a trifle overprotective at times. Now, what can I do for you? I take it that you are not sick?"

"No, sir. I just wanted to ask you a few questions, if I may."

"Well, I don't have much time. One of our local women is with child, and I may be called away at any moment. Babies tend to be notoriously inconsiderate of other people's schedules."

Mathew smiled. "I'll try not to be long."

As quickly as he could, he related what had happened to his vision the previous night in the forest and on the two occasions when he felt the odd tingling sensation in his arm. He also told the doctor about seeing the window move earlier that morning, seemingly on its own. The only change in his story was that he substituted the word "brigands" for "Orlocks."

Dr. Wycroft listened carefully, saying nothing. His intelligent blue eyes searched Mathew's face, frowning only once—at the mention of being able to see things impossibly far away. When Mathew finished, he asked a number of questions about whether Mathew had ever experienced such things before or if either his mother or father ever reported similar phenomena. He also asked if Mathew could ever remember seeing things or hearing voices that weren't there, to which Mathew replied no.

Coming around the desk, the doctor took up a candle with a bright polished silver disk behind it and held it close to Mathew's eyes, peering deeply into them. Next, he asked him to hold out his right arm and extend his hand, palm up toward him, and look the other way. With a small pin, he gently touched each of Mathew's fingers and asked him to indicate when he could feel the contact. Turning the pin around, he alternated touching different parts of Mathew's hand, arm, and fingers with both the sharp and blunt ends, asking which end was applied.

Apparently satisfied, the doctor returned to his seat behind the desk and said, "Well, young man, everything seems to be in order. I can see nothing wrong with you physically."

"I'm not crazy and I don't believe in ghosts," Mathew said evenly.

Dr. Wycroft smiled. "I do not believe in ghosts or demons either. And I also do not think you have lost your sanity. You seem like a rational, intelligent young fellow, so I must conclude that these things really did happen. It is merely the cause that escapes us. May I ask you one or two more questions?"

Mathew nodded.

"When the brigands attacked, do you recall how you were feeling at the time?"

"Scared," Mathew replied simply.

Dr. Wycroft nodded.

"But I wasn't scared sitting in the bathtub, and I didn't imagine seeing the window move."

Dr. Wycroft reached behind him, picked up a large odd-looking object, and placed it on the desk in front of Mathew. "Do you know what this is?" he asked.

Mathew frowned. "No, not really."

"It is a model of a brain," Dr. Wycroft said. "The model of a *human* brain, to be precise. You can tell this from the development of the frontal lobes." He pointed to a prominent rounded area covered by what looked like numerous grooves, bumps, and folds. "Animals do not have such development. For all that we doctors have studied, I must confess, we know very little of the processes going on in here. We do know certain things, of course, but they are rudimentary at best."

Mathew nodded, listening carefully.

"For example, if this part were to be damaged," the doctor said, indicating a small section on the side of the brain, "a man could hear, but would not understand any words that were spoken to him. But if this part were injured," he moved his finger only an inch away, "the same man could understand what was said perfectly, but would not be able to utter a coherent sentence. As to things that go on deeper inside the brain—here, in these frontal lobes, we can only make educated guesses."

"I received no blows to my head," Mathew replied. "Nothing even touched me."

"Ah, but that is the point. Nothing needs to have touched you."

"I'm sorry, I don't understand. I thought you said . . ."

Mathew's words trailed off as he noticed the doctor looking over his shoulder. Before he could turn, however, Dr. Wycroft jumped up and held his arms in front of him, as if to ward something off. A panicked look crossed his face and he screamed, *"No!"*

Mathew spun around, knocking over the chair and

reaching for his sword, only to find that there was nothing there. With his heart racing, he turned back to Dr. Wycroft, who had taken his seat again, and looked for all the world like he was about to order a cup of tea.

"Tell me what just happened," the doctor said.

"What happened?" Mathew sputtered. "What happened was you nearly scared me to death! I don't understand why you—"

Dr. Wycroft held up his hand. "My apologies. I was perhaps a bit overdramatic, but only to prove a point. When I asked you what happened, I should have qualified it by asking, 'What just happened to you physically?' Allow me to explain.

"When you perceived there was danger, you leapt to your feet and drew your sword, or started to do so. The tone of your muscles increased, preparing you to fight or flee, as the case might have been. I would also venture to say that your respiration quickened and, if I am not incorrect, the pupils of your eyes dilated.

"All of this happened, and *I never touched you*." The doctor smiled.

Mathew took a deep breath and bent down to right his chair.

"Do you see my point?" Dr. Wycroft asked.

"I think so," Mathew answered slowly, sitting back down in the chair.

"Excellent. Let us suppose further that my skill as an actor was not quite so proficient, and you only imagined—seriously imagined—that your life was in peril. I suggest to you that your body would have reacted in a very similar way."

Mathew's brows came together as the doctor's point became clear to him.

"Let me pose another question that may help a bit more," Dr. Wycroft said. "Do you have to think about it when you tie your boot laces or find the way to your home?"

"No, I guess not."

"Correct. And that is because your brain has learned these skills so well, it no longer has to go through a step-by-step process to accomplish what it already knows. It all happens on a lower level of your mind—the subconscious, if you will."

Mathew began to piece this new information together, while Dr. Wycroft leaned back and said nothing, watching him with interest.

"You are saying that I *imagined* some of what happened?"

"Not really," Dr. Wycroft replied. "What I am saying is, I fully believe *something* happened to you, and that it was as real to you as sitting here in this room. Since I can find nothing physically wrong with you, we are left with the mind as the source of our problem. This doesn't mean that your sanity is in question. It only means that you *perceived* something that caused a physical reaction as regards both your vision and the tingling sensations you described. With respect to the window, I regret I am not qualified to make an assessment. For that, I fear we may have to consult a carpenter."

He said the last part so seriously, Mathew began to laugh in spite of himself. The doctor smiled in response.

"At least it's a relief to know that I'm not going crazy," Mathew said.

"Hardly," the doctor said, rising and coming around the desk. "Stress—particularly stress that places one's life in peril—is a sufficient motivator to produce a physical reaction, even in the most stout-hearted of men."

Mathew nodded and got up as well. He began to fish around in the pocket of his cloak for some money to pay the doctor.

"That won't be necessary," Dr. Wycroft said. "I have prescribed no medicines, and I do not charge for speaking with healthy people."

Mathew thanked the doctor and walked to the door with him, past the baleful eye of his housekeeper, then bade him goodbye.

Before they parted, Dr. Wycroft said, "Your cousin told

me that he is a silversmith. Do you intend to enter that trade as well?"

"No sir, I don't think so."

The doctor eyed him narrowly for a moment, then said, "You may wish to consider medicine as a suitable profession. I suspect you possess the acumen for it. Mistress Woodall informed me that you and your family are on your way to visit relatives in Barcora. When you return, I should be happy to visit with you again on the subject."

Mathew reflected on Dr. Wycroft's comment while he walked down the street to the river. The homes along the block were all neat and well-kept, with gardens and flowers. It was something of a wonder to him that until this point in his life, he had never given any thought about what he would do when he reached adulthood. He had more or less assumed he would take over running his father's farm. But at the moment that possibility seemed increasingly remote. The whole thing disturbed him, and he pushed the thoughts to the back of his mind, along with several other issues.

For the time being, he was content to know his sanity was not in question. The idea of his brain producing an actual physical reaction in his body seemed so simple that he was astonished he hadn't thought of it himself. He'd heard stories of men and women performing great acts of strength in times of acute stress. *But green vision*? And seeing at night? The tingling sensation he could accept, particularly if, as Dr. Wycroft told him, his mind picked up on something he didn't consciously realize. The part about his vision, however, still disturbed him.

With at least a portion of his problems resolved, he felt his spirits rise for the first time in several weeks. In front of him the wide waters of the Roeselar continued on their journey to the sea. A few craft were on the river, some intending to put in at Elberton and some merely passing by. Mathew stopped to watch a tall two-masted vessel, its white sails billowing, come about and then heel over, tacking slowly into the wind while it closed with the shore. It was a graceful and beautiful thing to see.

Several streets from where he was standing, he could see the docks Akin had mentioned. A flurry of activity was already going on. Several ships were at anchor, secured by thick rope cables lashed to iron cleats in the docks. Bare-chested men worked in the afternoon sun, with tackle and hoists, loading crates of cargo into the ships' holds. All around him, merchants hoping to make a quick profit from the wools and silver pieces produced in Elberton, sold their goods to disembarking passengers directly from wagons.

Mathew observed the hustle and bustle with fascination as he walked along the street, searching for his friends among the crowd. Then he stopped and wrinkled his nose at a smell that was new to him. He realized it was coming from two long wooden buildings at the far end of the piers. If he had a handkerchief with him, he would have put it over his nose.

"That be the tanneries," a passing sailor volunteered, observing his reaction.

Mathew grimaced and shook his head. "Can you tell me where I might find a Captain Donal?" Mathew asked.

"Aye, lad. He be the master of the *Dancer*, that brig berthed three down."

Had he been less self-conscious, Mathew would have asked the man exactly what a brig was. He assumed it was a ship, but not wanting to appear uninformed, he thanked him, and began walking in the wrong direction.

"Lad, I said *brig*," the man called after him, loud enough for several people standing nearby to hear. "That's a flat-bottomed riverboat over there. Can ye not tell the difference?"

Abashed, Mathew reversed his direction, mumbled his thanks, and headed for a sleek-looking black vessel moored a short distance away.

The ship was large—the largest he'd ever seen. He guessed it to be at least two hundred feet in length and perhaps forty feet wide. Two stout masts, whose tops seemed impossibly high, rose majestically out of the deck. His eyes followed them to their pinnacle, and he shuddered involuntarily at the thought of someone actually climbing all the way up there to let out the sails. Even as a boy, he had never been fond of heights. The only reason he'd climbed trees with his friends was because his fear of being embarrassed exceeded his fear of heights.

While at anchor, all of the ship's sails were furled. Myriad ropes ran from yardarms and masts to the deck below and made an impressive sight, almost like a cat's cradle. It was the first real ship he had ever seen.

From the wooden pier, Mathew searched the deck for some sign of Father Thomas or any of the others, but he saw only one or two crewmen at work.

"Excuse me, is there a Captain Donal on board?" he called out.

A bearded man at the front of the ship—Mathew later learned it was called a foredeck—leaned over the railing and called back, "I'm Oliver Donal. And who might you be?" Despite the warmth of the day, the man was wearing a white shirt and long black coat and tie.

"Mathew Lewin, sir," he answered, walking along the dock toward him. "I'm looking for some friends of mine."

"Ah, so you be the other one. You've just missed them, lad. They left about fifteen minutes ago. Come aboard, come aboard, and let's have a look at you."

Mathew noticed a companionway in the middle of the ship as he walked past, but a rope netting that hung over the rail near to him seemed more expedient. He quickly unbuckled his sword and, holding it in one hand, clambered up and over the side.

The captain watched his progress with interest, giving him an approving nod when his feet touched the deck. "Oliver Donal, master of the *Wave Dancer*, at your service," he said, offering a thick callused hand.

"Mathew Lewin. Pleased to meet you."

The man raised his eyebrows and looked Mathew up and down briefly. "Growing them big in Werth Province, I see."

Mathew's expression immediately changed. Devondale was located in Werth Province. Ashford, where they had been telling people in Elberton they were from, was situated in Lankton Province, farther to the north.

"Relax, lad," Captain Donal said. "Your uncle Siward told me the truth. Why you're here and where you're bound is your business. He said you were a quick one. If Ceta Woodall vouched for the lot of you, that's good enough for me. Besides, she'd have my head on a platter if I didn't help," he added with a wink.

Mathew relaxed.

"Come. I'll show you the ship."

Oliver Donal was not a tall man, but he was powerfully built, and if his grip were any indication, Mathew decided he would be a good person to have on his side if trouble came. In contrast to his dark brown beard, his hair was a mixture of gray and lighter browns, bleached from long exposure to the elements. Like many men whose life was on the water, his face was deeply tanned and weathered.

Mathew soon found that the captain, though affable, could be blunt in his speech and manner. On one occasion, noticing one of his crew resplicing a line he had ordered replaced, he burst forth with a string of oaths, some of which Mathew had never heard before.

Mathew had resolved to ask what something was if he didn't know, and Captain Donal seemed more than willing to indulge his barrage of questions. The ship *was* more than two hundred feet from jib boom—a new term for Mathew—to the stern. The deck was yellow teak, with a polished brass rail running around most of its perimeter.

The captain showed him his own quarters at the rear of the ship, and where they would sleep during their run downriver to the Great Southern Sea before making the crossing over to Tyraine. "Sleep," Mathew decided, was an accurate word, because the room was little larger than a closet, but at least it was better than the thirty-six inches allotted for each of the fifteen crew members to sling their hammocks belowdeck. The problem, Captain Donal confided, was Lara. He wasn't quite sure what to do about her accommodations yet. The *Wave Dancer* was a working vessel, he explained, not fitted out for female passengers.

It was obvious Oliver Donal was proud of his ship, and perceiving Mathew's interest, he gave him a tour of everything from the cargo holds to the anchor cable, not to mention the ship's figurehead—a bare-breasted woman with long hair located at the bow. Fascinated with the newness of it all, Mathew tried to memorize the name and function of each object that was pointed out to him. Captain Donal, finding an apt pupil, seemed more than happy to oblige.

More than two hours passed before Oliver Donal, weary from speaking, bade Mathew goodbye. He shook his head and watched the long-legged young man walk down the companionway, reciting to himself the names of things, like mizzen mast, mainsail, and cable tier, as he went.

21

Elberton, the Blue Goose

BY THE TIME MATHEW REACHED WATER STREET, APTLY
named for its proximity to the Roeselar, he was famished.
Since he was too late for the midday meal, and too early
for dinner, he decided to stop at the Blue Goose Tavern,
which Effie had mentioned. Fortunately, the late afternoon breeze shifted, taking with it those distinctive odors
coming from the tanneries.

The Blue Goose was as different from the Nobody's
Inn as two places could possibly be. It took Mathew's
eyes a moment to adjust to the darkness after he walked
in. A long dark wood bar ran the length of the common
room. Two men dressed like sailors stood at the far end
and eyed him briefly before resuming their conversation.
The innkeeper also looked up at him and returned to polishing some drinking glasses.

It seemed to Mathew that the man had decided he was
invisible, for he made no move toward him despite a
number of attempts to attract his attention. In the hope of
having better luck with one of the serving girls, Mathew
took a seat at a table in the corner of the room. Whatever
prior attempts had been made to clean it were negligible
at best, much like the rest of the Blue Goose. There were
a few other people, men mostly, scattered about the room.
After spending ten more minutes being ignored, Mathew
decided to head back to the Nobody's Inn. Maybe he
could convince Effie to give him a loaf of bread or something until dinner. He started to get up when a voice
stopped him.

"Leaving?"

Mathew recognized the man as Will, the one who brought their packs up when they arrived.

"I don't seem to have much luck getting anyone who works here to take my order," he replied.

"They probably think you're not seventeen yet. Can't drink in this province less you are. It's a new law the duchess's advisers dreamed up. No one under seventeen can buy a drink anywhere in the Berne."

It surprised Mathew that anyone might consider him young-looking, given his height and the fact that he was carrying a sword.

"I'll be eighteen in two weeks," he replied, slightly offended.

Will stuck his lower lip out and shrugged. "Here now, Ed," he called to the bartender, "what's a man got to do to get some service? Me young friend here's seventeen and all but dead of thirst from being ignored in this place."

The bartender glanced over, scrutinized them for a moment, then gave a small nod to one of the serving girls, who was in the process of using a dirty rag to clean a table. The girl sauntered over, still carrying the rag, and took Mathew's order with the same enthusiasm she had expended on the table. A few minutes later she returned with a bottle of red wine and a sandwich that looked less than appetizing. The meat was stringy, but after a tentative bite, Mathew decided it was passable. Out of courtesy, he asked her to bring an extra glass for Will, who, uninvited, had sat down to keep him company.

"So you're from Ashford Town," Will said, downing his wine in one gulp.

Mathew refilled his glass. "Right. I'm Mathew Lewin," he said, extending his hand.

"Will Tavish. And what would be bringing you this far south, if you don't mind my asking?"

Mathew shook his head and repeated Akin's story about accompanying Lara to visit relatives in Barcora.

"She's a real eyeful, that one," Will offered with a wink. "Not promised to anyone, is she?"

Mathew resisted the urge to tell Will to keep a civil tongue in his head, and instead answered, "No." After taking another bite of his sandwich, he added, "She has a mean temper," pleased with himself for thinking of it.

"Well, you know what they say, 'fire on the outside, heat on the inside.'"

Will finished draining his second glass and put it down on the table, suggestively nearer to Mathew than himself.

Mathew took a breath and filled it again. "Have you lived in Elberton long?" he asked, changing the subject

"Pah. Not much longer than you. I was working a freight boat that stopped to pick up some cargo a few weeks back, you see. Captain got himself killed in a fight the morning we was to push off—rot his bones." Will spat on the floor for emphasis. "Left the crew high and dry. The authorities impounded the ship, and I've been on the beach ever since, waiting for the owner to show up and pay off."

"On the beach?"

"Dry-docked, boy. No gainful employment."

"But you work for Mistress Woodall, don't you?"

"That baggage. Do this, Will. Do that, Will. Take this here—put that there. It's enough to drive a man to drink," he said, with a less-than-transparent look at his empty glass.

Mathew frowned and refilled it again, but halfway this time.

"Thankee. Much obliged."

"I'm sorry to hear about your troubles. What do you plan to do?" Mathew asked.

A pair of shrewd eyes suddenly looked back at him. "Don't rightly know yet," Will answered, lowering his voice, "but there's a fortune in wool and copper tied up in the hold of that ship, let me tell you. Captain also had him a lockbox filled with silver coin. It's hidden under one of the planks in his cabin. I saw him stow it there one night m'self. He didn't know I was watching through the hatch, but I saw him hide it as plain as the nose on your face."

Will looked around the tavern before continuing.

"Haven't been able to get near it, though. They put a guard onboard when they impounded the ship. Seems the captain forgot to settle his port taxes before getting himself killed."

Mathew nodded and tried to appear sympathetic while he sought for an excuse to politely separate himself from Will's company without offending him.

"Two mates of mine is joining me here in just a little while. We've got a plan to take the vessel before anyone's the wiser," Will confided with a wink.

From the smell of Will's breath, which reached him from across the table, Mathew guessed that he'd been drinking for some time.

"You know—if a bright lad like yourself was to throw in with us, we might cut you in for a share. Not a full share mind you, but say a tenth part."

"That's very decent of you, but I've promised to take my cousin to Barcora."

Will sat back and looked at Mathew. He helped himself, unasked this time, to another glass of wine. "Seems there's a lot of you to take one girl to visit relatives. Even a comely one like her."

"We're a very close family," Mathew replied flatly.

Will didn't answer right away. He just looked into his glass.

"I suppose I'd better be getting on before they come searching for me," Mathew added, as casually as he could.

"Say . . . what about your uncle? He looks like a ready enough sort. Do you suppose he'd be interested? It'll take five to crew the ship."

"My uncle?" Mathew asked, then realized he was referring to Father Thomas. "No . . . I don't think he'd be interested. He's funny about things like that."

"Straitlaced type, is he?" The words came out slurred.

"A little more than most," Mathew replied.

"Just my luck to be beached in a place like this."

A little warning voice in the back of his head told
Mathew that the tone of the conversation was changing
along with Will's mood, which seemed to be increasingly
morose. Mathew decided the rest of the wine was forfeit
and reached into his vest pocket for his coin purse. He put
it on the table, in the hopes of attracting the serving girl's
attention. He was sorry as soon as he did. Will's eyes registered the purse, but looked away again just as quickly.
Unfortunately, the girl was nowhere to be seen. With
nothing else to do but wait for her to reappear, Mathew
causally rested his right hand on top of the purse and
poured himself another drink.

The shrewd look returned to Will's face. "Interesting
ring you've got there."

"Thanks."

"I've not seen any with its coloring before. Is it worth
much?"

"Actually, it's not mine," Mathew explained. "I'm
keeping it for the family of a friend of mine."

"Why don't your friend give it to them himself?"

"Because he's dead," Mathew said, getting deeper into
an explanation than he cared to.

"Dead? You don't say? What of?"

"A fever," Mathew answered, looking around in vain
for the serving girl once more. Instead he saw two men,
one short and heavy, and the other rail thin, approaching
the table. They were dressed like many of the other
sailors he'd seen that day. Will saw them too and waved.
Neither returned the greeting, but they came over, as
Mathew swept the coin purse back into his pocket, and sat
down. Mathew found himself effectively wedged in by
the fat one, who smelled like a mixture of sweat and fish.

"These are the mates I was telling you about. Bert . . .
Jack, this here is Mat Lewin, just in this day from Ashford
Town."

"Ashford?" the skinny one snorted. "I'll bet you're
glad to be clear of that place. I heard the Nyngaryns all
but flattened it. A big fight it was supposed to be too. A
bos'n's mate I know swore the passenger he talked to told

him Orlocks was in the fight as well. Can you imagine that?"

The heavy one shrugged and said nothing.

"Were many people killed?" Mathew asked.

"Don't know—but that's what generally happens in a fight, isn't it? Ain't that right, Bert?"

Bert gave him a sour look and picked up the wine bottle, downing the remainder of its contents. "We've got business to talk about, Tavish," he said, wiping his mouth on the sleeve of his shirt.

"I was just telling young Mat here that he ought to throw in with us. A bright young fella like him could do right well if he was to play his cards right."

"Tavish, you're a bloody fool," Jack spat out from across the table. "And that stupid tongue of yours is going to get us all hanged one day."

"It takes five to crew that ship, and you know it," Will shot back. "How's the three of us going to do it by ourselves? Young Mat's got family here. Five of 'em, so I counted, and what with them coming on hard times, with the news and all, it just seemed a natural opportunity to place in their path."

"You told others besides this boy?" Bert asked, going red in the face, and his tone becoming dangerous.

"I ain't spoke to no one besides him. What d'ya think I am?"

"I know what you are. You're a loudmouthed jackass who can't hold his drink or keep his big yap shut."

"A fine one you are to talk," Will said. "We've been two weeks rotting here waiting for you to come up with a plan to take that ship. And what's it gotten us so far? Nothing, I say."

"Well, now we're going to have to do something about *him*, aren't we?" Bert said in a vehement whisper, as if Mathew weren't seated right next to him.

The three men brought their heads together and began whispering fiercely to each other, still ignoring the fact that Mathew was there. He watched the exchange and made no comment. Instead he let his hand drift below the table and come to rest on the hilt of his belt knife. The conversation continued to escalate, along with their tempers. There seemed little question trouble was about to erupt, and that he was going to be in the middle of it, particularly in light of Bert's last statement. Fortunately, the long-absent serving girl chose that moment to reappear from wherever it was that serving girls go when you want them. Seeing the new additions to the booth, she wandered over to take their orders, with slightly more animation than she had previously shown.

Several more people were now in the room.

Mathew realized that if he didn't do something then, he might not have another chance, given the way Jack was looking at him.

"What can I get you gents?" the girl asked.

"I'd like to get another bottle of this wine," Mathew said quickly. "Elberton is a wonderful town. Did you know in Ashford, where I'm from, I can't even buy a bottle like this until I turn seventeen?"

The serving girl's mouth dropped open and she blinked in surprise. Then she turned and yelled *"Ed!"* to the bartender clear across the room, in a voice that would have done Captain Donal proud.

A moment later a livid tavern owner grabbed Mathew by his collar and physically pulled him from the booth, directly across a surprised Bert. The owner was accompanied by a large unpleasant looking helper carrying a thick club with leather wrapped around the handle. He seemed prepared to use it. Mathew thought that Jack and Will might intervene, but seeing the odds and noticing the man's club, they decided to give the idea further consideration.

"What do you mean coming in here and lying about your age?" the owner shouted, his face contorted in anger. "I could lose my license because of the likes of you, you wet-nosed little whelp." After practically dragging Mathew across the floor, which he resisted in a token fashion, Mathew found himself tossed unceremoniously out into the street.

"And don't let me catch you coming back here again, or I'll have Ern lay into you proper! You understand me?" Ed yelled.

Mathew got up and dusted himself off. It didn't take much to figure out that Ern was the scowling fellow next to him, slapping the club suggestively in his palm.

"I'm sorry, sir, but my cousin Will said you wouldn't mind—and that he was a good friend of yours."

Both men looked at each other, then turned and headed deliberately back into the Blue Goose. In a corner of Mathew's mind he recalled an old saying that went something like, *He who lives and runs away, lives to fight another day.*

Excellent advice, he decided.

He began to jog down the street, leaving the ever-increasing noises and shouts coming from the tavern behind him.

Shadows cast by homes and shops were lengthening as the light faded. Beyond the opposite bank of the Roeselar, the sun, now a large red ball, slowly descended to the tops of the trees.

Although Mathew had a reasonable idea of where the Nobody's Inn was located, his lack of familiarity with Elberton combined with the oncoming darkness became a problem. Still, running easily and chortling to himself about how Will and company might be faring at the moment, he turned at the end of the third street. After several minutes he slowed to a walk and surveyed his surroundings. Nothing looked familiar. A few more minutes of searching made it clear he was lost. The question was what to do about it. He rejected going back the way he'd come, because of the possibility of running into Will or his unsavory friends. Unlike Devondale, where the streets were laid out in a straightforward manner, Elberton's were much narrower and seemed to have more than their share of twists and turns. Without a landmark to guide him, Mathew decided one street was as good as the next. It stood to reason that he would soon figure out the proper

direction, but that turned out not to be the case. Wide at
first, the street he was on gradually got narrower and narrower, eventually coming to an end in a small courtyard.
Frustrated, Mathew had to turn back.

After fifteen minutes of making errors he began to recognize a few of the shops he had passed on his way into
town. He noticed that none of the windows contained any
merchandise to look at, which was curious.

*How can anyone have a shop if there is nothing for
people to buy?*

Then it dawned on him. The owners simply removed
their goods each evening, locking them safely away, then
put everything back out again in the morning. It seemed a
wasteful thing to do, until Will Tavish and his friends
came to mind.

Spring *was* coming, but not yet. A chill breeze blew down
the street, causing him to pull his cloak tighter. Ahead of
him a horse plodded along, slowly pulling a flatbed
wagon behind it. Mathew moved out of the way. Neither
he nor the driver said anything to each other as they
passed.

He thought about his conversation with Dr. Wycroft
again. Much of what the man said made sense. If fear and
stress could produce physical changes in a person's body,
that might be the answer . . . or at least part of an answer.
He admitted to himself that he *was* afraid in the forest,
very much so, but he'd been afraid of things before. He
remembered how scared he was at Thad Layton's farm,
and when he'd seen what the Orlocks did to Lee and
Garon. Those things were beyond anything he could have
imagined.

Had Mathew been less mature, his fear might have
shamed him. Instead he remembered something his father told him a long time ago, one of those rare occasions
when Bran actually talked about the war. He told Mathew
that he was once so scared on the eve before a battle, he
could barely stop his hands from shaking.

Even now Mathew could recall his surprise. He was

younger then, and simply could not believe his father was
afraid of anything. When he told Bran as much, his father
explained that heroes and cowards were both afraid; the
difference lay in what they chose to do about it. Bran had
also said that only a fool wasn't afraid. At the time, the
words hadn't had as much meaning for him as they did
now.

A movement up ahead interrupted his thoughts. Mathew
stopped walking. He wasn't paying close attention but
had the impression of something moving back into the
shadows on the corner. In the flickering orange glow of
the street lamp, it was difficult to tell what it might have
been. He looked more closely, peering into the darkened
doorways.

Nothing.

After a moment or two, he began to feel foolish. The
inn was only three or four blocks away at most, and the
others would probably be worrying by now.

Mathew shook his head and started walking again, deciding the only thing on the corner beside himself was his
own shadow.

"Going somewhere, are we?" said a familiar voice behind him. Mathew whirled around as Will Tavish stepped
out of a doorway. He had an angry-looking bruise on his
cheek and appeared quite the worse for wear. A second
later he saw Bert approaching from the opposite side of
the street, moving quickly for a man of his girth. Jack
rounded the corner in front of him. All three now wore
short swords.

"Think you're a funny one, don't you," Will sneered,
stepping closer.

Mathew drew his sword and put his back to the building.

"Now what's all this?" Bert asked, drawing his own
sword. "I thought we were friends."

"I know who my friends are," Mathew said, "and
you're not among them."

Jack looked around theatrically and said, "Funny, I
don't see no one here but you."

"Now I'm hurt—truly I am," Bert said. "After all we've been to each other."

He took a step forward but stopped as Mathew leveled the point of his sword at him.

"You know how to use that, boy?" Bert asked,

"Look, I don't want any trouble," Mathew said.

"Hear that? He don't want any trouble," Will mimicked, moving a little closer. "Tell you what. Us being reasonable sorts—we're willing to forget your poor manners. Why don't you just take off that ring of yours and toss it over here along with your coin purse, and we'll call things quits."

"I told you the ring doesn't belong to me," Mathew said.

"Oh, that's right. How forgetful of me. It belongs to your dead friend." Will mocked. "Well, he ain't going to miss it a bit."

That brought a derisive snort from Jack. Like Will, he took a step toward Mathew, but abruptly halted when Mathew's sword came around to point directly between his eyes.

"Three against one, boy," Jack taunted, his rat nose twitching and his sword ready.

Jack looked at the others, shrugged and appeared to relax for a second, then abruptly took a swing at Mathew's sword, trying to knock it aside. Fortunately, Mathew noticed a small leaning of his shoulder just before he struck, which telegraphed his intentions. A quick release of his back two fingers, alloweded the point of his weapon to drop, disengaging it around Jack's wrist. Instead of his blade contacting Mathew's, as he expected, Jack found himself still looking at the point of Mathew's weapon. If he was startled, it was only for a moment. He immediately tried the same thing again, with the same result, as Mathew again executed the maneuver his father had taught him. Jack took two steps backward, frustrated. He nodded to the others and they started to move in.

As soon as Mathew glanced away, Will saw his chance and lunged. Mathew easily deflected the attack, but instead of riposting against Will, he directed his riposte at Bert, who presented a far more substantial target.

Bert let out a howl as Mathew's blade found his shoulder. With a guttural noise Jack rushed forward with his sword above his head. His lips were pulled back in an ugly snarl. Mathew saw him at the last moment and twisted to the side, knowing that he would be too late to deflect the blow.

It never came.

Instead he heard a heavy thudding sound, and Jack dropped to the ground like a felled tree.

Mathew heard the whir of Collin's quarterstaff before he saw it crash down across Will's forearm. There was a loud crack. Will screamed and dropped his sword as the bone in his arm broke. Incredibly, at that moment the street lamps all along the block went out. Will stood there a moment in shock, then took off running and disappeared into the darkness.

Mathew turned back in time to see Bert lunge at him, his shoulder now soaked in blood. For a corpulent man, he was faster than Mathew expected. With a desperate effort, Mathew managed to parry the attack, deflecting it to the outside. Now completely off balance, Bert careened forward and crashed into him, driving them both backward.

Standing ten feet away, Collin saw Mathew draw back his sword and then hesitate for some reason. The combination of Bert's considerable bulk, along with his momentum, carried him into Mathew. A moment later they were both on the ground. He also saw the knife in Bert's hand.

"Mat!" Collin yelled, rushing to him.

Before Collin could reach them, Bert suddenly appeared to leap backward, away from Mathew. He landed on his behind with a heavy grunt. A combination of surprise and outrage filled his face and he scrambled to his feet, preparing to charge again.

In the heat of the moment, Collin registered what was

happening, but he had no time to think about it. A blow from his quarterstaff all but split Bert's skull, landing him face forward on the cobblestones. He lay there, not moving. Mathew was up on one knee, staring at a dark red stain slowly spreading across his left side.

"Oh, lord," Collin said, seeing the blood. "Are you all right? Don't move."

Mathew let out a breath and grimaced. "Help me to my feet," he said.

When Mathew got up, he pulled his shirt out of his breeches and gingerly lifted it, revealing a gash about six inches long just below his rib cage. Blood was seeping out of the wound. There was also a burning pain in his side.

"Oh, for the love of God," Collin said. "Let's get you back to the inn. Can you walk?"

Mathew nodded and felt around the perimeter of the wound with his fingers. "I don't think it's too bad," he said with a small wince.

"Wasn't that Will?" Collin asked, looking back down the street.

"Mm-hmm," Mathew said, peering down at the gash in his side.

"What did you say to make him so mad? And who are these two?" Collin asked, indicating the prostrate forms of Bert and Jack.

"His business associates, I think."

A small groan escaped Jack and he began to move slightly. Collin promptly hit him behind the ear with the butt of his staff, knocking him unconscious again. He looked at him for a second, and turned back to Mathew.

"Business associates? I don't get it."

"After I missed you at the ship, I stopped at the Blue Goose to get something to eat. That's where I met Will. He was pretty well drunk and blabbed about a plan of theirs to steal a ship with these others here. He even asked me to join them—not as a full partner, mind you, just a minor one."

"Naturally," Collin said.

They left Jack and Bert behind and walked slowly down the street toward the inn. Collin kept his arm around his friend's waist to support him. When Mathew finished relating the rest of his story, Collin shook his head.

"So all they wanted was your coin purse, Giles's ring, and some help stealing a ship. You have fascinating friends."

"I think Bert—that's the fat one you bashed on the head—said something like that earlier."

Mathew tried to grin, then grimaced at another pain. Collin frowned, but didn't say anything.

"How did you know I was here?" Mathew asked.

"I didn't," Collin replied, still watching him carefully. "I was on my way back from Effie's house—she lives on the next street. I saw you with those three. I told you, I didn't like Will's looks."

When they approached the door to the inn, Mathew pulled his cloak around him, to conceal the blood-soaked shirt. "Let me walk inside by myself," he said. "I want to get up to our room and clean this."

Reluctantly, Collin released his hold and let him painstakingly negotiate the steps. Two brass wall lamps hung on either side of the doorway. In the light they provided, he could see how pale Mathew's face was.

Father Thomas and Ceta Woodall were sitting in a booth in the corner of the common room, quietly talking, when Mathew walked in. It was obvious to Collin that Mathew was holding himself erect only with an effort. Akin, Daniel, and Lara were at another table, finishing their dinner.

"Well, the long lost soul finally returns," Daniel called out, seeing Mathew. "Where've you been all day, Mat?"

"Just walking around exploring the town," Mathew said casually, leaning against one of the large wooden columns near their table.

"You've certainly been gone long enough. Have you eaten yet?" Lara asked.

"Nope," Mathew replied. "I'm so hungry, I could eat

my boot. I'll just go upstairs, wash and be right back down."

Lara cocked her head to the side and looked at Mathew more closely. Her brows came together.

"You go on with your dinners," Mathew added. "I'll be back in a few minutes."

Across the room, Father Thomas noticed Mathew and paused in his conversation. He waved a greeting, as did Ceta. Mathew smiled and waved back, then headed for the stairs. Ceta started to resume her conversation, gently placing a hand on the priest's forearm, but she paused in mid-sentence when his expression changed. Suddenly, Father Thomas had become very interested in Mathew's progress. He slowly got to his feet, crossed the room in a few quick strides and started up the stairs. Ceta was right behind him. That was when Lara noticed drops of blood on the floor where Mathew had been standing. She excused herself, pushed her chair back and also headed for the stairs, leaving a confused Akin and Daniel sitting there.

"What's going on?" Daniel asked, looking over the top of his glasses.

Collin, who was standing by their table, leaned forward and lowered his voice. "Mat's hurt. He took a knife in the ribs. I don't think it's serious, but we need to go for a doctor right now."

"What? How?" Daniel said.

"He got into a fight with that fellow Will who works here and two of his friends. We need to go for the doctor."

"No," Akin said, getting up. "You both stay here. I know the way—it won't take me long."

"I'm coming with you," Daniel said.

Akin looked at him for a second, nodded, then grabbed the cloak from the back of his chair and both of them hurried out the door.

When Collin got upstairs, he found his room was crowded. Mathew sat on the edge of the bed with his shirt off, presenting a slightly comical sight. He held a blanket up to his chin while Ceta gently cleansed the wound with a towel. Lara dabbed his forehead with a cloth. His friend's expression was a cross between annoyance and mortification. He also noticed that the water in the basin was red.

"I tell you I'm fine," Mathew said, trying to get up.

"Siward," Ceta said over her shoulder. "You stay right where you are, young man."

Siward? Collin thought.

Father Thomas reached forward and put a hand on Mathew's shoulder, restraining him. "She is right, my . . . ah . . . Mathew," he said.

With a snort of irritation, Mathew sank back against the pillows. He exchanged glances with Collin, who turned his hands up and leaned back against the door frame, listening to the conversation.

"What happened to Will?" Father Thomas asked.

"I think Collin broke his arm," Mathew replied.

Ceta and Father Thomas turned to look at Collin, who shrugged and raised his eyebrows innocently. They frowned at each other and looked back at Mathew.

"And the other two?" Father Thomas asked.

"The fat one won't be hard to find," Collin answered. "Mat put a blade through his shoulder. The other one looks like a rat, and probably has a good-size headache right now."

"The first day in a new town, and you get into a fight," Lara said, shaking her head.

"Get into a fight?" Mathew sputtered.

"Well, what do you call it? You could have gotten yourself killed."

"But, I—"

"We will have to notify the sheriff of this," Father Thomas said. "Where can I find him, Ceta?"

Ceta? Well, things certainly seem to be moving quickly around here, Collin thought.

"I don't want you going outside," she said in a worried voice. "They could have more of their friends out there."

Father Thomas shook his head. "You needn't worry, I'll take Collin to protect me."

"I'm serious, Siward," she insisted. "This can wait until the morning when it's light."

"*No*, it can't," he said gently. "Particularly if their plan was to steal a ship and its cargo—not to mention attacking Mathew."

"But—"

"There are no buts," Father Thomas said firmly. "You know I'm right. Now, where can I find him?"

Ceta sniffed and stared at Father Thomas for a minute. "Fine, but I want you to promise to be careful—*and no going out looking for them.*"

"You have my promise," Father Thomas reassured her. He turned to Collin and asked, "Would you go to my room and bring me my sword and cloak, please?"

Ceta opened her mouth to say something, but Father Thomas put two fingers on her lips before she could.

"You did say to be careful."

She pushed his hand away and narrowed her eyes in response, but grudgingly gave in and supplied him the directions to the sheriff's home. It was on the other side of Elberton. Collin was back a moment later with the priest's things. Father Thomas gave Ceta a quick smile and squeezed her hand before they left.

Just as the door was about to close, however, Collin stuck his head back in the room and said, "Don't worry. I'll take good care of him."

His reply was a particularly icy look from the innkeeper. He ducked his head back into his shoulders and withdrew hastily.

Mathew thought he heard Ceta mutter something under her breath about "men" as she returned her attention to him. Finally satisfied that the wound was properly cleansed, she asked Lara to go downstairs and bring back a white sheet to use for a bandage.

After she was gone, Ceta asked him a few more questions about what he did during the day and how he was feeling. Eventually the conversation got around to Father Thomas. How long had Mathew known him? Why was a handsome man like him not married before? And so on.

When Ceta Woodall asked her last question, Mathew realized with a small shock that he didn't know *if* priests ever got married. He supposed they did, but the topic had never come up before. He'd answered most of the questions as best he could, but was greatly relieved when Lara finally returned with the sheet.

Ceta competently cut it into a wide strip and wrapped it around his middle, at the same time instructing Lara, who was paying careful attention, how often it would need to be changed. Mathew got the feeling that everything Ceta Woodall did was competent. When she was through, she gave a satisfied nod and excused herself to go downstairs and check on his dinner, leaving Lara and Mathew alone in the room together.

"Does it hurt much?" Lara asked. She sat down on the bed by his side.

Mathew moved his torso a little from side to side. "No. It feels fine."

"Mathew, why didn't you tell us something was wrong when you came in?"

"I don't know. I guess I didn't want to worry anyone," he answered, not meeting her eyes.

He looked out the window for a long time, and Lara sat there, quietly watching him.

"That's not true," he eventually said. "I was embarrassed."

"Embarrassed? But why?"

"When Will's friend lunged at me, I saw it coming. I really did. There was no trouble parrying the blade aside. I could have killed him easily. He certainly wanted to kill me—but I hesitated. I just couldn't bring myself to do it."

Lara reached out and brushed the hair off his forehead.

"It wasn't the same as it was with Berke Ramsey. I was in a blind rage then—madder than I've ever been in my whole life, I think. I never believed I could hate anyone like that. I can't explain it, but it was like something inside me snapped when I saw what he did to my father. I wanted him dead—more than anything in the world."

The words just came pouring out of him, and he didn't know how to stop them.

Mathew turned to look at Lara, his expression serious. "I'm not sorry for what I did in Devondale, but I just couldn't make myself do it again. I don't know. Maybe it means I really am a coward."

If she lived to be a hundred, she would never understand men's egos. Her grandmother had told her several years ago that men were strange things—easily predictable, yet complex at the same time. She was seeing that for herself now.

"Oh, Mathew," she said softly.

"I didn't want to get you involved in any of this," he said.

"You *are* such a big idiot," she replied. "You didn't *involve* me in anything, I involved myself. So did the others. It was *my* choice. I couldn't let the constable just take you away."

The scent of Lara's soap suddenly became more noticeable in the confines of the room. And all at once he was acutely aware of the warm glow of candlelight on her hair and her proximity to him. They stared at each other, not speaking. Her eyes seemed unusually large. And then her lips were on his.

When he thought about it later, and he did often, he knew that something between them changed there and then. They had kissed and petted before, but this was different. Very different. The passion was undeniable, but it was of a kind and quality that neither had experienced before. Deeper, and more intense than he was able to articulate.

When they separated, she didn't move away, but instead laid her head on his chest and closed her eyes while he stroked her hair. Mathew watched the orange candle flame by his bedside move and flicker, casting shadows on the walls.

Fifteen minutes later there was a light tap at the door. Lara immediately pushed herself up and walked to the mirror and began nonchalantly smoothing her hair. Unfortunately, in her haste to get up, she also pushed directly on Mathew's wound, causing his eyes to bulge. Realizing what she had done, she put a hand over her mouth in shock just as Ceta came in carrying a tray of food.

"Are you all right?" Ceta asked, seeing Mathew's expression.

"Just a passing pain."

Lara suppressed a giggle and looked out the window, blushing. Mathew, on the other hand, failed to see the humor in the situation.

"Oh good, here come Akin and Daniel, with the doctor," Lara said.

Ceta walked over and looked out the window as well. "I'll go downstairs and see them in. I do hope Siward comes back quickly."

"Will the sheriff arrest those men?" Lara asked.

"I'm sure he'll do what he generally does—scratch his head and look confused."

Ceta smiled and gave Lara's arm a squeeze before departing.

"See that he eats," she called out from the hallway.

Mathew turned over on his side and propped himself up on his elbow. "Do you know, I've been giving this some thought. Have you seen the way Ceta and Father Thomas look at each other?"

"Mm-hmm," Lara replied, still looking down into the street below.

"I'd say they like each other, wouldn't you?"

Lara turned, looked at him, and shook her head.

"Well of course they like each other, silly. Anyone can see that."

"Oh," Mathew said, a bit disappointed. He had just congratulated himself on his perception. "But they've only just met."

"So?"

"But I don't see how they can . . ."

Lara walked over to the bed and sat down, taking his

hand. "My mother said she knew the first time she saw my father. He and Ceta have been together all day."

"Really? Did you know the first time you saw me?" Mathew asked. There was a mischievous glint in his eye as he reached for her waist.

"In your case, it took a little longer," she said, putting a spoonful of stew in his mouth.

22

Elberton

SIWARD THOMAS WALKED MORE QUICKLY THAN USUAL.
His long legs negotiated the cobblestone streets of Elberton without apparent effort. It was not often that he was
confused, but there were a lot of things he needed to sort
out. Collin kept pace beside him. Aware that the priest
was deep in thought, he remained silent to avoid disturbing him. Along the way they passed the spot where Will
and his friends attacked Mathew. It was empty now and
Collin was content to note they had decided to make
themselves scarce.

Matters of right and wrong had always been clear to
Father Thomas, but lately things were becoming more
confusing. First Bran's death, then breaking the law, and
now his attraction to Ceta Woodall. To complicate matters further, there was Mathew's disturbing incident last
night in the woods. *Nobody* could possibly have seen the
exact number of Orlocks from that distance, let alone in
the dark. But Mathew had. True, it might have been a
lucky guess, but the boy said he was positive, and his
count was precise. Mathew, he knew, also was not given
to lying or exaggeration. His information had certainly
saved their lives. The question was, *how* did he know?
And for the moment Father Thomas had no answer.

Had he been less perceptive, Father Thomas might
have been inclined to attribute his decision to flee Devondale solely to his promise to Mathew's dying father. Bran
was his oldest and closest friend. Certainly there were
other options available. But with candor, he admitted to

himself that his own experience with the king's justice had colored his view of things.

The plan that he'd formulated so promptly was to get Mathew to the sanctuary at Barcora, then enlist the aid of the church in speaking with King Malach directly. Father Thomas was aware the archbishop had Malach's ear, providing the king was willing to listen. In recent years, Malach had grown increasingly inflexible in his decisions, relying more and more on his advisers, and less on his outspoken son, Delain.

It was at their urging that the ports were closed to the Bajani. *Fools*, Delain thought. *What did they think the Bajani were going to do when that happened?* The king's actions had all but ensured pushing Bajan toward Alor Satar. Dealing with Duren again was bad enough, but now he had Bajan, Nyngary, Cincar, and the Sibuyan all on his side, which made matters infinitely worse. If the news that Captain Donal and Dr. Wycroft related to him was accurate—and he had a feeling it was—the western alliance was in terrible trouble. On top of everything else, Duren had somehow managed to convince the Orlocks to leave their caves and side with him again—if Orlocks could properly be said to side with anybody. That made the least sense of all. It was inconceivable any sane person would voluntarily come into contact with those creatures.

This was only one point among many that he considered as they walked.

The Orlocks had clearly singled Devondale out to attack. *Why?* The town possessed no strategic value, and it made little sense from a military standpoint. Gravenhage and Mechlen both produced steel, and both had far greater resources. *Possibly there were explanations for these things,* he thought. But what the priest could not get out of his head was why a raiding party of twelve Orlocks would follow them for over a week. Certainly their encounter in the forest was not simply a chance meeting. The Orlocks wanted something or someone in their group—perhaps all of them.

Just before he killed the last one, he heard the creature

say, *There he is.* It was specifically referring to Mathew. True, the boy had spoiled their surprise at the Layton farm, but Orlocks had never been motivated by revenge before. There had to be something else.

And then there was Ceta Woodall. *Ceta.* They had been together most of the day, and her face kept intruding into his thoughts, even during the brief times they had separated. When he became a priest, he had believed the church would be his solace for the remainder of his life.

The Church and God will be your constant companions, and there will be little room in your life for pleasures of the flesh. If you harbor any doubts on this subject, choose not this path. His superiors had told him that when he trained for the priesthood.

He knew that most priests didn't marry after they made the commitment, but some did. Invariably, duties to the people of their community made having a home life and family difficult, and it took an extraordinary person to balance both. He had gradually come to believe that he was past such things. Apparently he was wrong.

Siward Thomas had been Devondale's priest for almost a decade now, and had reluctantly begun to accept middle age. True, there were women in the village who considered him a marriageable prospect, but he had always managed to gracefully avoid their well-intentioned efforts.

Ceta, with her large hazel eyes and slender figure, made him feel alive and young again. She was certainly the most attractive woman he'd ever met. There was an ineffable quality about her that he could not put his finger on. Priests were supposed to have answers, and it disturbed him not to have any for his own questions. Perhaps it would be best to speak with one of his superiors when they reached Barcora, he thought.

Collin cleared his throat. They were in front of the sheriff's home. Father Thomas didn't even remember the walk there. Although neither of them had heard Ceta's description of the man, what she said to Lara had turned out to be accurate.

To say the sheriff was disinterested in what happened would have been a gross understatement. His principal concern seemed to be whether his dinner was getting cold. Though he listened politely to their story, nodding occasionally, the entire conversation was punctuated by frequent glances at his supper. In the end, the sheriff promised to come by early in the morning and speak with Mathew. He also told them that he would notify the port collector to inform the guard patrolling the ship to remain alert for any signs of perfidy. Thus satisfied that his office was discharged, the sheriff showed them out and returned to his meal.

As the door closed behind them, Collin and Father Thomas exchanged glances and started back for the inn.

"We should thank God everyone isn't similarly endowed with his burning curiosity," Father Thomas observed.

It took Collin a second to digest the last statement before he burst out laughing. A few seconds later Father Thomas started laughing as well. The laughter acted like a release, a turning point in the events of the last week, when there had been very little to laugh about.

"I haven't had a chance to ask you, my son—how have you been doing through all of this?"

"Me? I'm fine," Collin replied offhandedly. He was still smiling, but after a pause, he added on a more serious note, "It's funny, you know, but I've been thinking about my family lately. My mother and father—my brother too. I miss them. The odd thing is, I even miss Devondale. When I was there, I couldn't wait to leave, and now . . . I don't know, it's all very confusing."

"I miss Devondale as well, Collin," the priest said. "I had hoped to get this journey concluded quickly, but now with the news about war, I'm not sure how things will play out."

"Father," Collin said, "I know we're going to Tyraine and then on to Barcora, but why?"

"It's my hope the Church will intercede with the king

or his minister of justice. If possible, I would very much like to prevent Mathew from going on trial, or spending several months in jail waiting for one."

Collin nodded slowly. "And then?" he asked.

"Then? . . . Then we go home."

Collin didn't speak for a minute. A light mist was falling, and he pulled his cloak closer around him. "What's Tyraine like, Father?" he asked eventually.

"Tyraine? Well, it's a city . . . far bigger than Devondale and Elberton put together. I'd say it's even bigger than Anderon. It has a huge harbor where ships from all over the continent come to trade. As a matter of fact, it's the largest port in the West. It's been many years since I've been there, but when I was, I had the impression of a place in a constant state of motion."

"Motion?"

"Mm-hmm. Even late at night, and well into the early hours of the morning, people were out on the streets."

"So you'll be going back to Devondale after we're done at Barcora?" Collin asked.

There was something about his tone that caused Father Thomas to turn and look at him. "Is it *that* obvious?"

"She's a neat lady," Collin said with a smile. "Sorry, I wasn't trying to pry," he added, realizing that he might have overstepped himself.

Father Thomas returned the smile. "Yes, I think she's special too."

"Have you told her you're a priest?"

"No," Father Thomas replied, a little too quickly. "The subject hasn't come up yet. I suppose I'd better have a chat with her when I get back."

"It might be a good idea."

Father Thomas glanced at Collin out of the corner of his eye. In the last few months, if not the last few days, the boy had matured a great deal. If anything, he had become more serious and thoughtful, despite his glib manner. When he recalled the sandy-haired, mischievous child who would occasionally let frogs loose in his class only a few years ago, the change seemed quite amazing to him. The priest counted Mathew lucky to have such a friend.

"Collin . . . do you know what happened between Mat and those men earlier?" he asked, changing the subject.

"I only got there at the end of it, Father. I was coming back from Effie's house when I spotted Mat and the others. He had his sword out, so I knew something was wrong. I got to him as fast as I could."

"Did you actually see him get injured?"

Collin nodded. "Mat wounded one of them in the shoulder—the fat one, I think. When I knocked his friend down, the man lunged with his sword. Mat parried the blade with no problem that I could see, but then he just held back. After that there was a scuffle and he charged Mat again. That's when the man's knife got through. Mat's lucky he's not dead."

Collin was about to mention about Bert suddenly leaping backward, away from Mathew, but changed his mind.

"And why do you suppose Mathew tried to conceal his wound from us?"

Collin shrugged. "You know Mat. He was probably afraid of looking silly. That's my guess."

"I see. I thought it might be something like that. And . . . what were you doing at Effie's house?"

Collin opened his mouth but suddenly couldn't think of a suitable reply. He was grateful the streets were dark and the priest couldn't see his face. He was still searching for the right words, so as not to compromise anyone's honor—Effie's in particular—when he heard Father Thomas chortling and realized that he was being teased. The priest put an arm around Collin's shoulders and they made their way back to the inn without further conversation, which suited him quite well.

The rain continued throughout the night and for the next three days. Father Thomas and Ceta spent most of their time in each other's company. Mathew was grateful to do nothing more than relax and read a book about the brain

Dr. Wycroft sent him. Akin made his way over to the silver guild to renew old acquaintances, and Daniel contented himself by refining and polishing the lenses for his farsighter invention. Collin found a card game with several men who were staying at the inn, and came away nearly five gold elgars richer.

On their fourth day in Elberton, Mathew woke in the gray first light of morning and slipped quietly out of bed. He moved softly, not wishing to disturb Collin or Daniel. Tentatively flexing his side, he concluded that except for some soreness, it would give him no trouble.

The previous day, Dr. Wycroft stopped by and looked at the job Ceta had done with the salves and dressings. He complimented her on her ministrations and said there was little else he could do. He did bring another salve, to be applied once a day in order to prevent infection, and also provided a supply of fresh bandages that he wanted changed daily. Lara promised to see to it. Interestingly, the man seemed embarrassed by what had happened and apologized on behalf of the town of Elberton. He was so serious and formal, Mathew only just managed to keep from smiling. At one point, when they were alone, the doctor asked if he had experienced any other problems since they'd spoken in his office. Mathew understood what he was referring to and said that he had not.

Now, Mathew walked quietly past his sleeping friends and looked out the window. The rain had abated but the streets were still wet. A blowing spray was coming in off the Roeselar. Behind him, Daniel stirred in his bed but didn't wake. Mathew rested his head against the wooden window frame and thought about Lara and how their relationship had changed four nights ago. After their kiss, he wanted to spend the night with her, but she demurred—though only just. With little choice in the matter, he grudgingly convinced himself it was just as well. At least he was spared a lot of nosy questions from his friends the next morning.

Ceta brought him two shirts that once belonged to her

late husband; she and Lara had apparently concluded that his was beyond saving. When he tried to pay the innkeeper, she thanked him but refused the money, saying that they were of no use sitting in a chest.

He pulled on his breeches and donned one of the new shirts—sensible dark blue and made of sturdy wool—then silently closed the door behind him and went downstairs. At that hour in the morning Mathew didn't expect anyone else to be up. He was surprised to see Father Thomas and Ceta sitting at a table together near the fire, talking. Father Thomas was holding her hand, and she was looking at him in that soft way only a woman could manage. Conscious of intruding on their privacy, he turned to go back but only got three steps before Father Thomas saw him.

"Good morning," the priest called out, without taking his attention from Ceta.

Mathew halted in mid-step. "I'm sorry. I didn't know anyone else would be around this early. I was just going out to the barn to say goodbye to Tilda."

"Tilda?" Ceta asked.

"His horse," Father Thomas explained.

"My horse," Mathew echoed.

Father Thomas had come to his room last night and explained his plan to enlist the Church's help after they reached Barcora. When the priest casually mentioned that they would have to leave their horses in Elberton, Mathew was taken aback. *Of course, we can't take the horses on a ship*, he realized. Nevertheless, he felt badly about Tilda. She had been with him for more than eight years, ever since he was little. The thought saddened him—one more thing to leave behind.

Ceta noticed the look in his eyes and promptly changed the subject by asking how he liked the shirts, meanwhile casting a critical eye over the one he was wearing. He thanked her again and said they were fine.

"Wonderful," she said, genuinely pleased. "Well, I imagine you two men are hungry, so if you'll excuse me,

I see Felker Whalen is here to make his delivery. After I've finished my business with him, I'll see to your breakfasts."

They followed Ceta's gaze to the large lattice window at the front of the room. A man was outside tying a horse and cart to the post. He was dressed like a farmer, and as they watched, began unloading crates of food from the cart. Ceta put a shawl over her head and went to join him. From a distance, Mathew could see that the exchange between them was animated. Ceta examined the eggs and vegetables one at a time, accepting some and rejecting the others, all to the pained expression of Felker Whalen, who looked to be arguing his case spectacularly, if unsuccessfully.

She returned a moment later carrying a pail of eggs and vegetables.

"If I don't watch that man closely, he'll deliver whatever he can get away with. We've been playing this game for years. He tells me I'm ruining him by paying too low, and I tell him he's trying to put me out of business with poor quality."

Father Thomas and Mathew exchanged amused glances and watched Ceta disappear into the kitchen. Five minutes later Collin walked sleepily down the stairs, squinting against the light. Father Thomas saw him and hooked his leg around a chair, pulling it into position next to them. Collin came over, sat down, and poured himself a cup of hot tea from the little pot on the table. No one spoke for a while; they just stared into the fire, sipping their drinks.

"You're up early," Father Thomas finally said to Mathew.

"Being stabbed doesn't seem to agree with me," he replied, stifling a yawn, and then added in response to Father Thomas's raised eyebrows, "I'm fine."

"Nice day," Collin observed sourly, looking out the window.

They both glanced up, and then back at the fire.

"Where's Daniel?" Father Thomas asked.

"Still asleep when I left him." Collin yawned while he stretched.

"Father, what time do we need to meet Captain Donal?" Mathew asked.

"In about two hours. He said first tide would be around mid-morning. I expect if we're on board by then, that will be fine with him."

Ceta reappeared a few minutes later carrying two plates of eggs and sausages. "Oh, dear," she said, seeing that Collin had joined them. "It looks like everyone's up early this morning. Just give me a second and I'll be right back. Did you sleep well?" she asked, setting the plates down on the table.

"Yes, ma'am. Mat didn't snore for a change."

"What? I don't snore—do I?" Mathew protested.

Collin rolled his eyes skyward and Father Thomas chuckled, taking another sip of his tea.

"Well, I hope *you* don't snore, Uncle Siward," she said, affectionately pinching Father Thomas's earlobe, then headed to the kitchen again.

There was a silence.

"You haven't told her yet?" Collin whispered, spilling some of his tea on the table.

"She knows I'm not your uncle, if that's what you mean," Father Thomas replied blandly. "Actually, we were just talking when you both came down."

"I meant about the other thing," Collin said, lowering his voice.

"I'm working on it," Father Thomas said dejectedly.

True to her word, Ceta returned with Collin's breakfast a short while later, which he attacked with gusto. He was finishing his plate when Effie arrived for work and came directly over to the table to say good morning. Before she excused herself to the kitchen, she bent over and said something in Collin's ear, causing him to turn several shades redder. Mathew thought he heard her ask Collin something about his back being all right, but he wasn't

positive. When she was gone, both Father Thomas and
Mathew turned to look at him with questioning eyes.

"Umm . . . I think I'll go upstairs and pack," Collin
said, and left abruptly.

Mathew sat quietly for a time, letting the fire warm
him, then decided that if he was going to say goodbye to
Tilda, he had better get it over with. Excusing himself, he
left Father Thomas to his own reflections. But before he
got to the door, the sound of a light footfall on the stairs
distracted him.

He looked back to see Lara coming down the steps.
She was wearing her gray dress, the one he liked. She
passed Father Thomas and exchanged a few words with
him, then walked across the room to Mathew with a shy
smile.

"Good morning," he said. "Did you sleep well?"

"Oh yes, and you?"

"If you consider sleeping with Collin sleeping well."

"Don't sulk," she said, patting his cheek. "Were you
going out?"

"I thought I'd say goodbye to Tilda before we leave.
Maybe I can find a carrot to bring her," he said, looking
around.

"You should probably try the kitchen, silly. I don't
think you'll find any carrots just lying around the common room."

Her last comment was so obvious he started to chuckle
in spite of himself. She always could make him laugh
when she wanted to.

"Would you like me to come with you?" she asked.

"To the kitchen?" he teased.

"To the stable," she said, hitting him gently on the arm.

"Sure."

A brief stop at the kitchen confirmed her prediction regarding the carrot. On their way out Lara waved to Father
Thomas, who waved back absently.

"What's the matter with him?" Lara asked in a low
voice.

"I think he wants to tell Ceta what he does for a living, and he's having a hard time finding the right words. He's a little worried how she'll react. It's funny, you know, I've never thought of Father Thomas being at a loss for words."

Lara nodded in agreement.

The stable was directly across from the inn, and they hurried across the yard to it. While Mathew was opening the double doors he had a brief moment of misgiving. What if Will Tavish was there? He considered going back for his sword, but decided it would be a waste of time. To no one's surprise, Will had never returned, and everyone figured they had seen the last of him. Overhead, gray clouds began to roll in from the west, accompanied by an occasional rumble of thunder in the distance. They made it inside just before it began raining again.

The interior of the stable was dimly lit by the bleak light of early morning, filtering in through two side windows. In the corner, to the right of the door, someone had stacked several large oil drums. Like many stables, when it rained the damp smell of wet hay mingled with the scent of the horses boarded there. Mathew counted eight stalls, four on either side, each with a horse in it, except for the one on the very end, whose occupant was a donkey. Tilda was in the third stall on the left. She raised her head when she heard his voice, letting out a snort.

Mathew and Lara walked over to her. Without being asked, she picked up a coarse brush in front of the stall and began to groom Tilda's flanks, while Mathew gently rubbed the old mare's nose. After a moment he remembered the carrot and held it out for her to eat. She finished it in three bites, whickering appreciatively. He put his arms around the horse's neck and gave her a hug.

"I'm going to miss you, old girl. We . . . just wanted to say goodbye and let you know that we'll come back as soon as we can."

The mare's big brown eyes watched him, and she

stretched her neck out, gently pushing his hand with her head. Mathew felt a tightness in his throat and swallowed.

"At least you won't have to put up with Collin's snoring," he said quickly, trying to hide his embarrassment.

Lara looked up from her brushing. "Collin? That's funny . . . I didn't notice him snoring while we were on the road," she said with a frown. "You do, you know," she added.

"Me?" Mathew said, pretending to be offended.

"Mm-hmm. Last night, when we were lying on the bed together, you dozed a little and you snored. You must have been tired."

"Me? I don't believe it."

"Honestly, I—"

Lara never finished her sentence. The light in the stable suddenly grew dim as the doors swung shut. They both turned to look at the same time. At first Mathew thought it must have been the wind. A loud peal of thunder rumbled outside, rattling the windowpanes. It sounded much closer.

"I'll get the doors," Lara said.

Mathew grabbed her arm before she could take another step.

There was something else as well. A smell—an unmistakable smell. He saw them before she did.

"Mathew, what?" Lara said, sensing that something was wrong. Then she followed his gaze and he heard her sharp intake of breath.

Two Orlocks stood in the doorway, and a third was just climbing down from the loft. *Fool!* his mind screamed. *Why didn't I take the sword?*

In desperation, Mathew looked around for another way out of the stable, or anything to defend them with, but there was nothing there.

"Get behind me," he said slowly, pulling her by the arm.

"Mathew—"

"I said, get behind me," he repeated, never taking his eyes off the creatures in front of him.

Strangely, the Orlocks didn't attack immediately, just as they hadn't attacked on the road that day after Thad Layton's farm. He registered the similarity. They just stood there, staring at them with flat emotionless eyes. Inside the stall, Tilda stamped her foot nervously and whinnied.

Slowly, carefully, Mathew and Lara began to back away. His heart was racing as he searched for a solution. At some unspoken signal, all three Orlocks began to advance. He watched them come, and anger at his own stupidity boiled in his chest. They were both going to die. He spread his arms away from his sides, shielding Lara, keeping himself between her and the Orlocks. The one on his right had a spear that came to a triangular point, and the others were armed with swords. Mathew watched them, gauging his distance as he readied himself to go for the one with the spear.

Maybe I can give her a chance to break for the door, he thought. *Only another few feet . . .*

He was not prepared for what happened next.

"Give it to me," the one in the middle said. It was the same hoarse whisper he remembered, but the words were clear enough for him to understand.

Mathew stopped retreating and looked at the creature.

Give it to me?

"I won't ask you a second time, boy," the creature said, holding out a slender hand. Its chest rose and fell, and he could hear it breathing.

"We will let you live, human," the one with the spear said. "You'd like that, wouldn't you?"

He didn't know what they were talking about. The one on the left was looking at Lara.

Lara? Give them Lara? he thought.

He was not going to simply hand her over and run. He'd see them in hell first. If they were going to die, it would be fighting.

Fool! his brain screamed at him again.

"My . . . what a pretty girl," the one on his right sneered, baring its teeth. The creature's tongue flicked briefly across its lips.

"Mathew," Lara whispered from behind him, her hands tightening on his shoulders.

The middle Orlock beckoned with its fingers once more, holding its palm out. "The ring, boy."

He wasn't sure he heard the last part correctly, and it was then that Mathew realized the creature was not looking at him but at his right arm, or more specifically, his right hand.

The ring? The thought lasted only a second as the Orlock on the left spoke.

"No more talk—*kill him*. The girl will make a nice . . . *toy*."

The Orlock's lips stretched back into a grotesque smile, or an approximation of what might pass for a smile on a human. Its sword came up.

The tingling sensation began slowly in Mathew's arm, and from somewhere deep inside of him, he felt a surge of energy unlike anything he had ever experienced. It caused him to gasp in shock.

It was difficult for Lara to say what happened next—her head was buried in Mathew's back, not wanting to see what was about to come. She heard him yell out, "*No!*" and felt his shoulders stiffen. The words seemed torn from his very soul. A split second later something warm passed by her face, followed by a brilliant white flash and an enormously loud bang that nearly deafened her. The windows on either side of them, along with the entire forward wall of the stable, exploded outward, along with both of the doors. The force of the concussion was enough to blow out the inn windows, along with those of several other houses, sending a shower of splinters flying in every direction. Daniel, who was just coming to get them, was picked up bodily by the blast and hurled backward.

The air in front of Lara seemed to ripple and distort itself for a moment, the way a pond does when a breeze passes over it. She was stunned by what had just happened, and stared at the opening that had been the front of the building. It was gone—destroyed. Rain and wind were blowing in, sweeping across the floor of the stable.

Of the Orlocks, there was no sign at all. Only a shallow depression in the dirt floor remained where they had been standing only moments before. Mathew slowly sank to his knees, and Lara had to grab him around the waist in order to hold him up. Through the open wall she saw people pouring out of the inn. Her ears still rang from the force of the explosion, and she was finding it difficult to think.

"Mathew?" she whispered. "What happened?"

The sound of her voice seemed to come from far away, but it appeared to steady him. She saw his eyes focus, taking her in, along with their surroundings. The air abruptly stopped rippling and returned to normal.

"Are you all right?" he asked, taking her by the shoulders. He looked her up and down for some sign of an injury.

"Yes . . . I think so. What about you? My God, what was that?"

He shook his head. "I don't know," he said. "I was thinking . . ."

Shouting interrupted him before he could finish his sentence. Mathew's eyes grew wide.

"The Orlocks," he said, spinning to look around him.

"They're gone . . . Mathew, they're gone," she said, turning his chin to face her.

Mathew blinked and slowly put a hand to his forehead, rubbing the bridge of his nose with his fingers.

"What is it?"

"I . . . it's just a headache. Let's get out of here."

She had to help him when his first step faltered. "Mathew . . ."

"No. I'm fine. Let's go."

When they got to the street, he disengaged himself from her arm. It was raining, but they hardly noticed. Akin and a heavyset man he didn't know were helping Daniel to his feet. His friend was cut in numerous places from the splinters.

"What the hell just happened?" Daniel asked.

"The oil drums inside the stable exploded," Mathew answered. "I think it was lightning."

"Lightning?" Daniel said incredulously.

The man who was supporting Daniel's arm looked back at the barn and shook his head. "Do you think you're all right to stand on your feet?" he asked, brushing some splinters off Daniel's shoulders.

"What? Oh, yes, I'm fine," Daniel said. "Thanks very much for your help."

"Just look at that, will you?" the man said, surveying the ruined stable. "We had a lightning strike a few years ago down by the docks. Completely destroyed one of them. You're lucky you're alive, son. Well . . . doesn't look like anyone got hurt, thank God. I guess we should get inside out of this rain."

"Thanks again," Daniel said, shaking the man's hand.

Father Thomas and Ceta were among the crowd that had gathered. Mathew signaled to them that they were heading inside.

"You were both in the barn when it happened?" Akin asked.

"Right," Mathew replied, but he didn't elaborate, leaving Akin open-mouthed.

After they entered the inn, Mathew went to the least crowded corner of the room, followed by Daniel and Lara, and then Akin and Collin.

"But I don't see how—" Daniel said.

He didn't finish his sentence, because Mathew stepped on his toes.

After checking to see that they were unharmed, Ceta went outside to get a closer look at the barn, and Father Thomas joined them. Mathew was grateful she wasn't with them at the moment.

"Thank God, you're both alive," the priest said. "When we heard the explosion and remembered you were both in the stable, I thought—"

"I'd better get upstairs and pack if we're going to make that ship," Mathew interrupted.

He knew they were all looking at him as if he had just lost his mind, but he didn't care. At the moment, all he wanted to do was to get away from the common room with its crowd of excited people, talking about what had happened, and possible prying eyes and ears.

"Yes . . . well, I guess I'd better change out of this dress," Lara said, picking up on Mathew's cue.

Father Thomas's consternation deepened, but then he caught on too. One by one they all proceeded up the stairs and into Mathew's room. Once everyone was inside, Collin and Daniel pushed two of the beds aside to make more room. Akin sat on the small wooden desk with his back against a rough plaster wall.

Mathew recounted what happened, and the others listened but said nothing. Occasionally, he looked at Lara, who nodded in confirmation. When he finished, he walked over to the window and stared down at the street below. Father Thomas and Akin exchanged troubled glances.

"But I still don't understand," Daniel said. "If lightning hit the stables, there would have been some kind of charring or blackening of the timbers. Even from where I was standing, I could tell that didn't happen. The whole wall exploded *out,* not in. The damage would have been going the other way if it was lightning."

"You said you were confused about why the Orlocks picked Devondale," Mathew said, speaking to Father Thomas. He was still looking out of the window. "And why a raiding party the size we met in the forest would bother to follow us for over a week. Well, I don't think they're following us. I think they're following me."

There was a long silence.

"What makes you say that, my son?" Father Thomas eventually asked.

Mathew watched a raindrop slide down one of the glass panes. "I don't know," he said, turning around to face the others. "But I think it has something to do with this ring."

"Your ring?" Daniel said, surprised.

"Giles's ring," Mathew corrected him. "I don't know what it is . . . and I can't explain it . . . but there's something odd about it."

He pulled the ring off his finger and looked at it for a second, turning it back and forth, then placed it on the table next to his bed.

"What are you talking about, Mat?" Collin asked.

"I'm not sure myself. I know it sounds crazy, but strange things have been occurring ever since I put it on."

"Such as?" Daniel asked.

Mathew took a deep breath and explained what had happened to his vision in the forest. He told them about it turning green, and being able to see in the dark through the smoke. While he was talking, Daniel walked over, picked the ring up and hefted it in his palm, then handed it to Akin.

"Heavy," Akin said. "I haven't worked with gold very much, but this is heavier than any ring of its size I've ever felt. And I've never seen this color before—if it is gold."

"You think this ring had something to do with what happened to you?" Daniel asked, his tone skeptical.

"I told you it would sound crazy. I went to see Dr. Wycroft several days ago. He said that when the body's under great stress, the brain can respond in strange ways. Some of it made sense. It's possible I'm imagining things, but I don't think so."

"Well, I never heard of anyone being able to see things a half mile away in the dark, or a person's vision turning green," Lara said.

"There's something else," Mathew went on. "Do you remember when we were in the forest and you were fighting the Orlocks that came after you?" he asked Father Thomas.

The priest nodded slowly.

"Do you remember what one of them said when he saw me? He said, 'There he is.' "

"That could mean anything," Daniel said.

"True. But when we were in the stable, they didn't at-

tack us right away. One of them spoke to me and told me
to give him the ring."

"He what?" Akin said, coming off the desk.

"That's right," Lara said. "I was there, and I heard it as
plain as I can hear you now." Her face was still pale from
what had occurred, but her tone was emphatic.

"I *did* hear what the creature said in the forest," Father
Thomas replied. "Mathew is quite correct. I simply did
not know what to make of it then. I still don't know that
this is the proper conclusion for us to draw."

Mathew sat down heavily on the bed, and Lara sat
down next to him, putting an arm around his shoulders.

"We led them here," Mathew said, staring down at the
floor. "Or more accurately, I led them here."

Silence.

"Then I think we need to be gone from this place as
quickly as possible," Father Thomas said softly. "Before
any more trouble comes searching for us."

"I agree," Akin said. "I don't understand what's so special about this ring, or why the Orlocks have any interest
in it. None of this makes the slightest sense to me. I'm
just a simple silversmith, but I'd like some answers. People I knew are dead. Thad Layton and his son, Stefn
Darcy . . . Maybe now there's a reason for it—or at least
part of a reason. I want to know why."

"You said there was a tingling sensation you felt when
you put the ring on?" Daniel asked.

"Right."

"Do you mind?" Daniel picked up the ring and looked
at Mathew.

Mathew nodded and stepped aside.

"Let's see, you had it on the fourth finger of your right
hand, didn't you?"

Mathew nodded again, as Daniel slipped the ring on.

They waited.

Daniel looked around the room. A minute passed, then
another.

"Nothing," he said, slipping the ring off. "Except it *is*

heavier than you'd think just to look at. But I didn't feel or see anything unusual."

He handed the ring to Collin.

"No thanks," Collin said, taking a step backward. "I'd just as soon have nothing to do with it, if you don't mind."

"C'mon," Daniel insisted, "we have to know whether it's the ring or Mat."

"Excuse me?" Collin asked.

"Just this . . . Mat said each time he put the ring on, he felt a tingling sensation. Now assuming he's not lying or crazy—sorry Mat—if we each try the ring, and one of us feels the same thing, then we know it's not him. On the other hand, if Mat's still the only one who feels it, then the problem *is* with him, or with some connection between the ring and him."

Collin scowled at Daniel, then took the ring and placed it on the same finger as Daniel had. He waited while everyone in the room kept their eyes fixed on him. After a couple of minutes, he shrugged and took it off, then handed it to Akin, who repeated the same experiment. The results were the same, just as they were when Lara attempted it. Father Thomas, who was the last to try it on, put the ring back on the table when he finished.

"Did anyone feel anything?" Daniel asked.

No one responded.

"All right, Mat . . . are you ready to try again?"

Mathew looked around the room. He was beginning to regret having spoken at all, nevertheless, he took the ring and put it back on his finger. The change of expression on his face was enough to tell everyone what happened.

"Well," Daniel said, "now we know it's not just the ring, or one of us would have felt something."

Father Thomas sat on the edge of Collin's bed during the conversation, trying to sort out the recent events in his mind. When he spoke up, his tone was measured and deliberate.

"I think Daniel is right," he said. "But I also do not believe we are going to find our answers here and now. As I said earlier, it's possible that we may have put these people in danger, so I suggest we finish packing and depart as quickly as possible. Akin, you and Daniel will follow us tomorrow on the *Douhalia*, as we discussed. I want you both to stay close until it's time to leave. Agreed?"

"Agreed," Akin replied.

"Fine. Let's meet downstairs in ten minutes."

Akin and Lara followed him out of the room.

"Do you still have that leather cord of yours?" Mathew asked Collin after the others were gone.

"Sure."

"Let me borrow it, will you?"

Collin rummaged through his pack, found the leather cord and tossed it to Mathew. He watched as his friend took the ring off his finger, threaded the cord through it, and placed it around his neck.

"Might not be a bad idea," Daniel agreed.

Outside, the rain finally let up, leaving a leaden sky and a few blowing clouds. The wind, as always, seemed to freshen crossing the Roeselar, and was sweeping through the town. Collin noticed Mathew's somber expression and put an arm around his shoulders.

"Don't worry, we'll figure it out."

Daniel also looked back from the hallway and winked. "Absolutely. You've got nothing to worry about—we're here."

Mathew gave them both a weak smile. "Actually, I was thinking about having to get on a ship in weather like this."

When they got downstairs, Father Thomas was back at the table by the fireplace talking with Ceta again. The boys walked quietly past and almost made it to the front door before a small shriek from the lady innkeeper stopped them in their tracks. They turned to see her put a hand over her mouth, get up and run into the kitchen, past a startled Lara.

"I may be going out on a limb, but my guess is, he just told her that he's a priest," Daniel observed.

Mathew and Collin responded by pushing him out the front door.

Ceta Woodall was in shock. She knew the dark-haired man she had grown so fond of over the last four days had reasons for concealing his identity. He had told her that much himself. What those reasons were, she could only guess at, or wait until he decided to speak. He had started to do so several times, but something always seemed to interrupt them. She was perceptive enough to guess that whatever it was, it had something to do with Mathew. Siward watched him protectively, and tended to fret about him when he was out of his sight. Her instincts, which she relied on heavily, told her to trust him, a thing that didn't come easily in her business. At night, lying in her bed, she chided herself on being naive and foolish. She hardly knew him. She told herself she was acting like a silly young girl, and at forty-two. *A woman my age ought to know better*, she thought. She hadn't allowed herself that luxury since her husband died. But there was something about the man—a gentle and quiet confidence that brought out her willingness to lay caution aside, along with her better judgment.

Siward had explained their plan to go to Barcora, but nothing beyond that. She got the sense that he very much wanted to share with her the burden he was carrying. Out of instinct more than anything else, she discounted the possibility that he was involved in any wrongdoing. Akin Gibb was a good man, and the girl, Lara, was cut from a solid, sensible mold that she could identify with. None of the company with him gave the slightest indication that they were anything other than what they seemed to be.

Whatever their secret, she was certain he would tell her before they left. She believed, wanted to believe, that these were good people. There was little question in her mind on that point. Ceta was aware that she had thought more objectively in the past, and probably still could, if only her heart didn't start pounding so when Siward was around.

They were leaving today. She'd even introduced them to Oliver Donal herself. What in the world was she thinking about? When was it—three or four days ago? It hardly seemed that long. Their departure was not something she wanted to dwell on, but she did think about it. In fact, she thought about it most of that night and into the early hours of the morning. When she applied her makeup, there might have been an extra touch of powder for her face, to prevent any unwanted blushing, of which she had done more than a little recently.

Men, she thought as she fought with a strand of hair that simply refused to stay in place. She finally gave up and sent a puff of air upward, blowing it out of her eyes. Unable to sleep, she put on the dark green dress that accented her shape and went out to the common room. Perhaps the cut was a little more daring than usual, but she had seen Siward's sidelong glances at her figure.

It was a pleasant surprise to find him awake at that early hour when the world was just opening its eyes. She had always been an early riser herself. They began to talk, only to be interrupted once again by what happened at that silly stable. For all she cared, God could have blown it up completely.

Of all the times for lightning to strike, she thought.

She only just managed to keep herself from screaming in frustration. After that, there was little else that could surprise her—or so she thought.

When Siward *finally* sat down with her and stopped hemming and hawing, he told her everything that her heart hoped he would say—and then he told her that he was a priest. The extra makeup she applied earlier didn't help as she felt her face going red.

A priest! And after the way she'd practically thrown herself at him.

My God, she thought, somewhat appropriately, considering the company. If that weren't enough, the bodice of her dress was so low.

*   *   *

Ceta Woodall, innkeeper of the Nobody's Inn of Elberton, couldn't recall running from anything or anybody in her life, but run she did, right through the kitchen, past the surprised cook and her helper, across a courtyard, out the back door, and into her home. She stood in the living room mortified. She had made a complete fool of herself, *and to a priest!*

She was not the only one who was stunned by her actions. Father Thomas, who admittedly had little experience as a participant in such matters, sat at his table, helpless. Lara witnessed the whole thing and was still standing in the same spot when Ceta ran by her only seconds before. When the priest noticed her there, he spread his hands helplessly and gave her a shy smile. She responded by mouthing the word "*go*" and pointing at the kitchen door.

Father Thomas shook his head dejectedly and sat there.

Lara stamped her foot in frustration and mouthed "*go*" a second time, pointing to the door more emphatically. It was a sufficient catalyst to put him in motion.

For the second time that morning, Ceta Woodall's employees were shocked, as a tall man with dark brown hair burst into their kitchen.

"Which way?" he asked.

The cook, a large pink-faced woman in her early sixties, looked him up and down for a minute. Her round face eventually creased into a smile and she made a gesture with her head, indicating the door. Father Thomas nodded and disappeared through it. As soon as he was gone, the kitchen employees broke into a fit of giggling.

The door at the back of the inn led to a surprisingly pleasant garden in the midst of a courtyard. A multitude of plants and neatly trimmed shrubbery seemed to be growing everywhere between rust-colored tiles. A wooden bench glider sat to the side of a path of tiny cream-colored pebbles that wound throughout the garden. Six cherry trees, situated at random around the courtyard, were already beginning to produce white and pink blossoms.

The garden's appearance was so unexpected that the priest paused and looked around. Recovering himself, he then walked deliberately along the little path to the only house there. The front door had a large dark brass knocker in its center.

He knocked softly on the door and waited. When no response came, he knocked again, only a little harder.

"Go away," a voice called from inside.

"Ceta, open the door. It's me."

"I know it's you. Go away."

"Ceta—"

"Go away, Siward."

"I don't want to stand out here discussing this."

He took a step back and looked in the window, which had the same small lead glass panes as the inn.

"Ceta, we need to talk . . . I need to talk to you."

He waited.

Father Thomas, already an educated man when he studied for the priesthood, was trained in the use of logic and reasoning. Over the years, he supplemented that learning through prayer and contemplation. He knew that maintaining a circumspect demeanor would enable him to stay calm and deal with difficult situations when others' emotions got the best of them. That was the fulcrum on which his logic and expertise rested.

He kicked the door in.

For the second time in the last hour Ceta Woodall gasped when her front door broke away from its hinges. In two quick strides Siward Thomas stepped in, took her in his arms and kissed her. Her head began to spin and her heart was racing so she was certain he would feel it pounding in her chest. Finally, she pushed away from him and stepped back, still breathing heavily.

"Ceta . . ." he said softly, like a caress.

"You must think I'm a complete fool, the way I threw myself at you."

"Not for one second," he said in the same gentle tone. He took a step toward her and she backed away again. "What's the matter?" he asked, taking another step.

"You're a priest."

"Don't you like priests?"

"What? Of course I like . . . that's not the point, and you know it. We can't . . . we shouldn't . . . I shouldn't have let you kiss me."

"What's wrong with my kissing you?" he asked, taking another step toward her.

"Stay where you are," she said, pointing at him. "You know very well what's wrong with it. Priests don't do that sort of thing."

He smiled. "Ceta, the Church doesn't generally encourage it, but priests *do* marry, you know."

There was a pause. A long pause.

"You're a Levad?" she asked, her eyes opening wide.

"Mm-hmm."

In the millennia that followed the ancient war, the Church persevered as it always persevered, becoming a bastion of knowledge and moral teaching, like a candle shining alone in the darkness. Mankind slowly pulled itself out of the devastation the Ancients wrought and began to rebuild. At some point along the three-thousand-year journey, a fundamental disagreement among members of the Church's hierarchy took place, centering on the interpretation of what was left of the holy writings. It caused a split, with fully half of the population turning to the Levads, as they called themselves, and the other half to the Ashots.

Though the basic precepts between the two sects were essentially the same, Levads were able to marry and celebrated the Lord's Day on the sixth day of the week, while the Ashots insisted the seventh day was correct and rejected the concept of marriage for priests. Congregants took all this in stride, occasionally making good-natured jokes about the differences between the two branches, and intermarrying when they fell in love.

* * *

"Oh, my God," she exclaimed. "When you said you were a priest, I thought . . . I mean, I was raised—"

Suddenly she was in his arms again. And this time their kiss was longer and deeper than the one before, somehow completing them, like parts of a whole coming together in a perfect, seamless fit. When the room stopped moving, she rested her head against his chest and looked out her window into the little garden she loved so much. She wanted never to leave this room. She wanted to freeze time where it was. Outside the window, a slight breeze moving between the trees like an invisible hand caused tiny white cherry blossoms to float through the air, giving the appearance of snow falling softly down. She closed her eyes, wanting more than anything she had ever wanted to save the vision and that moment in her memory forever.

"I broke your door," he murmured.

"I'll get another," she replied, keeping her eyes closed.

There was so much that they wanted to say, needed to say to each other. So many things to talk about. Walking with him to the docks was the hardest thing she ever had to do. But she was determined not to make it any more difficult than it already was. The sadness and impending sense of loss was almost too much to bear. So she bit her lip, forced a smile to her face and kept walking. They held hands, staying apart from the others.

When Captain Donal's ship lifted its anchor and moved slowly away from the land into the wide expanse of the river, it was all she could do to keep from bursting into tears. She reminded herself that she wasn't built that way, although she began to doubt it just then.

Siward said he would return, and she promised to wait for him. It would have to do.

23

Alor Satar, Rocoi

KARAS DUREN WAITED IN HIS PALACE GARDEN WITH HIS
sister for his niece to arrive. A table covered by a richly
spun gold cloth had been set out amidst a small grove of
olive trees. The garden, as Duren called it, was huge by
any standards, extending over several acres of well-
maintained land. Just to their right, water from one of the
cold springs that fed a small lake at the southern end of
property had been painstakingly diverted to form a small
pond. Splashing water flowed noisily over a series of
rocks and boulders, giving the impression of a waterfall.

Marsa Duren d'Elso, Queen of Nyngary, was twenty-
two years younger than her brother. She possessed many
of the same physical features he did. She was slender and
taller than most men, a fact that had always pleased her. A
mass of jet-black hair fell to her shoulders, framing a face
that was still startlingly beautiful after forty years. Her
large brown eyes, so dark they could almost be said to be
black, missed nothing. And like her brother, she wore a
ring of rose gold on the third finger of her left hand.

"You've made changes since I was here last," she said.

"A few," Duren agreed, taking a sip of the wine she had
brought him as a present.

Despite his efforts over the years, the loamy soil of
Alor Satar had never been able to produce anything other
than mediocre wines. Nyngary, on the other hand, farther
south, was known throughout the world for possessing
vintages of unmatched quality, particularly the potent

dark green that was Duren's favorite. On those occasions that she visited, which were infrequent at best, she always remembered to bring a case of it with her.

When the messenger had arrived from Alor Satar, bearing the news of her oldest brother's death, Marsa had raised an eyebrow and read the note without reaction. She then handed it back, and said, "Tell Karas I will come," and went back to pruning her roses. An hour later she sent a note to her daughter, informing her of her uncle's death and instructing her to pack for their trip.

It had taken them three days to reach Rocoi. On arrival, she found things much as they had been when she was a child. The streets and boulevards of the capital were still wide and clean, though they seemed somehow smaller than she remembered. There were a few more statues and fountains, evidence of her brother's penchant for art. Otherwise the palace remained much the same as when she had left to marry Eldar d'Elso, the king of Nyngary.

Immediately after Kyne Duren's funeral, Karas asked her to go for a walk with him. This in itself was unusual—her brother was not given to idle pursuits. Marsa assumed he wanted to review the deployment of their troops and finalize plans for the attack on the West.

Her husband had discussed the proposed campaign with her when Karas first presented it several months before. She was not surprised that he'd turned to her. It was typical of the man—he was paralyzed by indecision, and elected to defer his answer until giving the matter further study. Had she not exercised her influence over him, which came quite easily, the king would have gone right on thinking until he was old and gray.

Marsa knew her brother far too well to believe he would repeat the same mistake he'd made twenty-eight years ago. She had been quite young then, only a child herself, but she remembered everything as if it were only yesterday. If Karas had decided to take on the West again, she knew that he would not have reached such a decision lightly—or without the certainty that he would emerge victorious. Their minds were a great deal alike in that re-

gard. Her grandfather's passion burned as brightly in her
breast as it did in her brother's.

They walked across the tiled courtyard into the new
wing of the palace and he began to unfold his story about
discovering the ancient library. He told her of the knowledge he had gained from the books there, and of the great
crystal that seemed to reach forever into the depths of the
earth. She'd listened and absorbed all he said with little
comment. Duren even took her to the library and showed
her the books themselves, and the amazing white lights
that came on when they sensed movement in the room. It
was impressive, but her instincts told her that he was
holding something back. She decided to bide her time
and wait. Marsa d'Elso was very good at waiting.

She noticed the odd rose gold ring immediately. Karas
absently twisted it back and forth when he spoke. Initially she attributed it merely to his fondness for jewelry.

After they left the library, her brother appeared to be
struggling with himself to tell her the real reason he'd invited her. They walked together around the lake, eventually coming to a flight of stone stairs that led to the top of
a small hill. In the distance she could see the reddish
walls of Karas's palace and the balcony of the apartments
that she shared with her daughter.

A narrow path led away from the steps and into the
trees. It was just wide enough for them to walk in single
file. Ahead of them was a clearing, which Marsa recognized immediately. From where they stood, the palace
was completely out of sight, shielded by the trees and undergrowth. She'd seen that much of the ground under her
feet was blackened, as if there had been a fire recently,
but kept the observation to herself. In the clearing, someone had set out a table and two chairs. At the far end of it
stood a miniature house, abandoned long ago. Her father
had built it for her to play in as a child. She eyed it impassively. No particular emotions or fond memories
drifted back to her. She simply hadn't thought of it in
years. When her use for the house was over, it was gone
from her mind.

She turned back to her brother, waiting calmly for an explanation. Instead, he walked to one of the chairs and sat down, indicating for her to join him. That was when she noticed the small box on the table. It was finely crafted, made of rich burled wood. Duren opened the box, revealing three rings the same color as the one he wore.

Then he began to talk about his own ring. He told her of the ability the Ancients possessed to create things using their minds alone. He explained how their last war almost destroyed the planet and plunged mankind into darkness. She knew about the war, of course—everybody did. It was common knowledge. Relics of the Ancients' great buildings and roads existed in her own country, just as they did in Alor Satar. Finally, he told her about the eight rose gold rings the Ancients created at the very end, in the hope of averting disaster. That fact she didn't know.

While her brother spoke, he permitted a rare display of emotion to show on his sharp features. The hooded eyes suddenly seemed animated and alive, with an intensity that she could only remember seeing on one or two other occasions.

"Marsa," he said, reaching out to hold her hand. "I know what I have just told you is difficult to accept, but believe me, every word is the truth."

She looked at him, unsure about what to say. The story was fantastic.

"Perhaps a demonstration then," he added. "Observe."

Duren swiveled in his chair and pointed to the little house across the clearing, and it exploded. Bits of wood and glass flew everywhere. A few splinters reached them, but she didn't flinch, or even react. Her face remained impassive. Marsa d'Elso considered what she had just witnessed.

There was potential here, she decided.

"Observe," her brother said again, pointing at a large beech tree about fifty yards to their right.

Marsa felt a faint movement of the ground under her feet, which gradually increased in intensity. Suddenly, the earth began to shift, accompanied by a deep tearing sound. The branches of the tree seemed to shudder. The shuddering spread to the trunk itself, and the tree slowly began to topple over. It was both fascinating and terrifying at the same time. The tree hit the ground with a loud crash. When silence returned to the clearing, she found her heart was pounding rapidly.

She was also aware that her brother was watching her. "That was your doing, Karas?"

"I told you that it would be difficult to accept," he said, putting his hand on top of hers.

It was an odd gesture, coming from him, more planned than spontaneous, she thought. Searching her memory, she was unable to recall any overt signs of affection from him other than formal kisses on the cheek when ceremony dictated it.

Her breathing returned to normal, and she leaned forward on the table and said, "Why have you shown me this?"

"Because you are my sister, and I need someone that I can trust. I cannot be all places at all times. If we are to defeat the West this time, the war will be fought on several fronts. There are limitations as to how far I can reach. And our present allies will require, shall we say, reinforcement and sufficient motivation to bring events to a rapid conclusion. I have such power and ability that hasn't been seen in this world for three millennia," he whispered intently. "We can make the dream come true."

"And you think these other rings possess the same power?" she asked, looking into the box on the table.

"That, my dear sister, is what I propose to find out," he replied. "They will not work on just anyone. I have learned that much already. None of these," he said, indicating the rings in the box, "have ever been able to work for me. I've tested all three with my sons, Armand and Eric. Both are intelligent, competent men, but neither demonstrated any ability with them, or even the slightest reaction."

A silence followed while Marsa digested what he told her. Then she picked up the box and examined the rings more closely. Being careful not to touch them, she moved the box slightly in one direction and then the other. Sunlight filtering through the leaves reflected off the rose gold, seeming to deepen its color.

After a moment, she put the box back on the table and picked up the first ring. Nothing about it seemed the slightest bit remarkable, except for the weight. With a quick glance at Duren's hand to verify which finger he wore his own ring on, she slipped it on the corresponding finger on her own hand.

They waited.

Duren's eyes met her own, searching them for some indication that a connection was made.

Nothing.

She pressed her lips together, took the ring off, and replaced it with the next one. Once again she felt nothing.

"What am I supposed to feel?" Marsa asked as she took the last ring out of the box.

"With me, there is a brief shiver that courses through my arm and then disappears almost immediately. One of the ancient books says that it's a normal reaction. Sometimes a slight headache follows, but—"

Duren's words froze in his mouth. Immediately after putting the ring on her finger, Marsa's expression changed. Her eyes grew wide and her mouth opened in surprise.

In his excitement Duren stood up, knocking his chair over backward. "You felt it, didn't you?"

She rose as well, but more slowly and deliberately, and then suddenly she threw her arms around him. And for the first time in their lives, they hugged each other out of genuine affection.

"Yes, yes, I definitely felt something when I put it on. It was like . . . I don't know. Like when your arm goes to sleep after you lean on it too long. But it only lasted for a second."

Even as she spoke, she began to worry that the effect had simply come and gone in that fleeting second.

"What happens now? What am I supposed to feel?" she asked him.

"Nothing," he whispered, watching her carefully. "That's the way it works—at least with me. Just that brief tingling, and then it's gone. We need to test it, Marsa— carefully . . . very carefully. It takes a little time to learn how to control it. The first time I succeeded in accomplishing anything, I blew up a chair."

"I take it you weren't trying to blow the chair up, then?" she asked looking at the surrounding area.

"I'm quite serious, Marsa. The ring may not be a good match for you, and the results can be unpredictable at times."

"What do you mean, '*a good match*'?" she'd asked, turning back to him.

"The books are not clear, and much of it is still obsure to me. In the beginning, every man and woman in the world possessed a ring of their own. But then, for some reason, the Ancients began to destroy them, leaving only eight special rings—this was what they called them. Each was made for one person, and for one person only."

"Then how is it possible for us to use them?" she asked.

He shook his head. "I don't have the answer to that, sister. I only know that they *can* be used, or at least one of them can. I've been searching the volumes for almost a year. It has something to do with the energies our brains produce, but beyond that, I cannot say. The important thing is that after three thousand years, I've somehow made it work again. I believe this was meant to be a part of my destiny—of our family's destiny."

There was a long pause before Marsa spoke. "Why now?" she asked.

Duren knew what she was asking. He leaned back in his chair and looked away rather than meeting her eyes.

"I have been thinking," he said quietly. "What will people say of me when I am gone? That I was a philosopher? A poet? A conqueror? Such men have lived before, and all that remains of them is dust and broken statues. I grow increasingly aware there are rather less days ahead of me than behind. By itself, one would think this fact alone a sufficient cause for a man to reevaluate his life. To see that what he created has meaning—*endures,* if you will. I wish to leave a legacy to my sons and to you, my sister."

Marsa nodded slowly, her brother's meaning plain to her. Part of what he'd said was true, of course, but she had an incredible memory for details, just as her grandfather did. Even if Karas didn't remember their conversations years before, when she was still living at the palace, she did. What her brother wanted was to somehow best his father, even though he'd been dead for nearly forty years. Gabrel was never able to conquer the West. That would be Karas's measure of success. *Interesting*, she thought.

"I want to try," she said. "Tell me what to do."

He paused and took a deep breath. "All right, I don't think we need to blow anything up just yet." He smiled. "Let us start small. I want you to concentrate on an object . . . say, this chair over here. Form a picture of it in your mind and think about making it move. Just *see* the chair moving—nothing more."

Marsa didn't hesitate. Following her brother's instructions, she looked at the chair and closed her eyes, keeping the image vividly in her mind. Then she imagined the chair rising above the ground.

Karas Duren's sharp intake of breath caused her to open her eyes. Hanging between them was the chair, miraculously suspended, as though by an invisible rope. Her mouth fell open. Exultation and a rush of power filled her unlike anything she had ever experienced. She formed a picture of the table in her mind, and it suddenly lifted off the ground as well. Duren watched in open admiration as his sister manipulated the two objects. She moved them around each other and then up, all the way to the treetops, before bringing them back down again.

"Tell me what else I can do," she said excitedly. "I want to know everything."

Her brother held up his hand and said, "Slowly, Marsa . . . slowly. This is not something to rush into. You have much to learn."

For three days she and Duren worked together, refining her newly found skills. In doing so, they both learned something. While wearing the rings, each became aware of the other's presence, even when a considerable distance separated them.

On the morning of her second day, she decided to go riding with her daughter and a small escort into the rolling hills surrounding Rocoi. After stopping in a small village called Loring for their midday meal, she suddenly felt her brother in her mind. In no way that she could explain, she knew that he was seated in the library in a high-backed chair. The chair was made of red velvet and black wood, and he was reading one of the ancient texts. For a moment it was though she could see the book through his eyes. She saw the writing on the pages and the dust that clung to the binding. At the same time she felt his presence, she was certain he felt her as well. It was as vivid as if he were standing in front of her. She could see his head come up when the contact was made. By way of experiment, Marsa removed the ring, and the link was immediately broken.

In her apartment's private dining room that evening, they discussed what had happened over dinner. Duren confirmed that he felt her presence as well, and even described the precise section of the village she was in when it happened.

"I felt the exact second you took off your ring," he said. "It was as if there was a sudden emptiness. I knew you were still alive, of course, but it was as if you were somehow gone. I find it difficult to articulate."

"What do you think it means, Karas?"

"I don't know. Perhaps it means that there is a greater

affinity between family members." He shrugged. "Perhaps nothing."

She put her fork down and stared out of the balcony window. She could see the lights from Rocoi in the distance casting an orange glow against the sky. A minute passed and then another before she spoke.

"You told me that you sent the Orlocks after the fifth ring, but that they have had no success in finding either it or the person who now has it, is that correct?"

A brief look of annoyance passed over her brother's face, but was gone as quickly as it came. "Yes."

"And you believe this ring presents a danger to you—to us—if the owner learns of its powers?"

"I have told you this much already."

Marsa Duren d'Elso turned to face him and leaned back in her chair. "What do we know of him?"

"His name is Mathew Lewin, a country boy from a small town in Elgaria. He is tall, perhaps seventeen years old, and intelligent, or so my spies have told me. His father was recently killed . . . murdered, to be precise. In turn, Lewin killed the one responsible for his father's death."

"Really?" she asked.

"With his bare hands—choked him to death."

"Hmm."

"What does that mean?"

"If he used his bare hands, then either he knows nothing about the ring or he's unable to use it," she replied. "Why has he not been taken already?"

"Because he fled his village to avoid the law. The Elgarians have always been quite punctilious about their laws. The Orlock who returned last week followed them to a river town called Elberton. The creature was the only one who came back. The boy and his companions managed to kill fifteen of their party."

"*What?* How is that possible? How many are with him?"

"He travels with a priest, a girl, and perhaps two or

three others. The report was not clear." Duren waved his hand impatiently. "I'm afraid I had the surviving Orlock killed before he had an opportunity to be more specific. At any rate, others are following now."

"But I don't see how a boy could possibly—"

"Before the creature died, he told me about an explosion in a stable that killed the last three of his companions," Duren interrupted, speaking quietly. "So it seems he *can* use the ring."

"But how—"

"I do not know. I only know the ring presents a danger. Each of the rings are dangerous if they can be matched to someone with the ability to use them. It may even be possible for them to work with others. You should understand that by now."

"But we don't even know if any of the others still exist," she said.

"True. But we know about this one . . . and I mean to have it." Duren leaned forward, his dark eyes suddenly as hard as agate. "Between the two of us, we will crush the West into dust."

She held that image in her mind for a moment and the smile returned to her lips.

"Karas, should we not increase our chances of success, if at all possible?"

Duren's hooded eyes, which had been assessing the color of a glass of wine he was holding up to the candle-light, slowly turned toward her. Brother and sister stared at each other for a full minute without speaking.

"Teanna?" he finally asked.

"We have two rings left, and she *is* family."

His response was to raise his glass to her before he drained it.

Teanna d'Elso, Princess of Nyngary, looked at the invitation from her uncle requesting that she join him and her mother in the garden for their midday meal. Although not quite as tall as her mother, the eighteen-year-old favored

her greatly, both in looks and demeanor. She had inherited startling blue eyes from her father's side of the family, and her hair was a shade lighter, but otherwise mother
and daughter were difficult to tell apart, even when standing side by side. Teanna had always considered herself
fortunate to have inherited her mother's general composure and intellect. She was aware of this at a very young
age.

When she opened the door to her quarters, the two soldiers standing watch at the entrance snapped to attention.
She barely noticed them. She walked past the soldiers
and headed down the wide granite corridor that led to the
courtyard below, sparing a glance at the portraits lining
the walls. *My ancestors*, she thought. She felt the same
attachment to them as she did to most people. None.

The opulence of her uncle's palace was a contradiction to
its owner, she thought, who seemed an austere individual. Karas Duren tended to speak very little. He was an
observer, as she herself was. So were her mother and her
cousin Eric.

She supposed such things ran in her family.

Teanna passed through the courtyard, noting that water had been added to the central fountain since their arrival. She made a mental note to ask her uncle about the
artists who had crafted the work. It would be nice to have
a similar one for their own palace in Nyngary. Her father
would commission it. Teanna had no doubt that either
she or her mother could get what they wanted from him
with little difficulty. That had always been the case for as
long as she could remember. She loved her father, but
she had little tolerance for the man's indecisive nature.

The door hidden among the rows of boxwoods was
rusted, but it still swung open easily past the soldier
standing guard there. It pleased her to see that the man
looked away quickly, not meeting her eyes. Her mother
had taught her that fear could be a potent tool if one used
it correctly.

She followed the little path, under a spreading canopy

of olive trees, and found them waiting for her. A table had been set for lunch. Duren rose and made a slight bow to her, formal as always. She curtsied, then took a seat next to her mother.

"I'm so glad you could join us this afternoon, Teanna," Duren said, offering her a glass of chilled wine.

"Thank you, Uncle. I'm only sorry that Uncle Kyne could not be here to join us."

"And why is that?" Duren said, taking a sip from his glass.

The question took her aback. She had said it because she thought it would be an appropriate expression of grief at the passing of a loved one. But then the sight of Duren tossing the first handful of dirt on his brother's grave flashed in her mind. At the only other funeral she had attended in her short years, that of a distant cousin, the tossing of the first handful of earth had seemed to be a solemn act, attended by a good deal of tears. Her uncle, however, did so in the most offhanded way, barely pausing in his conversation with her mother, before they walked away from the grave.

She shrugged. "It seemed like the correct thing to say," she replied coolly. She decided that she would have to be more careful with her comments in the future.

Duren smiled. "Thank you, my dear. It's gratifying to see that your mother's candor runs in the family. We invited you here today because we wanted to present you with this little gift." Duren held open the box containing the rings.

The second she sat down, Teanna noticed that both her mother and her uncle were wearing identical gold rings with the same rose-colored tint.

She was also aware that though he was smiling, her uncle was watching her. Typically, her mother's beautiful face was an unreadable mask. Teanna looked at the box, picked up one of the rings and examined it closely.

Seconds passed. The wind blew through the trees, rippling the green leaves, and water continued to splash noisily over the stones into the pond beside them.

She took another quick glance at her mother. For a moment she thought she saw the barest hint of a smile.

Teanna placed the ring back in the box and selected the other, slipping it onto the third finger of her right hand.

Abruptly, the expression on her face changed and she stared at the ring, startled. When she looked up, her mother and uncle were smiling—genuine smiles, it seemed.

24

On the River Roeselar

THE TRIP DOWNRIVER WOULD HAVE PROVED INTER-
minably boring if not for Oliver Donal. The blunt captain,
with his wind-beaten face, proved not only a courteous
host, but a talented teacher as well. At times, it seemed to
Mathew the man was carved from a block of wood. He
could be found on deck at all hours of the day and night,
his sharp eyes missing nothing. The captain solved the
problem of where to put Lara by courteously vacating his
own quarters to her and moving in with the first mate, a
man named Zachariah Ward.

The weather improved throughout the first day, sparing
Mathew the embarrassment of having to deal with his
stomach. Unfortunately, things got worse at the beginning of the second day, when the river emptied into the
Great Southern Sea, which lower Elgaria, Sennia, Cincar,
and Vargoth all bordered.

Mathew's wonder at being on a real ocean was marred
when the waters became considerably rougher, forcing
him to spend the entire day in his cabin. He emerged the
following morning pale-faced, but steadier on his feet, as
his body grew accustomed to the ship's motion. By then
he was able to keep some food down, and tentatively
sampled a hot bowl of porridge and biscuits the cook
thoughtfully sent to him.

Several of the hands, and one in particular, named
Biggs, found it amusing that anyone could be sick in such
mild conditions. Twice Mathew heard him making jokes

about it to the other men as he walked past them. He ignored the comments, but they made his ears burn.

After the second day, and each morning for the remainder of the next two weeks, Mathew rose early and left his cabin to attend "class" with Jaim and Pryor, two brothers who were training on board the *Wave Dancer*. Captain Donal instructed them on how to read a navigation chart properly. He also taught them how to use a compass and sextant. Mathew learned that even though the land was out of sight, by calculating the position of the sun in the morning, taking a "reading," as Captain Donal called it, he could determine their position with a high degree of accuracy.

The math was a considerable challenge to the two brothers, as well as the patience of Captain Donal. Mathew, on the other hand, had no difficulty with the equations, most of which he was able to do in his head. In due course he learned that the boys were apprenticed by their father for two years to learn the trade. Pryor, who was fifteen, was a year older than his brother, Jaim.

Mathew found almost everything on the ship fascinating, from the complex series of lines that ran from the yards and braces, to the design of the ship's hull. He wanted to know how and why things worked the way they did, and finding a kindred spirit in him, the captain was free with his answers. To amuse himself, Mathew often passed his time practicing with the compass and sextant. He checked and rechecked routes, plotting them on Captain Donal's considerable store of charts.

At one point Mathew tried interesting Lara in what he was doing. She kissed him on the cheek, when nobody was looking, and told him to come get her for a walk around the deck when he was through tinkering.

Once the *Wave Dancer* reached the open sea, they began a leg of their journey that was to take them nearly 1,200 miles. Under full sail and making good speed, they were certain to be out of contact with the land for at least two weeks. This was due in part to the winds and prevailing currents in that part of the world. The entire experience of being on the ocean was astonishing and wonderful to Mathew. It was an odd feeling to look out and see nothing but water all around him. He learned from Zachariah Ward that the Southern Sea was harder to navigate than other bodies of water because of its unpredictable weather.

Standing in the bow the morning of their eighth day out, Mathew had to hold onto the brass railing to keep from being pushed backward by the force of the wind. Lara came up for a while to be with him, but went below after fifteen minutes. He thought it was exhilarating. For most of the day they had been "running before the wind," as Captain Donal put it, but during the last hour the wind shifted and freshened considerably, coming from the northwest over the port quarter of the ship.

Mathew soon learned what Zachariah Ward meant when he said that the weather could be unpredictable. In the west, the very direction they were heading, the sky began to darken, forcing Ward to call the watch and shorten sail. About two miles ahead of them Mathew could see a squall line forming. He was still watching it when he became aware of someone approaching behind him.

"Ho, Mat," Collin said.

"Where've you been?" Mathew asked, wiping some spray from his face as the bow plunged into a wave.

"Below, talking to Father Thomas."

Mathew nodded.

Collin glanced over the side at the foaming water below, then back at Mathew. "I've been thinking . . . this whole business about the ring is pretty strange, isn't it?"

Mathew took a breath and nodded again.

"Tell me again what exactly happened?"

"Why? We've gone through it already."

"I know, but I was upstairs when the stable exploded. I thought . . . maybe if we go over it once more, there might be something that we missed."

"I just don't see what good it will do. I've thought the

whole thing over till I'm blue in the face. Everything about it makes me uncomfortable. It's . . . just that . . . I don't know . . ."

Mathew's voice trailed off and he looked up into the foremast rigging.

Collin didn't say anything.

After a while Mathew turned back to him. "What is it you want to know?"

"Everything you can remember—*everything*, and don't leave anything out."

Mathew took a breath and began by recounting the details about what had happened in the forest. Collin didn't interrupt or make any comments until he was through.

"What were you thinking, just before it happened?"

"I wasn't wishing for my vision to turn green, if that's what you mean," Mathew said, annoyed.

"I know that," Collin said. "Do you remember anything about what you *were* thinking?"

Mathew's eyes became unfocused for a moment. "I remember wishing that if I had that farsighter invention of Daniel's—you know, the brass tube and the glass lenses—that I might be able to see just how many Orlocks were out there. I think that's about right. I was pretty scared at the time."

Collin nodded to himself. "And what about in the stables, Mat?"

"Well . . . the Orlocks were starting to come at us, and one of them said, 'Give it to me,' or something like that. I thought he was talking about Lara. But then he pointed and said 'the ring.' It was as clear as can be."

"And . . . ?" Collin prompted.

"And I was pretty sure that we were both going to die," Mathew said, his eyes still distant. "I didn't remember to bring my sword with me. I got furious with myself for being such a dolt."

"And?"

"And and and," Mathew said irritably. "The last thing I remember just before it happened was thinking that I would see them in hell." Mathew looked into his friend's brown eyes. "Look, I was angrier than I've ever been in my life. It was mostly at myself, but then I remembered what they did to Garon and Lee, and that just added to it."

"You'd see them in hell, that's what you said?"

"I didn't say it, I thought it. I was trying to find a way out—any way. We were trapped. I thought we were going to die. Do you understand?"

"Sure," Collin said.

His expression was serious, which Mathew didn't see often in him.

"Mat, would you put the ring on for a second?"

"What? No. I think it's best if I keep it off. I'm giving it to the first member of Giles's family I can find."

"I'd like you to try something—"

"No," Mathew said emphatically. "Was this Father Thomas's idea?"

"Uh-uh. I think he feels the same way you do—just keep it off for a while and see if any other odd things happen."

"Well, that's good advice as far as I'm concerned," Mathew said. "It stays off. What'd you want to do anyway?"

Collin shrugged. "I'm not sure. I wanted to see if you could make something happen when you were completely calm. I was thinking that maybe being angry or scared out of your mind might be the key."

"And what if I made something happen like before? It would sink the ship, if not blow it up completely. I don't even know what caused the other things to happen in the first place, and I certainly don't want to try and find out in the middle of the ocean."

"Hmm . . . you may have a point, Mat Lewin." Collin grinned. "And you're not that great a swimmer."

Mathew found that he was gripping the railing so hard, his hands hurt. The whole business about the ring made him uncomfortable. Not having answers was like trying to grab smoke. With an effort, he forced himself to relax and smiled back at Collin. Over the last week, the same thought had occurred to him several times. Twice when he was alone, he had started to slip the ring back on his finger. But each time he had resisted the temptation and placed it back on the leather cord again.

Mathew was spared any further thoughts on the subject when another wave broke over the bow, spraying them with water. Now only a mile away, it appeared the approaching squall line had expanded in either direction, obscuring the horizon. Mathew knew the hazy areas ahead of them were probably sheets of rain; there wasn't much possibility of going around them.

For the second time that morning, Zachariah Ward was forced to call out the watch to shorten sail.

"Will you look at that?" Collin said, pointing.

Mathew looked and saw one of the strangest sights he had ever seen. Just off the port bow, a huge funnel of water had lifted itself out of the sea and was twisting and spinning over the churning ocean.

"Waterspout," Zachariah Ward said from behind them.

They turned to look at him and then back at the phenomenon gliding across the ocean. The tail of the waterspout appeared to move and dance as the whole thing changed shape, from wide and symmetrical to elongated and lopsided.

The first mate watched it pass astern of the *Wave Dancer* and gave a curt nod, satisfied it would present no immediate danger to the ship. Mathew was about to ask him how such things happened when Collin suddenly said "Hey!" and took a step forward, holding the back of his head.

All three of them looked down to see a gray fish, slightly less than a foot long, flopping around the deck at their feet. A second later another fish landed on the deck, followed by another.

"What in the world?" Collin exclaimed, still feeling the back of his head. "I thought someone hit me."

When they looked around, they discovered that the deck was littered with fish, flopping everywhere. Before anyone could speak, Mathew saw Captain Donal coming forward. He had a dark, menacing look on his face.

"What is the meaning of this?" he demanded.

"I don't know," Collin said. "I was just standing here—and this fish hit me in the head."

"*What?* Are you trying to tell me these fish just fell out the sky, sir?"

"But it's true," Mathew stammered.

"*True!* You both have the effrontery to give me the lie on my own quarterdeck?" Captain Donal's face was red and he was shaking with rage.

"We're not lying," Collin said. "It happened just like that. I swear."

Several crew members, hearing the raised voices, stopped what they were doing to stare. A few started to draw closer, and soon a small crowd had gathered. Mathew looked around and started to worry.

"A fish just hit you in the head, you say?" Captain Donal said, his voice dripping with sarcasm.

"Well . . . yes," Collin said, noticing the men around him for the first time.

"Hit him in the head. Do you hear that, Mr. Ward?" Captain Donal sneered.

"I do," the first mate answered. His face was now even more serious, if such a thing were possible.

"Well, I don't see any wings on this fish, do you?"

"N-No," Collin answered, "but it happened that way, I'm telling you."

The captain looked at Mathew, who nodded in agreement, not knowing what else to say. He noticed one of the men had a belaying pin in his hand, and another was holding a grappling hook. None of them looked happy. The captain's face was so red he looked as if he were going to explode.

"Again you give me the lie. This will go hard on you, sir. Fish everywhere on my ship—all over my nice clean deck! Did any of you men ever hear such nonsense? Boyish pranks, I call it."

There was a general murmur of agreement from among the crew, and they began to move toward them in a menacing manner.

Collin said, "Look, Captain, I swear—"

"Silence," roared the captain. "Mr. Ward, what do you think we should do with these two?"

"Hmm," the first mate replied, rubbing a whiskered chin and looking them up and down.

"Keel-haul 'em," someone in the crowd called out.

"I say over the side with them," another man growled. Mathew recognized him as Wimby, a master's mate.

Mathew could not believe what was happening. The world had just gone crazy. Fish were flopping everywhere, seeming to have fallen out of the sky; the captain was raving at them like a madman; and the crew looked as if they were ready to hang them for what happened. Then out of the corner of his eye he noticed that Captain Donal was shaking. With a start he realized that the man was quivering with laughter as he wiped tears from his eyes. A second later the entire crew burst out laughing. Even the grim-faced Mr. Ward was laughing so helplessly, he could barely stand.

Mathew's eyes found Collin's. They had stumbled into an asylum of lunatics.

"You should see your faces," Wimby said, pointing.

Indeed, Mathew's and Collin's faces had turned a bright shade of red, even in the darkened conditions around them.

"It's the meridian," Captain Donal explained. Still chuckling, he bent down, picked up a silver-colored fish, and tossed it over the side.

A few crew members slapped the boys on their backs and returned to their duties while the crowd began to disperse.

"Tradition has it that when a virgin crosses the meridian for the first time, his mettle must be tested," Zachariah Ward added.

"Virgin?" Collin asked.

"First time at sea," Zachariah Ward said, clapping him on the shoulder. "Welcome to the Great Southern Sea."

Collin staggered forward a step and said, "Thank you . . . I think."

"But the fish . . ." Mathew said.

Most of them were gone from the deck now, with the crew tossing them back over the sides as they left.

"The waterspout," Captain Donal explained. "Picks 'em clean out of the water. I actually saw one drop a small shark on a deck once. I almost swallowed my teeth the first time it happened to me. Spouts are common enough at the meridian, especially at this time of the year. Be glad we're not at the equator. The initiation there would have been much more . . . interesting."

Mathew didn't want to know about what happened at the equator. But a thought occurred to him. Before he could ask, Captain Donal, who was brushing a tear from the corner of his eye with a thick finger, appeared to read his mind.

"Don't worry about your lady friend. The tradition only applies to men."

"Oh," Mathew said. "That's good."

He could just imagine how Lara would have reacted. She would have probably started throwing fish at the crew, he thought. But the picture did make him smile.

"You gentlemen might consider repairing to your quarters," the captain said. "I imagine we're in for a blow.

He was looking over the port quarter at the squall line coming at them. The sky had continued to grow more threatening, and seas were running at eight feet or better. Rain was already beginning to fall with some force, angled by the wind. Another wave crashed over the bow, soaking everyone, as the *Wave Dancer* plowed into the storm. A part of Mathew's mind marveled at the power of the sea, and another part marveled that his stomach had gotten used to the pitch and roll of a ship.

"Mr. Ward!" The captain had to shout to make himself heard above the wind. "Top gallants only, if you please."

"Aye aye, sir," came the first mate's reply. "Hands to the rigging!" he bellowed. "Take in all sail! Top gallants, only! Let's look lively, lads!"

Mathew could hear the order being repeated below. In seconds the remainder of the watch came pouring up onto the deck and began scampering barefooted up the rigging. It wasn't long before the sails magically began to disappear. With Collin ahead of him, they made their way amidships, using the railing to keep themselves balanced.

In less than a minute the storm was fully on them as the *Wave Dancer* clawed her way forward. The wind had backed again and was coming even more strongly from the west. To the starboard, Mathew saw Captain Donal and Zachariah Ward hunched over against the elements, fighting their way back to the wheel, where Brown, the ship's master, struggled to keep the *Wave Dancer* on course.

"Put the helm over, and bring her into the wind!" the captain shouted.

The deck was already awash from the waves breaking over it.

Just as he was about to follow Collin down the ladder, a faint sound attracted his attention. With all the noise from the wind and the water crashing over the side, he couldn't be certain, but it sounded like a scream. Mathew looked down into the companionway and saw nothing. A quick glance around the deck revealed nothing. The crew were coming down the rigging, having finished securing the braces.

There it was again!

Mathew looked up this time. Shielding his eyes from the blowing rain, he saw a man dangling by his foot at the top yard of the mainmast. Without stopping to think, he jumped to the rigging and began to climb. The ship was rolling so badly, he nearly lost his footing in the first ten feet and he had to hold on to the shroud until the *Wave Dancer* righted herself. Once past the main yardarm, Mathew paused for a second to catch his breath, wiping the water from his eyes. Whoever was up there was unable to free themselves. The man was being thrown back and forth helplessly. Mathew felt the ship rise up the crest of a huge wave, the bow lifting out of the water, only to be followed by a sickening plunge as the *Dancer* dove down the trough.

Fighting down his fear of heights, Mathew began climbing again. The deck was now far below him, pitching madly. Angry whitecapped waves continued to buffet the side of the hull. From the stern, he saw someone point up at him, Zacharias Ward, he thought. He passed the second yard, not bothering to rest this time, and holding on the slick rope as tightly as he could. The deck was a dizzying distance beneath him. Above, on the topgallant yard, the man swung back and forth, the sail booming around him. Twice Mathew's boots slipped and almost caused him to lose his foothold on the sodden ropes. He decided there was no other choice but to go barefoot, as he had seen the men do. Wrapping his arm around a nearby brace for support, he carefully pulled off his boots and dropped them.

Good, he thought, *at least I'll have an excuse to get another pair when we get to Tyraine, if I live that long.* All it would take was one slip to plunge him to his death. The wind and the rain were making the going more difficult and his shoulders were beginning to ache.

Up. Need to go up. Keep moving, he told himself.

Mathew didn't know how long it took him to get to the topgallant yard. Surprisingly, without his boots he found that his feet were more secure on the ropes. From below him, he could see that two more men had started to follow him up, but there was no time to wait for them. The man had stopped moving above him. His arms were hanging limply down from his shoulders, and his head lolled back and forth with the ship's movement. For a moment Mathew thought he was already dead, but when he wiped the rain from his face again, he was sure he could see the man's eyes focus on him. He climbed the remaining fifteen feet to the yardarm and moved out onto it, slowly and cautiously, the force of the wind again nearly breaking his handhold. He secured a purchase on the footrope and began to slide his way out to the helpless sailor, who was still being thrown around like some broken rag doll.

Halfway there, he thought.

Another seaman arrived and started to move out toward him. He was followed by a man Mathew recognized as Biggs, who had made fun of his seasickness on their first day out. When he got nearer, he recognized the helpless sailor, a fellow named Vickers. The footrope had somehow gotten twisted around his ankle, holding him fast. The skin was rubbed raw, covered in blood. A third man appeared on the yard and was trying to make his way out to them.

Mathew realized that whatever he was going to do, he would have to do it alone, because no one could get past him on the yard and there was no time to go back. He could see the rope around the man's ankle was so twisted, there would be no choice but to cut it. The problem was what to do after that. As numb as his fingers were, he doubted if he had the strength to support Vickers once the rope was cut.

He was still considering his alternatives when he heard Biggs yell from the shrouds, "Hang on, she's leaning to."

Mathew watched in horror as a wave of considerable size crashed into the starboard side of the ship, sending a shudder up the mast and out onto the yard where he clung.

Level with the horizon only seconds before, he suddenly found himself looking down into the boiling sea as the yard tilted vertically upward. Mathew fought with all his strength to hang on. The *Wave Dancer* rolled to its side and continued to roll. For an interminable moment it looked like the water was rushing up to meet him, then slowly the ship began to right itself. He felt himself moving in the opposite direction. It was a sickening feeling.

The first man, an assistant sail maker named Chalmers, moved closer to him. For reasons Mathew couldn't begin to understand, he was grinning. Through the wind and the spray, Chalmers looked like some sodden ghostly apparition with a knife between his yellowed teeth.

"I'm going to try and cut him loose!" Mathew yelled.

"Is there any way you can get past me to get a hold on his belt when I do it?"

The man looked down at Vickers, who was hanging below them and shook his head.

Mathew muttered a curse to himself. He needed to find a solution quickly. Biggs had now joined them on the yard and both men were watching him. Then he saw it— far above, at the pinnacle of the mast, a block and tackle. It contained a halyard that ran down to the sail itself. The other end was secured to the mainmast at the deck.

"Biggs," he yelled, "I want you to cut the rope to that tackle above us. We're going to tie it to him and lower him down. They'll need to give us the slack from below and then brace for it."

Biggs looked up at the tackle, nodded, and began to slide back to the mast. Using hand signals since the noise level was too great to be heard, he communicated what Mathew wanted to the third man, who relayed it to those below. In a minute Biggs gathered the freed rope and was carrying it back out to him. Mathew was only ten feet from Vickers, and he resumed inching toward the man. Vickers looked up, seemed to recognize him, and understood why he was there. He made a weak, flailing gesture with one of his hands. Inch by painful inch, Mathew drew nearer, until the man was almost in reach.

Just a little more, he thought.

In order to reach Vickers, Mathew knew that he would somehow have to brace himself on the yardarm and then get low enough to tie the rope around the man's belt. For some reason, the memory of hanging from his knees on Rune Berryman's apple tree came back to him. So did the image of falling out of that same tree and breaking his arm.

It'll be more than my arm if I fall now, he thought.

Mathew took a deep breath, gritted his teeth, and hooked a leg over the yardarm. Very carefully, he threaded his other leg through the space between the sail and the yard and let go. The deck and water rushed up at

him as he swung backward upside down, held only by
the strength of his legs. He shut his eyes for a moment.
When he opened them, the world was still upside down.
By extending himself fully he was just able to reach
Vickers's waist and tie the rope Biggs had passed him
through the man's belt. All the time he felt Vickers's eyes
on him, as well as those of the other men who were clinging to the yard.

"Listen to me!" he shouted. "I'm going to cut the rope
around your ankle. Biggs and two other men are up here.
They've got the rope braced. We're going to lower you
down. Do you understand?"

Through his pain, Vickers managed to give him a faint
smile and a weak nod.

"All right, on three now," Mathew called out. "One,
two—"

"Hold fast," Biggs yelled, "we're heeling over again."

Mathew immediately swung himself upright and
braced. Just as before, the ship lurched when another
wave slammed into its side and started to roll once more.
He had just succeeded in pulling his leg free when an unexpected gust of wind, far stronger than any of the previous ones, caused the sail to suddenly backfill, breaking
his grip. Unable to hold on any longer, Mathew thrust
himself, all arms and legs, away from the yardarm toward
one of the stay lines. The deck hurtled up to meet him. At
the last possible moment he succeeded in grabbing hold
of the line, or else he surely would have plummeted to his
death. He clung there for a moment while he collected
himself and regained his breath. He wiped the sweat
from his eyes and then slowly, painfully, pulled himself
back up hand over hand. Biggs reached out to help him
the last few feet. Fortunately, the roll wasn't as bad or
prolonged as it was before. In a moment the ship began to
right herself.

It took him a while to get back into position. Fatigue
was beginning to set in, but he shut it out of his mind. After a glance to see that everyone was still with him, he

called out again. "On three. Ready? One . . . two . . .
three."

Working rapidly, he pulled the dagger from his belt
and sawed through the rope. The last strand separated
with a snap and Vickers, now freed, swung out crazily,
suspended by the line above him. Chalmers and Biggs
grabbed for him and stopped him just before he would
have collided with the mainmast. At a sign from Biggs,
those on deck cautiously began to lower the man. War-
renton, the third sailor on the yardarm, made the descent
with Vickers to help guide him along. Once they were under way, the others swung out to the main brace, and to
Mathew's chagrin, slid efficiently down to the deck. He
was relegated to climbing awkwardly back down the
shroud.

By the time he reached the deck, a small crowd had
gathered. He was so tired and weak he could barely
stand. Oliver Donal and Zachariah Ward were there along
with Biggs, Chalmers, and a few others. So was everyone
else from his party. Several of the crew removed their
hats and knuckled their foreheads to him. Captain Donal
threw two massive arms around him in a hug, nearly
crushing the wind out of his lungs.

"'Pon my soul, if you don't have the makings of a seafaring man in you!"

Someone in the crowd raised a cheer, and the others
immediately picked it up. He was too exhausted and
numb to care at the moment, but he managed a smile.

"Vickers?" he asked, wanting to deflect the attention
from himself.

"Below, with the surgeon's mate, where you should
be," Zachariah Ward replied, pumping his hand, a look of
admiration in his eyes.

Mathew nodded and started toward the companionway.
He had only gotten a few steps when a grizzled-looking
sailor named Kessington came forward, saluted, and said,
"If you please, sir, you'll be needing these. I recovered
your boots for you before they was washed over the side.

A little wax and polish and they'll be good as new. Don't you worry none."

Wonderful, he thought. "Thank you, I'm very grateful."

The man's weathered face split into a grin. Mathew felt tired enough to go to sleep right there on the deck, but instead he squared his shoulders and walked stiffly to the stairs leading below.

Father Thomas put a hand on his shoulder and smiled at him as he went by. Collin was waiting there as well.

"Can't let you out of my sight for a minute. Obviously you have a death wish, or you're so desperate to get rid of those boots you're likely to try anything."

Mathew smiled, but was unable to think of anything intelligent to say. He just waved and descended the ladder. He felt a little silly, soaked to the bone, dripping wet, and carrying his boots under one arm.

Lara was waiting at the bottom.

As soon as his feet stepped off the last rung, she was in his arms, her face buried in his chest. Then she started kissing him, his face, his forehead, his eyes, and finally his lips.

"I was so worried about you," she whispered in his ear. "When the ship started to roll over, I thought . . . I thought . . ."

"Shh," he said. "I'm fine. Nobody got hurt."

"And then you started to fall." She was crying. "I saw you grab onto the rope and climb back out onto the beam," she said between sobs, "And I know how much you don't like heights, and—"

"Yard. It's called a yard," he corrected gently.

There was a pause.

"What were you thinking?" she said, pounding her fist into his chest.

"I wasn't thinking of anything," he said, rubbing the spot where she'd hit him. "I couldn't have just left him there, could I?"

Lara looked at him, then sniffed, and wiped a tear from the corner of her eye.

Mathew put his arm around her shoulders and they

walked slowly to his cabin. Now that the excitement was over, his energy seemed to be draining out of his body. What he wanted was to lie down and close his eyes for a few minutes. After that, he'd go see how Vickers was doing. The ship continued to roll with the waves, and they gave the appearance of two people who had had too much to drink, swaying from one side of the corridor to the other as they walked.

When they got to his cabin, they hugged again. Mathew mumbled something in her ear amounting to a suggestion that she come in with him.

Her response was to open the door and gently push him forward. But she didn't follow.

"Aren't you coming in?" he asked. His tongue felt thick.

"In your present damp and depleted condition, I doubt you'd survive it."

He was certain there were several good arguments to counter that, but he was too weary to think of them. So he was relegated to raising his eyebrows and adopting a wounded expression.

Lara giggled. "And looking like a lost puppy won't do you any good either."

She stepped back just in time to avoid his grab at her waist.

"But what if I fall out of bed and hurt myself in my weakened condition?" he asked.

She drew a long breath. "Truly pathetic," she said, shaking her head.

A second later he found himself looking at a closed door and listening to the sound of her feet echoing down the wooden planks of the corridor.

25

Great Southern Sea, 300 Miles Out

HE DIDN'T KNOW EXACTLY HOW LONG HE'D BEEN asleep, but from the angle of the sun coming through the little window in his cabin and its reddish glow, he guessed that it was late in the day. The ship's motion quickly told him that they were no longer fighting the storm.

On the little stool beside his bed he found a pair of dark blue breeches, a clean white shirt, hose and a pair of shoes, along with a note from Brenner, the captain's steward.

Mr. Lewin:

Captain Donal's compliments, sir. We had to guess at the sizes, but I think these will do until your clothes are properly dried out. I'm mending the shirt that was torn and will return it to you this evening. The captain requests you join him for dinner in Miss Lara's cabin at four bells of the evening watch.

Brenner

Mathew swung his feet out of bed, dressed, and stepped into the corridor. The lamps weren't lit yet. That wasn't done until the evening watch, so there was still plenty of time before afternoon watch ended. During the

second day on board, he learned the ship's bell was rung
for each half hour of the watch.

Mathew's memory had always been a good one, and he
recalled that the sickbay was located on a half-deck at the
stern of the ship below *"Miss Lara's cabin."* The layout
of the ship had never presented any difficulty for him. For
some reason, however, Collin had trouble finding where
things were, much to his annoyance—and Mathew's
amusement.

Because of his height, Mathew had to stoop as he
walked along the corridor. His own cabin was amidships,
so it took him only a minute to make his way back to the
stern. Bales of cargo, all securely lashed down, lined the
passageway and cargo holds. Not a spare inch was
wasted on a seagoing vessel. There was no door to the
tiny area they used as a sickbay, just a curtain hung from
an archway, separating it from the cargo holds.

Vickers was on a cot lying on his back, his left foot
heavily bandaged. When he saw Mathew, he started to rise.

"None of that, now," Mathew said, stopping him. "I just
came to see how you were doing. Stay where you are."

"Aye aye, Mr. Lewin," he said, propping himself up on
his elbows. "I'm doing just fine, sir, thanks to you."

"And how's the leg?" Mathew asked.

"Nothing broke, so Weldon says. Just need to stay off
it for a few days. It's probably sprained some."

Weldon, Mathew remembered, was the surgeon's
mate, which was all they had on a ship the size of the
Wave Dancer. He also recalled the bloody mess the rope
made of the man's ankle. It would take quite a bit more
than a few days to mend, but he had learned these sailors
were a tough, stoic lot. Shipboard injuries were a fact of
life, and they all seemed to accept them in stride.

Vickers told him he was from Stermark, in Queen's
Province. It came as a surprise for Mathew to learn the
man was married and had two small children at home.
Like so many others, Vickers had heard the news of
Duren's attack and was worried about his family.

"As soon as we finish unloading our cargo in Tyraine and the captain pays off, I'm headed back north to get them out of there," he said. "The fellow that told me the news also said people had seen Orlocks taking part in the fight. I don't know as I believe that. You know how people get when stories get told and retold."

Mathew felt the muscles in his neck tighten. For the last few days he had tried his best to forget about their dead, cruel faces—without success. He even dreamed about them. Battling the elements, he decided, was infinitely preferable to looking into those hate-filled eyes. Vickers's words brought it all back again.

"You may well believe it," he said, looking toward the corner of the cabin at a small black rat that poked its head out from behind a box. The rat twitched its nose speculatively, testing the air. Mathew reached for a bandage roll and threw it. The rat eyed him for a second, then turned in a leisurely manner and disappeared behind the crate again.

"They comes with the ship," Vickers observed philosophically.

Mathew returned his attention to Vickers, who leaned back on his elbows.

"About the Orlocks, sir, do you believe it's true? I mean, I always thought they were just so much stories, you know."

"I'm afraid it's true, Vickers. They attacked Ashford— that's the town where I live," Mathew said.

The lie came no more easily to him than it did before. He was aware that Father Thomas had told Captain Donal the truth about where they were really from along with the reason for their journey. According to Ceta Woodall, he was completely trustworthy. She had also pointed out that he had a right to know the truth before putting himself in harm's way. For safety's sake, however, it was agreed that they would use the fictitious story with the crew.

Mathew went on, "They killed a farmer and his son and others."

Vickers shook his head and made a sign against evil with his hand. They talked for the next half hour. Vickers thanked him for saving his life and promised to do the same if the situations were ever reversed. Neither felt comfortable discussing what had happened, and each tacitly concluded the less said, the better.

Afterward, on his way up to the main deck, Mathew passed several crew members who doffed their hats to him. One of them, a tough-looking old sailor named Griffin, knuckled his forehead and said, "Good on ye for what ye done, Mr. Lewin. Good on ye."

Mathew returned an embarrassed smile and climbed the companion ladder, emerging on deck just aft of the mainmast. He wandered over to the starboard rail. Two sailors who were mending rope discreetly moved to the other side of the ship to give him privacy. He was aware of all that—aware that they were treating him differently than they had before. It made him slightly uncomfortable. As far as he was concerned, he simply did what was needed at the moment.

It was hard to believe that only a short while ago the ship he was now standing on so easily was flying up and down waves larger than most buildings he'd seen. The water was relatively calm at the moment, broken only by occasional rolls and swells.

No matter how hard he tried to think of other things, his mind kept returning to the conversation he and Collin were having before the storm hit. He was conscious of the ring hanging around his neck, and being honest, he had to admit he was frightened of it. For the better part of the week little else had occupied his thoughts, and he had refused to put it on again. Absently, Mathew touched the wound in his side. It throbbed, but not unduly so.

In his spare hours he had pored over the two books on the human brain Dr. Wycroft was kind enough to let him borrow before they sailed. He learned that the brain was possibly the least understood organ in the human body. It was so complex, with so many interconnecting structures; he doubted that a lifetime of study would make things much clearer. After hours of reading, he began to form a theory that a connection existed between the ring and the thoughts his mind produced. At the same time he knew it couldn't be every thought. That was the problem. Why some and not others? He'd worn the ring for quite a while and certainly had the chance to think about lots of things. None of them just materialized. A split second before the explosion in the stable, he was wishing for something to blast the Orlocks from the face of the earth. He recalled as much during his conversation with Collin. And that was exactly what happened. Just before the Orlocks attacked them in the forest, he wanted desperately to see how many were out there. Same result.

The sun, now a yellow disk, sank lower on the horizon, bathing the water with a warm light and creating myriad sparkles that appeared to move with a life of their own. It was beautiful, he thought.

Slowly, gradually, his hand moved to the ring, still suspended around his neck by the leather cord. The familiar chill went through his arm as soon as his hand closed around it. But this time there was something different. Directly in front of him, floating in the air over the starboard quarter, was a small patch of fog. He was certain it wasn't there a moment ago. The early evening sky was clear, apart from a few clouds. He spared a glance at the opposite side of the deck. Both of the sailors had finished their tasks and were walking aft. He turned back to the fog. After a moment, he decided that it wasn't fog at all, more a blurring of the air. There was nothing to either the right or left of the phenomena. It was more like trying to look through a gossamer curtain covering a doorway, he decided. But the doorway seemed to have no distinct boundaries. It kept moving and changing shape.

Curious, he watched it closely, grateful that no one else was around. He had no feelings of nervousness or stress now—only curiosity.

The fog, or whatever it was, was brighter in the center and had light radiating out softly from its sides. Mathew thought he could make out images on the inside, but they were indistinct and hazy. He concentrated harder. Without warning, it moved closer to him, or he closer to it, he wasn't certain which. The images in the center began to clear, coalescing into recognizable shapes. There were trees and a path with shrubbery running into a small glade. The clarity astonished him, and he could almost feel the rough texture of the pebbles beneath his boots.

Cautiously, he peered around the glade and realized he could detect no sounds at all—from anything. Part of his mind acknowledged the sound of waves slapping against the side of the ship as it moved through the water, and the wind humming in the rigging, but these things were separate and apart. The light was almost gone then, except toward the horizon, where streaks of red and crimson contrasted with the ever-deepening blue sky. From the shadows in the vision he could tell it was sometime in the late morning or perhaps the early afternoon, yet on board the *Wave Dancer* it was nearly dusk.

Three people, a man and two women, now quite distinct, sat at a small table covered with a gold cloth by the side of the path. They were talking with each other. Mathew could see their lips moving. On the table was a bottle of red wine and three glasses. He was there, but not there.

One of the women was quite beautiful. He couldn't quite see the face of the other one, but she appeared to have the same black hair as the first, which fell loosely to her shoulders. From the clothes they wore, Mathew thought they might be some type of royalty. When he was twelve, Lord Kraelin and Lady Ardith had visited Devondale, and the fineness of their garments were still vivid to him. The first woman was dressed in a gown of white with long sleeves that came to a point at her wrist. The other woman was in silver. The man was clad completely in black—his boots, shirt, and cloak. Mathew could only see him from the side, but his features were sharp and he had an aquiline nose. Just behind them, water ran noiselessly over rocks down a small hill into a pond, making no sound at all. His left hand gripped the ship's rail tightly while he continued to watch, trying to make sense of what he was seeing.

And then the man slowly turned.

In the process of lifting his glass of wine, the man appeared to freeze. Slowly, his head swiveled around in Mathew's direction and a pair of hooded eyes looked directly up at him. A second later the woman on his left also turned. The one with her back to him never did. Although he saw her shoulders stiffen, she kept looking straight ahead. The hint of a smile played at the corners of the man's mouth. It was cold and mirthless. The woman's face was utterly devoid of any expression, though she was clearly aware of Mathew's presence, if it could be called that. There was little doubt in Mathew's mind they were looking at him. Their scrutiny unnerved him so much he took a step backward, letting go of the ring around his neck in the process.

Instantly the image was gone as if it had never existed. Only the rise and fall of the sea and the lowering clouds bathed in the last light of day remained.

Mathew stood there on the foredeck and considered whether he was losing his mind. He recalled a visit to Gravenhage with his father when he was much younger, when he saw a man wandering erratically down the street. The man was talking to himself and to other people who weren't there. Sometimes he shouted, but most times he just rambled on incoherently. Seeing him approach, his father gently moved him to his other side, shielding him. Mathew recalled being scared when the man crossed the street and came toward them. None of what he said made any sense. He was unshaven and badly needed a bath, and his hair was as unkempt as his clothes. At first he looked confused, then angry, and then he started to cry, before moving on. Bran watched him go, keeping his arm protectively around Mathew's shoulders, and shook his head sadly. When they rode home together, he asked his father about what happened. Bran told him that sickness sometimes affected the mind as well as the body.

The images of his father were so clear they were painful. He remembered the night by the river when Father Thomas had told him the pain would lessen over time, and he wished with all his heart it would be so. And soon.

In the end he made the only decision he could. Mathew smiled to himself and looked out over the water, resting his elbows on the rail. It was possible that he was crazy, but he didn't think so. People in Devondale, plain spoken and stubbornly practical, were made of sterner stuff. Eventually, Collin's suggestion about doing an experiment drifted back into his mind again.

Answers were what he needed, and answers were what he was going to get.

26

Great Southern Sea

CAPTAIN DONAL'S CABIN WAS A GOOD DEAL LARGER than his own. It actually consisted of two separate rooms and was comfortably decorated. The large stern windows created a light and open atmosphere through which the ocean could be seen foaming in the ship's wake. Overall, they added to a feeling of spaciousness at odds with the cramped life Mathew had come to expect on board the *Wave Dancer*.

In the first room, a plain oak desk and two side chairs were placed against the ship's starboard side. Behind the desk was a dark mahogany bookcase, about five feet high, filled with the books and memorabilia that Oliver Donal had collected over thirty years at sea. Several thick rugs were scattered about each of the rooms of the great cabin, as it was called. The sleeping quarters, now occupied by Lara Palmer, contained a bed of good size, like the captain himself, and a headboard with a small carving of a ship in the middle. Two storage trunks were placed at the foot of the bed. Above the bed was a painting of a lovely dark-haired woman and a pretty young girl, standing on either side of Oliver Donal. Mathew later learned they were his wife and daughter. After some consideration, he decided the artist had done a good job capturing the captain's features. In the second cabin, a dining table and six chairs were arranged for Oliver Donal's dinner.

When he and Collin arrived shortly after six bells, they saw Father Thomas and Lara standing by the stern windows talking to their host. The rain had long since stopped and the windows were opened to allow in the first warm breezes that promised spring. Lara was wearing his favorite gray dress, and she had added a thin gold chain that circled her waist. It reminded him of the one Ceta wore.

Captain Donal's bearded face creased into a broad smile when they entered. He excused himself and crossed the room to shake their hands. Mathew noticed his beard was scented.

"Gentlemen, be welcome. Mistress Palmer has graciously consented to allow the use of her cabin for dinner this evening," he said, with only a touch of sarcasm. "I trust you are suffering no ill effects."

"No sir," Mathew replied.

"Good lad," he said, placing a hand on Mathew's shoulder. "You must really learn to take some instruction in flying before you start leaping about my rigging again."

He turned to Collin, "And you, no more attacks by flying fish?"

Collin grinned and shook his head. "It really looked like that's what happened—to me anyway. I was just standing there talking to Mat, and wham, a fish hits me in the head."

"You probably deserved it," Lara said, coming over to them.

Captain Donal began chuckling to himself all over again. There was a brief single knock at the door, followed by Zachariah Ward, who entered the cabin after the captain called out, "Come."

"Ah, Mr. Ward, there you are. I take it you have met everyone here already?"

"I have," he said, typical of the spare manner of his speech. "Your servant, ma'am," he added, making a small bow to Lara.

"Excellent. It seems that we are all accounted for. If you will all take your seats. Mistress Palmer, if you'll allow me," he said, holding out a chair for her.

Lara inclined her head graciously and allowed herself

to be seated. She gave Mathew a smug look when he
found himself seated between Father Thomas and Collin,
a bit to his disgruntlement. A few minutes later Brenner
began serving the food. The sun was practically gone
from the horizon and evening stars were beginning to appear. From somewhere, Brenner produced two long wax
candles in silver holders and placed them on both ends of
the table before withdrawing again.

"A gift from my wife on our last voyage out," Captain
Donal said, noting Collin's interest.

"They're very nice," said Collin. "I have a friend who
is a silversmith in our village. I'll bet he'd like them."

The two candlesticks were the only things that didn't
seem to fit with the furnishings in the rest of the cabin.
Both were ornately carved, and it was obvious that a
great deal of work was involved in producing them.

"They're from Ritiba, or so my wife says. She refused,
however, to divulge how she came by them. I secretly
suspect there's a story there somewhere."

"If you've ever met the captain's wife, you'd know
there's a story there," Zachariah Ward observed dryly.

"You see?" Oliver Donal said, looking around the
table. "That's the problem with marrying a homely
woman—they have nothing better to do with their time
than to corrupt my crew and subvert discipline."

Mathew cast a quick glance at the portrait in the second cabin. Whatever words might be used to describe the
woman whose visage hung there, "homely" was definitely not one of them.

When he looked back, he noticed that the captain and
first mate were laughing quietly to themselves. A private
joke, he guessed.

"I think you men are terrible," Lara said. "What would
your poor wife say if she heard such talk?"

The captain turned and smiled at her. "Your pardon,
Mistress Palmer. We generally do not have the pleasure
of ladies on board a working ship. If the truth be known,
you're about the age of my own daughter, who I suspect
would defend her mother's honor with equal vigor."

Collin leaned over and whispered in Mathew's ear, "See, I told you they all belong to a club. Say something about one of them, and every woman for a thousand miles seems to know."

Mathew did his best to suppress a smile, but not before catching a raised eyebrow from Lara. Fortunately, Brenner chose that moment to bring out the soup, which smelled wonderful. Mathew watched the steam gently rising from the bowls in anticipation.

Looks can sometimes be deceiving. Despite its appetizing aroma, the broth was tasteless, little more than warm water. Watching Captain Donal and Zachariah Ward make liberal use of the salt shaker, Mathew decided to follow their lead. It was easy to see that Collin shared his opinion.

Zachariah Ward observed their reactions and said under his breath, "God made the food, but the devil made the cook."

For some reason, Lara and Father Thomas didn't seem to mind the tasteless concoction. Neither did the captain, so not wishing to offend his host, Mathew decided to make the best of it.

"What are you plans after we get to Tyraine, Captain?" Father Thomas asked.

"Well, I'm carrying a fair number of crates of finished cloth and leather that should bring a good price in the market there—particularly with talk of a war going on. If I can locate enough Nyngary wine, I'll trade some of the silver I have and make a run over to the Coribar Islands. I can pick up a barrel of wine for six gold elgars and sell them for eleven. The islanders have always been more than willing buyers, especially for the green vintage, since their priests started sticking their noses into local politics."

"Really?" Father Thomas asked. "What do the Coribar clergy care about people drinking wine?"

"Nothing," Captain Donal said sourly, scratching his beard with two thick fingers. "It's all just an excuse to gain influence, in my opinion. Wine was as convenient as anything else. They succeeded in getting the governor to impose a tax on all the local wine producers, which nearly put them out of business. So now they import more than they produce. There's no tax on imports, at least not yet. It's turning a lot of farmers into merchants."

Alongside Captain Donal, Zachariah Ward nodded in agreement.

"Interesting," Father Thomas mused. "The Church of Coribar has always had its own agenda and it's not always obvious. They tend to take a long view of things."

"You seem to know a lot about their priests, Master Thomas. Have you been to the islands before?" Zachariah Ward asked.

"Oh, I visited there many years ago, just before the start of the Sibuyan War," Father Thomas replied mildly, taking a sip of his soup. "This soup is quite good, by the way."

The first mate frowned and looked down at his bowl.

"Well, I'm glad you're enjoying it," Captain Donal said. "I've been after the cook to put more salt and seasoning in it for years, but he seems to be reluctant to do so."

With a quick glance over his shoulder at the door, the captain leaned forward and lowered his voice.

"I suspect that my wife may be at the bottom of this. She's not a great one for salt. Says it makes her puff up like a blowfish and it's bad for the heart. If I want to get any taste out of what she feeds me when I'm home, I have to sneak in my own salt when she's not paying attention."

Before Father Thomas could think of a suitable reply, Zachariah Ward spoke up. "What were you doing on Coribar, if I may ask?"

"You may," Father Thomas replied. "Twenty years ago, the relations between Coribar and Elgaria were somewhat more distant than they are today, largely because of the dispute surrounding which of the countries had the right to govern Senecal."

"I remember that," Captain Donal said. "Malach claimed the peninsula was an Elgarian possession, and Calvino claimed it for Coribar. They nearly started a war over it."

"True," Father Thomas agreed, taking a sip of pale yellow Nyngary wine. "For as long as anyone could remember—more than five hundred years, if memory serves—no one gave much thought to the Senecal peninsula at all. Then one day a farmer digging in his field struck an odd metal object. After a good deal more digging, the object was unearthed. It turned out to be a machine of the Ancients, and suddenly everyone was interested in Senecal.

"The priests of Coribar promptly reoccupied a temple that had been abandoned for years, decreeing, somewhat conveniently, their study of the sacred writings revealed that the peninsula was originally the home of their god, Alidar. Apparently he resided there in the distant past—when he was still mortal.

"The people of Senecal, supremely unimpressed with those who lived there in the past, showed even less interest in embracing Coribar's god than their ancestors had. They appealed to King Malach for help. Never one to miss an opportunity, Malach promptly sent a regiment there on the pretext that an old treaty actually made it a protectorate of Elgaria. I point out that neither side made any mention of the discovery or its considerable monetary value."

"What type of machine did they find?" Mathew asked.

"It was a type of vehicle—a coach, if you will," Father Thomas said.

"A coach?" Zachariah Ward asked. "All that fuss over a coach?"

Father Thomas took another sip of his wine, shook his head, and put his glass down.

"This coach was like nothing seen ever before or since. It rode on four soft black wheels of the most unusual material. The body was long, perhaps twenty-five feet in length, and came no higher than my chest." He indicated the height with his hand.

"From what I could tell, it was made of a silverlike metal. It wasn't silver, of course, but it seemed to have threads spun into the very heart of it. No blade of ours was able to scratch the surface. There were two doors on either side that opened straight up rather than out, the way our doors would do. And on the inside of the coach—I use this for lack of a better word—were four seats, and a wheel to steer it. Very much like the wheel of this ship, actually."

"You saw this yourself?" Zachariah Ward asked, his eyes widening.

Father Thomas nodded. "It had glass all around it so that anyone sitting inside could look out. Again, it wasn't glass like the same kind our windows are made of. It was something different and much stronger. The seats were oddly shaped too, curved and deeply cushioned."

Father Thomas's face became more animated than Mathew could remember in quite some time. The images the priest was painting fascinated him, and he leaned closer, listening intently along with everyone else at the table.

"Now I am truly lost. Why would a coach need a wheel to steer it?" Zachariah asked.

"Because this coach," Father Thomas said, pausing for dramatic effect, "operated under its own power—at least it did for a very short time. What I am saying is, there was no need for a team to pull it."

That raised Zachariah Ward's eyebrows, and he sat back in his seat, plainly skeptical.

"The most amazing thing was that we were actually able to navigate it for a few hundred yards, before it failed."

"You mean you sat in it?" Collin exclaimed, his eyes wide. "How could it have worked after all this time?"

"I did. And so did the commander of our company, a fellow named Royd. He was the one who figured out how to make it go. Strange, the way memory works, but I haven't thought of him in years. He lives in Anderon, I think. As to how it worked, I confess I haven't the slightest idea."

"Incredible," Captain Donal said, leaning back in his chair.

"Did they ever find anything else in Senecal?" Mathew asked, his mind already skipping to the next logical question.

"As a matter of fact, they did," Father Thomas replied. "A number of books were recovered, along with other items. Nobody had the slightest idea what those items were. Some type of machines, I thought. Of course, the priests of Coribar sent word about the find to the governor—particularly in light of our arrival. He in turn notified the duke, who decided to come and see things for himself. Soldiers from our company were still assisting the locals with the digging when six ships sailed into the harbor bearing a full regiment of his soldiers. A standoff ensued, as you may have guessed, since the forces were approximately equal. We were under orders to maintain the status quo until an emissary from the capital arrived."

"And how was it resolved? I'd always heard that Malach got the better of the bargain," Captain Donal said impatiently.

Father Thomas smiled at the memory. "Well, as it turned out, a case of green Nyngary wine proved to be instrumental in helping liberate some of the very things Duke Rinalo's soldiers were protecting. While they were celebrating, four men, myself included, slipped into their camp and . . . ah . . ."

"You stole the treasure!" Captain Donal roared with laughter.

Father Thomas looked embarrassed, but replied, "That perhaps captures the spirit, but I wouldn't put it exactly in those words. Actually, I always felt a little badly for the duke's men."

"Why?" Lara asked.

"Um . . . it seems I was the one who sent them the wine. Their commanding officer was less than pleased when he found the soldiers . . . and several local women together the following morning. Senecalese women tend to be notoriously . . . ah . . ."

Captain Donal burst out laughing again. Even the

dour first mate started chuckling to himself, while Lara turned pink.

"So I take it the things you recovered are now in King Malach's possession?" Mathew said.

"All except for the books. They were sent to the sanctuary at Barcora for safekeeping and further study. Copies were made, of course, and delivered to Anderon."

Mathew leaned back in his chair and looked at Father Thomas. The more time he spent with the priest, the more sides the man seemed to have.

"A wonderful story," Zachariah Ward said, shaking his head. "What are your plans once we drop you in Tyraine?"

"To go on and visit with family for a while. Lara's sister was recently with child, so there is a new relative we have yet to meet—a boy, I believe I was told."

Across the table, Lara nodded in confirmation.

"Your family lives in Tyraine?" the first mate asked.

"No . . . no . . . just outside the city in the foothills. Their farm is close to the passes."

Mathew heard Collin mutter under his breath, "He lies as well as I do."

"Well, I don't doubt the young ones will find Tyraine . . . interesting," Captain Donal said, addressing Father Thomas. "I certainly did at their age. The first time I saw it, I was a sail maker's apprentice on the *Maid of Malogan*, but that was more years ago than I care to remember."

"I haven't seen Tyraine in at least fifteen years," Father Thomas said. "I wonder if it's changed much."

"Not very . . . busier perhaps. It might be best to keep the girl close, though. If you'll pardon my suggestion, Tyraine can be a little rough on the uninitiated," Captain Donal said, addressing the last part of his comment directly to Lara. "Wouldn't you agree, Zachariah?"

The first mate nodded soberly.

"Is it much worse than Elberton?" Lara asked.

" '*Worse*' isn't the word I would choose. Let's just say different," Captain Donal answered. "Actually, Elberton is more of a backwater town compared with Tyraine. I would do no less if it were my own daughter."

The oft-quoted expression among seafaring merchants who traveled to and from that coastal city was that you could get anything you wanted in Tyraine. The residents there, perhaps because they were the southernmost city in Elgaria, and consequently the farthest from the influences of the government, were known for their liberal outlook. Taverns tended to stay open into the small hours of the morning, and it was not uncommon to see people hurrying home after an evening of revelry just as the sun was rising.

The clergy tried its best to shape the population's prevailing attitude toward more productive and conservative pursuits, at least the way the Church viewed them, but with only limited success.

Tyraine's newest mayor was the fourth in four years. Recently appointed by her grace, the grand duchess, he promised at the time he accepted his badge of office that change would be swift and certain. His first priority, he told her grandly, would be to see that taxes were again collected, and promptly delivered to the royal treasury at Longreath Castle. He was certain he could accomplish his task within two months at most.

After finding his first tax collector hanging by his heels from the watchtower in the city center plaza, the mayor began to suspect there might be more complexities to the job than he originally anticipated. The second tax collector fared less well than the first, being coated with tar and unceremoniously dumped, by persons unknown, onto the mayor's very own doorstep.

The beleaguered mayor, a man in his early sixties, wanted nothing more than to put in his remaining years and retire in peace to an attractive country estate that he had already picked out. He began to see his dream moving farther away. Consequently, he placed the question before his advisers, who had little useful to offer. Finally, in desperation, he sent a request to Longreath Castle for several additional men to supplement the already over-worked constable's office—along with two cases of green Nyngary wine. A week later the duchess sent back a wheel of Lirquan cheese and a polite note expressing her confidence in his administrative abilities and wishing him every success in his new position—but regretfully declining the additional men.

As it turned out, significant inroads to the problem occurred at a dinner with several of the city's more prominent merchants. Using his own funds, the mayor hired two very large and disagreeable-looking Felizian mercenaries, who made it their business to stand in the doorway and assist him in collecting his guests' overdue taxes when the dinner was over.

Buoyed by his first official success, the mayor began to see his country home more clearly in his mind once again. Tyrainian merchants, being resourceful people, fell back on the time-honored custom of raising prices and passing along the reductions in their net revenues to their customers. Thus, all parties were temporarily satisfied, except perhaps for the customers. That is—until the Vargoth fleet sailed into the harbor.

Still more than three hundred miles away, the *Wave Dancer* moved steadily closer to Tyraine.

Mathew felt light-headed and yawned. "I think I'll take a turn around the deck and get some sleep," he said. "This wine seems to have gotten the better of me."

"Why don't you stay for a moment?" Collin suggested. "They're about to bring out dessert."

Lowering his voice so only his friend could hear him, Mathew whispered, "If it tastes anything like the rest of the meal, I'll probably live longer if I pass it up. I suggest you do the same."

"I think I'll chance it," Collin replied. "Stay for another minute or two and I'll go up with you."

Mathew let out a resigned breath and shrugged. "Your funeral."

A look passed between Collin and Lara, but it was gone so quickly that Mathew wasn't sure he'd seen it. And the wine certainly didn't help.

A moment later the room went dark as Captain Donal and Father Thomas both leaned forward together and blew out the candles. The door to the cabin opened, and silhouetted against the lamp in the corridor, Vickers held a cake ablaze with candles. Right on cue, exactly as Lara arranged it, Father Thomas began to sing "Happy Birthday," along with everyone else.

Mathew was speechless. He'd totally forgotten it was his birthday, the glow of the candles almost matched by the color of his flushed face. When the song was finished and he blew out the candles, Father Thomas shook his hand. Captain Donal clapped him on the back, almost dislodging a bone. Lara whispered something in Mathew's ear that turned both it and his other one red, then kissed him on the cheek, which was followed by a hug that lasted longer than it might have, raising both Captain Donal's and Father Thomas's eyebrows at the same time.

While they were still congratulating him and wishing him well, Zachariah Ward spoke up. "You might be interested in knowing that a few months ago Captain Donal celebrated his birthday here on the *Wave Dancer*. Now, being a loyal crew member, I gave my oath not to reveal how old he is, but I can tell you the crew also presented him with a birthday cake on that auspicious occasion, just as we did here for Mr. Lewin. The captain wanted to blow all the candles out too, but sadly, the heat drove him back."

He said this in such a bland manner that it took Mathew a second to realize he'd just made a joke. Seconds later the entire cabin was laughing—Captain Donal loudest of all.

One by one, after sampling the cake, which turned out to be a far better effort on the cook's part than the dinner, people bade each other good night and returned to their cabins. Mathew and Lara, however, climbed the compan-

ion ladder and stood on the stern deck, just above her
cabin. They watched the sea pass foaming by and listened
to the dozens of little noises a sailing ship made. Far out
in the distance, across the port beam, they were able to
make out the green and red running lights of a ship heading in the opposite direction. Each deep in their own
thoughts, neither spoke.

Overhead, the stars shone brightly under a black velvet
sky, and to the west, a full silvery moon rose, inching
higher and higher toward its zenith.

27

Great Southern Sea

FOR THE BALANCE OF THE VOYAGE, MATHEW CONTIN-
ued to refine his skills at navigation and sailing, with the
help of Captain Donal. Following the midday reading and
after consulting the charts, he concluded they would
reach Tyraine early the following morning and told the
captain so. It was a fair day, with light breezes blowing
from the northeast over a glassy calm sea. A few white
clouds appeared here and there against a brilliant blue sky.

He looked over his shoulder and waved to Lara, who
had just come up on deck. Over the last few days, she'd
gotten into the habit of watching him take his readings.
Usually, she stood by the opposite rail so as not to disturb
him. He had no idea why she had any interest in his do-
ings, but it didn't bother him. In fact, he liked her atten-
tions.

Today she was wearing a pale yellow dress, a gift from
Ceta. It left her shoulders bare and threw Mathew's concentration askew. Captain Donal, standing beside him,
looked over his shoulder at the calculations he had made.

"You have the knack, Mr. Lewin. You definitely have
the knack," the captain said. He tended to be a good deal
more formal when on deck. "Yes, I quite agree with you.
We'll reach Tyraine tomorrow. Excellent work, sir.
Carry on."

When he was gone, Jaim, the younger of the two
brothers, dejectedly tossed his ruler on the table and said,
"I don't know how you do it, Mat. I really don't. We've

been trying to learn this for more than four months now. You come along and learn it in a few days."

"I'm sorry, Jaim. Numbers were always easy for me. Would you like me to go over them again?"

"It's like trying to read Cincar, as far as I'm concerned. I'll never get it. My father thought this was a good idea. The first chance I get I'll probably run the ship aground."

"I doubt either of us will ever get the chance," Pryor said, sounding as unhappy as his brother. "You see the way the captain looks at us. The other day he told me I'd be more use as fish bait."

Mathew didn't know what to say. He liked both boys and wished he could find some way to help. What Jaim had said was true, however—the charts and celestial observations he made daily in plotting their position presented little difficulty for him. Even as a young boy, Mathew could often recall being invited to sit in as a fourth at cards with Truemen Palmer, his wife, and Father Thomas. Once they explained the odds and probabilities to him, the game seemed easy, though it did require sharp concentration. Performing the calculations themselves came quite naturally.

"Look, there's no use going on about it," Mathew said. "Let's try again together."

Using a crate for a makeshift table, he unrolled one of the charts and once more attempted to explain how to determine their position using triangulation. In a few minutes Jaim looked hopelessly lost, and Pryor was not much better. A footstep behind them attracted their attention and they turned.

"Hard at work, gentlemen?" Zachariah Ward asked.

"Yes, sir," Pryor mumbled.

"Why so glum, then?" the first mate asked, observing the boys' faces.

"It's all this math and angles—it's giving us fits, Mr. Ward."

Zachariah picked up the sheet Pryor was working on and scrutinized it a moment. "Perhaps if you allowed for the declension of the sun you might have a better result.

This course you've plotted will take you directly to Melfort as opposed to Tyraine."

"Melfort?" Pryor said. "But isn't Melfort three hundred miles to the north—"

"And inland?" Jaim said, slumping down to sit on the deck with his back against the table.

"My point exactly," Zachariah replied.

Pryor looked miserable. "I don't know, Mr. Ward, maybe the captain was right about using us—me, that is, for fish bait."

"I doubt any self-respecting fish would take the time to eat you in your present state of ignorance," the first mate replied. "However, I do have an idea. Just the thing to lift your sagging spirits. Being that this is Mr. Lewin's last day with us, Captain Donal and I have arranged a little contest."

"Contest?" Pryor asked.

"Indeed, sir, indeed," Captain Donal said, coming back over to join them as Jaim scrambled to his feet. "A race, if you will. The afternoon watch versus the evening watch, to determine the champions of the *Wave Dancer*. Pipe the hands up, if you please, Mr. Ward."

Mathew and the two boys looked at each other excitedly. In moments both watches poured onto the deck and assembled amidships, waiting for the captain to address them. Collin and Father Thomas came up to see what the commotion was about. Even Vickers was there, his foot still heavily bandaged.

"Men," the captain called out, "if the winds hold fair we should make Tyraine on the morrow. As you know, our guests will be leaving us there. Now at dinner last night, Mr. Thomas put the question to me as to which watch contained the better men. A discussion arose between Mr. Ward and myself—on purely an academic level, mind you—with Mr. Ward maintaining one position and myself the other. This matter, of course, needs to be settled definitively."

Several of the older hands smiled knowingly in anticipation of what was coming.

"We therefore propose a race," Captain Donal went on. "Two teams of five men each, starting from aft on the quarter deck, to the top of the mainmast and back again."

"If you will cast your eyes upward," the first mate called out, "you will note, in anticipation of your zealous efforts, an attractive yellow scarf now flies from the topmost tackle."

Some twenty heads looked skyward at the same time to the pinnacle of the mast. Mathew looked up along with everybody else, shielding his eyes from the glare of the sun. A yellow scarf was clearly visible at the top of the mast—*just visible*, he thought.

"This scarf, an item of considerable value, has been generously donated by Mistress Lara Palmer as a pennant to the victorious team that brings it safely back—along with, I might add, a kiss from the lady herself *and* a silver elgar for each man from the captain."

A cheer went up from the men.

"You will have two minutes to select your teams," the captain shouted over the cheering. "I suggest you young men join your respective divisions," he said, speaking to Pryor and Jaim.

Both boys, their faces all smiles, scrambled down to the mainmast where the rest of the crew was assembled.

Mathew caught Lara's eye, put his hands on his hips and elaborately mouthed the words, "*A kiss?*"

She stuck out her tongue.

Before he could say anything else, seaman Biggs approached him.

"Begging your pardon, Mr. Lewin, but would you be good enough to run for our watch?" he asked. "Your friend is going with the evening watch, and it will even things out a bit."

Mathew saw Collin standing with the men on the starboard side. "Well, I'm not sure it will," he replied, "but if it's all right with the captain, I suppose I can give it a go."

A quick glance at Captain Donal indicated there were no objections, and he accompanied Biggs to the port side. Jaim, Weldon, and Brown were waiting there. Remembering the dizzying view from the mainmast top, Mathew wasn't at all sure about the wisdom of his decision.

Father Thomas walked over to join Captain Donal and Zachariah Ward.

"All right lads, take your places," the first mate called out.

After a brief conference, it was decided that Mathew would go first, then Weldon, and Brown, with Jaim and Biggs bringing up the rear. Each watch shouted good-natured jibes at the other as they lined up, waiting for the captain's signal. Mathew saw that Collin would be first for the evening watch. Captain Donal stepped to the middle of the deck and raised his hands for silence. The remainder of the crew had all come up, along with Brenner and the cook. People seemed to be everywhere as the excitement built. Some were hanging from the rigging, shouting encouragement.

"What are the rules, Captain?" someone called out.

"Only these: You climb to the top of the mainmast as fast as you can and get down the same way. Each of you must touch Mistress Palmer's scarf. Last man to run brings the scarf back and claims the prize."

That brought another chorus of cheers and whistles.

"Good luck to you all, and may the best team win."

"Don't worry, we will!" Chalmers called out from the other side.

"Here we go, lads," the captain bellowed. "One, to be steady . . . two, to be ready . . . three, and you're off!"

Mathew dashed forward, running as hard as he could for the mainmast shrouds. He and Collin reached them at about the same time and began to climb. Cheers and encouragement broke out throughout the ship, and he fancied he could hear Jaim's high-pitched voice screaming below him. Up and up they climbed. Collin reached the crow's nest first, with Mathew only a few feet behind him. Mathew gritted his teeth and redoubled his efforts as they passed the yardarm. Opposite him, Collin cursed when his foot slipped, giving Mathew a narrow lead. Still higher they climbed, past the topgallant yards and into the next set of shrouds that led to the royals, and from there to the very top of the mast. Mathew's shoulders were beginning to ache, and he tried not to think about the ridiculous thing he was doing, nor how high he was. Just below him, he could hear Collin coming up fast, making up the ground he had lost. He knew his friend would catch him in a moment.

When Collin drew level with him again at the royals, his face grimacing with the effort, Mathew spared a glance at the people far below, and regretted it as soon as he did. It slowed him enough that Collin overtook him, and Mathew saw that he would reach the scarf first. Seconds later Collin did just that and started back down. Mathew reached up, touched the scarf, and followed as rapidly as he could. From the deck the cheering and shouts drifted up to his ears.

Collin was now twenty feet below him and descending quickly, increasing his lead. Recalling how Biggs and Chalmers got to the deck in the storm after they secured Vickers, Mathew decided his only chance of keeping the race even was to do the same. As soon as he reached the royal yardarm, instead of continuing downward through the shrouds, he quickly slid out using the footropes to the mainstay brace and swung himself awkwardly out onto it. With a deep breath and a prayer, he wrapped his arms around the stay and started to slide. The deck came at him with frightening speed, and he had to squeeze his limbs for all he was worth to slow his descent. He heard Collin curse when he shot past, reaching the deck with a lead of at least three full seconds. He hit the ground harder than he would have liked, turned, and charged down the port rail toward his team.

Weldon tore off after Mathew slapped his hand. While Mathew doubled over and gasped for breath, his team-mates slapped him on the back. Captain Donal spared him a brief, admiring glance. Both Father Thomas and the captain seemed to be enjoying themselves as much as the participants.

On the opposite side of the deck, Kessington took off

toward the mast. He was lithe and quick, and by the time he and Weldon passed the mainsail, they were almost even. Scrambling upward, they reached Lara's scarf at the same time, with Kessington perhaps a hand span ahead. Both men came down the main brace so fast, it almost made Mathew ill to realize he had done the same thing. The shouts from the crew were deafening. Even Vickers was jumping up and down on his good leg, screaming as loudly as the others.

Brown and Fullers, the ship's cook, went next. Mathew had high hopes for his side on this pairing. Fullers was a short man with a large belly, while Brown seemed relatively fit. However, it was soon apparent that for all his bulk, Fullers climbed like he was born to it, while Brown had difficulty negotiating the shrouds. Nevertheless, he made a good effort, reaching the deck only a few seconds after Fullers, who came pounding down the side, his belly bouncing with every step.

Jaim and Pryor took off like two arrows shot from the same bow. Although Pryor was the older and stronger of the two, Jaim was clearly faster. Mathew's heart went to his mouth when Jaim let go of the brace on the descent and dropped the last fifteen feet to the deck, reaching it ahead of his brother and then running down the side like a madman. If Mathew and Brown hadn't caught him, he'd surely have been unable to stop. Jaim collapsed laughing on the deck as his companions congratulated him.

It was down to the last man, and the race stayed even as Biggs and Chalmers, two topmen, left their starting positions. By now Mathew was yelling as loudly as everyone else. Both men moved up the shrouds at an astonishing pace, barely even touching the ropes. They climbed past the crow's nest and the topgallants, then up into the royals. The day had begun to warm considerably, and Mathew could feel his shirt sticking to his back. He cupped both his hands on to the side of his head, squinted, and could see that his teammate had a half body length lead over his rival, certain to get there first. But just as Biggs reached out for the yellow scarf fluttering

elusively in the breeze just beyond his fingertips, he lost
his footing and at the very last moment Chalmers shot by
him to grab the prize.

A collective groan went up from at least half of the
ship as Chalmers swung out to the main brace and began
to slide down hand over hand. After reaching the deck, he
trotted up to the captain, waving the scarf triumphantly
above his head.

Lara stepped forward to receive it, and Chalmers succeeded in surprising everyone there by sketching an ungainly bow to her, to which she replied with a deep
curtsey. Lara placed the scarf around Chalmers' neck, tying a loose knot in the front, and gave him a kiss on the
cheek. This brought another round of cheers from the
men, louder than before.

Captain Donal dutifully passed the elgars out to the
victors. Both teams met in the middle and shook hands,
congratulating each other according to the custom. Pryor
and Jaim, Mathew noted, appeared considerably happier
than when they were calculating, accepting good-natured
claps on the back from the crew and nods of approval
from the captain and Zachariah Ward.

Mathew turned around to see Collin.

"Sneaky. Very sneaky indeed, using that brace, Mr.
Lewin," his friend said, grinning.

Mathew grinned back, and they shook hands.

"'Pon my soul, sir," Collin added, doing a fair imper-
sonation of the captain, "I've thought it before, but I'm
almost ready to concede that you may actually have some
small possibilities."

"I think I'll go below and wash some of this tar off my
hands and change my shirt," Mathew said. "I assume
you've already made plans for spending that money when
we reach Tyraine?"

Collin tossed the silver coin up in the air and caught it.

"Oh, I imagine something will come to me."

Lara watched the crew slowly disperse as they went back
to the routine of running the ship. She also watched

Mathew's head and shoulders disappear down the companionway behind Collin.

Something had changed.

She knew him better than anyone in the world, and she could tell that something was different. It was not just in the way he carried himself—straighter and more confident. It was in his voice as well. She'd heard it when he told her to get behind him in the stable—unlike any tone he'd ever used before. Initially, she'd attributed it to the situation, but the difference, however subtle, had held. Mathew was no longer the self-conscious boy she'd known all her life in Devondale. The problem was, he acted one way in public, and another in private. When they were alone, he seemed distracted and distant.

She heard the jokes about him being seasick, and knew how they affected him. He was so afraid of being embarrassed, so unsure of himself. Of course, he refused to talk about it.

Ever since the frightening incident with Vickers, the crew had noticed the change as well. His whole attitude around them was different, and they responded by treating him with deference and respect. If he was aware of it, and she had no doubt that he was, he chose not to mention it.

Typical, she thought.

She knew that men tended to hold things in. Bran had been that way. So were her father and her uncle—at least according to her mother. But she had come to expect that Mathew would be different. From the time they were little, they always had an unspoken communication with each other. Her mother and father had it. Lara supposed that Mathew and Collin did as well. At home in Devondale, everyone more or less expected that she and Mat would get married one day. *Perhaps*, she thought. But some things needed to change first—like talking to her when he had a problem. At the moment he seemed to be retreating into himself, except in public, where he managed to appear quite at ease. Only she knew how much of the facade he showed to others was real and how much was an act.

Last night she'd known exactly where to find him—alone in the bow of the ship. He was holding the ring in his hand and staring straight ahead into the ocean at something, but when she looked, she saw nothing there.

For the rest of the day Lara contented herself by walking on the deck or reading a book Captain Donal had loaned her. She saw Mathew only briefly. He came up on deck for a minute, but went back down again with only a brief wave to her. On the opposite side of the ship, Collin saw her, put down the rope he was using to practice tying knots and wandered over to talk. They smiled at each other.

"Have you noticed Mat acting a little strange lately?" he asked.

"Um-hmm," she replied, looking at the companion ladder where Mathew had just gone down.

They turned then, as Father Thomas walked toward them. He was wearing dark green breeches and a light yellow shirt open at the throat.

"Are you enjoying the day, my children?" he asked.

"No," Collin replied glumly, causing the priest to raise his eyebrows.

"Indeed? With the flush of victory still upon you, I would have thought your spirits might be high. And you, my dear," he said, noticing Lara's expression. "Are you similarly afflicted?"

"Yes, Father," she replied.

"Ah, perhaps we should talk . . . assuming you wish to, that is," he suggested. The casual manner of his speech suddenly disappeared.

"It's not us, Father," Lara said. "We're worried about Mathew. He's been acting strangely for the last few days."

"I've noticed only that he appears more sure of himself, but that can hardly be a problem."

"It's this whole business with the ring—the explosion and what happened in the forest," Collin said. "And there've been other things too—little things."

"Tell me what you are referring to, my son," Father

Thomas replied, reaching for the rail to steady himself as the ship rode over a swell.

"Well, that night, back in Elberton, when those men attacked Mat, there was something else. I didn't think much of it at the time, but now . . . I'm not so certain," Collin said.

"What do you mean?" Lara asked, looking at him.

"There were three men, as I told you—Will Tavish, who worked at the inn, a fat one, and a skinny rat-faced fellow. The fat one was a large man, bigger than the cook on this ship, I'd say. They had Mat cornered. I never heard any of their names, except for Will. The skinny one already had a sword out and took a swipe at Mat's blade. Mat just avoided it.

"I started running as soon as I saw what was happening. Before I could get there, Rat-Face saw an opportunity and lunged. Mat was quick enough to parry him, but he riposted on the fat one instead. It surprised everyone. The man let out a howl and rushed at Mat, knocking them both backward.

"Now this is the odd part," Collin said. He lowered his voice and looked at each of them in turn. "At the exact moment the man jumped for Mat, all of the street lamps along the block went out. A second later, the fat man came flying backward. It had to be at least eight feet, is my guess. Everything was happening so fast, but now that I think about it, I don't know."

"Couldn't Mathew have pushed him?" Lara asked.

"At the time, I thought he did. And I suppose it's possible," Collin said. "Mat's stronger than he looks. But the man was better than three hundred pounds. You had to see it."

No one said anything for a while. Father Thomas's arms were crossed in front of his chest and his face had taken on a very serious aspect. Lara struggled internally about whether to mention what she had seen. Eventually she made up her mind.

"There's something else you ought to know too," she

finally said. "For the last week, maybe more, Mathew has been coming up on deck late at night by himself. Several nights ago I followed him onto the deck. I think he's been experimenting with the ring."

Lara quickly told them what she had observed.

When she finished Father Thomas shook his head and muttered, "I had not thought this possible. But it seems I've been as blind as everyone else."

"I don't understand, Father," Lara said.

Father Thomas rubbed his hands across his face. "Do you remember the story I told at dinner about my visit to Senecal many years ago?"

They both nodded.

"More was recovered in that forsaken place than anyone knows," Father Thomas said.

"You mean other than the vehicle and the old machines?" Collin asked.

"Precisely. There were books and records about what actually happened to the Ancients," he explained, keeping his voice down. "Even I don't know the full story. That's why we must get to Barcora as quickly as we can. They've been studying these things for years."

"But what has that to do with Mathew?" Lara asked.

"Do you remember what I taught you in school about the Ancients, my child?"

"I think so," Lara replied, "but I still don't—"

"While we waited in Senecal for King Malach to send a ship and transport what we found, I was approached one night by a man named Brother Samuel, a priest of my Church. I was not a priest then, just a soldier. He asked if he could examine the artifacts, and I saw nothing wrong in that. To my surprise, Samuel paid scant attention to either the vehicle or the other machines. He was interested only in the books and records. Each day for three days, from early morning until late into the evening, he stayed in the tent we put up to house the objects. My curiosity aroused, I began to sit with him to see what he found so interesting. Of course, I could not understand most of the words the Ancients used. You see, languages change over time, and they lived more than three thousand years ago—"

Father Thomas abruptly stopped talking, and waited for two sailors carrying a coil of rope to walk by. When they passed, he continued.

"Samuel was not only a teacher, but a scholar of history. I learned a great deal from him in those three days. The records he found spoke of the war the Ancients fought. They were our ancestors, my children—and they destroyed themselves utterly and completely. All of their great works crumbled back to the earth from which they came, and in the end so little of them was left, we had only stories to go by.

"On the second evening, Samuel showed me a book. It was badly damaged, and whole portions were missing, but much could still be made out. It was written by a man of science, his name lost forever in the eons that followed the destruction. He wrote of a desperate search to find the last remaining rings his people created toward the end. No mention was made of whether they were rose gold or not, nor was it ever clear why they wanted them, but I believe the rings were thought to be dangerous and powerful enough to destroy the world. There were other books, but this one, more than any other, held our attention. Samuel was pushed to the limit of his abilities to decipher the words written there. We read on through the night until the sun began to rise, desperate ourselves to solve the mystery of what happened—but it was not to be.

"We learned only that their end came quickly— quicker than any of them suspected, or had the power to avoid. The author of that book wrote of unseen horror and misplaced hope, although what he meant by that, I never learned."

"And you think Mat has one of those rings?" Collin asked.

"I don't know, my son. Honestly, I don't. I have not been entirely certain what to make of the things Mathew has told me. One portion of the book talked about the search to find the rings, yet another spoke of the need to destroy them. It was unclear to us if the author was talking about the same thing."

Collin let out a low whistle.

"What do we do, Father?" Lara asked.

"We travel to Barcora, with all haste. My belief is that we will find many of the answers we seek there. The sanctuary has the largest library in the western world, and the priests have had more than fifteen years to study what was recovered."

After a pause, Collin said, "We need to tell Mat about this."

28

Alor Satar, Rocoi

DUREN AND HIS SISTER MARSA PAUSED IN THEIR THIRD game of kesherit when there was a knock at the door of her suite. Reflexively, she smoothed her dress and turned. Duren merely looked up, saying nothing. It became apparent after a moment he had no intention of saying anything. It was, after all, her suite.

"Enter," she called.

The door promptly opened and four large men dressed in the uniform of Duren's personal guard came in. Between them were two Elgarian soldiers, their hands bound behind their backs. Their faces were bruised and swollen and their uniforms filthy, encrusted with blood and dust. From their haggard looks and red-rimmed eyes, it appeared they hadn't slept for quite some time. The taller of the two was a man of lean features and hard gray eyes. Even bound, he still had a commanding presence. His name was Gerard Idaeus, general of Elgaria's northern armies and commander of the defense forces of Anderon. The other, slightly shorter man was powerfully built, with a tenacious-looking face and piercing blue eyes. He was Aeneas Kraelin, duke of the Queen's province and cousin to King Malach.

Her brother, Marsa concluded, was still sulking, having lost two games of kesherit to her in succession, and probably wouldn't be fit to speak with for a while yet, so she took the lead.

"Gentlemen, we are so pleased you could join us," she said smoothly. "Oh dear, you do look extremely uncom-

fortable standing there. Captain, two seats for our guests,
I pray you."

The captain hesitated for a moment, until Duren
glanced in his direction, then he promptly retrieved two
chairs for the prisoners. When neither man made a move
to sit, the captain and the soldier next to him grabbed
them roughly by the shoulders and yanked them backward into the chairs, then positioned themselves on either
side of the prisoners.

"I very much regret the necessity of your hands being
tied" she said. "If you will give me your assurances that
you will make no attempt to escape or to do any harm,
I'm sure we can dispense with the restraints."

"I'll give you nothing," Duke Kraelin snapped.

The captain lashed out with the back of his hand, striking the duke across the face. His head rocked back and a
trickle of blood started to run down his chin from the corner of his mouth.

Marsa d'Elso stood up in one fluid motion, sparing
only the briefest glance at her reflection in a gold-
trimmed wall mirror on the wall. "Come, your grace, can
we not act as civilized people?"

The Duke blinked hard to clear his vision and looked
at her.

"Yes . . . I know who you are," she continued. "I am
also aware your companion is Gerard Idaeus, commander
of King Malach's northern army. I trust his majesty is
well. He was to be found nowhere in the city, or so I've
heard."

Aeneas Kraelin drew himself up in his chair and managed to wiped the blood from his mouth on the shoulder
of his uniform.

"Civilized? You talk about civilized? You attack us
without warning. Thousands are dead—burnt to death, or
blown to pieces by your magic, and you talk to me about
being civilized? Your *soldiers* killed women and children. And you have the gall to speak to me about being
civilized."

The soldier who had just struck him drew his hand back again, but a barely raised finger by Marsa d'Elso stayed the blow.

"Magic?" She laughed. "I assure you we used no magic, although I can understand why you might think so. In fact, now that I think of it, I imagine it must have appeared very much that way. But you have our assurances—we did nothing of the kind. Did we, Karas?"

Duren looked sideways at his sister and said nothing, his expression unchanging.

Gerard Idaeus spoke for the first time. His voice sounded dry and cracked, but his eyes were intense.

"What do you call walls of fire springing up out of nowhere? Holes opening in the earth to swallow men? Buildings toppling by themselves?"

"Such are the fortunes of war, I'm afraid." She rather liked the turn of that phrase. "Captain, would you be good enough to bring these men something to drink?"

When the captain hesitated again, she added, "Now," the veneer of politeness dropping away.

"You needn't bother," the duke said. "We do not drink with our enemies."

"Such needless posturing, your grace. Surely, this is unnecessary."

"Cut our bonds and I'll be pleased to show you what is necessary," Idaeus said.

"Always the soldier, hmm? How tedious. You may be aware that the people of Alor Satar are wonderful story-tellers. They are also wonderful listeners. Right now, you have our undivided attention. My brother and I would very much like to hear where King Malach and his son have fled to with the remainder of your northern army."

"You'll find out soon enough," Idaeus replied.

"Will we?" Duren spoke for the first time, getting up from his chair.

The captain returned carrying two silver goblets of water. Lord Kraelin shook his head and turned away. Idaeus did the same.

"Yes . . . Duren," Duke Kraelin said, deliberately omitting his title. "I was at the Great Hall twenty-eight years ago when you crawled out on your stomach. Your words mean as much now as they did then. Send us back to your dungeon and have done with us. We have nothing to say to you. It's only a matter of time before—"

Aeneas Kraelin never completed his sentence. His mouth moved and breath could be heard coming from his lips. But his ability to speak vanished when Marsa d'Elso sent a thought that severed his larynx exactly as her brother had taught her. Blood foamed from the duke's mouth, his eyes widened in shock and his mouth opened to scream, but no sounds emerged. He stared at Duren's sister, who stood watching in fascination as two lines of blood ran down the man's chin, a faint smile on her face. Unlike her brother, she didn't mind the sight of blood at all. Karas, she noted, chose to direct his attention to the floor. The feeling of power surging inside her sent a thrill up her spine. It was simply delicious, intoxicating.

Next, she envisioned the small mallet-shaped bones that were located just after the opening of Kraelin's ear canals. With a thought, she snapped them off, just the way she'd practiced on the bodies Karas had sent her. All sound suddenly ceased for the duke, a complete and utter silence descending upon him.

It wasn't just enough to simply think about something, Karas had told her. To make use of the ring one had to have a concept of the result they wanted to achieve. Marsa was a quick learner. The duke stumbled up from his chair and staggered about the room, his mouth open and bleeding. His head thrashed wildly back and forth. To Marsa it looked like he was playing some grotesque pantomime.

Gerard Idaeus watched what was happening in horror. "My lord," he cried. "My lord, what is it?" And then turning to Duren, he yelled, "Do something."

Duren regarded the man without blinking. "You must forgive my lack of sensitivity. Obviously, such a sight distresses you, General," he said.

An image began to form in Duren's mind of the human

eye—Idaeus's eyes, to be exact. At the back of the eye-ball was a thick cordlike structure, a nerve root, the physicians had explained to him. And from that nerve, hundreds of smaller nerves projected themselves, run-ning all the way to the very back top portion of the brain. He had never done anything like it before, but he decided detaching the thickest of the nerves would probably be sufficient.

Idaeus let out a gasp as a curtain of blackness dropped in front of his face, shutting out all light and depriving him of his sight forever. He too stumbled from his chair and in shock reeled backward into the soldiers behind him, who promptly shoved him away, knocking him to the ground, fearful that whatever was afflicting him might also affect them. The commander of King Ma-lach's northern army tried to get to his knees and fell onto his side. Behind him the soldiers laughed.

One of them came forward, grabbed Idaeus by the back of his collar and growled, "Let's see who crawls out on his belly now," which brought barks of laughter from his companions. His face was next to Idaeus's but the general saw only a bottomless black cavern.

At a motion from Marsa d'Elso, the soldiers dragged both men out of the apartment, closing the door behind them. Duren grimaced at the small trail of blood left be-hind by the duke and promptly looked away.

As soon as they were alone, Marsa ran across the room and hugged her brother. "Oh, Karas, did you see it? Did you see what I did?" she asked excitedly, throwing her arms around him.

Duren smiled—genuinely, for him—and put his arms around her waist, pulling her closer. "I'm very proud of you, Marsa," he said, not really meeting her eyes but looking down at the swell of her breasts. "We seem to be a family of many talents."

"I want to learn everything," she murmured in his ear, still keeping her arms around his neck.

"Patience. We'll have to wait until the physicians send us another body to practice on."

"But why?" she asked, feeling one of his hands moving lower, to the top of her buttocks.

It came as no surprise to her. She had seen the sidelong glances, and felt it when his hands lingered on her shoulder or waist a moment longer than they should have.

She responded by pressing her hips forward against his and obtaining the reaction she wanted.

"Living people?" he asked incredulously. "You want to practice on living people?"

The tip of her tongue flicked out, just touching his left ear, while her hands moved upward from his neck into his hair. A moment later her tongue explored his ear again, deeper and more sensuously. His hand moved lower, and she made a little noise she knew men liked to hear. Looking over his shoulder, she saw in the large gold mirror that her daughter had entered the room. Their eyes met only for a moment, and a faint cool smile appeared briefly on Teanna's face before the girl turned away.

"Well, I suppose anything's possible," Duren whispered, chortling to himself.

29

At Sea, 20 miles east of Tyraine

MATHEW WAS SITTING ALONE ON THE MAINMAST YARD-arm. He needed time to think and be by himself, and a ship offered very little in the way of privacy. There were so many things going on in his head at once. Earlier that morning, Father Thomas had come to his cabin and told him about his discussion with Collin and Lara. Mathew listened quietly without interrupting. When the priest was through, Mathew walked across the room and locked the door.

Collin and Father Thomas exchanged puzzled glances.

Without saying a word, Mathew slipped the leather cord over his head and put the ring on. The familiar tingling came and went. "Do you see that candle next to you, Father?" he asked.

Before the priest could answer, the candle lifted off the desk and floated gently through the air to Mathew's hand. There was a sharp intake of breath from both of them, followed by another when the candle's wick flared and a flame appeared, then went out again just as quickly.

No one spoke. Eventually the silence became uncomfortable.

"How long have you known, my son?"

"A little over a week," Mathew said. "It's taken me a while to learn to control it."

"The explosion back in Elberton . . . ?" Collin asked.

"I'm pretty sure that was me too. I was thinking about something like it a second before it happened. You and I talked about it."

"But how could you do something like that?" Collin asked.

"That's the problem," Mathew said. "I have no idea. To be honest, until recently I've been too afraid to try doing anything else."

"Well, that's a relief," Collin exclaimed, blowing out a breath.

"What else have you been able to do, my son?"

"Two nights ago I created a waterspout—just a small one. I did the same thing again last night."

"What do you mean, *'created a waterspout'?*" Collin asked, his brows coming together.

"I mean, I just pictured it in my mind, and it lifted right out of the water."

"And that block and tackle that fell, almost killing me yesterday?" Collin asked. "Was that one of your experiments too?"

"Not in the way you think. I saw it fall and caused it to miss at the last moment. I was almost too late getting the ring on. Thankfully, no one was paying any attention to me. Everything about this scares me to death."

"Thanks . . . I guess," Collin said.

"There's something else I should tell you," Mathew said. "Several nights ago when I put the ring on, I saw things, or rather, people."

The priest's face was somber and serious. "People? What do you mean, my son?"

"At first I thought it was my imagination, but then the same three people reappeared each time I put it on. I'm positive about that. I think they knew I was there too, because—this is hard to explain—they looked at me, or at least two of them did. One was a man. The other two were women. I could only see one of the women, but I got the feeling the third one knew I was there even though she never turned around."

"You were *there*?" Collin asked.

Mathew took a breath. "It was like looking through a window . . . or a doorway. I knew I was here on the ship, but part of me was wherever they were at the same time."

"I don't get it," Collin said.

Mathew shrugged. "I told you, I didn't think I could explain it . . . but that's what happened."

"Have you any idea who they were or where it was you saw them, Mathew?" Father Thomas asked in an odd tone.

"Yes . . . I think so. The first time was in a garden of some sort. The second time was in a large room with lots of marble and fancy furniture. I think it was a palace, from the look of it. At first, in the garden, they didn't know I was there, but then the man turned and smiled at me, if you can call it that. It was frightening. There wasn't a trace of warmth on his face."

Mathew looked from Father Thomas to Collin. Neither said anything.

"Father . . . do you know what Karas Duren looks like?" Mathew asked, breaking the silence.

Mathew could already see the answer on Father Thomas's face before he began to speak.

"I saw him once at the Great Hall when the peace accords were signed, but that was almost thirty years ago. He was a tall man, slender and arrogant in his bearing. He had dark hair and—"

"Hooded black eyes," Mathew finished, slumping down into a chair.

Collin looked from his friend to the priest. Then he threw up his hands and said, "Oh, this is just wonderful."

"You said there were three people," Father Thomas prompted.

Mathew nodded. "Like I told you, I never saw the third one, except from the back. She had long black hair. The other woman's hair was the same color. She was tall, slender, and very beautiful. She was wearing a silver gown. This is odd, but in spite of how she looked, her expression was as cold as Duren's—maybe colder. I don't know how to explain it, but I could almost tell what they were feeling about me—all of them. It wasn't pleasant."

"You sometimes have that effect on people," Collin observed, sounding more like himself.

Mathew ignored the remark. "The woman who did

look at me wore a thin circlet of gold around her head. I remember that. There was something else too," Mathew said, closing his eyes in concentration. After a moment he gave up. "I suppose it'll come back to me. Do you have any idea who she is, Father?"

Father Thomas pressed his lips together before answering. "It could be any number of people. I don't believe it's Duren's wife. She's fair-haired, and not tall in the way you describe her. My guess is that it's Marsa Duren d'Elso, Karas Duren's sister. The description sounds right. She also happens to be the Queen of Nyngary."

"Well what do they want from me?" Mathew asked dejectedly.

"Your ring, I suspect," Father Thomas calmly replied.

"Land ho!" one of the seamen shouted.

His voice yanked Mathew out of his reverie.

"Where away?" Zachariah Ward called out from the ship's wheel.

"Two points fine off the port bow."

Mathew looked but wasn't able to make out anything from his vantage point. A moment later, Collin climbed up to join him. Both boys stood up using the footropes to balance themselves. On the distant horizon, where the sky and sea merged, Mathew was able to pick out a hazy irregular shape just barely visible above the sea.

"There," he said, pointing.

Collin followed the line of his arm and saw it too as word spread quickly around the ship. Soon everyone was on deck to watch the landfall. Mathew took special pride in the fact that he had accurately plotted the last five days of their trip across the Southern Sea by himself, albeit with Zachariah's approval.

"Well, gentlemen, what do you see?" Captain Donal called up to them.

"Just a shape," Collin answered, looking down. "Doesn't look like much right now."

"Temper your patience, sir. In about another hour, if

the wind holds, we should round the point and be in Tyraine harbor."

The wind, however, chose not to cooperate, shifting directions before their feet touched the deck. They spent the next hour tacking eastward and had to beat their way back, with only minimal progress. Throughout the morning the sun continued to rise, burning off most of the haze that covered the land ahead of them. When their last tack was completed, Mathew was certain he could make out more than just a vague outline on the horizon. A short time later the rocky coastline of lower Elgaria came into view. Craggy hills mixed with trees and exposed rock rose up steeply up from the beach to form the famous cliffs of Tyraine.

Lara joined them by the rail, her brown cloak thrown loosely over her shoulders despite the early morning's warmth. Almost unconsciously, she slipped her arm through Mathew's and leaned her head on his shoulder. They watched as the ship moved toward a jagged point of land that jutted out into the water like a crooked finger. Captain Donal sent one man into the chains at the bowsprit to take depth readings and another man aloft to the crow's nest to watch for shoal water.

From the navigation classes, Mathew knew what that meant. Having spent all of his life in Devondale, he had never thought about the land dropping away from the shore in an uneven manner with rises and falls of its own. Captain Donal explained that changes in the water's color, particularly close to a shoreline, were good indications there was land just below the surface. A ship could easily run aground if its master wasn't alert. White water and breaking waves were other signs to watch for.

Mathew tried passing his new knowledge along to Lara, and although she gave every appearance of listening politely, he decided that was all she was doing. Ultimately he gave up, and resolved that he would confine his discussions on the finer points of sailing with those who better appreciated them.

The sky continued to brighten to a deep brilliant blue, and the warm breeze on Mathew's face felt good. In a short while they would sail into Tyraine harbor. He knew he should have been happy, but of all the people on the ship, he was least looking forward to it. Over the last few days, he had felt more at ease than he could remember in quite some time. Life was simple and uncomplicated there. *Definitely something I can get used to*, he thought. As if she could read his mind, Lara squeezed his arm tighter, and Mathew closed his eyes, letting the seductive rise and fall of the *Wave Dancer* take him.

The tranquillity of the moment lasted only until a low whistle from Collin attracted his attention. The rugged face of a sheer cliff was passing slowly to the starboard side of the ship, and opening before them was the full expanse of the Tyrainian harbor.

From what members of the crew had told him, Mathew expected Tyraine to hold a good deal more vessels than Elberton did. But not this many! It was immense. There had to be at least forty ships of every kind and description dotting the harbor. Every available space at the docks was taken. Masts and yards with furled sails were everywhere.

The harbor itself was shaped like a horseshoe, with the city of Tyraine rising majestically behind it, extending up into the very hills. He had thought Gravenhage was big, but this dwarfed it by a long shot. He looked at Collin, whose mouth was open. Lara seemed equally taken aback, although she managed to conceal it better.

Building after building of all shapes and sizes rose up from the landscape. Mathew counted at least eight different towers, all taller than Gravenhage's central one. Just off to the right, his eye picked out a large, prominent, gold-domed structure that reflected sunlight like a beacon.

"Will you look at that?" Collin said. He was staring at the same thing and could barely conceal the awe in his voice.

"The Temple of Alidar," Father Thomas said from behind them.

They were so fascinated by the sight, none of them had heard him approach.

"I thought they only worshiped him in Coribar," Collin said.

"Their priests have had a temple here for many years. The city tends to be quite tolerant of all religions. Even the Bajani have a mosque here. It's the one with the two spires up on that hill to your left."

"But I thought that everybody in Elgaria was the same as us," Collin said.

"Most are. In fact the majority are. But we do have a number of other religions throughout the country. I've always tried to think of them as new customers," Father Thomas joked.

"Well, I for one am astounded," Collin said. "See, it's just like I told you, Mat, we don't know anything about anything. There's a whole world out here just waiting . . ."

Collin's voice trailed away, and Mathew and Lara turned to look at him. He was watching Father Thomas. The smile had disappeared from the priest's face and his expression was suddenly serious.

"What is it, Father?" Lara asked.

"Too many," he replied absently.

Mathew could see that he was concentrating on the ships anchored in the harbor, his lips moving silently, counting them.

"What's too many?" Collin asked.

"The ships. And if I'm not mistaken, those six over there are from Vargoth."

"Is that bad?" Collin asked again.

"Possibly. The problem is that we lack any real news. Unless things have changed a great deal over the last sixteen years, it would be unusual to have more than one or two Vargoth vessels—three at most—in the harbor at the same time."

"That doesn't mean there's anything wrong, does it?" Collin said

"Perhaps not," Father Thomas said, not taking his eyes from the ships. "Another problem is that if we *are* at war, we don't yet know who stands with whom. And by my count, there are at least fifteen vessels from Vargoth tied up at the piers and more in the harbor. I don't like the look of it."

Mathew was about to ask a question of his own when a cry came from the crow's nest,

"Two galleys putting out oars, and two more closing from the stern."

It was true. Just after they rounded the point passing the harbor mouth, Vargoth ships stationed on either side of the entrance set a course to converge on them. At the same time, the two galleys at the docks, noting their presence, were now steadily moving toward them. Any chance of escape was effectively blocked.

Mathew recognized the heavy tread of Captain Donal approaching. He was joined a minute later by Zachariah Ward, who looked even more grim-faced than usual. After surveying the situation, they exchanged a meaningful glance.

"This doesn't bode very well, I'm afraid," he said to Father Thomas. "I would say we've sailed straight into a trap."

Father Thomas nodded slowly. "You think Vargoth has sided with Duren?"

Captain Donal's frown deepened before he answered. He leaned over the rail, studying the approaching ships, then looked to the stern.

"I'd say there's very little question of that, sir. We're caught like fish in a net."

"Is there any chance we can turn and make a run for it?"

Father Thomas asked the question without conviction. The answer was already obvious on Captain Donal's face.

"The *Dancer*'s faster and handier than those ships, but we'd not make the headland before they were on us."

"How long do we have?

"I'd say fifteen minutes, no more."

Father Thomas's brow furrowed in concentration while he considered the possibilities. Mathew turned back to look at the approaching ships once more. Those that had set off from their anchorage were large ungainly affairs, considerably bigger than the *Wave Dancer*. Each was equipped with a catapult that could pound an enemy's vessel into submission. Even from his distance, he could see the broad black and gold pendants of Vargoth flying from their masts.

Mathew thought about it for a minute and realized that he knew very little about either Vargoth or its people. To the best of his knowledge, he couldn't recall ever having met anyone from that country before. He knew it lay somewhere to the east of Elgaria and well to the south of Alor Satar at the tip of the Great Southern Sea. He could remember his father telling him it was a barren, hard country that hired its soldiers out to those who could pay.

Mathew watched the graceful rhythmic oars moving back and forth together, giving the strange ships the appearance of a bird in flight. In its own way, he thought it was a beautiful sight.

"Where's the least likely place to look for someone on this ship?" Father Thomas asked after a moment.

"The cable tier," the captain answered, watching the galleys drawing nearer.

"Mathew, Collin, this is what I want you to do—get yourselves down there now. Mathew, do you know where it is?"

Mathew nodded.

"You're to stay there until after dark, then make your way to a tavern called the Stone Pheasant. You shouldn't have any trouble finding it. Walk up five streets from that center dock next to the large gray ship. Can you see it?" he asked, pointing.

"I see it," Collin said.

"Fine. It doesn't make any difference which street you take; they all lead to a large square called the Plaza Marcus. There's no way to miss it. Go across to the other side. At the very left corner you'll find a street, called Montaigne. Follow that street to the tavern. It will be about a twenty-minute walk. Do you both understand me?"

Father Thomas's voice had turned rapid and urgent.

"Right," Mathew replied.

"My *niece* and I will be registered under the name of Miles Vernon, a trader in gems from Tardero. If all goes well, we'll be meeting a friend of mine there."

Mathew opened his mouth to ask who the friend was but never got the chance. A huge fireball, flung from the Vargoth ship closest to them, roared overhead, causing everyone to duck. It splashed down in the water no more than fifty yards from their stern, the sea boiling around it.

"Mr. Ward, pipe the hands to the braces and heave to, if you please. Take in all sail."

"Aye, Captain. Take in all sail," he echoed, following the custom of repeating the last order.

"And you, gentlemen, will please make yourselves scarce," the captain said. "Take a set of spikes and hammers down there with you. It will look like you're working. In case you're discovered, you've been on the ship for three months—runaways from Wakefield. Mathew, you're John Tabor, and you Collin are Sammy Shelton— both apprentices. Now off with you."

"But—" Mathew said, turning to Lara.

"Just go," she said, pushing him. "Uncle *Miles* and I will be fine. I seem to be acquiring a lot of new relatives on this trip."

"What about Daniel and Akin?" Mathew asked. "They'll be here tomorrow on the *Douhalia*, and they're going to sail right into the same trap we have."

"Akin can take care of himself," Father Thomas replied in a low voice. "You'd both better get moving now. We don't have much time."

Mathew looked over the port rail at the lead ship. As soon as it became obvious that Captain Donal didn't intend to run or put up a fight, they also shortened sail and dropped anchor. Two boats were being lowered over their side. The other ship, on their starboard side, already had a boat in the water. Both were filled with soldiers.

Mathew slipped the leather cord holding the ring over his head and handed it to Lara. She promptly put it around her own neck, tucking it out of sight down the front of her dress. Then he and Collin looked at each other and dashed for the ladder.

Father Thomas also disappeared belowdeck. He re-emerged minutes later, wearing a long dark blue robe and a jeweled belt around his waist. He had changed his breeches and donned a new shirt with a white silk scarf. To all outward appearances he looked exactly like a wealthy foreign merchant. Seeing him, Captain Donal raised his eyebrows.

"I see that you're a man who plans for the future," he said under his breath.

"The Lord helps those who help themselves," Father Thomas replied quietly.

Their conversation got no further, as fully armed soldiers began to clamber over both sides of the ship at the same time. Father Thomas and Captain Donal watched at least thirty Vargothan mercenaries deploy themselves along the deck. Two minutes later boats from the stern ship tied on and another twenty men came onboard. Watchful and alert, none of the soldiers spoke, but they stood ready to act at a moment's notice.

Father Thomas pulled Lara closer to him and put a protective arm around her shoulders. To his experienced eye, these men appeared both professional and tough. Their black cloaks were thrown back, and though no weapons were out, he could see their hands resting suggestively on the hilts of their swords.

The wait didn't last long. A man in his late fifties, followed by another man, climbed through the entry port. Both were dressed as soldiers. The first wore a silver starburst insignia on the left breast of his cloak. His hair was almost completely white and his dark brown eyes bespoke intelligence. He had a hard, slender physique. The second was a large man, rougher in appearance than the first, with a scar running from his right eye to his upper lip. He looked cautiously around the deck with his hands on his hips. The first man took only a second to pick out

Captain Donal. Father Thomas gently guided Lara to his opposite side, then casually leaned against the railing as the man approached them.

"You are the captain of this vessel?" the first asked without preliminary.

"I am, sir. My name is Oliver Donal. And perhaps you'll explain the meaning of your actions."

Without any warning, the man lashed out, striking Captain Donal across the mouth with the back of his hand. The captain's head snapped sideways and he took a step forward, but ten blades drawn at once by the nearest soldiers forestalled him. Slowly, keeping his eyes on the man, the captain raised a finger to his lower lip and wiped the blood from it.

"Good. It appears that you have sense as well as courage. I find that refreshing. My name is Abenard Danus, commander of the occupation force of Tyraine. You are now subjects of the Empire of Alor Satar."

The statement brought an immediate buzz of reaction from the crew, causing several of the soldiers to step back, drawing their weapons. A look from the large man next to Danus restored order.

"Cooperate and you'll be treated well," the large man said, pitching his voice to carry. "Resist and you'll hang from those cliff's yonder till the skin falls from your bones and the crows eat your eyes." Though he made the pronouncement blandly, Father Thomas had no doubt that he would carry out his threat without a second thought.

When the man continued pointing in the direction of land, Father Thomas and several crew members turned to look. Startled gasps came from everywhere at the same time. It took every bit of Father Thomas's willpower to keep from reacting. The memory of that sight promised to stay with him for as long as he lived.

All along the cliffs ran a continuous line of gallows with people hanging from them. What made the sight all the more startling was that even from their distance, the priest could tell the bodies were not just men, but women and children as well.

"This is Notas Vanko, my second in command," Danus said. "I suggest you take heed of his warning. He is a man of considerably less patience than I."

Somehow, Father Thomas doubted the last statement.

"If you are expecting rescue—do not!" Vanko called out. "If you hope to escape—do not! For there is no escape. Anderon is destroyed. Your king and his coward of a son have fled the city, and are hiding like frightened children in the forests. The army of Elgaria has been scattered like the wind. Stermark and Toland were taken two weeks ago, as was Tyraine. The choice is yours—you may serve the Empire as loyal subjects, or be ground to dust by it. Either way, it makes little difference to us. There is always more wood to make gallows with."

Father Thomas could see the muscles knotting in Captain Donal's neck and shoulders. And when he grabbed the captain's thick forearm, he had no question the man was about to act, probably killing them all in the process.

"You certainly took long enough to meet us," a strangely accented voice said.

Mathew, hiding below in the cable tier, heard the words and looked up sharply. The accent was unusual, one he had never heard before, but it almost sounded like . . . *Father Thomas!*

"Who the devil are you?" Danus snapped.

"Raise your hand to me and I'll have it cut off and fed to the dogs," Father Thomas replied in the same accent. "I am Tarif Ja'far Bruhier, brother of Arif Asad. Perhaps you will explain why it took you so long to reach us and the reasons these fools fired on my ship? Do you realize we could have been injured?"

Notas Vanko started to draw his sword, but a slight shake of the head by Danus restrained him.

"We were not told to expect a visit by anyone from Cincar," Danus replied calmly, looking narrowly at Father Thomas.

"Excellent. I see you are sufficiently educated to know who we are, but I am still waiting for an explanation,

Commander. I doubt that Lord Duren would care to have his allies treated in such a manner—particularly the Sultar's brother and his own daughter."

Danus examined Father Thomas coldly, then turned his attention to Lara, who raised one eyebrow as she met his gaze. For the first time, Father Thomas thought he could detect the barest hint of uncertainty in the man's eyes.

"As I have said," Danus told him, "we were given no indication to expect anyone from your country for at least several weeks. I repeat, what is the purpose of your visit?"

Father Thomas placed both hands on his hips. "Do you honestly believe this is the appropriate place for us to have such a discussion? My brother told me he and Duren would choose the governor carefully, but . . ." He let his voice trail off, allowing the impact of his words to reach Danus.

The commander glanced from Captain Donal to Father Thomas and then at Lara, who promptly turned her back on him as if he were no longer worthy of her attention. Instead, she looked over the railing at the city of Tyraine, praying he wouldn't hear her heart thumping.

As the seconds passed, Father Thomas slowly slid his hand closer to the dagger in his belt.

"Colonel," Danus eventually said to his companion, "leave a sufficient number of men aboard this vessel to ensure that the crew provides you with their . . . fullest cooperation. Cut the hands off of any man who resists. Lord Bruhier and his niece will transfer to my ship and accompany me to my residence . . . as our *guests*."

Father Thomas put one hand over his heart and made a slight bow.

"Your hospitality is appreciated, Commander. I must tell you, however, that though these men are Elgarians, they are bound by oath to my family. They have risked much to take us this far. I am similarly bound by the honor of my house to uphold our agreement."

"And that would be?"

"To dispose of their cargo as conditions dictate . . . less the customary taxes and gratuities to the present administration, of course."

"Of course," the commander replied. "Perhaps you are right. We will discuss it further aboard my ship. If you and . . . ah . . ."

"Forgive me. I present the princess Lina Palmeri Batul Asad, Commander. I regret my niece cannot converse in your language as yet."

Lara kept her back turned to both men, continuing to gaze straight ahead. When Father Thomas touched her shoulder, she turned and listened, or gave the appearance of listening, while he rattled off a series of words she thought must have been in the language of Cincar. The only thing she recognized was his repeating the name *"Lina Palmeri"* again. Fortunately, he punctuated it by gesturing in her direction. Not knowing what else to do, she inclined her head in what she hoped was a good imitation of the way a lady of nobility might act. She was much relieved when Danus bowed to her. Father Thomas repeated the introduction to Colonel Vanko, who nodded curtly, though deferentially in her direction.

"Captain, we will be parting company now, I'm afraid," Father Thomas said to Captain Donal. "Would you be kind enough to have one of your men send our things to Commander Danus's ship?"

"Of course, your highness. And may I say it has been a great pleasure serving both you and the princess," Captain Donal replied with grave formality, as he bowed to them.

A short while later they found themselves onboard the Vargoth warship with Abenard Danus. Lara succeeded in keeping both her emotions under control and her face impassive as she surveyed the surroundings. Just knowing that Father Thomas was nearby proved a steadying influence. He squeezed her arm reassuringly on the ride over in the small boat and smoothly covered for her when she almost thanked Commander Danus for warning her to be careful climbing the wet steps. Once on deck, she moved to the far rail, separating herself from the others as she conceived a princess might do.

This ship was clearly different from the one she had just left. At the front—the bow, Mathew had told her—there was an evil-looking contraption she assumed was the catapult that fired at them. Instead of an open area, a wooden canopy ran the entire length of the ship covering the deck. She asked Father Thomas about it later and he explained it was to protect the crew from arrows in battle.

From the corner of her eye she could see Colonel Vanko speaking with one of the soldiers, a heavyset burly fellow. The man snapped a closed fist across his chest in salute and dashed below. He reappeared seconds later carrying a small wooden boxlike contraption and promptly began climbing the foremast, the box suspended from a leather strap looped over his shoulder. When he reached the crow's nest, he paused and opened and closed a lid at the front of the box. The sun's rays struck an angled mirror inside it, producing light flashes. From one of the towers well up into the hills of the city came a series of flashes in response.

Behind her, Commander Danus and Colonel Vanko were talking with each other, but she was only able to make out bits and pieces of their conversation. In the end it was decided that Colonel Danus would leave twenty men onboard the *Wave Dancer.* They informed Father Thomas, who, as Tarif Ja'far Bruhier, shrugged with apparent unconcern. Lara decided to follow his example, sparing only the merest glance backward. She carried out the charade and tried not to think of Collin and Mathew hiding belowdeck.

Only the rhythmic sound of fifteen sets of oars breaking the water, and the wind passing through the rigging could be heard as the city of Tyraine loomed nearer. It truly was larger than anyplace she had ever been before. She was immediately struck by the colors of the houses and buildings. In Devondale, homes or public buildings tended to be white, gray, or brown. These, however, were painted in shades of purples, turquoise, and yellows, in addition to the more conservative colors. Before they reached the dock, her ears were assailed by all manner of noises. Everything seemed in a state of ongoing activity, with people pushing past one another and walking in all directions. Up and down the broad street fronting the harbor peddlers sold fish, vegetables, fruit, and a variety of different merchandise from the back of their carts. If Tyraine was a city under occupation, she marveled at the flexibility of the local population to adapt to the circumstances.

Shortly after the ship tied up, a plank was run out for them. Lara, Father Thomas, and Commander Danus walked down it, but Vanko stayed on board, citing official duties. An ornate black coach drawn by two horses was waiting for them. It was an elaborate affair with gold scrollwork and tufted velvet seats. Even the interior walls were lined with silk damask, which Lara guessed must have been extremely expensive.

Not quite sure what to do, she gently pulled on Father Thomas's sleeve and whispered in his ear, "Is this for us?"

Already halfway around to the other side, Commander Danus paused and looked at them quizzically.

"My niece wishes to tell you the coach is acceptable, and thanks you for your courtesy," Father Thomas said, replying to the unasked question.

Danus smiled and made another little bow.

Although Lara admitted later that her actions might have been a trifle showy, she did not get in the coach. Instead, she deliberately waited for Vanko to return and open the door for her—which he did while muttering under his breath. As soon as they were properly settled, the driver, also a soldier, started off.

If the scene at the dock had proved a surprise, it was nothing compared with their ride through the streets of Tyraine. Gravenhage was no more than a small town compared with it. The streets were wide enough to qualify as boulevards, and it seemed every one was lined with trees and ornate lamp posts. More than once they passed through expansive plazas with large fountains and statues spouting water from their mouths and other openings, some of which made her blush. Through it all, she concentrated on giving the appearance of only mild interest and not meeting the commander's eyes. During the ride, Father Thomas made polite conversation with Abenard Danus.

"Tell me, my friend, have you encountered any problems establishing order among these people?"

"Only in the beginning, but we found a solution. Since then we have encountered little resistance. Perhaps you noticed the hills just above the city? The former mayor is the third from the left."

Although Danus's manner of speech was mild and offhanded, his words were chilling. Father Thomas's only reaction was to suppress a yawn.

"Indeed," he said, looking out of the window toward the hill. "Are those children and women I see up there, Commander?"

"Indeed," Danus answered, slightly mimicking Father Thomas.

The priest drew his head back into the coach, his pleasant aspect replaced by something much harder. "I do not care for the tone of your voice."

"And I really don't care what you think," Danus snapped. "You may well be Tarif Ja'far, and your brother may also be the ruler of Cincar, but until I can verify those facts, you will be treated with courtesy but remain in the home of the mayor. He seems not to have a use for it at the moment." Danus smiled. "Do I make myself plain?"

Father Thomas leaned forward, speaking very slowly. "Your words are clear enough. That is well. I was told to expect this of you. You asked what my purpose is here. I will be just as candid. You are aware we must choose a man to govern this province. History has shown us that great generals do not always make great leaders. I am here at the direction of Lord Duren and the council to make such assessment for myself. Do I make *myself* plain?"

Before Danus could answer, Father Thomas went on.

"Talent for conquest is one thing—the ability to rule is quite another. Even someone of a military point of view must understand that commerce and trade have to resume in time. This port and this city are central to our plans. The reports only just reached us that you had priests hung, and that you sacked their churches as well. What kind of fool are you? You'll be lucky if you don't find yourself keeping the mayor company when Duren finds out."

The last statement was a calculated gamble on Father Thomas's part. He made it not knowing if there was the slightest grain of truth attached to it, but it had the effect he wanted.

"The priest's death was an accident," Danus shot back. "The man who did it was executed immediately. I have no way of knowing what you have heard, but I have followed the council's orders to the letter."

"Fool," Father Thomas hissed under his breath. "This is your responsibility and you seek to pass it off to another. You disappoint me."

"Disappointment be damned. We've done our job here—the job your armies could not do alone. Fortunately, the issue of who you are can be resolved quickly. I expect al Mouli and Lord Duren to arrive here in three days. Your general, Naydim Kyat, will also be present by then, for the farspeak. Then we shall see if any disappointment is warranted."

Father Thomas was not prepared for the last statement. He hadn't the faintest idea what a "farspeak" was. To make matters worse, it now appeared that he had only three days to get them all out of Tyraine before the Cincar general arrived and sealed their fate. He issued a silent prayer that Akin and Daniel's ship would not be delayed.

A dangerous game, he thought.

And so gambling further, he played his next card.

"You are no doubt aware that we have an agreement with your King Seth. The Alliance will honor that agreement. You may be the right man for governor and you may not. Certainly, you have friends who seem to think

so. But let us make certain no further *accidents* happen.
You will be held personally responsible."

Danus's reaction betrayed him. At the mention of the
words "friends" and "governor," the man visibly relaxed,
nodding in agreement.

Thinking about the situation later, Father Thomas concluded that a leopard could not change its spots quite so
easily. That Duren wanted Elgaria was plain, but he also
sought to establish himself as ruler of Lirquan, Telegium,
Mirdian, and the rest of the western nations. Whatever
else could be said, there was little question he held a special hatred for Elgaria, the nation that spearheaded his
major defeat in the past. Long after the peace accords of
Luzon were signed, they uncovered Duren's plan to di-
vide Elgaria into smaller territorial possessions of Alor
Satar and eliminate its very existence.

"Perhaps my words have been too harsh, Lord
Bruhier," Danus said. "I am a soldier first and a politician
second. These are difficult times. You and the princess
shall have freedom while you are here. I can assure you
the quarters I have selected are most comfortable. Not
what you are used to, I'm afraid, but comfortable nevertheless. I must insist however, while you are under my
care, you allow me to assign two of my men to . . . *assist
you* . . . for your own protection, of course."

Father Thomas put his arm across his chest with an
open palm covering his heart and bowed in his seat. "It
shall be as you say, Commander. I do require your assis-
tance in another matter, however. A Mirdite ship called
the *Douhalia* should arrive sometime tomorrow. Your soldiers will take special care to see no harm comes to it. On
board that ship you will find a slender blond man and a
young boy with gray eyes. I cannot reveal their names but
I can tell you that they carry information extremely valuable to the Alliance. Let me stress again, *no harm is to
come to either of them*. They are to be brought directly to
me. Under no circumstances are your soldiers even to

have conversation with them. I will not tolerate a mistake on this point."

No stranger to espionage, Danus regarded Father Thomas carefully, then nodded. "Does this have something to do with the meeting?" he asked.

Father Thomas deliberately paused and drew an exaggerated breath. "You are a quick man, Commander. The reports do you justice. But you will understand I am not at liberty to speak of this yet."

Danus nodded soberly once more. "I do have one more question, Lord Bruhier. The princess and you are dressed, shall we say, rather plainly. I am confused as to why you have chosen to travel alone without an escort."

"The reasons for our dress should be obvious to someone of your intelligence," Father Thomas replied. "The merging of cultures requires that it take place smoothly, with as little disruption as possible. Is it not better the new rulers of this country appear similar to the people themselves—kindred spirits, as it were?"

Danus chuckled.

Father Thomas looked out the window as the coach rolled past another fountain—a pagan god rising from the sea, holding a trident. Streams of water arched toward the giant figure from a series of jets around the fountain's circular marble base, and when the wind blew through them, it created a mist.

"And for the second part of your question," Father Thomas continued, "as you yourself have suggested, there will be an adequate enough escort here in a few days for the farspeak, won't there?"

He sat back and smiled at Danus, who began to chuckle to himself.

30

Tyraine

IN THE DARKNESS OF THE CABLE TIER, MATHEW strained to hear what was being said on deck. The best he could do was catch scattered pieces of conversations. What he did know was that Father Thomas and Lara were no longer on the ship, and the *Wave Dancer* had started moving again.

There were all manner of sounds and activity going on above them. The room they were in was stifling hot. What little air was available came from an opening the anchor cable ran out of. In no time at all they were both sweating profusely. To make matters worse, his stomach was turning tricks.

Then the voice of Captain Donal boomed out directly above them. "Mr. Ward, prepare to let go the anchor on my command."

"Aye aye sir," came back an equally loud reply.

Collin and Mathew looked at each other and immediately jumped backward away from the turnstile.

"Ready, Mr. Ward?"

"Ready to let go of the cable, sir."

Mathew smiled, mentally thanking Captain Donal and Zachariah Ward for their warning. Had they been next to the turnstile when it released, it surely would have crushed them to death.

A second later the huge rope cable began to pour through the opening as the anchor was let out. In their confined space, the noise seemed unnaturally loud. A splash against the side of the ship, followed by the deck canting slightly to the right, told Mathew the anchor was at rest on the harbor's sandy floor.

"What are we supposed to do now?" Collin whispered.

Mathew was about to reply when the sound of footsteps coming along the passage from the forward part of the ship froze the words on his lips. He could tell there was more than one person, and from the noises they were making, he was certain it was not any of the crew. Whoever it was, they were moving crates and banging open doors. Only a short distance away he heard a voice say, "I don't see why we're doing this."

"The sergeant said we're to look over every inch of the ship. The order came direct from Vanko himself. You heard him, same as me."

Another crash as a crate was knocked aside.

Mathew thought quickly. There was no way out of the room they were in, and at best they had only seconds before they were discovered. When they first made their way into the cable tier, he had noticed a half-finished bottle of rum left in the corner from some crew member's private celebration. Without hesitation, he grabbed the bottle and poured some of it on the front of his shirt and then took a long swallow. Another mouthful found its way onto Collin's shirt.

"Hey," Collin protested in a fierce whisper.

"Take a swallow and start singing," Mathew snapped.

"What?"

"Start singing."

It took a moment for Collin to realize what Mathew wanted. Then he downed a long drink and launched into a bawdy tavern song he had heard in Elberton. Mathew joined him, rapping an accompanying rhythm on the deck with his hand.

The footsteps outside paused for a moment, then rapidly started down the corridor toward them. They were still singing when the door to the room was thrust open and a bright light from a lantern nearly blinded them.

"Put that out you fool," Mathew said drunkenly, holding a hand up against the light. "Do you want the captain to hear?"

"Hey, close the door, mates," Collin said, starting to rise. Before he could fully get to his feet he bumped his head on one of the beams and sat down heavily on his backside, cursing for good measure.

The two soldiers looked at each other. The first one shook his head, took a deep breath, then reached into the tiny room, grabbing Mathew by the back of his neck. The second one did the same with Collin. Despite their apparently drunken protests, they found themselves being dragged back through the passageway and up onto the deck. They stood there somewhat unsteadily on their feet, still held by the soldiers.

"Hey, we don't know these men. Who the hell are you?" Collin slurred.

The second soldier, holding Collin up by the arm, smacked him across the back of his head and said, "Keep your manners, pup. You'll live longer that way."

Collin swung a wide punch at the man, who easily avoided it, causing him to spin by, off balance. The soldier planted a boot squarely across Collin's rear, knocking him to the deck. Out of the corner of his eye Mathew saw Captain Donal and a man he took to be an officer of some sort approaching them.

"All we could find was two drunken rats singing down in the cable tier," the first soldier said.

"Them, and this bottle of rum they was drinking," the second soldier added.

Captain Donal's face was red with rage. "So that's where you were," he roared, grabbing Mathew by the front of his shirt. "Caught stealing rum from the ship's store again and hiding like two children! This is the last straw. The last, I say. D'ye hear me? I'll have no more of you aboard this ship, father or no father."

"Now what do we have here?"

"Two boys, as got into the captain's liquor—is my guess, Sarge," the second soldier replied.

"Who are you calling a boy?" Mathew growled. "I've beaten bigger men than you. You don't scare me any."

The soldier holding Mathew looked up wearily and cuffed him across the ear.

"Hey!" Mathew said.

"Are they the only ones you found?"

"Right, Sarge," the first soldier answered.

The sergeant turned to Collin, who was still sitting on the deck, and said, "Get him to his feet."

The soldier reached down and hauled Collin up.

"Hold out your hands," the sergeant ordered.

"What for?" Collin said suspiciously, earning him another clout across the back of his head.

"Do as the sergeant says, pup. He's not as friendly as I am."

Reluctantly, Collin held out his hands, and the sergeant examined them.

"Now you," he said, turning to Mathew, who shrugged and put his hands out.

"Where do you hail from?" the sergeant asked, stepping closer to Mathew, but before Mathew could respond the man pushed him away. "Whew—they smell like a distillery."

"They're from Wakefield," Captain Donal answered. "And sorry's the day I let their father talk me into taking them aboard my ship. They've been nothing but trouble from the very beginning. Well, that's all over with, d'ye hear me? You'll get yourselves off my ship before I throw you off myself."

"What about our pay?" Collin asked.

The captain wrinkled his nose and turned his head away, bellowing, "Mr. Ward, get these two drunken louts off of my deck this instant!"

"Just a moment," the sergeant interrupted. "Open your shirts, the both of you."

"Huh?" Collin said.

Before they had time to react, both soldiers grabbed their arms at the elbows in viselike grips. The sergeant stepped forward and pulled Mathew's shirt open, then did the same for Collin.

"I told you they weren't wearing any gold rings," the captain said. "They're lucky if they've got a copper elgar between them."

The sergeant looked at their naked chests, then nodded and gave an abrupt jerk of his head toward the side railing. Seconds later Mathew and Collin found themselves unceremoniously deposited into Tyraine's harbor. Their packs came flying after them, to the laughter of the soldiers and crew lining the rail.

Collin shook his fist in anger back at them, bringing a fresh outburst of laughter. Then they turned and floundered their way toward the dock. As they started swimming, his quarterstaff landed with a splash ten feet in front of him and he was forced to dive to retrieve it. A few men unloading barrels from a flatbed wagon stopped to watch them climb out but did nothing to help. Instead, they shook their heads at the ridiculous sight of two sodden young men emerging from the water.

"Mat, those comments about the gold ring . . ." Collin said.

"I heard them. Let's get out of here. We're attracting way too much attention as is."

"Where are we going?" Collin asked, bunching up the tail of his shirt and wringing a stream of water out of it.

"As far away from this place as we can get. Father Thomas said to meet him at the Stone Pheasant. That's where we should head. Where's the street he showed us from the ship?"

"Over there." Collin pointed

After drying off as best they could, they started walking. Fortunately, the day was warm and their clothing began to dry quickly.

"At least we don't smell like we took a bath in the captain's rum anymore," Collin said when he stopped to take a stone out of his boot on the next street corner. "Have you ever seen anything like this?"

Mathew shook his head. "I thought Anderon was big,

but this place is huge. This street has got to be at least three times as wide as our main street."

"How much money do we have between us?" Collin asked.

Mathew stooped down, opened his pack, and fished out his coin purse. He hefted it in his hand, then spilled the contents out into his palm.

"I've got twelve silver elgars and five coppers. You?"

"Eight silver, four copper," Collin replied, locating his purse.

"What happened to the rest?" Mathew asked.

"Some crew members taught me a game with dice. I didn't do so well," Collin grumbled.

"Well, it's more than enough for a week's lodging— meals too, I think. I'll have to remember to thank Captain Donal for throwing our packs at us. I'd have regretted losing my sword."

"Zachariah nearly hit me in the head with my own staff," Collin said.

"Be thankful he remembered it."

The directions Father Thomas gave them proved accurate, and they had little trouble locating the tavern. Surprisingly, it was not very large. The building reminded Mathew of Devondale's Rose and Crown. Thankfully, no one paid them much attention when they entered. Over the fireplace was a tapestry depicting a now familiar hunting scene. Mathew looked at it and wondered whether all taverns contained the same pictures.

While they were waiting for the proprietor to appear, the room's leaden atmosphere became apparent. It was the same mood Mathew had noticed in the streets. Despite all the activity, few people made eye contact, content to attract as little attention as possible. He had hoped Tyraine at least might be different, closer to Devondale, but that wasn't the case. It hadn't taken him long to understand why.

A few minutes earlier, when they had entered the plaza Father Thomas told them about, the gallows lining the hills above the city became visible once more. There were few times in his life Mathew could remember being struck totally speechless, but he knew that sight would stay burned in his mind forever. Although still a considerable distance away, they were far closer now than they were on the ship. Silhouettes of women and children were unmistakable, moving back and forth in the breeze. It was almost too much to bear. When Collin saw it, he let out a string of oaths under his breath. Unable to look away, Mathew kept his eyes locked on the macabre scene, wishing to God he had never seen it. Eventually, Collin had to pull him by the elbow.

They were not in the Stone Pheasant long before the landlord appeared. A loose-limbed, shambling sort, he looked them over suspiciously through a pair of rheumy eyes.

"What can I do for you gentlemen?" he asked, noting the condition of their clothes.

"I apologize for our appearance," Mathew responded. "We had a disagreement with our former employer."

"Disagreement? Looks more like you've been for a swim in the harbor to me. Smells like it too," he said with a sniff.

"That's how the disagreement was concluded," Collin said.

The landlord gave a short quick bark that started as a laugh but ended in a series of coughs.

"We're looking for a man named Miles Vernon. We're supposed to meet him here," Mathew said.

"Don't know anyone by that name," the landlord said when he finished coughing. "But there's a lot of new people in the city these days. Can't say I know everyone. You're welcome to look around, though. You want something to eat?"

"Thank you," Mathew said. "I suppose we could do with a meal and a bottle of wine. What are you serving today?"

"Meat and potatoes with new spring vegetables. It's good too. Had some myself a while ago and I'm still standing." The innkeeper began laughing at his own joke, which only produced another series of coughs.

"I hope that's not from the food," Collin whispered under his breath.

After recovering sufficiently, the landlord said, "Take that table over there. I won't be able to serve you any drink, unless you're over seventeen—duchess's new law."

"It's all right," Mathew said. "We're both eighteen."

"As old as all that?" the landlord joked, not unkindly.

"You'd think with the war, the rule would be relaxed a bit," Mathew said.

The landlord shrugged and led them across the room. "No such luck," he said. "The Vargoth army's told everyone they're going to enforce all the laws of the province—and some new ones too. It's not good for business, but I can't complain. At least I'm still *in* business." Lowering his voice, he added, "That more than I can say for some."

Collin commiserated, shaking his head.

"Do you know where we can get a room? It's possible the man we have to meet may not arrive until tomorrow."

"I've got a room upstairs. I can let you have it for two silvers a night."

"Two silvers!" Collin exclaimed. "That's more than twice the price it should be."

"Times are hard. I can't say I like it any better than you do, but you won't find a room in the city any cheaper. I'll throw in towels and a bath to boot."

Following a brief conference with Mathew, during which the landlord politely looked away, the transaction was concluded. They sat down to wait for their food and Father Thomas.

31

Tyraine

THE FOLLOWING MORNING AFTER HE HAD FINISHED breakfast, there was a discrete rap at the door. Father Thomas opened it to find a Vargoth mercenary standing there.

"Commander Danus said to inform you when the man you were expecting arrived. We have him downstairs. He claims his name is Thad Layton, a silversmith from Astara, and the boy with him is his apprentice."

"Very good. I'll be down presently."

Father Thomas finished dressing quickly and descended the stairs. Seated in the living room amidst the comfortable furniture of the former mayor were Akin and Daniel. As soon as Akin saw him, he opened his mouth to speak, but Father Thomas cut him off with a raised hand.

"You are late, Master Layton," he said, using the Cincar accent for the benefit of the soldiers, who were obviously listening, though pretending not to.

Akin immediately closed his mouth as soon as he heard Father Thomas use the name of their deceased friend.

"The Sultar will not be pleased by this delay."

There was the briefest of pauses before Akin responded. "My apologies, but we were unavoidably detained."

"Your excuses are of no concern to me. We have paid you well, and if you want to continue to be paid, I suggest you plan your actions more carefully in the future."

Turning to the soldiers, he said, "Do you know where Commander Danus is?"

"I think he's down at the docks with Colonel Vanko, examining the Mirdite ship that just brought these two in, my lord."

Inspecting their plunder, more likely, Father Thomas thought.

He made a gesture of annoyance for the benefit of the soldiers. "Very well. Tell him to join me when he is through. The rest of you leave us, but remain close by. I must speak with this man."

As soon as the soldiers were gone, Father Thomas embraced them both but put a finger over his lips before either could speak. He quickly crossed the room and pulled the curtain back an inch or two, peering out the opening. Satisfied that they were alone, he came back.

"Thank God you're both all right."

"We're fine," Akin replied, "I didn't know what to make of it when those soldiers came for us."

"The city is taken, as you must have already guessed," Father Thomas said. "Unfortunately, this is not the worst of it. Those soldiers are mercenaries from Vargoth. It seems Duren has convinced them to enter the war on the side of Alor Satar. They've murdered hundreds of innocent's already."

"We saw on the way in," Daniel said gravely.

"It's worse than you think," Akin said. "The day after you left, the Nyngary army crossed the border and entered Elberton. Duchess Elita sacrificed her personal bodyguard trying to stop them. It was no use. They were slaughtered to a man."

"Is—"

"Ceta is fine," Akin said quickly.

Father Thomas suddenly felt like he had been hit in the stomach. He looked at his hands and realized they were shaking. He tried to stop them and couldn't. "I never should have—"

"There was nothing you could have done," Daniel said, coming over to put an arm around the priest's shoulders. "She sends her love, by the way. You should have seen her—bashed one soldier over the head with a frying pan

and told him to mind his manners under her roof. And he
did too."

Father Thomas put his hands over his face and drew a
long deep breath. When he took them away, his eyes were
red-rimmed. "She's all right?"

"I swear, Father. She's a strong woman. You'd have
been proud of her," Daniel replied. Akin nodded in
agreement.

Father Thomas closed his eyes.

"There's more I have to tell you," Akin said. He waited
until he had the priest's attention and continued. "From
the time they arrived, it was obvious the Nyngaryns had
no interest in Elberton. They were there for one reason
and one reason only—to find Mathew."

"What?"

"It's the ring," Daniel said. "They interrogated everybody in Elberton, asking whether they knew anything
about it, or him. Eventually they found Will Tavish; or
rather, he found them. Now their fleet is on the way here."

"Their fleet?"

"Thirty-five, maybe forty ships, and all of them packed
to overflowing with Nyngary soldiers. We heard that
some of them were carrying troops from Cincar as well."

"This is incredible," Father Thomas said.

"The captain of the *Douhalia* cut the anchor and snuck
past them at night," Akin said. "We got out just in time.
They can't be more than a day behind us. Are the others
here too?"

Father Thomas shook his head. "Just Lara," he replied.
"We hid Collin and Mathew when the Vargoth galleys in-
tercepted our ship. I'm sure they weren't taken or I'd
have heard of it by now. Our plan was to meet at a tavern
called the Stone Pheasant. It's not far from here."

"Just out of curiosity, Father, exactly what are *you* doing here?" Daniel asked.

A smile slowly spread across the priest's face. "They
think I'm the brother of the Sultar . . . and that Lara is his
daughter," he answered, rubbing his chin.

"You can't be serious!" Daniel said, getting to his feet. Akin's mouth just fell open.

Father Thomas shrugged, looking slightly abashed. "Greed is a powerful motivator, my son. I merely appealed to the commander's baser instincts. But in light of what you have just told me, we have even less time than I'd hoped for."

"That babble you were speaking was Cincar?" Akin asked. "I confess I didn't understand a word of it. Where did you ever learn it?"

"Oh, here and there," Father Thomas replied offhandedly, not really meeting Akin's eyes. "The important thing is *they* didn't understand it either. Right now we have to figure out how to get out of this place without the company of those soldiers outside. Then we need to find Collin and Mathew as quickly as possible and leave this city. Commander Danus was accommodating enough to tell me the armies of Bajan and Cincar will be here in two days."

"How in the world are we going to get out of here?" Daniel asked. "They took our weapons and there are five armed guards outside."

"I still have my sword," Father Thomas said.

"That's one against five. Not very good odds," Akin observed, looking out the window.

"Then we need to level them a bit," Father Thomas replied. "This is what we will do . . ."

When Father Thomas and Lara failed to show up at the Stone Pheasant, it was obvious they were more than just a little delayed. Collin and Mathew took turns waiting for them in the common room. Alone in a strange city occupied by mercenaries, their situation began to look increasingly bleak. Each new alternative they considered was as unacceptable as the last. And as Collin pointed out at least three times that day, there was the small matter of money to consider. At best, their funds would be gone in two, possibly three more days. The merchants they came into contact with were all sorry, most of them genuinely so, but they were still . . . well, merchants. Neither of them wanted to consider the possibility that Father Thomas and Lara might not return at all.

When Mathew came downstairs, two soldiers who had been there most of the afternoon were still in the same places they'd occupied before he left, except now they were now joined by a third.

"I see our friends are still here," he said, settling into a seat across from Collin.

"Shh, I want to hear this," Collin whispered, moving closer to the edge of the booth.

From the volume of the conversation, it was obvious that at least two of the three soldiers were well into their second bottle of wine. Mathew glanced at the mirror on the wall. They were all large men, dressed in the same manner as those who had boarded the *Wave Dancer*. Each carried a sword across their backs, as was the custom in Vargoth. Their black capes were thrown haphazardly across the top of Collin and Mathew's booth. Mathew reached forward casually, picking up their own bottle of Sennian red wine, and poured a glass.

"Keep yer flamin' voice down, I tell you," the newcomer said.

"And I tell you, I was there—so was Bill. We both saw it with our own eyes," the one who wasn't Bill replied.

"What of it, then?" the first man growled.

"If it wasn't magic, you tell me what it was. I couldn't have been fifty yards from Duren when he knocked down the gates and half the wall at Anderon."

Mathew stiffened at the mention of Duren's name. Collin met his eyes for a second, then looked away, concentrating on the conversation behind them.

"I never believed in magic until I saw what he did," the other man said. Mathew assumed it was Bill speaking. "He just raised his hands and the gates blew to pieces. There was a crash like you've never heard before. Ern's telling it straight."

"And that wasn't the worst of it," Ern went on. "He

sent balls of fire into the middle of their ranks. They broke and ran just like they did in the field that morning. Them that didn't get away were roasted to death. And Duren just stands there on that hill, smiling all the while."

"So?" the new man said. "We didn't sign up to go on a picnic, did we?"

"Yeah, but it ain't natural," Bill replied. "And that's no way for a soldier to die."

"What'd you care how they die, as long as they do?"

"I don't know," Ern said. "Soldiers is one thing. But he burnt women and children too. Had 'em dragged out to the market plaza and burnt 'em alive. I saw that with my own eyes and no one can say I didn't. I'm telling you, he's as crazy as they come. And that sister of his—"

"He must have killed thousands, if he killed one," Bill added.

"And I'm telling you for the last time, lower yer flamin' voice."

There was a clinking of glasses on the other side of the wooded partition separating the booths. It was followed by a silence. Mathew realized his heart was pounding, and took a couple of deep breaths to slow it. Collin's face was pale and his eyes were locked on Mathew's, watching him.

"How can you be sure the sister's coming here?" Ern asked after a moment.

"I'm not sure of nothing," the new man said. "I'm just repeating what the colonel told my captain. That's why we're moving everything up toward Tremont. The Bajani and the Alor Satar are chasing what's left of their army from the north, and we're coming at 'em from the south. With the Nyngaryns and Cincar closing them off from the east, they'll be trapped—nowhere to go. In two days it'll be over. Easy money for us."

"What about the west?" Ern asked.

"They'd have to cross the mountains into Sennia, and the Sennians are staying out of it so far, so are the Mirdites."

"Do you think the Orlocks will show up here as well?

They give me the shakes just looking at them." It was ` Bill's voice again.

A heated exchange followed among the occupants of the booth, but it was mostly in angry whispers. Neither Mathew nor Collin were able to hear what was said.

It was still going on when Collin said, "I've heard enough of this. Let's get out of here."

"One of us has to be here in case Father Thomas and Lara show up," Mathew replied.

He was as shaken as Collin by the conversation he'd just heard, but his mind was trying to settle on what they had to do next. The first priority was to somehow get word to the Elgarian army. And that promised to be no easy task. He didn't know where Tremont was, except it was someplace north of them. He was also unfamiliar with the countryside. They needed Father Thomas. But if the priest didn't come soon, it might be too late.

"I'll stay," he said.

"Fine," Collin answered, sliding out of the booth.

Mathew grabbed his friend's arm as he started to leave and pulled him closer. After seventeen years, the look on Collin's face was familiar to him.

"Listen, this is not the time to do anything stupid. We need to find Father Thomas and let him know about this."

Collin started to pull away but Mathew held onto his arm. He could see what was building in his friend's eyes.

"And what if he's dead already? What if they're both dead?" Collin whispered fiercely.

There was a mixture of anger and frustration in his voice, and something else too—accusation. Mathew slowly released his fingers.

When Collin got outside, he turned left and started walking rapidly. He was angry. Angry at their situation. Angry with himself for the words he had used to Mat, and furious that so many people had been needlessly murdered. He felt like throwing back his head and screaming, or better yet, hitting somebody. But what would that accomplish?

It might make me feel better, he grumbled to himself.

After about two blocks he came to a halt and took a deep breath. There had to be *something* they could do. Two more days and the Elgarian army would be trapped and destroyed. He'd never been to Alor Satar, or even met anyone from that country, but if they were anything like the Vargothans, there was little doubt in his mind that Elgaria was in dire trouble.

Uncertain what to do or which direction to take, he walked a little more, then stopped next to an alleyway that ran between two buildings. A woman with two young children was coming up the street toward him, and he stepped aside to allow them to pass. When they got close enough, he could see she was young and had a pretty face.

Probably not much older than me, he thought.

She glanced at him nervously, then looked away, pulling the children closer to her. Fear and apprehension beclouded her features. She disappeared around the corner without looking back. It was the same expression he had seen on a number of other faces since they'd arrived in Tyraine.

Collin shook his head sadly. This was no way for anyone to live. Duren had no right to do this to them—to anyone. People's lives were their own. It was what he'd grown up knowing in dull, boring Devondale. Except no one ever mentioned it. *A fundamental concept* was a favorite expression of Father Thomas. Now . . .

This is no good, he thought. *Got to go back and tell Mat I didn't mean anything by what I said.*

Just as he turned to go, a hand clamped over his mouth and he felt himself being lifted off his feet and carried into the alley. Collin reacted immediately, lashing backward with his foot. He struck something solid, which felt very much like the trunk of a tree. The blow had no effect at all on his assailant. He fought wildly, trying to free himself from the grasp of whoever was holding him. The man was incredibly powerful, and Collin's efforts had no more effect than a child against an adult.

"*Collin . . . Collin*, it's all right. It's me. *Stop fighting.*"

He knew that voice.

A second later the hold around his chest relaxed and his captor set him down. He turned and found himself staring into the smiling face of Fergus Gibb. Standing next to him was one of the largest men Collin had ever seen.

"Fergus!" he exclaimed, throwing his arms around him.

They embraced with the warmth of two lost friends finding each other in a strange place.

"What? How?" Collin sputtered when they separated.

"I'm sorry." Fergus laughed, drawing Collin deeper into the alley. "Truly I am. But it was the only way we could get you off the street quick enough without attracting attention ourselves."

"I don't understand. How did you get here?" Collin asked.

"Siward Thomas sent me. I've been here for over a week waiting for you. Oh . . . excuse my lack of manners. Collin, this is Gawl. He's one of us."

Collin looked up at a bearded face. He was almost six feet tall himself, but this man was huge. He was easily a foot taller than him and looked like he weighed at least 325 pounds—all solid muscle.

"One of us? He looks more like three of us."

Two bushy eyebrows came together briefly, then the large face broke a wide grin, showing a mouth full of white, even teeth. It changed him a great deal. Gawl extended a hand, completely engulfing Collin's hand in his own.

"Well said, young friend. Obviously, Fergus, we have found a man of wit as well as manners," Gawl's deep voice rumbled. "You were not only polite enough to step aside for that woman and her children, but most accommodating to us as well. I trust I did not hurt you."

"No, but you nearly scared me to death. I'm sorry I kicked you."

"Think no more on it." Gawl smiled again. "I have grown accustomed to this rough and tumble life . . . though only with the greatest reluctance."

"Gawl is a sculptor," Fergus said.

"A sculptor?" Collin said, looking at Gawl again. He blinked as a pair of warm brown eyes looked down at him.

"Indeed. Soldiering is only a sometime vocation with me. I have a studio just outside Barcora. Has anyone ever told you that you have a most interesting bone structure? Perhaps you'll allow me to do your head sometime."

The remark did little to increase Collin's sense of comfort as he stood next to the giant. "You're a Sennian?" he asked, shifting the subject away from Gawl's *"doing his head."* Whatever that meant, he was perfectly willing to leave his education on the subject for another time.

Gawl bowed slightly in response.

"How did you know where to find me?" he asked, turning to Fergus.

"We were watching you from across the street, hoping you and Mat would step out of the tavern. When you did, we followed. But you were walking so fast, it took us several blocks just to catch up."

"I don't see why you didn't just come in."

"Well . . . it seems the mercenaries found two of their soldiers dead with broken necks. They've been searching the city looking for a large fellow who was seen in the area. And if I'm not mistaken, there were three Vargothan soldiers keeping you company in the common room. So we felt it best not to attract attention to ourselves."

Collin looked from Fergus to Gawl, who smiled at him, showing his teeth again. This time, it only seemed to give him a feral aspect.

"I see. Mat and I have been waiting for Father Thomas and Lara. We were supposed to meet them at the Stone Pheasant yesterday."

"Father Thomas?" Gawl said in a deep base voice. "You did say *Father* Thomas, didn't you?"

"Yes," Collin replied.

"Siward Thomas is a priest?" he asked, looking at Fergus.

Fergus spread his hands and shrugged.

Collin was unprepared for Gawl's reaction. The man

put his head back and began to laugh. It was a rich, booming sound.

"For God's sake, Gawl, hold it down. You'll have every soldier within five blocks down on us."

"Forgive me," he said, wiping a tear from the corner of his eye with a thick finger. "I have heard much in the past few weeks, but I simply was not prepared for the news that Siward Thomas is a priest. This is just wonderful," he added, still chuckling to himself.

"I take it, then, you know Father Thomas?" Collin asked.

"Oh, yes," Gawl answered, struggling to hold back a fresh round of laughter. "We served together many years ago in the last war. Another unfortunate distraction that kept me from my work, as it turned out."

"I was about to tell you, *before I was interrupted*, that we know where Father Thomas and Lara are," Fergus said. "It seems they're staying at the house of the mayor, or the late mayor, I should say."

"The mayor's house? They're prisoners?"

"If they're in prison, I'll gladly exchange our accommodations with them," Fergus said. "No, they arrived yesterday—with an escort, in Danus's own coach. He's the Vargoth commander, by the way."

"Perhaps Siward has convinced him to convert," Gawl suggested, starting to chuckle at his own joke again.

Fergus chose to ignore that. "My brother and Daniel got here today," he said, "and were also brought there, but we have no idea why, or what's going on."

"We need to go back and get Mat," Collin said. "We overheard some soldiers talking at the tavern. Father Thomas needs to know what they said."

Collin quickly retold what he and Mathew had heard about the four armies converging on what was left of the Elgarian forces.

Gawl's face gradually lost all traces of humor while he listened. When Collin was through, he and Fergus looked at each other.

"This is serious," Gawl said. "We're going to have to act, and act now."

Fergus slowly nodded in agreement, his face having grown as grave as Gawl's.

"It's more serious than you know, Collin. The Elgarians are camped not fifty miles from here at a town called Tremont. That, by the way, was where I met Gawl. Everyone thought we'd have at least a week before Duren arrived. Delain's plan is to take Tyraine back in three days, hopefully with the help of Sennians and Mirdite reinforcements, assuming they get here in time."

"Delain? Prince Delain?"

Fergus nodded.

"Correct," Gawl said. "We have no choice but to act now." He had a hand on Fergus that covered most of his shoulder. "Go back to the tavern and bring the other boy. We'll meet at the mayor's house."

He turned and disappeared into the street before Collin had time to think.

An hour later Mathew found himself standing with Fergus and Collin in a park directly across from the mayor's home. Gawl found them shortly afterward. As far as Mathew could tell, the situation had gone from bad to worse. Two more Vargothan mercenaries had joined the guards already there. When he saw them, Gawl shook his head and mumbled something Mathew couldn't quite make out. Mathew watched Gawl carefully look over the house and the surrounding area with an almost detached interest. It was obvious he was assessing the strengths and weakness they would have to contend with.

Eventually, Gawl told them to wait where they were and vanished once again among the trees. Mathew watched him go, impressed that so big a man could move with that much speed and stealth. A short while later he returned and informed them he had procured a sufficient number of horses that were tied up at the opposite end of the park. Under the circumstances, Mathew thought it best not to inquire exactly how he accomplished it.

Twice they caught glimpses of Father Thomas and Akin through the windows, but they had no chance of signaling to them. The answer to their problem came in a form that Mathew never would have suspected. Just as Gawl was beginning to outline his plan, he heard a sharp intake of breath from Collin. Everyone turned to see what he was staring at, including Mathew, whose mouth had dropped open.

There on the second floor of the house, one of the tall glass windows stood open with the curtains pulled aside. In clear view to anyone who glanced up was the naked back of a woman bathing, her long chestnut-brown hair thrown over one shoulder. Humming, she languidly lifted one arm and run a sponge down it. It took Mathew a second to realize the woman was Lara.

In shock, he started to get to his feet, but Gawl restrained him with a warning hand on his shoulder. The two of the soldiers stationed across the street from the house were also looking up, obviously enjoying the show. One of them motioned his companions over, putting a finger on his lips and pointing toward the window. Mathew felt his face flush and started to rise again. Before he could do so, Fergus tapped him on the shoulder, frantically pointing to the ledge at the side of the house. He watched in amazement as Daniel emerged through a window on the second floor, then inched along a thin ledge until he was directly over one of the guards at the corner. On the opposite side of the house Akin squeezed through a window and moved toward the other guard. The soldier stationed in front of the door didn't leave his post but craned his neck to see what was going on.

"Isn't that . . . ?" Fergus's voice trailed off, finally recognizing his brother poised on the ledge above the man.

Meanwhile, Lara continued to hum, running the sponge up and down her arms and around her back with a complete lack of concern. When she stood up and walked across the room to get a towel, turning sideways in the process, the soldiers in the street nearly fell over themselves trying to get a better look.

"Can I borrow your bow?" Collin whispered to Fergus.

"What are you going to do?" Fergus replied, slipping the bow over his head and handing it to him.

"Even things out a bit."

"But their backs are to us."

"Maybe you'd like to ask them to turn around," Collin hissed under his breath. He pulled the arrow back to his cheek.

Fergus opened his mouth, then closed it again. Almost at the same time, Akin and Daniel both jumped. Daniel's feet struck the guard with a sickening thud. From clear across the street Mathew heard the sound of bones snapping. Daniel got to his feet, took the soldier's sword, and flattened himself against the side of the building. The man he had landed on didn't move. Akin mistimed his jump and nearly missed the guard completely. Fortunately, the man was so surprised by someone dropping out of the sky that he froze long enough for Akin to bring a poker down on his head.

Collin rose and fired in one smooth motion. There was a buzz as the arrow cut through the air and found its mark in the center of the nearest soldier's back. The soldier froze and slowly looked down at the arrow sticking out of his chest before dropping his sword and crumpling to the ground. Then Gawl drew his broadsword and charged across the street with Mathew and Fergus right behind him.

When they saw their companion go down, the remaining three soldiers, hardened professionals, immediately drew their own weapons. Collin fired again as he ran and a second soldier took an arrow in the stomach.

Apparently, the sight of a bearded giant charging down on them with a raised sword was enough for one of the soldiers, who turned and fled. The remaining guard was more resolute and stood his ground. Gawl barely broke stride before smashing his blade out of the way and cleaving him nearly in two. Mathew saw it all happen, surprised by his own lack of emotion as Gawl pounded down the street after the other man.

Seconds later Father Thomas climbed through the ground floor window, then reached back to help Lara out. Akin spotted his brother, and after an expression of disbelief, he limped over, grabbing Fergus in a fierce hug, tears filling his eyes. Father Thomas was surprised, but clearly overjoyed to see them. After she finished tucking her shirt into a pair of men's breeches and buttoning the top button of her blouse, Lara ran over and hugged each of them in turn.

"Mathew, I was so worried about you," she whispered in his ear. "We couldn't get out of here, and I was just going out of my mind."

She was about to add something slightly more intimate, when she noticed an odd look on his face.

"What's the matter?" she asked.

"When I saw you in the window, I almost . . . I mean, I just—"

"Father Thomas needed a diversion, and I suggested it," she replied. "I thought it was effective, didn't you?"

His mouth opened, then closed while he searched for some suitable reply, but no words came out.

Lara's eyes got wide and her mouth opened. "Why, Mathew Lewin, I believe you're jealous," she teased, brushing back the lock of hair that had fallen onto his forehead.

He caught her hand and took her by the shoulders, putting on his sternest expression. It only made her giggle, which was not exactly the result he intended. Lara covered her mouth with her hand, trying to contain herself. With a snort he turned around, intending to have a word with Father Thomas, but had to wait as Gawl reappeared at the end of the street.

"Did you get him?" Fergus asked.

Gawl flashed a wolfish smile.

"I wish he wouldn't do that," Collin muttered.

"What?" Mathew asked.

"Smile."

"You're slowing down in your old age," Father Thomas said.

"The inexorable march of time, I'm afraid," Gawl replied dryly. The next moment both men threw open their arms and began laughing as they hugged. Though Father Thomas was nearly as tall as Mathew, Gawl towered over him by a good eight inches.

"Ah, Siward, I cannot tell you how good it is to see you."

"I wish it were under better circumstances, my friend," Father Thomas said, holding Gawl's forearms. "I have missed you. You look well, truly you do."

"Time enough to reminisce later," Gawl said. "It's best if we get off this street as quickly as possible. One of Danus's patrols may show up at any moment. I have horses at the opposite end of the park."

"Agreed," Father Thomas said. "Akin, are you able to walk?"

"Yes, I think so," Akin said, putting some weight on his ankle. "It's just a little sore from the jump."

Akin's foot, as it turned out, was worse than he let on. By the time they reached the horses, it had begun to swell and discolor, forcing him to lean on Fergus for support. He swung into his saddle with difficulty, wincing from the pain. The rest of them mounted quickly and set out along the street that led up into the hills.

32

On the Cliffs Above Tyraine

AS THEY RODE, FATHER THOMAS AND GAWL CONSTANTLY checked behind them for signs of pursuit. The houses began to grow fewer and fewer, and they finally reached the crest of the ridge that overlooked Tyraine.

Just after they cleared the lower treeline, the rows of gallows abruptly became visible.

Lara gasped and looked away. Father Thomas closed his eyes and said a silent prayer. Both Akin's and Fergus's faces grew stony, though neither said anything. They just stared fixedly at the road ahead of them. Mathew felt his stomach knot at the sight of the bodies of two young children.

"Damn them," Collin muttered by his side. "I hope every one of those Vargothan bastards rot in hell."

Mercifully, they did not have to stay on that road much longer, and it was a welcome relief when they veered off into the trees. Their somber silence was broken by Father Thomas, who told Gawl about his conversation with Abenard Danus.

"Siward, this is very serious," Gawl said when he'd heard it all. "Not only do we have less time than we imagined. We lack the manpower to do anything about it."

Father Thomas opened his mouth to speak, but Gawl anticipated his question.

"Sennia will not be here for at least three more days," he said with a shake of his head. "We cannot move to the north, and the Vargoth army is behind us. Even if Sennia could break through, Elgaria will be caught in the vise."

"How many men does Malach have with him?" Father Thomas asked.

Gawl shook his head. "Malach is dead, Siward," he said quietly. "He was killed when Duren took Anderon. Gerard Idaeus and old Duke Kraelin were both taken in the battle. They may still be alive—we don't know. Fortunately, Delain and Rozon managed to rally what was left of the forces and fled south. There are perhaps eleven thousand troops remaining. We are outnumbered six to one. Duren caught everyone completely unaware."

Father Thomas nodded. "Akin told me what happened to Elita's bodyguard. What about the rest of her army?"

"They are in the north to meet the Sibuyan. Delain sent messengers, but no one knows if they've gotten through. The rest of the Elgarian forces are spread throughout the country."

Mathew and Collin listened in silence as the grim news unfolded. Daniel and Lara heard it too and exchanged worried glances. The more Mathew heard of the disaster that had befallen his country, the more the sense of isolation he'd been feeling for the last several weeks continued to grow. His father's memory tugged at the corners of his consciousness once again. Despite his best efforts to think of other things, he recognized the now familiar tightening in his chest and wished that he could speak with Bran just one more time.

The shadows around them darkened, growing longer as the sun dropped lower in the sky. Throughout the rest of the day their horses continued to climb over the rugged countryside. The road itself, although not terribly wide, was in good condition and appeared to be cut through the middle of a mountain. Far to their right, occasional breaks in the forest revealed glimpses of the ocean and parts of the Elgarian coast. What pleasure anyone could take in such beauty was marred, however, by the reappearance of gallows on the lower ridge, and what seemed an endless line of bodies hanging from them.

Again they rode in silence, until Gawl, who seemed to know the area well, told them the town of Tremont was in a valley about ten miles to the north. A few minutes later he led them off the road and deeper into the forest along a small path.

Fifteen minutes later they came to a small clearing where a magnificent double-tiered waterfall cascaded out of the rocks above them and emptied noisily into a small pond. Delicate green ferns grew all around, and pine needles covered the forest floor.

"Marvelous," Akin said, painfully dismounting from his horse.

"It's called Crystal Falls," Gawl said.

Despite the rushing splash of the falls, a sense of calm pervaded the place. Mathew got off and led his horse over to the pond to drink. When the horse was through he tossed some water onto his face and behind his neck. The unexpected beauty of the waterfall and the quiet calm of the glade had a relaxing effect on everyone, even the horses. Mathew looked up to the crest of the falls, shading his eyes against the filtered sunlight coming through the trees. From where he was, the water seemed to be pouring out of a crevice in the rock.

Behind him, Gawl said, "There's a cave up there that goes back into the mountain. Years ago, I followed it for more than a day before turning back. It contained the most wonderfully shaped rocks I've ever seen."

"This is just beautiful," Lara said, looking around.

"A wonderful spot, Gawl. I needed to see this," Father Thomas said, rubbing the back of his neck.

"Let's let the horses rest for about twenty minutes. Would you agree, Siward?"

Father Thomas nodded and went over to talk with him, while Daniel and Fergus helped Akin find a seat on the ground. After refilling his canteen, Collin sat down with them, leaving Mathew and Lara together.

Mathew spotted a narrow path by the side of the waterfall that disappeared into the trees. Curious to see where it went, he started down it. Lara watched him for a few seconds, then ran to catch up, taking his arm. She looked at him a few times while they walked, but he didn't return her glances. After another hundred yards of silence she poked him in the ribs with her knuckle. He scowled and brushed her hand away.

"Are you still angry with me?" she asked, playfully poking him again.

Despite his best effort at maintaining a stern visage, a small laugh escaped through his nostrils. Lara tried to restrain her own laughter, but not as successfully as she would have liked. Abruptly, Mathew veered off the path, grabbing her by the wrist and pulling her with him. He placed her back against a tree as her arms wrapped around his neck.

"You shouldn't be so upset, you know," she said. "It wasn't easy on me either."

Mathew pursed his lips and took a deep breath. "I did admire your courage."

"Oh . . . is that what you were admiring, Master Lewin?"

Mathew smiled and looked down at the clothes she was wearing. He slid one hand around to her buttocks, moving her closer to him, as the other hand played idly with the top button of her blouse . . . which accidentally came undone. Lara glanced down at the button, then up at him. In the low forest light her eyes seemed unusually large.

"Women's clothing is very complicated," Mathew said, noting that she was wearing a camisole underneath.

"Really?"

"Wearing so many things must restrict one's circulation."

"I see," Lara said, taking a small nip at his ear.

"Definitely," Mathew said, as he undid another button. "I've been reading medical books, you know."

"Liar," Lara whispered in his ear.

"Trust me. It's a scientific fact," Mathew said, pulling on the ribbon that tied the camisole closed.

He blinked as yet another white lace garment became visible. *It's like a bloody suit of armor,* he thought.

"It's a bustier," Lara said, giving him a weak smile. "They're the latest fashion. Ceta let me borrow one. Do you like it? They're supposed to be very sexy."

"I'm beside myself," Mathew said in a flat tone.

Lara gasped when he placed both hands under her and lifted her off the ground. She responded by wrapping her legs around his waist—and he responded. They might have made love then and there, but it was neither the right time nor place. Eventually, they sank to the ground and held each other and kissed.

As they lay there looking up at the sky through a tangle of tree limbs, Lara said, "Mathew, do you remember those hunting trips you, Daniel, Garon, and Collin went on to Rockingham last year?"

"Mm-hmm, but I believe it was two years ago," he said, and made a small circle with his tongue at the nape of her neck that produced a tiny moan. "Why do you ask?"

"Oh . . . I don't know. Collin mentioned that you met some girls at the inn when you stayed the night."

Mathew frowned for a moment, pretending to think. "I recall now. Yes, I do believe there were two girls . . . sisters, from Broken Hill. They were passing through with their families to visit relatives."

"What were they like?"

"The families?"

"The girls, monster."

"Hmm," Mathew said, stalling for time and making a mental note to give Collin a swift kick when he saw him. "I don't remember much about them. They were several years older than I was, I think. Why?"

"Oh . . . I was just wondering, that's all. I don't know why you boys had to go on those silly trips by yourselves. I suppose they made you all feel more manly."

"In fact, I'm feeling very manly at the moment. And if we had a little longer, I'd be happy to demonstrate that to you," Mathew said, slipping his hand inside her shirt. Lara's eyes rolled up and she let out another gasp as his mouth came down on hers.

* * *

Fifteen minutes later they walked up the hill together holding hands. They got to the campsite in time to hear Father Thomas ask Gawl, "Do you think there's any possibility the Sennians can get here in less than three days?"

"No. And it's all the fault of the Church and their butt-pinched priests," Gawl growled. "Sorry, Siward. According to the Church, it's heresy not to observe the spring rites. They succeeded in getting the council to delay committing troops until the holiday is over, which won't be for another three days—and it's a full day's journey from Barcora. There was nothing I could do. My hands are tied."

Akin and Fergus heard the comment and looked up at Gawl. So did Lara and Mathew.

Gawl noticed the puzzled glances, frowned, then said to Father Thomas, "It has just occurred to me that I have not been properly introduced to everyone here."

Father Thomas raised his eyebrows and a significant look passed between the two men that spoke of their long familiarity with each other.

"Well, then," he replied, "I believe you have already made the acquaintance of Fergus, Collin, and Mathew. So that leaves . . . let's see . . . Master Daniel Warren, Master Akin Gibb—who is Fergus's brother, of course—and Mistress Lara Palmer . . . I have the honor to present to you Baegawl Alon Atherny, a sometime soldier by his own description, a sculptor by choice, King of Sennia, and, I'm proud to say, my friend."

Collin's mouth gaped open, then he snapped his fingers as the recollection came to him. "My father told me about you! I remember it now. You won the Olyiad Games years ago."

"Not won. Survived," Gawl replied.

The Olyiad were the most famous athletic games in the world. Held every four years, athletes from all countries, regardless of their politics, were invited to Sennia to participate in the various competitions. One of the events was something called the decathlon. It was unique to the country of Sennia, and held with the blessing of the Church. The decathlon consisted of ten events, one of which involved killing a bear with only weapons the contestants could fashion themselves. The winner of the competition was crowned king. Any man who was able to achieve victory in three successive games became permanently enthroned. Until Gawl, no one had done so for over three hundred years.

Looking at the broad face of the man standing in front of him, Collin was inclined to feel sorry for the bear. He also remembered the remaining three contestants of the decathlon met each other in mortal combat, and it occurred to him that "survived," as Gawl had put it, was precisely the right word.

"Wasn't that a long time ago?" Collin asked.

"Not that long, young friend. I trust your father is well? I'm sorry, but circumstances did not give me the opportunity to ask before now."

"He's fine, sir," Collin replied.

"It's Gawl to my friends, and Askel Miller's son would be considered a friend. Your father, by the way, is one of the finest archers I've ever seen."

Gawl then turned to Mathew and said, "I heard the news about Bran, and I cannot tell you how saddened I was to learn of his passing. Please accept my deepest condolences."

"Thank you," Mathew said, coming forward to shake his hand. When he got close enough, Gawl took him by the shoulders with two massive hands and whispered in a voice meant for him alone, "As I loved the father, so shall it be with his son."

Mathew glanced up into the face above him and was met with a benign smile. He and Gawl looked at each other for a time without speaking, before the big man nodded and then turned to Lara.

"My lady, you honor us with your presence and courage."

Lara blushed slightly as her fingers absently touched the top button of her blouse. "You are the first king I've met," she replied, curtseying.

"Indeed? From what I have heard, I suspect that will not long be the case."

They let the horses rest and drink awhile longer in that green glade before returning to the road. Gawl once again led the way.

"We should be in Tremont in under an hour," he told them. "The army is camped in a field about three miles north of the village by a—"

"Uh-oh," Akin said, turning back in his saddle. *"Company."*

Everybody looked at the same time. A column of Vargoth mercenaries was snaking its way up the road. Though still well below the crest of the plateau, the mercenaries' armor could be seen glinting between the trees.

"How many are there?" Father Thomas asked, reining his horse.

"Too many," Akin answered. "At least thirty, I'd say."

Daniel pulled the brass tube from his pack and trained it on the line of soldiers who were moving steadily along the road. The others watched him with curiosity. After a moment he said, "There are thirty-three, and that fellow Danus is with them.' "

Daniel saw the puzzled expression on Gawl's face, and handed the tube to him. "Close one eye and look through this part with your other," he said.

Tentatively, Gawl put the object up to his eye and peered through. After a second he pulled his head away and examined the tube closely, then shrugged and put it back to his eye. When he was through, he handed it to Fergus, who displayed much the same reaction.

"What in the world is this?" Gawl asked.

"I call it a farsighter."

"Fascinating," Gawl said. "An interesting group of companions you travel with, Siward." He turned back to Daniel and added, "When we have the luxury of more

time, perhaps you'll explain how this *'farsighter'* works.
I would love to learn more about it."

"How long do you think we have?" Akin asked.

"Ten minutes, no more," Father Thomas replied.

Gawl nodded. "Ride," he said, wheeling his horse
around.

Despite their lead, progress was painfully slow. The
road was narrow and not in the best of conditions. Most
times they were only able to ride two abreast, and often
they had to fall back into a single file. Sparse vegetation
dotted the hills on either side of them, eventually giving
way to bare rock. They urged their horses forward. Unconsciously, Mathew reached back in his saddle to where his
sword was tied, reassuring himself that it was still there.

Twice, as the elevation of the road increased, they were
able to catch glimpses of the mercenaries coming up rapidly behind them. There was little doubt they were gaining ground. Next to him, he could see Collin surveying
the terrain. Mathew didn't have to ask to know what his
friend was thinking.

"There are too many," he said.

Collin glanced at him and pointed partway up the slope
at some bushes. "There's enough cover up ahead by that
crystal formation on the ledge for someone to conceal
themselves. When the Vargothans ride through, I can
slow them down."

Mathew shook his head. "You'd only get off a few
shots."

"It would buy the rest of you some time," Collin replied.

Mathew shook his head.

"Well, we have to do something," Collin insisted.

A minute later the problem was rendered academic.
They reached a bend in the road and saw another twenty-
five mercenaries riding toward them over the crest of a
distant hill, no more than five miles away.

Father Thomas threw up a warning hand and skidded
his horse to a halt. The rest of the party reined in behind
him. Gawl saw it at the same time and muttered something under his breath.

"Trapped," Fergus said, unslinging his bow.

Mathew looked at Collin and saw he was doing the same thing.

Father Thomas guided his horse around in a circle, seeking some means of escape. Going up was out of the question. They'd make easy targets for the Vargoth archers. The way back was blocked, as was the road before them. But unless they got through to warn their people, the Elgarian army—and Elgaria itself—was doomed. Mathew gripped the reins so tightly they hurt. That was the moment he made his decision. He walked his horse slowly over to Lara, who had been watching him carefully all the while, and asked, "Do you still have the ring?"

Her large brown eyes held his for a moment before she loosened the top button of her blouse and pulled the leather cord out over her head. She handed it to him without a word.

Near them, Gawl rumbled, "Give up be damned, Siward. I have no intention of swinging from one of those ropes on that ridge. If I'm going to die, I'll take as many of these maggot-eating Vargothans with me as I can."

"I'm sorry I got you into this, my friend," Father Thomas replied softly.

"We're not dead yet."

Mathew could hear the sounds of swords being drawn, but he was still looking at Lara. He was vaguely aware of men shouting and the clash of horses' hooves on the road behind him.

Mathew untied the knot and pulled the leather cord through the rose gold ring. It dropped into the palm of this hand. The metal felt cold to the touch, colder than he remembered. He looked down, willing his hands to stop shaking.

Then Lara smiled at him, and he smiled back.

Pulling his eyes away from hers, he let the leather cord slip through his fingers to the dusty road. He put the ring on the fourth finger of his right hand. The familiar chill was there again.

"Mathew," Lara said quietly to him.

"It's all right," he replied. "Tell the others to keep back."

"Mathew," she repeated more urgently as he pulled on his reins and began walking his horse back up the road toward the mercenaries.

The others shouted at him, but Mathew ignored them, concentrating only on what he had to do.

Two hundred yards from his friends, he dismounted and slapped his horse on the rump, sending it back toward the rest of his party. They were still calling to him. A quick glance in their direction revealed that Gawl had drawn his broadsword. He and Father Thomas stood in the center of the road with their backs to each other. Fergus was helping Akin up the side of the slope, toward the sparse cover on the right. Collin and Daniel were proceeding up the opposite side. Only Lara remained in her saddle, exactly where he had left her.

Far above Mathew, the smoother outcroppings of rock gave way to jagged, more exposed surfaces. He looked back in time to see Abenard Danus and his men emerge from the shelter of the trees at the far end of the road. When they spotted him, they immediately reined in their horses, wary of an ambush. The commander of the Tyraine occupation force and Colonel Vanko dismounted and began walking toward him, searching the area carefully with their eyes. When they were within fifty yards, they stopped.

"The boy from the ship," he heard Vanko say. "Not playing the drunken seaman anymore, are you, boy?"

Mathew didn't answer.

"You're Mathew Lewin, aren't you?" Vanko called out, his hands on his hips.

"I am," Mathew called back.

"Give up. You have nowhere to go, boy. There's a full patrol of our men coming up the road behind you as we speak. Why don't you throw down your weapon? Tell your friends to do the same and you'll find us merciful."

"Like you were merciful to the women and children along the ridge?"

It was Danus who replied. "War is hard, son," he said.

"We have no desire to kill you. We're only following orders. Throw down your weapon and we'll let you live."

"What about my friends?"

"We'll let them live as well," Vanko answered, too quickly. "We're just after the ring."

"Why?" Mathew called back.

Danus shrugged. "It's not for me to say. I'm just a simple soldier doing his duty."

While they were keeping him occupied, four Vargothan archers were stealing their way up the sides of the slopes, using the shrubs for cover. Behind him, Daniel called out, "Mat, there are two on your right and another two on the left."

Mathew nodded, without turning around. "Tell your men to fall back, Colonel," he called out.

That brought a bark of laughter from the mercenary. "And what are you going to do if we don't?" Vanko said. "Stop all thirty of us by yourself? Face it, boy, you don't have to be a soldier to understand the odds. At least this way you'll have a chance of staying alive—which is more than your Captain Donal managed to do. You may have seen him hanging on the ridge on your way up."

Mathew felt his stomach turn over at Vanko's words. *Captain Donal dead?* His mind began to race. Why were they were still talking to him when they could have ridden them all down in seconds? There was something holding them back.

All of the feelings of hurt and loss of the past few weeks began to flood back into him, building in intensity, until at last those emotions were replaced by something else—something colder and infinitely more deadly.

"You haven't answered my question," Mathew said tightly. "What do you want with the ring? And whose orders are you following?"

"Lord Karas Duren of Alor Satar, your liege and the ruler of this country," Danus replied, executing a mock bow.

"*Wrong answer*," Mathew said softly to himself.

* * *

A moment later it seemed to Collin that the mouth of hell suddenly opened in that narrow pass. He had been moving sideways along the slope, hoping to get a clear shot at either Danus or Vanko, to give Mat cover. He had no clue what his friend was trying to do. Either Mat was playing his last trump card or he had completely lost his mind. There *were* too many. He knew that. Father Thomas had said as much only a moment ago. *Well, at least I'm going to do the same thing as Gawl—take as many of those maggot-eating sons of goats with me as I can,* he thought.

And then it happened.

The air in front of Mathew appeared to blur and bend. At the same time, a terrible groaning sound began deep in the earth itself. It seemed to come from the very rocks around them. Suddenly, the ground under his feet heaved violently, knocking him down.

He saw Vanko, Danus, and the rest of the Vargothans freeze in mid-motion and look around. A tiny pebble went skittering by Collin's right hand just as he was about to stand up. It was followed by another, and then another. When he looked, his mouth dropped open in shock, then he bolted up and ran like he'd never run before. He barely succeeded in getting out of the way before the highest outcropping of rock tore loose and came crashing down on the mercenaries. The tremendous roar nearly deafened him.

When he thought he was clear of the avalanche, Collin looked back and watched in stunned disbelief as the area of moving air in front of his friend formed itself into a translucent ball of blue fire that began hurtling up the pass, sweeping everything before it like a gigantic wave. The four archers who had been creeping toward Mathew saw it as well. They dropped their bows and broke from cover, fleeing in panic.

The explosion that rocked the pass caused Collin to lose his balance again. A second later the archers were gone, as if they had never been there at all. All that was left was a huge cloud of dust hanging in the air and the crackle of trees burning. Of the Vargoth soldiers, no sign at all remained. They were either burned alive or lay buried under tons of rock.

Two hundred miles away, Ra'id al Mouli, Kalifar of Bajan, and Karas Duren walked among their troops. Duren was dressed that day as an ordinary soldier. Ra'id al Mouli wore his usual black robe trimmed in silver, and the traditional head wrapping of his country. They were discussing Duren's plan to deal with the remainder of the Elgarian army when Duren felt the surge. It caused him to miss a step, and he turned and looked to the south.

It was the Lewin boy—there was no question in his mind. After their second contact, the boy had succeeded in blocking him, out of instinct, he suspected, as opposed to anything intentional. Whatever he had just done was incredibly powerful, so much so that the barrier between them dropped for a brief moment. Duren felt his presence and instantly knew it was him.

The first time they touched, the contact had scared him. Duren admitted that to himself, but there was a fascination to it. He simply could not believe a common farmer's son possessed that much power in so short a time. It had taken him almost a year. From that brief encounter, he had learned the boy's name and where he was from, while Lewin learned nothing in return. The young fool didn't even know what it was he possessed. Duren had sensed that. The boy had no idea what he could do with the ring, which made him the stronger of the two.

When they mind-touched for a second time, only two weeks later, Duren was shocked to discover how profoundly Mathew's mastery of the ring had increased. He could sense intelligence there, along with sorrow, fear, and uncertainty. Some of those he attributed to the recent murder of the boy's father. He supposed such things were only natural. Though the Orlocks had failed to retrieve

the ring, the information they brought back about young
Master Lewin was invaluable. To know your enemies'
weakness was everything.

In his mind, Duren reached out for his sister. Her voice
replied almost immediately.

"What was it Karas? I felt it all the way out here."

"It was him—the boy."

*"But so powerful! I'm in the middle of the ocean.
We're still at least a full day out."*

*"Get here as fast as you can. We will meet the Elgari-
ans tomorrow. With you hitting them from the east and
Vargoth from the rear, we'll crush them out of existence."*

*"But Karas, shouldn't we be concerned with him?
Anyone with that much power . . . it's frightening."*

*"The young fool has finished himself. He'll need days
to recover, and days are not what we're going to give him,
Marsa. Besides, he's no match for the both of us together."*

"Karas—"

"Just get here as fast as you can!"

Duren broke the link, abruptly aware that Ra'id al
Mouli was speaking to him.

"My lord, are you quite all right?"

"Yes . . . yes . . . just a brief communication with my
sister."

"Indeed? And the queen and the army of Cincar are—"

"Still at sea, but they should arrive sometime tomorrow
to join us," Duren said.

Ra'id al Mouli shrugged. "With or without them, I fear
the Elgarians' fates are sealed. Our forces are far greater,
and with the mercenaries coming up their backs, there is
little they can do. It is unfortunate that it should have
come to this."

"Unfortunate, Kalifar?" Duren asked, surprised.

"Unfortunate," al Mouli repeated. "This was not a situation of our making. I have no desire to shed more blood
for its sake alone. What the Orlocks did at Anderon and at
Melfort was unconscionable."

Duren smiled. "The Orlocks have their own reasons

for what they do. And it does not always coincide with our own. They are a useful tool—a means to an end. You are too soft, Kalifar, as I have said before."

"I do not understand why they returned after these many years," al Mouli said. "I am truly perplexed."

"As I have said, their purposes are known only to them. Perhaps they see an opportunity for their species in this conflict. Who knows?"

"But it *is* well known how the Orlocks feel about the world of men, my lord. After thousands of years, I find it unlikely their mind-set should have changed—unless you can provide me some insight on the subject."

Duren spread his hands expansively. "My dear Kalifar, their needs are not so much different from our own. Perhaps they have grown weary of living in caves under the earth. Perhaps they wish nothing more than to share the sunlight and warmth of day in a country of their own."

Ra'id al Mouli felt his stomach constrict. "But . . . they are eaters of human flesh."

His voice was barely more than a whisper as the enormity of Duren's plan became clear.

"We all have our little faults," Duren remarked.

"*What* have you promised them?" al Mouli asked slowly.

"Oh . . . southern Elgaria," Duren replied, picking a bit of lint from his clothes.

In a nearby tent, Armand Duren and his brother Eric looked up from the map they were studying as they issued last-minute instructions to their generals.

"The Kalifar seems a bit out of sorts this morning," Eric observed.

Armand let out a long breath. "Then I suppose it wouldn't be a good time to mention it was you who raided the border towns in the first place," he answered, keeping his voice low.

"Perhaps not, but I did think my men looked rather striking as Bajani soldiers, didn't you?"

* · * *

Mathew watched the dust settle softly back to earth. Nothing moved beneath the mass of rock that had come crashing down into the pass. The mercenaries were all dead—buried. When he decided to form the fireball, he had no idea whether it would work. He just pictured it in his mind. He felt very much alone. Just then the headache was already beginning. So was the fatigue, but he'd expected that. The more he used the ring, the more he'd grown accustomed to the weakness that seemed to follow right after each use. In the past it had usually disappeared after a few minutes. The explosion in the stables had taken him almost half a day to recover from.

Things seemed to be spinning around him. He heard footsteps and turned to see whose they were. If Collin didn't grab him, Mathew would have fallen to the ground. Lara was there too. She put her arm around his waist. Even dressed in men's clothes she looked pretty. She smelled good too. His mother smelled like flowers, he recalled. Try as he might he couldn't quite get his mind clear.

Walk, he told himself.

That was what he had to do. With a quick glance over his shoulder at the tons of rock lying across the path, he put one foot down, then another. Collin walked on one side of him and Lara on the other.

With each step, Mathew's legs grew steadier under him. Except for the headache, his mind was clear by the time he reached Father Thomas, who watched him carefully as he approached. So did Gawl. He realized that they weren't sure what to expect. He felt perfectly all right, he just wished they would stop looking at him as though he'd sprouted a pair of horns.

The silence became uncomfortable.

"Maybe you should ask Harol Longworth for your money back," Mathew said. "I think he sold you a defective ring."

Out of the corner of his eye he saw Akin visibly relax and smile. So did Fergus. Then Father Thomas chuckled and reached out, pulling him to his chest. Soon everyone was laughing and talking at the same time, patting him on the back. Only Gawl was still frowning.

"Perhaps you can explain to me what just happened, Siward," he said. "I know what I saw, but I find it difficult to believe in magic," he said quietly, dangerously.

"It's not magic, my friend," Father Thomas said, kissing Mathew on the forehead. He turned to face Gawl. "What you just saw was the science of the Old Ones—the Ancients. I'm certain of it now. None of us are sure why or how, but I think Mathew has somehow tapped into it."

"How after thousands of years?"

"I don't know," Mathew said, answering Gawl's question. "I wish I did. One thing I *am* positive about is that this ring is the link."

Mathew pulled the ring off his finger, placing it in the palm of his hand, and held it out. Gawl's eyes narrowed but he pointedly made no move to touch it.

"I think we should discuss this later," Fergus said. "We still have the problem of the other patrol. They should be here any moment."

"And we can't go back," Daniel said, looking at the opposite end of the pass, now blocked by boulders.

Mathew was about to say something when he felt a tremendous blow to his shoulder that knocked him to the ground. His left arm suddenly went numb and there was a searing pain in his back.

Lara screamed.

Painfully, Mathew rolled to his side and saw Collin nock an arrow and fire. A second later Fergus did the same. Pandemonium broke out all around him. When he looked down, blood was dripping from his fingertips. He realized that he'd just been shot. The arrow was sticking out of his chest, just below his left collarbone.

Father Thomas grabbed him by his other arm and was trying to pull him to the side of the road.

"One on the left," he heard Collin yell. "Two more on the right."

"Here come the rest," Fergus shouted as he fired an arrow.

He heard a man scream as arrows from both Collin and Fergus found their mark in his chest at the same time. Buzzing sounds from more arrows filled the air as the mercenaries began to arrive. To his right, Daniel went down with a shaft through his thigh.

When you're shot, it's usually the shock that kills you and not the wound, his father had once told him.

Mathew fought to clear his head. Twice he tried to form thoughts of wind or fire, but whatever connection he had to the ring seemed to have deserted him. Through a haze, he saw Lara and Father Thomas, swords in hand, standing in front of him.

It was safe to say that the last thing the mercenaries expected as they made their way up the remaining grade into the pass was the insane charge of Gawl, who crashed into them screaming at the top of his lungs and wielding his huge broadsword, followed by Fergus Gibb and his limping brother Akin.

Mathew managed to get unsteadily to his feet and draw his sword. To his surprise, instead of seeing just the black uniforms of Vargoth, he also saw flashes of scarlet and gold cloaks among them as well. He blinked and looked again. Soldiers of both the Elgarian Royal Guard and Duke Kraelin's troops burst into the pass. They were hacking down the Vargothans left and right. Meanwhile, Gawl, roaring his fearsome battle cry, waded in among them, dealing death with every massive swing of his sword. It was frightening to watch.

In the midst of the battle, Mathew spotted a tall figure on horseback clad in battered gold chain mail rise in his stirrups and yell out, "To me, Elgaria! Rally to me!"

A contingent of soldiers formed around the man and drove the mercenaries up into the pass. The Elgarians went mad, fighting with terrible ferocity. More black uniforms were going down before the onslaught than were standing.

Abruptly, four of the mercenaries broke away from the fight. "There!" one of them shouted, pointing at Mathew. "He's there!" and charged directly at where he, Father Thomas, and Lara were standing.

Mathew was having trouble focusing. The pain in his shoulder was almost unbearable. Father Thomas and Lara stepped forward to meet them. The soldiers were barely twenty yards from them now. With the arrow still lodged deep in his shoulder, Mathew steadied himself and staggered to his right. Blood continued to flow freely down his left arm. He braced himself.

Mathew saw Collin dashing back to help, but knew he would never make it in time. The first soldier was nearly on them.

Then Father Thomas moved. With precise timing, he sidestepped the first man, ducking under his blade. In a flash he thrust his own sword deep into the man's side. The soldier screamed and crumpled, falling face forward to the ground. Mathew tried to get between Lara and the next man, but his legs seemed to be made of lead. He was close enough to see the beads of sweat on the Vargothan's face. The man's cold, hard eyes were intent on her. With his lips pulled back in a snarl, he thrust his sword directly at Lara's chest.

Lara saw it too. Just as Father Thomas had taught her, she executed the parry. Her hand yielded backward, turning the blade aside and using the man's own momentum against him. The mercenary realized what was happening too late, and tried desperately to twist his body out of the way to avoid the point of the blade she left in line with his chest. Shock and anger registered on his face, followed by surprise as he careened forward, impaling himself on her weapon. He was dead before he hit the ground. Lara put her foot on the soldier's chest and pulled her weapon free. The third soldier died when Collin's arrow took him in the back of the neck, firing as he ran.

Neither Father Thomas nor Lara was in time to stop the fourth soldier, who crashed past them and directly into Mathew. With every bit of speed he was still able to call upon, Mathew parried upward, sweeping his line from low to high, deflecting the thrust that surely would have ended his life. He immediately lowered his shoulder and drove forward, catching the man full in the abdomen. With the last strength left in his legs, Mathew lifted straight upward and arched his back, tossing the soldier over his head.

Off his feet, the soldier desperately reached for anything he could get hold of. He found the arrow lodged in Mathew's shoulder and grabbed it. The pain was excruciating. Mathew gasped in shock as breath left his body and a black curtain settled over his eyes.

33

Lower Elgaria, Town of Tremont

HE HAD NO IDEA WHERE HE WAS OR HOW LONG HE LAY there. From somewhere far off, he heard voices, distant and faint. Gradually they got louder, and he felt himself swimming up to a world of light and sound once again. When Mathew finally opened his eyes and looked around, he found he was lying on a cot. His left shoulder was bandaged and his arm was held fast across his chest in a sling. He tested the shoulder, moving it just a bit. It hurt, but not objectionably so—less than he thought it would, actually. Cautiously, he began to orient himself to his surroundings. The terrible fatigue he felt earlier seemed to be gone, along with the headache. He rolled over onto his good side, propped himself up on one elbow and saw Lara asleep in a chair on the opposite side of the room. There was a blanket covering her. The light coming through the window was gray, making it difficult to tell whether it was early morning or dusk. *Morning*, he decided after a moment. Raindrops dotted the windowpane.

In the opposite corner of the room, his sword was propped up against a chest of drawers, and someone— Lara, he assumed—had folded his breeches and shirt and placed them at the end of his bed. With a start, he realized the ring was no longer on his finger. It was back on the leather cord, hanging from his neck again. He didn't even remember taking it off.

Mathew swung his feet to the floor and reached for his clothes. The fact that he was still alive and Lara was sitting nearby, he took to be a positive sign.

He was quietly slipping his foot into his breeches, trying not to wake her, when he heard her say, "You have a cute bottom."

It surprised him so much he nearly lost his balance and fell over.

She laughed—a rich silvery sound.

"You nearly scared me to death," he said, catching his breath. "How long have I been asleep?"

"All of yesterday and through the night. The sun's only just come up," she said, glancing out of the window.

"Where are we?"

"In Tremont," she replied.

He realized that he was standing with one leg in his breeches and one leg out, so he hopped to the other side of the bed and finished dressing. Out of the corner of his eye he could see Lara watching him. When he slipped his arm out of the sling to put his shirt on, she got up from the chair and quickly crossed the room to help him.

That was when he knew something was wrong.

Normally, Lara would have ordered him back into bed, but she was helping him. *Not exactly in character*, he thought.

He winced as she stood on tiptoe and pulled the shirt over his head, gently guiding his left arm through the sleeve.

"What is it?" he asked.

She looked up at him but didn't answer right away.

Mathew's chest tightened. "The others?"

"Shh," she said. "They're fine. The doctor's seen Daniel and he'll recover. He probably won't be able to walk for a while. Everyone else is all right. You should have seen Gawl. He's the most frightening thing. He really is the King of Sennia, Mathew."

"Then what is it?" he asked again.

Lara leaned forward, put her head on his chest and gently rubbed her face against his good shoulder. "When I saw that arrow strike you, I thought you were . . ."

Tears welled up in her eyes. A second later she began sobbing and kissing his face all at the same time. He always felt particularly stupid when women cried around him, and at that moment it was the last thing he wanted to deal with. But not knowing what else to do, he responded by stroking her hair and soothing her until she calmed down.

"I love you," he whispered in her ear.

It was the first time he could recall actually saying those words, but they were natural and honest—and he meant it with all his heart.

Lara pushed away from him and stepped back. She searched his face and found nothing but candor there. She pulled him closer to her and put her head back on his chest.

"I love you too," she said softly.

They stood there holding each other for a time. Neither spoke, but it didn't matter. Eventually, Mathew became aware of the voices he heard earlier, and realized they were coming from the floor below him.

"I'd better go," he said in her ear. "I need to talk with Father Thomas."

"He's downstairs. They're expecting you."

Mathew frowned. "Expecting me?"

Lara took a deep breath.

"You might as well hear it now. You'll hear it soon enough anyway. There's an Orlock army thirty miles from Ardon field. That's where our people are camped. Duren's soldiers and the Bajan army are expected in the morning. Since last night, our people have been busy holding off the Vargothans. They've been trying to break through on the Coast Road. No one can use the cliff passes anymore, thanks to you."

"Has there been any word about the Sennians or the Mirdites?" Mathew asked.

"Prince Delain says the Mirdites are making a forced march, but they probably won't arrive in time. Neither will the Sennians."

"In time?"

Lara looked like she was about to say something else but then decided against it. Instead, she turned and looked out the window, watching the rain.

"Lara." Mathew spoke her name quietly.

She didn't turn around. She just continued to stare out of the window, her arms crossed in front of her, holding her elbows. "I'm scared, Mathew." Her voice was barely more than a whisper. "Duren's on his way here, and we're so badly outnumbered. What's going to happen to us?"

"I don't know," he said quietly.

"There are so many of them. The stories they've been telling about what happened at Anderon are just—"

"Shh," he said, gently turning her to face him.

"But—"

He cut her off with a shake of his head.

She looked up at him expectantly, her eyes bright with tears. There was a mixture of hope and uncertainty on her face. He knew she wanted him to solve the problem, to make things better. Only he wasn't sure an answer existed.

Mathew hugged her again, then turned and quickly left the room.

Once in the hallway, he leaned against the wall as his mind was suddenly assailed by images of the mercenaries' faces looking up in horror at the tons of rock poured down on their heads. He closed his eyes tightly and took two deep breaths, telling himself they were the same people who had killed little children and women without mercy or compassion. An image of their faces buried beneath the earth and boulders almost caused him to stagger. Mathew clenched his jaw so tight it hurt. It seemed impossible to shut them out of his consciousness, but finally he managed it. He took another deep breath, then swallowed, located the staircase, and went down.

The room was filled with soldiers, at least twenty of them. They were dressed in the colors of the Elgarian army as well as in the brown cloaks of Duke Kraelin. It only took him a second to pick out Gawl seated against the back wall with Father Thomas and two other men. One was Jerrel Rozon and the other was the man he had seen in the pass.

The moment Mathew crossed the room, many of the conversations seemed to trail away. All four men at the table got up as he approached. Gawl, of course, dwarfed everybody. The King of Sennia's face relaxed into a smile that didn't seem nearly as intimidating as he remembered it. He extended a hand that swallowed Mathew's completely.

"This is the young man we were talking about," Gawl's deep voice rumbled.

The man next to him nodded and said simply, "I am Delain. Well met, Master Lewin. Well met, indeed."

With a shock, Mathew realized that he was standing in front of the Prince of Elgaria and immediately started to bow, but Delain stopped him.

"Time enough for all that later," he said, extending his hand. "I believe circumstances prevented our being formally introduced yesterday. Mathew, isn't it?"

"Yes, sir," Mathew replied, flustered.

Delain was an inch or two taller than him, with a slender frame. He possessed a fine rich voice and a handsome face, with dark hair that was going gray at the temples. On his forehead, about an inch over his left eye was a recent scar that ran into his hairline.

"Be seated, Mathew," Delain said, and he and the others seated themselves as well. Then he turned and addressed a grizzled-looking veteran with an eye patch at the table next to theirs. "Targil, this young man must be hungry. Do you think we might convince the proprietor to bring him some food?"

"At once, your highness," the man replied, getting to his feet. "I'll see to it myself."

"Oh, and Targil—"

"I know," he replied, holding up his hand. The man looked directly at Mathew with his good eye and gave him a quick wink before heading off toward the kitchen.

"The owner of this establishment is a sanguine fellow who tends to short the portions of inattentive guests with admirable impartiality," the prince explained.

Mathew smiled and nodded, mindful that Gawl had said they were discussing him.

"I see our surgeon has you wrapped up. How are you feeling today?"

"Quite well, your highness. Thank you."

"Delain will do. At the moment, I'm the prince of a kingdom on the verge of extinction, and the ruler of a country whose capital and palace have been destroyed. I should have seen this coming and acted sooner."

The apology wasn't directed to Mathew or anyone else in particular.

"Delain," Gawl chided from across the table, shaking his head slightly.

"No, my friend. The fault is mine," Delain said.

Mathew could hear the bitterness in his voice.

"My father and thousands of my people are dead because I failed to perceive what was going on around me. Unless we can find a way to stop Duren and the Orlocks, Elgaria will be lost."

"Well, we're not dead yet," Father Thomas said.

The others who stood around the table nodded in agreement, except Delain, who smiled sadly and scanned the room.

So much pain, Mathew thought.

"They're not invincible, your highness," Rozon said. "We've good men here yet and Duren is still a long way from his goal."

"Not as far as you might think," the prince answered.

"Then shouldn't we do something?" Mathew asked.

"That seems to be the question, doesn't it?" Delain answered. "But what? Man for man, I believe we could hold our own until the Mirdites and Sennians arrive to reinforce us. But this power of Duren's . . . I confess, I am at a loss as to how to fight against it."

"Our men do not lack courage," Jerrel Rozon said, "but it is difficult to send them against walls of fire and buildings collapsing about their heads."

The general added a brief nod of acknowledgment to Mathew.

"Forgive me, your high—Delain, but there are no buildings where the Orlocks are camped," Mathew said.

He heard the words coming out and felt his face growing red at the same time, but having committed himself, he had no choice but to proceed.

The prince looked at Mathew. "Your point?"

"I admit I don't know much about these things, but it seems to me we're waiting for Duren to come to us. So are the Orlocks, or they wouldn't have made camp. They would have attacked immediately."

Mathew glanced quickly at Jerrel Rozon, who folded his arms across his chest and sat back in his seat.

"The boy's right, Delain," Gawl said. "We're evenly matched with the Orlocks. I say we meet the problem before it meets us."

Delain glanced around the table and saw similar sentiment on the other faces. When he didn't respond right away, Mathew had the impression the prince was wrestling with something.

"Let us say we do commit our army to engage the Orlocks," Delain finally said. "We'll still have to deal with Duren on the morrow, and thus far we have been less than successful in doing that. We lost at Anderon, Stermark, and Toland. We have fewer men now than we did three weeks ago, and if the information you provided Gawl is correct, it appears Nyngary and Cincar have cast their lot with Alor Satar. How can we hope to prevail against such odds?"

"We'll do what we can do—what we must, your highness," Jerrel Rozon said.

"There is enough blood on my hands already. The thought of thousands more . . ." Delain's voice trailed off and he stared into the large cup of tea in front of him, absently stirring it with his forefinger.

Mathew watched him carefully. While the prince was preoccupied with his own thoughts, it occurred to him just how heavy a burden Delain was carrying. Not just for himself, but for all the soldiers he led and all of the people of his country. They were fighting for its very existence.

"Duren holds a particular hatred for my family," Delain went on after a minute. "It was to my father that he surrendered at the end of the Sibuyan War. I was younger then, not much older than you, Mathew, but I can still remember. I could almost feel the hatred flowing from him when he walked past me in the Great Hall."

Targil returned carrying a plate of eggs and cheese for Mathew. He looked quickly from Delain to Jerrel Rozon, and then at Gawl, before shaking his head and putting the plate down.

"Thank you," Mathew said. Targil replied with a curt nod and returned to his own table.

"I have decided to give myself over to Duren and sue for peace. At least it will stop more people from dying, and perhaps some part of what we are will survive."

Jerrel Rozon and Father Thomas were immediately on their feet. Gawl, however, remained where he was, watching Delain.

"Your highness!" Rozon exclaimed under his breath.

"What you are saying is madness," Father Thomas said. "Duren can't be trusted and he can't be reasoned with. You know that as well as I do."

Several heads began to turn in their direction. Rozon saw them and sat down again, motioning for Father Thomas to do the same. Rozon's voice was not much more than a whisper when he spoke.

"I served your father, God rest him, and now I serve you, but what you are proposing *is* madness. No good can come of it." It was obvious he was making an effort to control himself.

Delain looked at him, then shifted his attention to Gawl. "You think that I act the fool as well?"

Gawl didn't reply right away. "You're a good man, Delain. But yes, I agree with Siward and Jerrel. If you had your head brought to Duren on a pike, it would make no difference. Our situation *is* bleak, I grant you that. The Mirdites and my Sennians will probably get here only in time to bury us. But I say this to you . . . I would sooner use my last breath to spit in Duren's face than spend one minute under his thumb. I say attack the Orlocks now. We'll deal with Duren when the time comes."

Delain shook his head and was about to speak when Mathew began talking. When he looked back on it years later, he was unable to explain where he got the courage to do so.

"Duren hates for the sake of hating."

Everyone at the table turned toward him. Mathew felt the words catch in his throat, but he pushed himself to go on, speaking slowly and deliberately.

"He loves nothing, and he wants—not for any reason, but for wanting alone. One of the things he wants is death—for you, me . . . everyone in Elgaria. Delivering yourself to him won't change anything."

Delain's smile was benign. "But how could you know this?"

"It's hard to explain," Mathew answered. "I've felt his mind a number of times now. I know how that sounds, but I swear on the honor of my name, I speak the truth to you."

The prince raised his eyebrows and sat back in his chair. "Ah . . . the ring. Father Thomas has been telling us about it. I arrived too late to see what you did. I mean no offense, Mathew, but—"

"I was there, Delain, and I saw it with my own eyes," Gawl rumbled. "So did Siward—excuse me, Father Thomas. There's no exaggeration in what we told you."

"And that is the ring you spoke of," the prince said, pointing to the ring hanging around Mathew's neck.

"It is," Father Thomas replied.

Mathew slipped the leather cord over his head and pulled the ring free.

"May I?" Delain said, holding out his hand.

Mathew hesitated. He was aware several people around the room were watching. He placed the ring in Delain's palm.

The prince turned it over and looked carefully at the writing on it. "The old language," he mused, half to himself. Then, to everyone's surprise, he placed the ring on his finger. Father Thomas immediately started to get up, but Gawl restrained him, putting a hand on his forearm.

"Am I supposed to feel anything different?"

"There's generally a slight tingling in my arm."

In truth, what Delain had just done made Mathew angry, surprisingly so, but he held his tongue and kept his expression neutral.

"I feel nothing."

"It doesn't seem to work with anyone else, except Mathew," Father Thomas said tightly.

Delain held up his hand and said, "My apologies. I should have asked your permission before doing that." The prince pulled the ring off his finger and handed it back to Mathew.

"Explain to me, Mathew, how you were able to do those things Father Thomas and Gawl told me about. I confess that all this talk of magic rings is difficult to accept."

Almost a full minute passed before Mathew answered.

"The truth is . . . I don't know. It's a matter of thinking about something and then making a picture of it in your mind."

"I see. Could you turn this goblet into gold, then, if you wanted to?"

"No. I don't think it works like that," Mathew answered.

"What about creating a hundred catapults for us to use in an assault?" Rozon asked.

Mathew knew what a catapult was, and he had a rough idea of how it worked, but the skepticism was so plain on Rozon's and Delain's faces, he closed his mouth without saying a word.

Delain watched him for a moment, then said, "Would you excuse us, please?"

Mathew got up from the table and crossed the room, looking neither right nor left.

34

On the Cliffs Above Tremont

IT WAS STILL RAINING. MATHEW STOOD UNDER THE eaves of the inn looking out at the town of Tremont. There wasn't much to see. If anything, Tremont was even smaller than Devondale. A few shops were scattered up and down the street. The roofs of the homes were still made of thatch instead of the newer tile or slate people had begun to use recently. The smell of sea air was not nearly as prominent there as in Tyraine, he noted.

Mathew watched the raindrops splashing down in a small puddle and leaned against the doorway. He felt like a fool. Yesterday in the pass when he struck back at the Vargothans, he had felt Duren's presence and that of his sister as well. It was only for an instant, but he knew it was them, just as they knew him. He told Delain that Duren hated for the sake of hating alone. There was no exaggeration in those statements. Even in that fleeting contact, he could feel the full force of the man's emnity for him, for Elgaria—for almost everyone and everything. It frightened him, and Duren knew it.

They were badly outnumbered. And now Delain wanted to give himself up to Duren to save Elgaria and his people. It was a noble plan, but one doomed from the start. Oblivious to the rain, Mathew started to walk. His father was dead. Giles was dead. And soon Elgaria would be dead too.

There were no paved streets in Tremont, just hard-packed dirt. Mathew pulled his cloak around him, letting his long legs carry him away from the inn. It was obvi-

ous from the expressions on their faces they hadn't believed him.

He didn't know where he was going; he just felt the
need to move. In a few minutes he reached the end of the
town. The street became a road that split in two different
directions. A small patrol of soldiers on horseback, weary
and tired, was just returning.

He watched them approach and stepped aside, out of
their way. One of them looked down and gave him a
friendly grin.

"Wet day for a walk, son," the man said.

Mathew smiled up at him and wiped the rain from his
face with his forearm. "What news?" he asked.

"We hold. The Vargothans haven't been able to break
through the bottleneck under the cliffs, though lord
knows they've been trying hard enough. But we hold."
There was a mixture of pride and determination in the
man's voice.

"Do you know where this road goes, by any chance?"
Mathew asked, indicating the right-hand fork.

"Up to the cliffs, I believe," the soldier said. "Is everyone in this province crazy, or are you all fond of walking
about in the rain?"

"Sir?"

The soldier lifted his chin, indicating something over
Mathew's shoulder. Mathew turned and saw the familiar
figures of Collin and Akin Gibb coming up the street in
their direction. Akin was still limping but considerably
less pronounced than the day before. They waved when
they saw him.

"Friends of yours?" the soldier asked.

Mathew nodded. "I'm afraid so. They follow me
everywhere. Can't seem to get rid of them."

The soldier chuckled and pulled on the reins of his
horse, turning it for the town. "Don't stay out too long,"
he called over his shoulder. "We'll need every able body
come tomorrow morning."

Mathew waited patiently for his friends to catch up.

"Odd day for a walk," Akin said when he got close enough.

"That seems to be the general sentiment," Mathew replied. "I take it you two aren't just out for a morning stroll."

Akin grinned and shook his head. "Father Thomas sent us after you. What are you up to, Mat?" he asked. "It's wet out here."

Mathew noticed Collin watching him. He glanced quickly at his friend, then looked away. He wasn't much good at keeping things from him. "It might be best if you both went back," he said.

"But why?" Akin asked.

"Because there is something I have to do and I'm not sure how safe it'll be."

There was a silence as the rain continued to fall on the hoods of their cloaks.

"It's the ring again, isn't it?" Collin asked finally.

Mathew's lips tightened.

"Well, I don't know about you," Akin said, addressing Collin, "but I love a good walk in the rain."

"Go back," Mathew repeated. He turned on his heel and started up the road leading to the cliffs.

He didn't have to look to know that both Akin and Collin were still there. All three walked in silence for nearly a half hour. They were thoroughly soaked by the time they reached the pass where the Vargothans lay buried. Mathew surveyed the slope that rose up to his left.

"What are you looking for now?" Collin asked.

"That." Mathew said, pointing to the crystal outcropping above them. It was the same one Collin had pointed out the day before.

Collin and Akin exchanged puzzled glances and turned back to him.

"You might want to stay down here," Mathew said, starting up the side of the slope. He knew saying it was useless, but he said it anyway. Both of them started to scramble after him.

Ultimately, he was glad they came. Having only one arm free made the going difficult. The rocks were slippery from the rain, and twice he would have fallen had Akin not been there.

"What's so special about those crystals?" Collin asked.

"There was something I saw yesterday," Mathew answered, half to himself, "just before . . ."

Using the partially exposed roots of a tree for an aid, Mathew pulled himself up a small incline to a narrow ledge. A rough path ran alongside it, literally cut into the side of the hill. It appeared to curve up and around to another ledge just above them. Because of wild shrubs and the way the hill was sloped, it would have been unlikely for someone standing in the pass to even suspect a path was there. Parts of the ledge were broken away or littered with rock and debris. Mathew walked over to where the path curved back in the opposite direction. Eight steps were cut into the face of the hill. They were badly weathered and broken, but it was clear they were not put there by accident. When he climbed up, Akin and Collin followed.

The crystals were now less than fifty feet away. There were six of them, hexagonally shaped and at least twice the height of a man. They were arranged in a perfect circle, with one much larger column in the center. It extended straight up, disappearing into the overhanging rock. Except for the one that had been shattered by a rock slide, they all appeared to be intact. Mathew, Collin, and Akin stood there staring at the bizarre structure.

"All right," Akin said. "Obviously, this is no accident."

Mathew nodded and touched the nearest one, lightly running his fingers over the surface. "Do you remember what Father Thomas told you about the things they found on Coribar?" he asked.

"Sure," Collin replied. "It was some type of coach the ancients used—a vehicle, he said, and some machines nobody knew anything about . . . oh, and some books too."

"Not at the dinner," Mathew reminded him. "It was a

day or two later, when you and Father Thomas told me
about what he read with the other priest."

"Right. It was about the rings the Ancients created, and
there was something about . . . crystals," Collin said,
characteristically snapping his fingers.

While he was talking, Mathew took the cord off his
neck and put the ring back on.

Akin saw him do it but made no comment.

"You were saying something a while ago, when I
asked you what was so special about these crystals," Collin prompted.

Mathew nodded. "A split second before I struck at the
Vargothans, I could have sworn I saw a red glow coming
from them. Everything was happening so fast, I couldn't
be certain. I just assumed it was the sunlight or something. Then when I woke up this morning, I remembered
the conversation we had on the ship."

"And you think these are the crystals that Father
Thomas was talking about?" Akin asked, his tone a mixture of skepticism and puzzlement.

Mathew shook his head. "Not the same ones, obviously.
But you said yourself they didn't get here by accident."

"We've seen crystals rocks before, Mat," Akin said.
"Why should these be any different?"

"I intend to find out."

Mathew looked around and noticed a dried bush about
thirty feet from them. He took a breath and formed the
image of fire in his mind. A second later the bush burst
into flames. At the same time, the barest hint of red light
coursed through the center crystal, then disappeared.

Collin and Akin saw the flash too.

"All right," Akin said, running a hand through his hair.
"What does it mean?"

Mathew didn't respond right away. He kept his gaze
fixed on the bush as it crackled and burned itself to char.
When he finally spoke, it was measured and methodical,
as if he were reasoning his way through a mathematical
problem.

"I'm not sure, Akin. But this ring and these crystals are connected in some way."

"Connected?"

"In Elberton, I must have used a lot of power to destroy the Orlocks. It drained me until the following day. I didn't have a lot of strength physically and then the headache came. It took me almost a full day to recover. I had no idea why at the time. The same thing happened yesterday. Immediately afterward, I couldn't do anything at all. I tried when the other mercenaries showed up, but the fact was, I could barely stand. Then I took that arrow . . ."

"Well, you're standing now," Collin pointed out.

"I know," Mathew said, "but I shouldn't be. That's just my point. I should be flat on my back. Only this time, my strength returned much faster."

Collin frowned as he realized what his friend was saying. By all rights, Mathew shouldn't even have been able to get out of bed yet.

Mathew reached up and undid the clasp holding his cloak, letting it drop to the ground. When he slipped his arm out of the sling and started to undo his shirt, both Akin and Collin looked at him like he had lost his mind.

"Mat, for God's sake, what do you think you're doing?" Collin asked, alarmed at his friend's behavior.

"Help me get these bandages off."

"Are you completely crazy?"

"I hope not. We'll see in a second."

Collin hesitated for a moment and then started to do as Mathew asked. Akin watched, incredulous, concluding they had both gone insane.

When the last bandage fell to the ground, Mathew turned around. There was a fresh pink scar about three inches long where the arrow had gone into his shoulder, but otherwise the wound looked completely healed.

A sharp intake of breath from Akin and a sharper curse from Collin confirmed what Mathew already knew. He bent down, picked up his shirt and pulled it over his head. Then retrieving his cloak, he threw it across his shoulders. He avoided looking at either Collin or Akin while he did so. He wasn't sure what to expect from them when he turned around.

"If I hadn't seen it with my own eyes, I'd never have believed it," Akin said.

"And this is the same fellow who gets sick to his stomach before fencing meets?" Collin said. "How's it possible?"

"I don't know," Mathew answered. "Obviously, it has something to do with the ring, and these crystals too, I suspect. But the fact is, I'm getting stronger each time I use it. When I woke up today, I could barely feel where the arrow had gone in."

"What are you going to do, Mat?"

"In Tyraine you said something about evening the odds."

Neither Akin nor Collin responded.

"Do you suppose we can see the water from up there?" Mathew asked, looking up at the hill's summit and squinting against the rain.

"Water? Do you mean the ocean?" Akin asked, looking up as well. "I imagine it's high enough, but—"

Without waiting to hear the rest of what he had to say, Mathew stepped around him and continued along the narrow track. Collin and Akin followed. It was only a brief climb to the top, and moments later they found themselves looking out across the countryside stretching below them. As Akin had guessed, the ocean was clearly visible in the distance to the east; so was the Coast Road, which snaked along the cliffs. To the north they could see the valley where Tremont was located, along with the tops of a few buildings poking out above the treeline. Beyond that and well to the west lay Ardon Field, where the Elgarian army was camped. Farther to the west, the first line of mountains rose up that separated Elgaria from Sennia.

"I think you should go back now," Mathew said without turning around. He stood there, feet wide apart, staring out at the sea toward the horizon.

"Why?" Akin asked.

"Because there's something I'm going to do. To be honest, I'm not even sure that I can, or if I'll be able to control it."

There was a pause before anyone spoke.

"Father Thomas sent us to get you," Collin said. "I guess we'll stay and go back together."

Mathew nodded slowly. Knowing Collin as well as he did, the answer came as no surprise.

Collin glanced over the ledge at the crystals and saw a red glow coming from the base of the largest one, in the center. He touched Akin's arm, pointing to it. The wind suddenly began to pick up, whipping their cloaks around their bodies. Overhead, angry rain-darkened clouds were gathering. A distant roll of thunder pulled Collin's attention away from the crystals. All of them had brightened and were beginning to pulse.

Mathew hadn't moved. Both of his hands were clenched in fists by his side as he continued to stare at the sea. It seemed he was watching something. Following his gaze, Collin looked out at the horizon and could see the sky lit by flashes of light. Had he brought Daniel's farsighter with him, he thought, he could have seen the storm that seemed to come out of nowhere, tearing into the Nyngary and Cincar fleets that were within an hour of the Elgarian coast.

On board the ships, everything was in chaos. One minute the seas were calm and the next they were buffeted by tremendous winds as the storm broke in a frenzy about them. Only one person among the forty warships actually knew what was happening.

The second Mathew struck, Marsa d'Elso knew. His face and his mind were familiar to her now. Men were shouting and running in panic in all directions, but she stood calmly on the quarterdeck of her flagship, oblivious to the chaos. It was amazing, fascinating, how strong he was. The boy was tall with a fine face and blue eyes. The rain had plastered his dark hair to his head and she could see drops of water on his face. There were others with him—another boy, with sandy-colored hair and broad shoulders, and a blond-haired man. Without knowing his exact location, she knew it would be difficult for her. Only a vague outline of the coast was still visible to her, and the storm was making things harder. She would just have to guess, she decided. Her brother, having no direct line of sight, wouldn't be able to help except by linking and increasing her own strength. But Karas didn't seem to be worried, and there were things he knew that she had yet to learn. Above her, a long terrible groan came from a mizzen spar, followed by the sound of wood snapping. It broke loose from the mast and came crashing to the deck, killing a sailor. She stepped over the body and walked to the rail, holding onto it for support. In her head she heard the voice of her brother whisper, "*Now!*"

A moment later Marsa d'Elso lashed out with all the strength she possessed.

Two hundred feet below them and more than a mile distant, Mathew saw trees exploding along the Coast Road as bolt after bolt of lightning hit them. He was so shocked he nearly lost his concentration. A second series of strikes tore into the face of the hill several hundred yards from them, sending showers of earth rocketing straight up into the air.

Akin flinched and ducked his head. "Was that you?" he called out over the wind.

Mathew shook his head. "It's her . . . and the brother, but I don't think they know exactly where we are." His voice was little more than a croak. Beads of perspiration had formed on his face as he fought back. Mathew's jaw muscles were knotted and the veins at the side of his neck stood out bright blue.

A loud booming crack to their left shattered the air, and the top of an old spruce tree disintegrated in a brilliant flash of light.

"They may not know," Collin yelled, "but it looks like they have a pretty good idea."

He was able to spare a quick glance at the crystals again and saw that their glow had intensified to an angry red.

Ignoring the eruptions shaking the earth around him, Mathew shut out everything else and drew on himself.

When Duren first heard his sister's voice in his mind, he could not believe the Lewin boy had decided to attack or that he was physically capable of such a thing yet. True, the boy was strong, but there was no way he could have regained sufficient strength after what he'd done the day before. When he probed Mathew's mind, gently, subtly, he was shocked. No matter. He was certain that he and Marsa were more than a match for him. The boy was concentrating so hard, he would never know until it was too late. It would have been nice to have his exact location, but it was impossible to tell with the storm. Probably on a hill someplace near the Elgarians, from the brief glimpse he had. Wherever it was, he was certain the young fool needed to have a clear view of the water to have created a storm of the magnitude Marsa reported. She would continue to draw him out, making him work harder and harder. That would give him time to make his move.

As soon as she linked with her brother, Marsa felt her strength surge. Almost at once the storm began to weaken. Karas was right—the boy was no match for both of them together. It was a shame in a way, she thought. She had begun to form interesting plans concerning Mathew Lewin. For the past half hour she had hurled bolt after bolt at him with no effect other than to keep him busy, which was exactly what Karas wanted. She knew it would be the purest luck for one of them to find its mark. More likely, they struck the Elgarians defending the Coast Road. That would be acceptable. It was possible she had even hit their mercenaries, which would have been not only annoying but also a waste of good money.

With the storm's ferocity beginning to dissipate, she

turned her far vision to the rugged coastline through the breaks in the clouds. It took her only a second to pick out where they were. The boy Lewin may have shielded himself, or thought he had done so, but his friends were vulnerable. She was too far away to stop their hearts or make the blood boil in their veins, so she contented herself with something more creative.

Collin had to look twice to believe it. Until Akin tapped him on the shoulder and pointed toward the Coast Road, he had been watching Mathew, wanting to help but not knowing what to do. It was obvious that Mathew was engaged in a battle of some kind with Duren and his sister. He accepted that much as true. Somewhere out on the horizon, a tremendous storm was raging. Thunder rumbled in the distance and lightning flashes lit up the sky for miles in every direction. Equally plain, especially once things began to explode all around them, was the fact that the Queen of Nyngary and Duren were fighting back. But what he was not prepared for was the wall of orange fire at least fifty feet high and several hundred yards wide that suddenly sprang out of nowhere and began rolling rapidly in their direction, consuming everything in its path. In no time at all it had reached the base of their hill. They could feel the intense heat as the firewall started to climb.

Collin looked around for some means of escape. He had to get Mat off the hill before it was too late. It was one thing to fight a man, but a wall of fire?

When he heard Akin say "My God," under his breath, he spun around and saw a blue wall of fire, as big as a house, roaring toward them from the opposite direction, cutting them off completely. Somewhere in the back of his mind he acknowledged that they were going to die.

Mathew was instantly aware when Duren joined with his sister. Already strained to his limit, their combined attack almost proved too much for him. But Duren had given away his timing a split second before he struck. Mathew clearly heard the word *"Now"* spoken in his mind at the same time Marsa d'Elso did. At the very last moment he was able to throw up a shield over Akin, Collin, and himself as the fire exploded around them. The force of the explosion was enough to knock all of them to the ground. He pushed himself up to his knees knowing he would have only moments before Duren and his sister realized they had failed.

The storm continued to clear around her, and the Queen of Nyngary looked out across the water. She could not believe her eyes. Of the forty ships in the armada, only five remained. Several were floating hull up, having apparently capsized when the waves hit them, and the sea was littered with wreckage. Marsa d'Elso watched in amazement as the bow of a Cincar ship slipped soundlessly beneath the water and disappeared. Men were clinging to pieces of masts, railings, or whatever would float. When rays of sunlight began to break through the clouds, the scene was even more horrible than she had imagined.

Not generally given to public displays of anger, Marsa d'Elso was unable to control herself. A look of rage contorted her beautiful face. *How could a mere boy have done this?* she thought. He was still alive; she was aware of that, but weak—vulnerable. *I will make him pay. Oh, yes. People will talk about his fate in whispers for centuries to come.*

The captain of the ship was coming toward her. She composed her features and waited for him, but the man suddenly stopped and his mouth dropped open. Puzzled, she turned to see what the fool was gaping at. To her amazement, she saw two enormous waterspouts lift themselves out of the sea and slam into her ship with the force of a battering ram. Spars and rigging started to snap everywhere as the ship began a slow roll over . . . over . . . and down.

35

Lower Elgaria, 75 miles north of Tremont

KARAS DUREN FELT THE LINK WITH HIS SISTER BREAK. His mind reached out for her and found nothing. The only image that came to him was a brief glimpse of the Lewin boy on his knees with his head down, atop a blackened hill—still alive. *Still alive!*

The soldier who entered his tent blanched at the fury written on the man's face and withdrew immediately. Outside, Ra'id al Mouli, sitting astride his white stallion, saw the soldier emerge from the tent almost as quickly as he had entered, with a face as white as ash. This was followed by a guttural scream of rage from within the tent.

I am in league with a madman, he thought.

Soldiers all around him turned to look at one another in puzzlement and discreetly moved farther away.

Clearly, something has happened, he thought. *But what?* More important to him at the moment was how it would affect his people. He had known for weeks the bargain he made with Duren was a bad one. The situation now was exactly as he feared. Having grabbed a lion by the tail, it was impossible to let go. Quietly, he cursed Malach for closing the ports and leaving him no options.

Women and children. His mind still recoiled from the thought of their being given to the Orlocks at Anderon. He'd found out too late to stop it. Their deaths made no difference to Duren, but al Mouli considered himself a man of honor. One did not make war on women and children. There was no honor in such actions, only shame. To fight a man face-to-face and see his eyes was one thing, but killing many men promiscuously with fire from a distance was another entirely.

The man seated next to him on an elegant black horse with a silver bridle was General Darias Val, commander of the armies of Bajan and a boyhood friend. Val had hard angular features with piercing brown eyes, and a large nose that looked as if it had been broken a number of times. Unlike his companions, he chose not to wear the customary head covering of his country. Most of the dark brown hair of his youth was gone, and what remained at his temples was now gray.

At a glance from al Mouli, Val nudged his horse closer. The two men spoke quietly for a minute, keeping their expressions neutral. They looked around at the assembled troops. To a casual observer, nothing would have appeared out of the ordinary. They were simply two friends passing their time in idle conversation. The only indication that something might have been out of place was the tightening of Darias Val's hands on the reins of his horse and a sharp glance in the Kalifar's direction. A second after their conversation was concluded, they shook hands and Val touched his hand to his forehead, lips, and heart, then turned his horse and rode slowly toward the far end of their camp.

Those soldiers who noticed him either saluted or bowed according to their custom, but with the preparations for the army's departure under way, there was little time to consider what the Bajani general was doing. At the end of the camp he turned his horse to the west and began picking his way through the trees, circling well around the camp. Eventually he came to the road that would lead him to Tremont. The advance scouts he'd sent out the previous day told him the Elgarians were camped at a place called Ardon Field. This was where they apparently had chosen to make their last stand. Certainly their situation was hopeless. Even if the Mirdites could reach them in time, he would still carry an advantage in numbers they could not overcome.

What the general did not know, could not know, was

that the odds had recently shifted a great deal. The Nyngary and Cincar fleets now lay at the bottom of the ocean. But even had such information been available to him, it would have made no difference. Darias Val was a loyal man. Loyal to his country and to his lifelong friend, Ra'id al Mouli. No matter that he was a soldier and the other was the Kalifar. Certain things never change, which was why his mission was so important. Unseen by anyone else, just before he turned his horse around Ra'id al Mouli had slipped a letter into Val's hands.

The Kalifar was not only a religious man, but an ethical one as well. The horror of watching children being herded up like cattle and delivered to the Orlocks for food was a sin so great that no amount of obeisance could ever wash it away. For weeks the general had known that al Mouli could not live with such shame. It was only a matter of time before his friend realized that for himself and took the necessary steps to separate them from the monster they were allied with.

He dug his heels in the animal's flanks and bent low, urging the stallion to greater speed. If al Mouli could buy him an extra hour, there might be enough time to stop the Elgarians before the trap was closed. In all likelihood, the Kalifar had signed their death warrants by his decision. *Better one or two than thousands*, he thought. Val touched the breast pocket of his shirt, feeling the outline of the letter he carried, reassuring himself that it was still there.

Just over a hundred miles from where Darias Val rode, Collin Miller opened one eye and looked around. The dark clouds above his head were breaking apart, revealing a bright blue sky behind them. Satisfied that he wasn't dead, he opened the other eye. The rain had stopped, and while the wind was still blowing, it was no more than a sharp breeze. Mathew was in front of him, on his knees, head hanging down.

"Good lord," he heard Akin say.

The silversmith got to his feet, went to Mathew and

put an arm around his shoulders. "Are you all right?" he asked quietly.

Mathew didn't respond right away. Collin heaved himself to his feet, walked over to them and squatted down in front of his friend.

"Hey," he said, trying to get Mathew's attention.

"I'm tired," Mathew said after a moment. "Help me up, will you?"

A wave of relief passed over Collin. Both of them grabbed him under the arms at the same time and lifted him to his feet. Mathew swayed for a second, then steadied himself.

"Are you feeling better?" Akin asked. His voice was filled with concern.

Mathew swallowed, blinked, and glanced at the area around him. The land, the trees, the bushes and grass were burned black for hundreds of yards in every direction. Only a twenty-foot radius around where they were standing was unaffected. Below, he could see the broad swath of destruction the firewall had cut as it roared toward them.

"I can't say I care much for your new friends," Akin observed.

"They probably feel the same way about me," Mathew answered.

"Are you all right?" he asked again, searching Mathew's face closely.

Mathew rolled his shoulders and turned his head to both sides before responding. "Yes . . . I think so. I'm a little weary, but my strength seems to be coming back. It's quicker than it was in Elberton or even yesterday."

"Good," Collin said. "Let's get off this hill before they come back and want to play some more."

The smile slowly evaporated from Mathew's face. "One of them won't be coming back at all."

Both Collin and Akin frowned at the comment.

"Which one?" Akin asked quietly.

"The sister," Mathew said, staring down at his feet. "I didn't have any choice."

"It's all right, Mat. We understand," Akin said, seeing the expression on Mathew's face, then looking at the destruction that seemed to be everywhere. "What about . . . ?"

"The Nyngary and Cincar fleets are gone."

"Gone?" Collin said. "What do you mean—"

"Exactly what I said, *gone*. Dead . . . they're all dead. Every last one of them." Mathew closed his eyes tightly, trying to shut out what he was seeing.

"Mathew . . ." Akin said softly.

"We'd better get back," Mathew eventually said. "I doubt any of this is going to improve Duren's disposition very much."

"That lightning and the storm we saw out at sea . . . ?"

Mathew nodded, tight-lipped. He walked over to the edge of the hill and looked down at the crystals. They were dark now. The realization of what had happened, what he'd done, began to weigh on him. He steeled himself with the thought that they were enemies coming to invade his country, to kill his people, but it gave him no comfort. This time it wasn't just one person, or thirty . . . it was thousands.

Visions of bodies and wreckage rising and falling on the ocean swells materialized with frightening clarity in his mind. Ships slipped soundlessly beneath the waves as men desperately clung to decks gone vertical, their bows lifted out of the water. Death was everywhere. The dead eyes of sailors and soldiers alike stared at him from beneath their watery graves.

Collin started to go to him, but Akin touched his forearm and shook his head. Being older, and with a lengthier perspective on life, he understood Mathew's need for solitude at that moment. The enormity of what the boy just told them he had done was obvious, at least to him. Despite the massive abilities Mathew seemed to possess, the fact remained that he was still eighteen years old.

No one talked much on the way back to the town. Mathew walked a little apart, alone with his thoughts. Akin saw the tears in his eyes and said nothing.

When they got to the tavern, there was a mild commotion going on. Two soldiers were holding a man dressed in a knee-length black robe by the arms. Next to him was a magnificent-looking black stallion with a silver bridle. Several townspeople were there, everyone talking at the same time. The man, however, remained calm—almost disdainful of the crowd. Despite his years, he looked fit and hard as agate.

"What's going on?" Collin asked one of the soldiers.

"We caught this Bajani spy on the road about fifteen minutes ago. Claims he has to talk with Prince Delain."

"I take it you know what a flag of truce is, do you not, soldier? Have done with this foolishness and take me to the prince at once."

There was an unmistakable air of command about the man.

"You keep your filthy mouth shut until you're spoken to," the soldier on his right growled. "I wouldn't trust one of you Bajani cutthroats if my life depended on it—flag or no flag."

"Your life *does* depend on my talking to the prince. Yours, and everyone in this town—if not your country as well. I repeat, *take me to him immediately.*"

The soldier, confused and clearly out of his depth, replaced confusion with obstinance and struck the man across the face with the back of his hand.

Mathew stepped close to Collin and whispered in his ear, "Go get Father Thomas."

"Right," Collin said. He darted around the crowd, which had now grown larger by several people. A minute later Father Thomas emerged from the tavern and walked directly up to the soldiers.

"Bring this man inside," he said to the soldier without preliminary.

"But he could be a spy."

"Then he's an exceedingly poor one to have ridden here under a flag of truce, wouldn't you say?"

"Maybe we should wait for my sergeant," the soldier persisted. "I seen you talking to Prince Delain and all, but—"

Father Thomas leaned forward. "Now, soldier."

The soldier hesitated for a moment, then motioned toward the tavern with his head. The man looked at Father Thomas, raised an eyebrow and nodded slightly. He turned to the soldiers holding his arms and pointedly looked down at their hands. Both of them let go and stepped aside, allowing him to pass.

Once inside the tavern, Father Thomas led Mathew, Collin, and the visitor to a private room at the rear. He closed the door behind them and turned to face him.

"I am Siward Thomas," he said. "Unfortunately, neither the prince nor any of his staff are here right now. What can I do to help you?"

"Your courtesy is appreciated," the man said with a slight bow. "My name is Darias Val. Regretfully, I can only speak with the prince himself. Please believe me when I say that it is a matter of the greatest urgency. Many lives are at stake. I pledge by the honor of my family that I speak the truth. How long ago did he leave? I must know."

"I cannot give such information to you, General Val."

Val blinked at the use of his title, then pulled up a chair and sat down heavily. "Then I am afraid that all is lost."

Father Thomas sat down at the table directly across from him and looked at the man. "Surely, there must be some—"

He never got the chance to finish his words. A low humming sound interrupted him. It filled the room and seemed to come from everywhere and nowhere at the same time. In seconds the hum increased to a whine, followed by a flash of white light against the wall. The light began to shimmer and move, eventually forming itself into the shape of a man. When the noise stopped, Karas Duren stood there looking at them.

Father Thomas was on his feet in an instant, followed by Darias Val. Instinctively, Mathew backed away, reaching for his sword. Then he realized that Duren had not moved. There was something odd about his body. It wasn't completely solid. In fact, light seemed to pass through it. Behind Duren, soldiers and horses could be seen walking past the opening of a tent. To Mathew, it was almost like looking out of a window. It reminded him of the images he had seen on board the *Wave Dancer*. The others noticed the anomaly too. Duren was there but not there. The heavy lidded eyes searched slowly around the room for a moment, before coming to rest on Mathew.

"You are too late. The trap is already closed." The voice had a dry sound, like the crackle of dead leaves under foot.

"Too late for what?" Mathew asked.

A small cold smile appeared on Duren's face, but the dark eyes remained fixed on him.

"Poor fool," Duren whispered. "Only at the end will you learn the power you have stumbled on. But power without knowledge is worthless. Surrender and I will be merciful."

"Merciful?" Mathew said. Coming from Duren, it was a strange word. "If you thought you could win, you wouldn't be talking to us now."

"You think you are strong enough to stop me, boy?" Duren said, his eyes boring into Mathew's heart.

"I don't want to fight you. But Elgaria isn't yours. You have no right to hurt people."

"No right to hurt people? Interesting words from one who strangled a helpless man to death with his hands."

Mathew took a step back. The sheer hatred emanating from Duren, apparition or not, was so palpable that he could almost feel it.

Duren saw his reaction and began to laugh. It was a frightening thing to watch.

"You have very little choice in the matter, as you shall soon learn. When I am through with you, you will curse your mother and father for having brought you into this world. And you," he said, looking directly at Darias Val, "see now the fate of a traitor, just as your people have seen."

Slowly, Duren lifted his right arm until what he was holding in his hand became visible. The head of Ra'id al Mouli stared back at them through lifeless eyes, his mouth open in a perpetual scream. Blood drained from his severed neck.

Everyone in the room recoiled in shock. Father Thomas closed his eyes, murmuring a prayer for the man's soul, while Darias Val's face turned to stone. Though his stomach convulsed at the sight, Mathew forced himself not to look away. Assailed by what he was witnessing, and by Duren's hatred, it took a supreme effort not to react. He was frightened, but determined to stand there whatever it took.

His father's words about fear and being afraid came back to him then. When Bran, large and stolid, told him he had been afraid during the war, Mathew had been confused and shaken by the admission. It was the same conversation he recalled that night in the forest when the Orlocks attacked. He remembered the rest of it now. After taking a long draw on his pipe, his father had told him that heroes and cowards were both afraid. The difference lay in what they *did* about it. Duren wanted fear, fed on it, but he was not going to get any more of it out of him. Even if his actions amounted to nothing more than sheer bravado, Mathew resolved to stand where he was.

The cold, malevolent smile continued to play across Karas Duren's face, and he turned his attention back to Mathew, locking eyes with him.

"I will have it," he whispered. "I will have it all."

Then he was gone. Only the reverberations of a distant chime hung in the air, eventually becoming too faint to detect.

"You were right about the news not improving his disposition," Collin said.

Darias Val's face was ashen as he sat back down in his chair again. "It appears that I am too late." He shook his head sadly.

"Too late for what, General?" Father Thomas asked.

"To warn you."

"Warn us?" Akin asked. "Warn us about what?"

"Your soldiers have gone to meet the Orlocks," Val said. He held up a hand to forestall the inevitable denials. "You need not bother telling me otherwise, I already know this to be true. When they get there, they will find no one. The Orlocks will be here very shortly, and Elgaria will be caught in a vise when Alor Satar arrives. Their army is not far behind me. Nyngary and Cincar will join them, striking you from the east. And Marsa d'Elso is, I fear, worse than her brother. I am truly sorry."

"Then why are you here to tell us this?" Father Thomas asked.

"Because Duren is a madman. He seeks only death, not victory. He doesn't simply want your country, he wants to obliterate it from the earth itself. Ra'id al Mouli realized this. The letter I bear is an offer of peace between our nations."

"Ra'id al Mouli? The king of your country?" Akin asked.

"Kalifar," Val corrected. His voice sounded tired. "None of this matters now. That was his head Duren was holding. All is lost."

"Not yet," Mathew said.

The commander of the armies of Bajan turned to look at the boy Duren had addressed. Val saw that he was a tall young man with a slender frame, still filling out as he grew to manhood. The blue eyes were bright and intelligent, but why Duren should have spoken to him as he did was a puzzlement.

"It cannot be stopped," the general said. "Your army has already left."

"Then we'll just have to get them back," Mathew said. "If the armies from Nyngary and Cincar were coming here by ship, they're not going to arrive."

Val heard the statement. The boy made it without arrogance or mockery. Searching his face, he found no deception, only a very serious-looking young man.

"How could you possibly know such a thing?" Val asked, not unkindly.

"He's telling the truth," Akin said from across the room.

Val looked at both of them and frowned. "Even so, the Orlocks will be here before your army can return. It would take time to carry the message to them, and time again for them to ride back. By then it will be too late."

Mathew paid scant attention to what Val was saying. There was something strange in what Duren had just done.

Power without knowledge. That's what Duren had said to him.

Something was bothering Mathew. He had been unable to put his finger on it while Duren was speaking, but there *was* something curious about what just happened—apart from being overly dramatic. Then it came to him. Thus far, with the exception of him being able to link with Duren, his sister, or the other woman on the one occasion he saw her, the ring had only been effective when he was able to see what he was trying to manipulate. He was fairly certain Duren couldn't have known where he was, because he didn't know himself until a few minutes ago. True, Duren might have touched his mind through the ring link, but this was not the same thing. And then there was the noise. No, he decided finally. It *was* different— something he didn't know about. What Duren did had nothing to do with being able to identify where he was. *Power without knowledge.* But how?

Maybe the simplest approach is the best? he thought. *Perhaps all I need is a picture in my mind.* Mathew closed his eyes and concentrated on forming an image of Delain. Conversations were still going on around him, but after a few seconds they faded into the background, replaced by a low hum.

Later he was able to describe it as looking into a pond where the water had just been muddied. He saw the shadowlike shapes of horses and men. They were moving, though indistinct. Then the waters abruptly cleared.

Three men were riding at the head of a column of soldiers. Delain was in the middle, on the same dun-colored horse Mathew had seen the previous day. Gawl was next to him, and Jerrel Rozon was on a white horse opposite the prince.

There were sounds now—horses snorting, low conversations, and a woodland bird singing off somewhere in the distance. He saw Rozon draw his horse up short and raise his arm, halting the column. Gawl and Delain did the same. Mathew knew they were reacting to the noise, the same way everyone in the room had before. At the same time, he was aware that Father Thomas and Val had stopped talking. Delain and Rozon were looking around in an effort to identify where the sound was coming from. A number of soldiers, confused by what was happening, did the same thing. Gawl made no move other than to draw his sword and wait.

There were trees lining both sides of the road they were on, and Mathew picked one nearest to them. Almost at once the same flash of white light reappeared, and he felt rather than saw himself standing in front of the tree. The truth was, standing there made him feel silly and self-conscious, since he had absolutely no idea of what to do next. Nevertheless, he reasoned if he could hear them, they ought to be able to hear him, so he started speaking.

"Delain, it's me, Mathew Lewin."

The Prince of Elgaria, who was looking in the other direction, let out an oath and spun in his saddle toward the tree.

"Mathew? What?"

"Listen, we have very little time. I don't know how long I'll be able to do this. You're riding into a trap. The Orlocks were there to draw you out. They're circling around to Tremont to catch you from behind. Duren's going to attack from the front and try to pin you between them. You have to get back here."

"How is this possible?" Delain asked. "And who are those people behind you?"

"I don't know how it's possible," Mathew answered

honestly. "Duren was just here, or at least his image was. I'm only imitating what he did. I can't explain it."

"We would have seen it if the Orlocks were on the move. And as I recall, you were the one who suggested that we take the initiative this morning."

"The Orlocks have found a way through the underground caves that connect their camp with Tremont, my lord," Darias Val spoke out.

Mathew motioned to him. Val hesitated only a second before stepping closer to the window of light floating before him.

"General Val?" Delain said, incredulous.

"Indeed. I am just as mystified as you are, my lord, though I am pleased you remember me. It has been more than ten years since we last met. Ra'id al Mouli sent me to you . . . though I must tell you he is now dead . . . murdered by Duren. He charged me to carry a letter to you—this letter," Val said, withdrawing the envelope from his shirt pocket. "It bears an offer of peace between our countries."

Delain stared at the letter he held and then glanced at Jerrel Rozon before he answered.

"How do I know that I will not be riding into a trap? The last time I checked, we were enemies."

"You do not know, but I swear for the second time this morning upon the honor of my name and family that I am telling the truth. Duren is a rabid dog. Would to God Ra'id had seen this in time."

Confusion clouded the prince's face as he tried to understand what was happening.

"Is that Siward Thomas with you?" Gawl's deep voice asked from his saddle.

"It is, my friend, and I confess to being just as confused by all this as you are," Father Thomas said, stepping forward to stand next to Mathew.

"How do we know this is just not some trick of Karas Duren's?" Gawl growled.

Father Thomas's brows came together and there was a pause before he answered.

"A number of years ago in Baranco, there was a particular lady you had become friendly with. She had red hair and was . . . ah . . . shall we say, quite a healthy girl. Unfortunately, she neglected to mention she was married. When her husband came home unexpectedly, there was . . . umm . . . a disagreement. I think we can use that term. And you were wounded in the—"

"Yes, yes, exactly," Gawl interrupted. "That is certainly Siward Thomas, Delain."

Rozon leaned forward in his saddle and looked around the prince at Gawl, who was keeping his attention fixed on the road.

"You need to hurry," Mathew said. "I think we have very little time left."

Delain stared at the translucent images that had so strangely appeared to him for a full minute. Then the prince wheeled his horse around and shouted, "Elgarians, ride!"

Mathew broke off contact. The window he was looking through compressed itself, getting smaller and smaller until it was only a bright point of light. It disappeared as the same forlorn chime sounded from far away.

When he turned around, everyone was staring at him as though he had just grown another head.

"Stop that," he snapped. "I didn't ask for any of this, and I don't understand it any more than the rest of you."

Power without knowledge, a voice whispered in his head.

"So," Darias Val said, looking directly at the ring on Mathew's hand. "This is the source of Karas Duren's power. Both he and his sister wear the same one. Until just now, I thought it only an ornament."

"We can talk about it later," Mathew said. "Do you know how long we have until the Orlocks get here?"

Val nodded slowly. "It was planned that both our army and Alor Satar would strike the front of Elgarian lines on the eighth hour after midday." Val paused and looked out the window. "I'm afraid you do not have much time, perhaps three hours, no more."

"Where will they be coming from?" Father Thomas asked.

"I don't know the exact location of their caves. Orlocks are not forthcoming with such information. The plan was of their making. I only know that one of the caves lies to the southwest of the town. If possible, I would like to remain and fight with you."

"Against your own people?" Collin said.

Instead of replying, Darias Val smiled, showing a full set of very white teeth. "Never."

"Then what's so damned funny?" Collin asked irritably.

"I was amusing myself to think that the great and perfect lord of Alor Satar has made a small mistake."

"Mistake?"

"It is a custom among my people that when a Kalifar dies, the faithful honor him by observing a mourning ritual for a period of seven days." Val's smile became even wider and he crossed his legs, looking extremely smug.

Father Thomas blinked as the impact of his words sunk in. "Then?"

"My people will not fight while they mourn their leader. It seems your odds have just gone up—assuming your legions can get here in time. Otherwise, this is as good a day as any to die."

Father Thomas put his hand on Val's shoulder and said, "Thank you. We would be honored to have you with us. But if you will pardon me, there is much I need to do now."

Val nodded soberly. "I would accompany you and lend what little help I can."

"And you, my son," Father Thomas said, turning to Mathew, "is there anything that ring of yours can do to help?"

"I'm not sure. But I intend to try, Father."

"That's all anyone can ask. Get Lara and Daniel and meet us at the north gate as fast as you can. If they're coming at us from the south, we'll make them fight their way up the streets and alleys. The people who live here know the layout of their town, and the Orlocks do not."

"Can we use that old castle up there on the hill?" Collin asked, looking out of the window.

Father Thomas and Akin came over and peered out the window with him. Val pushed himself out of his chair to join them and examined the site with a professional eye.

"Better still," he said eventually. "The creatures would have to attack uphill, and except for that breech in the side wall there, most of it appears intact. It is only that . . ."

Val's voice trailed off, and he turned to look at Father Thomas. The priest finished the sentence for him. "It may turn into a box with no way out."

Val spread his hands. "Still, it's better than having your people with their backs to a wall."

Father Thomas closed his eyes and rubbed the bridge of his nose with his fingers. "Let us hope the Lord is watching Tremont today. Akin, get those soldiers to spread the word. Have them get everybody up to the castle. Collin, off with you. Get Lara and Daniel up there as quickly as you can."

The boys nodded and made for the door.

"Where are you going to be, Father?" Akin asked.

"I will remain here in the town with the men. We will gradually fall back before the Orlocks, until we reach the castle. If they want this town, they will have to take it inch by inch. Hopefully, we can buy enough time until Delain returns."

Listening to the plan unfold, the Bajani general stuck out his lower lip and nodded in approval. "You have such interesting priests in your country," he observed.

"You have no idea," Akin said over his shoulder, leaving Father Thomas and Darias Val in the room alone together.

Father Thomas was about to say something when he noticed Val looking at him strangely.

"Would you not say it is a strange thing for the prince to leave a priest in charge of defending this town?"

Father Thomas raised an eyebrow but didn't reply.

"You appear most well-informed for a man who follows your profession, Father," Val went on. "It has been many years since I had contact with the Elgarians, but I seem to remember that Malach had a brilliant young general. I believe his last name was Thomas as well. He commanded the southern armies of your country. By any chance, did you ever make his acquaintance?"

Father Thomas looked down at the ground, then out the window. "We meet many people in our lives."

"There was also something else about a duel and a baron's son, but alas, the details escape me now."

Father Thomas shook his head slowly and the two men looked at each other for a time.

"The Bajani army is one of the best trained in the world. Do their generals fight as well as the soldiers?" the priest asked.

"Ah . . . that we shall see." Val smiled. "With your god and mine watching over us, victory is assured."

Father Thomas was not sure about the last statement. As they left the room together, he hoped that God was watching very closely indeed.

36

Tremont

MATHEW AND COLLIN BOUNDED UP THE STAIRS AT THE
back of the common room. They found Lara and Daniel
together in his room, watching the pandemonium that
had broken out below from a window. Daniel's leg was
set between two wooden splints and heavily bandaged.
Though obviously in pain, he was able to move around
with help. In minutes they managed to get him downstairs and on his way to the other end of town, where the
North Gate was located.

Tremont had only one main street. It wound through
the town in a long S shape. A number of smaller alley-
ways and warrens branched off at different junctures, but
all eventually returned to it. Word of the impending attack spread rapidly, and the townsfolk responded without
hesitation.

Collin stopped a man on a wagon and asked him to
give Daniel a ride to the castle. The man agreed and told
them to get on. Daniel, wanting to stay and help, complained bitterly and had to be persuaded. They had less
luck with Lara.

"Mathew Lewin," she said hotly, "if it weren't for me
you'd be in jail or dead now, so I think the least you
would do is welcome my help."

Mathew winced. Her statement may have been literally
true, but still it didn't sound particularly good when she
said it. Realizing it would be pointless to argue with her
any further he threw his hands up in frustration. Collin,
who believed that a battle was no place for a woman, was

about to add his agreement, but a glare from Lara that could have started a fire changed his mind. The fact that she was carrying a sword may have also had something to do with it.

Men and women were busy blockading the street with wagons, bales of hay, wine barrels, and anything else they could find. The North Gate was only a five-minute walk from the tavern. Twice along the way they saw Father Thomas and the Bajani general instructing men where to place the barricades and positioning the archers. Mathew also noticed that five or six women were present with bows of their own, but wisely chose not to say anything about it. A small "Hmph" from Lara told him there was no need.

While they were walking, he made a rough count in his head and estimated that they had about eighty altogether, *not the ideal defense force, considering what they would be facing. It will have to do,* he thought. At the gate they found more hastily erected barricades. The people of Tremont lined them, stern-faced, ready to defend their families and their town. In age, they ranged from younger than Mathew to at least as old as Silas Alman back home.

The road from the gate up to the castle was lined with the elderly and with mothers carrying their children. Lara noticed one woman struggling with two small infants in her arms and went over to help, taking one of them from her. Collin and Mathew spotted another young woman with three children trailing after her and scooped up one in each arm. All of them trudged up the hill together.

The woman turned out to be the children's eldest sister, the same age as they were. Her mother was still down in the town with her father.

"I'm Erin Cardith," she said, smiling at Collin. She was a pretty girl with a fine figure and long dark hair.

"Collin Miller, from Devondale. This is my friend, Mat Lewin. That's Lara Palmer over there."

"Pleased to meet you. Are you with Prince Delain's people?"

"No. We're just here to help out with the town's defenses." Collin grinned.

Erin's eyes got a little wider. "Oh, I see."

Mathew's eyes got wider too, but he rolled them skyward and kept quiet.

At the top of the hill they passed through a large stone archway that marked the entrance to the castle. Erin explained to them that the structure was once an old abbey, abandoned after a fire more than three hundred years ago. No one in Tremont could remember when they started calling it a castle, but everyone had done so for as long as she could remember. It actually consisted of four separate buildings surrounding an expansive courtyard made of gray rectangular stones. Grass grew in those places where the stones didn't quite meet.

It surprised Mathew that the two large wooden doors guarding the entrance were still there at all. They were badly weathered and cracked. After a closer inspection, he had little hope of their withstanding much force. But they were better than no doors at all. He and Collin tested the hinges and found that with a little effort they could get them to close.

The buildings were all constructed of yellow and brown brick, and almost all of the windows on the first floor had rusted iron crossbars in front of them, which Mathew thought unusual for an abbey. Odder still were the windows on the second floor, noticeably narrower than the ones below. Portions of faded red and white tile roof still remained on three of the four buildings. The building to the left of the entranceway's roof was almost completely gone. Not much more remained of the original structure than the outer shell. Through the window openings, Mathew could see that the timbers were blackened, which was consistent with the fire Erin had told them about.

What attracted his attention most was the old bell tower at the rear corner of the courtyard. Shaped like a large rectangular column, it was the most prominent feature of the complex, rising at least fifty feet above the tallest building there, the most castlelike. Staring up at it, he imagined that at some point in the past it must have been used for more than just ringing a bell. Evenly spaced stone ramparts ran completely around it.

At least a hundred people were in the courtyard now, with Delain's soldiers busy directing and positioning the men. Women ushered younger children to the rear of the buildings and then returned to help. Most of the men had axes or swords, and a few had pikes and halberds. Mathew was pleased to see that better than thirty of the townspeople were also carrying longbows. Off to one side, in the doorway of a building, four younger boys were busy piling arrows and spare swords into stacks under the direction of an elderly white-haired man on crutches. Everyone went about his or her task quickly and without comment.

"How can I get up that tower?" Mathew asked Erin.

"Through that door there in the middle of the building, I think," she said, pointing. "There's an old staircase at the very end that goes up to the top, but you'll have to be careful. I'm not sure how strong the steps are. We used to play here as children, and they weren't very sturdy back then."

Mathew and Collin looked up at the tower.

"Oh, one more question," Mathew said. "Do you know of any caves south of the town?"

Erin frowned and made a clicking sound with her tongue. Mathew suppressed a smile—Lara had the same habit when she was concentrating.

"Um-hmm," she said after a moment. "There's one that I remember. Some of the boys liked to camp out in it, though I could never understand why. I guess they wanted to do whatever boys do when they camp. They tried to get me to stay the night once, but it was so yucky I decided not to."

"Yucky?" Collin asked, raising his eyebrows.

"You know, just . . . icky."

Mathew and Collin exchanged puzzled glances. Lara, however, nodded in agreement, apparently understanding what Erin meant.

"How far is that cave from here?" Mathew asked.

"Not far. I'd guess it's just about two miles . . . probably less. It couldn't be much more than that."

"Do you think I'd be able to see it from up there?" Mathew asked, looking up to the tower.

"I'm really not sure," Erin replied. "You might. It's between two hills, partway up. I haven't been there in a long time, but I remember the trees covered the entrance until you're almost right on top of it."

That's just wonderful, Mathew thought. He was about to ask something else when Lara said, "There's Daniel. I'd better see how he's doing. He doesn't look happy."

"And I'd better get the children settled," Erin said. "I'll be back as soon as I can."

Collin watched her walk away and said, "Do you know, I always suspected they have their own language."

Mathew shook his head. "Let's go see what it looks like up there."

"Only if it's not too *icky.* Hang on for a second. I have an idea."

Collin dashed across the courtyard to Daniel. He returned a few seconds later carrying the farsighter.

The door Erin had pointed to was made of a heavy dark wood, reinforced with two bands of rusted iron and nails across it. Like everything else in the castle, it was badly weathered, but surprisingly, it swung aside with only a little effort. The hinges made a creaking sound that seemed unnaturally loud in the confines of the building. When they were inside, they paused, allowing their eyes to adjust to the dim light. A central hallway ran down the length of the floor, with a number of smaller rooms on each side. It was made of stone, as were the walls, and seemed solid enough. A dank, musty smell hung in the air.

"Nobody's been in here for years," Collin said, looking at the layer of dust on the floor.

Mathew nodded, turning to look at their footprints. Some kind of gray-green mold grew on the walls, and cobwebs stretched between the doorways and across the corridor. Behind him, he heard Collin muttering under his breath. Ever since they were children, his friend had disliked spiders, snakes, and other things that crawled. Though Collin would no doubt have resisted saying so, the place was, well . . . yucky.

Exactly as Erin had said, there was a stairway at the end of the building. Mathew tested the first few steps. The wood groaned but held under his weight. Behind him, Collin walked into another cobweb and cursed again. Vines of ivy, untended for ages, crept up along the outer walls, and grew in through broken windows. The steps themselves were covered with leaves and debris blown in over the years by the wind. They proceeded cautiously, stepping over parts of an iron handrail that lay on the steps between the first and second floors.

When they finally reached the roof, they both took a deep breath, grateful to be out of the stale air. It was obvious to Mathew that whoever built the castle had done so with its defense in mind. Because of its elevation, the tower provided a clear view of the town and surrounding area for miles in every direction. He could not remember ever having been in a building quite as tall before. Beneath them in the courtyard, preparations were still going on as people readied themselves for the imminent attack.

The sinking sun was just above the tops of the mountains, bathing the landscape in warm reds and purples. He walked to the south side of the tower and gazed out over the countryside, searching for the cave Erin had told them about. Collin joined him. He rested his elbows on the edge of an opening in the wall and lifted Daniel's farsighter to his eye, scanning slowly back and forth over the hills. They looked for a full minute without any success.

"The damn trees are so dense, it's hard to see anything

clearly," Collin said irritably. "They could be just about . . .
wait . . . see there? At the base of the hill on the left."

He handed Mathew the brass tube.

Though no cave was visible, he could clearly see a
number of white shapes moving in the trees. Mathew felt
his stomach tighten, remembering the Orlocks' ghastly
faces. He handed the farsighter back to his friend.

There was a pause before Mathew spoke.

"Collin, do you think Karas Duren is a monster?" he
asked, running his fingers lightly over his ring.

"What? Yeah, I guess so. He kills for no reason at all.
It's like you said earlier, the man just . . . hates."

Mathew nodded and went silent again, staring out
across the landscape.

"My guess is the cave's got to be just beyond those
trees," Collin said. "It looks like there's a farm of some
sort over to the right. That first group is probably a scout-
ing party they sent to check the area before the rest arrive. I was just thinking . . ."

Collin's voice trailed off as he looked around. He was
alone on the roof.

"Mat?"

Collin walked around the tower to see if Mathew had
wandered to the other side, then returned to his spot on
the south wall and looked over the edge of the ramparts.
Down below in the courtyard he saw Mathew run out of
the building and dash past several surprised villagers,
who had to jump to get out of his way.

"Damn!" Collin shouted, pounding his fist on top of
the wall. A second later he was racing down the steps.

When Lara saw Mathew burst out of the doorway of
the building, she jumped to her feet to ask what was
wrong, but he was gone so quickly she never had a
chance. Not long afterward Collin came tearing out of the
same door.

"Collin," she called, taking a step forward.

"Stay here!"

"But—"

"I said, *stay!*" he roared at her. Then he was gone.

* * *

Mathew raced down the hill toward the town. The men at the North Gate called after him, but he didn't have time to slow down and explain. He knew there wasn't much time left. His first thought was to reach the stables and his horse as quickly as possible. Then, directly ahead of him, he saw a merchant was loading his possessions onto a flatbed wagon in front of a shop. A second horse was tethered to a post on the opposite side of the wagon. In three strides Mathew bounded up and across the wagon and onto the horse's back, knocking the startled man to the ground in the process. A sharp tug on the reins, and Mathew wheeled the horse around and charged off down the street.

He bent low over the animal's neck, urging every ounce of speed out of it that he could. The houses and buildings of Tremont flew by. In less than a minute he was clear of the town and into the forest, galloping for the Coast Road. From what Erin had said, the hills were somewhere to his left. The problem was, so were the Orlocks. Forty yards ahead he spotted a single-track path that appeared to go in the right direction. Praying he still had enough time, he skidded the horse to a halt and jumped down.

No sense in announcing my arrival. Just give me a clear view of the cave, he thought.

Quietly unbuckling the scabbard from around his waist, he slid his sword out and rested the scabbard on the ground. The Kayseri steel, with its odd grainlike lines, glinted dully in the low forest light.

Mathew followed the path, moving as quickly and silently as possible. At home he had always been good at stalking rabbits, and though these weren't rabbits, he decided the principle was about the same. In a short while the trees thinned out. His heart sank when he saw that there was nothing but an open field between him and the base of the hill where the cave should be. What he did see, however, made him catch his breath. At the end of the field, well to his left, were at least two hundred fully armed Orlocks emerging from the trees. More followed behind them.

Knowing he had to get to the cover of the trees on the other side of the field, Mathew dropped to his stomach and began to angle his way through the high grass. He estimated that it was perhaps a hundred yards to the trees. If his luck held—and he prayed that it would—he had a good chance of circling around the creatures before they saw him. Their fetid odor reached his nose. It took him more time than he wanted to reach the end of the field, and it seemed he held his breath the entire way. The trees were now just in front of him.

At last he was able to see the base of the hills Erin had mentioned. He hoped the cave opening would be visible. Close by, he heard branches snapping and leaves crushed underfoot as more Orlocks entered the forest. His own heart was pounding so badly, he was certain even a deaf Orlock would be able to hear it ten feet away.

Got to get closer, he thought.

From the sounds around him, he guessed that the number of Orlocks had at least doubled since his first glimpse. Mathew crouched low behind the last tree he could use for cover and searched the face of the twin hills for any sign of a cave.

Then he saw it. Two Orlocks, fully dressed in chain mail and hardened leather armor, were making their way down the side of the hill. Their cloaks were dappled shades of green and brown that blended with the forest and undergrowth. If not for the fact they were moving, he might have missed them completely.

The cave opening was not what he'd expected. It was little more than a crack in the rocky face of the hill, perhaps eight feet high, and only wide enough to permit two or three of the Orlocks at the same time. He thought that perhaps several hundred had come through already. If Delain's estimate of their numbers was accurate, at that rate it would take hours for the rest to get through. Whatever the reason for the delay he was willing to take it.

Mathew made his decision.

The only way the Elgarians had a chance would be to meet Duren head-on instead of fighting on two different fronts. It was true his people were badly outnumbered, but he was determined to do something to make sure those numbers didn't get any worse.

He'd shut his eyes and just begun to concentrate when a hand closed over his mouth. He lashed out backward with his left arm and struck something solid. Mathew threw himself forward and rolled to his right.

A very annoyed Collin Miller looked back at him, rubbing his ear.

"Collin?"

"Of course it's me," he hissed. "What the hell do you think you're doing, rushing out of there like a madman? There are Orlocks everywhere. Some friend. I come to rescue you and you punch me in the ear."

"I'm sorry," Mathew whispered back. "Look up there."

Collin looked and then nodded. "Great. That makes a thousand Orlocks—and us. Maybe we can challenge them to a name-calling contest."

The comment made Mathew smile in spite of himself. "I've got something else in mind," he said. "Get ready to run like your life depended on it."

A million expressions to choose from and he picks that one, Collin thought.

The sounds around him were getting too close for his comfort. In the distance, there were three blasts of a horn, and moments later another horn of an entirely different timbre answered.

He was trying to place exactly where the sounds had come from when the ground under his feet began to move. Collin froze in place, looking around in shock. So did the Orlocks coming out of the cave.

Mat!

Mathew's body was rigid. Every muscle seemed to be straining against some tremendous unseen force. The rolling and heaving of the ground continued and Collin fought to keep his balance. Seconds later a deep groaning sound unlike anything he had ever heard in his life began. It felt like it was coming from the earth itself. Collin saw that the Orlocks were scrambling out of the cave as fast as they could. He looked up at the hill in disbelief as the rock itself began to move. It wasn't much at first. Bits of earth started falling from the ledge above the crevice and a few small rocks clattered down the hill. Soon the bits of earth accelerated, becoming a shower. Then it happened again. A long protracted groan, like the land itself was in pain, gradually became louder and louder. Unbelievably, the cave entrance was closing. Larger rocks were crashing down the hill now, smashing into the base below. The shocks transmitted through the ground reached them more than seventy yards away.

He saw one Orlock desperately try to squeeze itself through the space that remained—and fail. The right side of the hill moved inexorably toward the left, trapping and crushing the creature. It screamed and continued to scream, horrible to hear. Unable to watch the Orlock's agony any longer, Collin looked away. Blood seeped down over the bare rock. There was a final muffled shriek from the Orlock, followed by silence when the doorway slammed shut. At the same time, the ledge above the cave let go, tearing itself away from the rest of the hill. It cascaded down with an ominous rumble, until millions of tons of earth and rock sealed off any trace of the opening that had been there only a moment before.

When it was over, Mathew took a step backward and would have fallen if Collin hadn't been there to catch him.

"Mat," he whispered urgently. "Are you all right?"

Mathew stared at him blankly as if he didn't know where he was. Collin took him by the shoulders and said, "*Look at me*. Mat, we've got to get moving. They'll be on us soon."

"I just need a minute."

Mathew's voice sounded thick and the words came out slurred, like a person who'd drunk too much ale.

"C'mon, I'll help you."

Collin put an arm around his friend's waist. On his left, the voices were closer, dry rasping sounds. They still had to make it across the field, and he had no idea how they were going to do that and stay alive.

"All right, one step at a time," he said. "Hang on."

With Collin supporting him, Mathew took a stumbling step forward and then another. Crouching low and moving through the trees, they managed to reach the perimeter of the field in just under a minute. To his surprise, Mathew appeared to be getting stronger.

"Do you think you can make it to the trees on the other side?" Collin asked.

Mathew shook his head and was about to say something when a chorus of shouts close by stopped him.

"Go," Mathew whispered, pushing Collin away.

"*Like hell!* If they don't kill me, Lara certainly will. We both stay or we both go. That's it. You were the one who said run for your life, so let's get the hell out of here."

Mathew's mouth tightened and he took two deep breaths.

"*Now.*"

Collin still had him around the waist when they emerged from the cover of the trees and began a jagged trot across the field. Tall blades of grass whipped at his face as they ran. Behind them the Orlocks were coming, and they were coming fast. By the time they were halfway to the other side, Mathew felt his strength returning and his stride smoothed out. Collin noticed it as well, and released his arm from around his waist. In another fifty yards they'd be into the trees.

Instinctively, Mathew reached for the power once again, forming the image of a firewall in his mind.

Nothing happened.

A wave of panic gripped him, only to be replaced by a hollow feeling in the pit of his stomach, as though a part of himself had been torn away. Collin, who must have

sensed his momentary hesitation, turned toward him.
Mathew shook his head, gritted his teeth, and increased
his pace to full speed. Both of them charged through the
underbrush into the trees, running as hard as they could.
Neither had to look to know how close the Orlocks were.
They dodged under branches and around trees, avoiding
the heavy roots that threatened to grab their ankles.

Mathew's lungs were burning from the effort, but he
kept going, fighting through the pain. Beside him, he
could hear Collin breathing heavily.

"There," Collin gasped.

Relief swept over him when he saw that his horse was
still where he'd left it, with Collin's mount now next to it.
They were no more than fifty yards away. Collin reached
the horses first and jumped into the saddle, with Mathew
only a step behind. He had no sooner seated himself
when a lance embedded itself in the tree next to him, followed by another and then another. The Orlocks came
rushing through the trees at them, screaming.

"*Ride!*" Collin yelled.

Mathew dug his heels into the horse's flanks. At the
same time, long-nailed white hands reached out to grab
him. The horse reared and bolted forward. Somewhere in
the back of his mind he remembered that he'd left his
scabbard behind. In front of him, Mathew could see
chunks of earth flying up from the hooves of Collin's
horse. Moments later they both broke clear of the forest
and charged down the road toward town. Soon the south
gate of Tremont came into sight, as did ten Orlocks, an-
gling sharply toward them from the woods on their left.

When Father Thomas heard the sentry at the gate yell
"Riders coming in," his heart missed a beat. He had seen
Mathew tear by him down the street only a little while
ago, followed by Collin. When Bran lay dying in his
arms, he had sworn an oath to his oldest friend to care for
and protect his son, and he had never broken an oath in
his life. How long ago did that happen? he wondered. His
mind was in turmoil. To go after the boys meant leaving

the town with women and children who were unprepared and unprotected. And he doubted that any right-minded Elgarian was going to start taking orders from a Bajani general, including the three soldiers Delain had left behind. It left him as the only one with enough military experience to hold things together. But for how long and against how many Orlocks? And where was Delain?

He prayed the prince would arrive in time. His heart told him the Elgarians would come, but his head said they wouldn't. When he heard the horn blasts earlier, north of town, he knew the battle was joined—a battle that would determine the fate of nations and people for generations to come.

In the end, it was the women and children of Tremont that decided him. He could not let the Orlocks have them. Torn between his responsibility to the boys and the people there, he made his choice.

Twenty years before, near the close of the Sibuyan War, the regiment he had commanded was the first to reach the town of Lindsey. He could still remember the screams. The worst sight of all was the badly mutilated body of a child, not more than five or six years old. The boy was still barely alive, though by what miracle, he would never know. Despite years of combat, he had recoiled in shock. The little boy's lips were moving and he forced himself to bend down, putting his ear close to the child.

"Please kill me." The whisper had been barely audible.

That sight of pity and horror had never left his mind. He could still see the boy's one remaining eye slowly filling with tears that rolled down the side of his face as he took the dagger from his own belt. A tiny hand, broken and covered in blood, reached up for his. The boy managed the faintest of smiles as Siward Thomas plunged the dagger into the child's heart, begging God to forgive him for what he had just done. Bran Lewin, who was there, put an arm around his shoulders and held him until he stopped crying.

In the days that followed, when the Elgarian army had hunted the Orlocks and killed them without mercy, a dark rage buried deep inside of Siward Thomas was loosed, with a ferocity he had not believed he possessed. The recollection of it frightened him even to this day.

No, I will not let the Orlocks have them, he thought. *They will find no one left alive if they breach the final barrier.*

Father Thomas tore up the stairs two at a time. He reached the catwalk that ran around the inside perimeter of Tremont's defense wall just in time to see Mathew and Collin flying up the road on their horses toward the gate. He also knew they weren't going to make it. A band of Orlocks coming at them from the left was going to cut them off before they got there.

"Archers, ready!" he roared at the top of his lungs. *"Fire!"*

Twenty arrows flew through the air, and a number of Orlocks went down. Mathew and Collin were no more than 150 yards from them now.

"Open the gate!" he yelled.

A second volley of arrows cut down more of the Orlocks. Hundreds of others were coming out of the forest close behind. He saw Mathew and Collin break to their right, riding down two of the creatures. A third leaped onto the back of Collin's horse and tried to pull him from the saddle. The horse reared, throwing the creature off. Collin pulled the reins sharply and turned his horse to the left, charging forward at a full gallop.

"Go, go, go!" every man on the wall screamed, urging them on.

Father Thomas ran down the steps, jumping from the last four of them to the ground as the gate swung open and they rode in. As soon as they jumped off, the priest immediately grabbed each of them in a fierce embrace. He opened his mouth to say something when someone called out, *"Here they come!"*

"Ready, lads. Make each shot count," another man yelled.

Pulling his attention away, Father Thomas ran back up the steps again, ducking just in time to avoid an Orlock spear. More followed. Most either embedded themselves harmlessly in the thick wood of the gate or sailed over the heads of those defending the wall.

"There are about six or seven hundred still left," Mathew said between gulps of air, crouching down next to Father Thomas. "They're right behind us."

"So I see. Are you both all right?"

Mathew and Collin nodded.

"Has there been any word from Delain?" Mathew asked.

"Not yet. Our people have engaged the enemy to the north. The question now is whether they can get through in time. What did you mean '*still left*,' my son?" Father Thomas asked.

Mathew quickly explained what had happened, and Collin filled in the details he left out. Father Thomas's eyes widened.

After a few minutes the spears stopped coming.

"Where's Akin?" Collin asked.

"He's at the other end of town with our Bajani friend," Father Thomas replied. The priest poked his head up and saw a mass of yellow-haired Orlocks advancing toward the gates.

"Mathew, is there anything you can do about them?"

Once again Mathew reached for the power and found only emptiness. "Not yet, Father," he said.

"Then I suppose we will have to do what we can. *Get ready, men!*" he called out, checking each side of the battlements. "If they breech the wall, we fall back to the tavern, and then to the North Gate. Does everyone understand? If the creatures want Tremont, they'll have to take it inch by inch."

"You tell 'em, Father," a heavyset dark-haired man to their right said. The man turned to Mathew. "Nice mount you rode in on, son. Hope you did some good out there."

The tunic the man wore was stretched tightly over his stomach, and in his hand he carried a bow as if it were a toy. It wasn't until much later that Mathew learned his name was Edwin, and it was his horse he had taken earlier.

A pretty red-haired girl of about fourteen came running down the street with two bows and full quivers for Collin and Mathew. She curtsied and then dashed back up the street.

A huge roar went up from outside the wall as the Orlocks began their assault. Sparing a quick glance through one of the timbers, Mathew saw the creatures streaming out of the trees from all sides and running for the gates. Some of the Orlocks had painted black circles around their eyes and mouths, giving them an even more grotesque and frightening aspect. One of the men on his right noted the same thing.

"It doesn't make them any more attractive, if you ask me," he said, drawing a bead on the nearest one with his bow.

Arrows began buzzing through the air from all points along the catwalk, and though Orlock after Orlock fell, others seemed to take their place just as quickly. Mathew couldn't say how long the fighting went on, but he found himself drenched in sweat and his mouth bone dry.

During the first wave it became clear why the Orlocks had thrown their spears into the wall. Running over the bodies of their own comrades, either dead or still living, some reached the bottom of the wall and began climbing, using the spears for a ladder. On the far left end of the catwalk several made it over the top, only to be cut down by the Tremont defenders.

Throughout the waning afternoon as the sun settled lower and lower, a number of women and girls from the town brought food and water to the men. The younger boys carried fresh supplies of arrows to replace the ones that were lost. To his surprise, several times during the day Mathew saw a number of women take up positions along the wall. Their faces as determined as the men, they fired down on the Orlocks.

The second wave was considerably worse. More and more Orlocks fought their way to the top, killing at least ten men and two women before they themselves were killed. One of the Orlocks dragged a man with him over the wall as it fell backward with an arrow in its chest. Mathew glanced up and down the length of the catwalk. He didn't think they would be able to withstand a third assault. When he looked at Father Thomas, he saw the same thoughts written on the priest's face. At most there were thirty men left, with hundreds of Orlocks still out there. Looking through the timbers, he could see them pulling the bodies of their dead companions away—for food. He pushed the thought from his mind.

Once more he tried to reach for the power and once more he failed. It worried him more than he let on. Something was very wrong. By this time his ability to access the ring should have returned. It was already taking longer than the previous day, when he had all but drained himself to the point of not being able to speak. His strength had come back then, just as it had each time before. But his ability to use the ring had not returned. He was certain there was a reason for it. There had to be.

Power without knowledge. The words kept going around in his head. There was something else, but it was like trying to grasp smoke. He kept wrestling with the problem until a cry from the wall attracted his attention.

"Get ready!" Edwin yelled at the top of his lungs.

Mathew jumped to his feet and had to look twice to confirm what he was seeing. The Orlocks were attacking again. Hundreds of them had spread out in a broad line and were running for the wall. If that wasn't bad enough, a small group in the center was pushing two burning wagons loaded with hay, gaining momentum with every step.

Father Thomas rapidly surveyed the situation and yelled out, "Back! Everyone fall back. Abandon the wall."

They began scrambling down the ladders along the catwalk. Mathew had just reached the ground when a loud crash followed by a shower of sparks rising up into the early evening sky told him one of the fire wagons had hit. Thankfully, the gate held. A second crash followed, and Mathew saw a crack appear in the heavy cross timber that bolted the two gates together.

"Back!" Father Thomas called again, grabbing his arm and pulling him along.

They ran up the street, checking over their shoulders as the Orlocks began to climb over the wall. Collin and Edwin paused long enough to loose arrows. Collin's found its mark in the middle of an Orlock's chest, while Edwin's arrow struck his target in the stomach. Both creatures screamed and fell backward. Edwin frowned, pulled a copper elgar out of his pocket and tossed it to Collin.

"You were closer," he said, and resumed his lumbering trot up the street.

Collin grinned and pocketed the coin with a quick wink at Mathew, who could only shake his head.

Just before they rounded the curve of Tremont's main street, Mathew spared another glance over his shoulder. The entire wall was on fire. While he ran, he caught glimpses of men positioned behind barrels, in windows, and crouched in the doorways of shops along the way. Two lines of barricades had been hastily erected across the street. He also noticed there was a thick line of hay directly behind one of the barricades, which puzzled him.

A loud crash told him the gate had fallen and Orlocks were pouring into the town. For the next hour, the archers Father Thomas had hidden released flight after flight of arrows at the creatures, quickly changing their position after each volley. This slowed the Orlocks, but Mathew knew it wouldn't stop them for long. For the third time he tried to use the ring and failed. Each time he did, it was like trying to remember a dream. It was there, but just beyond his grasp.

When they finally arrived at the tavern, most of the advanced archers who had been cutting down the Orlocks were falling back as well. One of them, an elderly man with a shock of white hair and a deeply lined face, came up to Father Thomas and shook his head.

"They're coming up the street now. We couldn't hold them any longer," he said.

"You did as well as anyone could ask of you," Father Thomas said gravely. "Get back to the North Gate and tell the men to be ready. They must not be allowed to pass there."

The man nodded and ran off.

Father Thomas watched him go. The vision of the slaughter at Lindsey returned to his mind, gripping his heart like a hand of ice. The oath he swore to himself earlier, at risk of his eternal soul, also came back to him, as it had done throughout the day. *No*, he thought fiercely, *it will not happen again*.

He had spoken to the men privately, and all of them understood. If the Orlocks made it to the castle, they would find no one living to torture or maim. The weight of such a decision rested on his mind like a mountain. He was a priest, sworn to comfort those who were in pain, and life was a precious thing to be preserved. Briefly, he thought of Ceta Woodall waiting for him back in Elberton, and of never seeing her again. The possibility knifed into his heart, and only with the greatest of efforts did he force it back down again.

The Orlocks rounded the street fifty yards from the first barricade and, seeing the men waiting beyond, rushed at them. Exactly as planned, when seventy or so of them had climbed the first barricade, the "dead" man lying half under an overturned wagon sprang to life and lit the hay with a torch that lay smoldering next to him. A line of fire roared up and became an impassable wall, separating the first group of Orlocks from the second. The man scrambled out from under the wagon and dashed for one of the stores, disappearing into it. Behind him and on both sides of the street, archers opened up on the first group of Orlocks, who were cut off from their companions.

Despite the storm of arrows, still some made it through. Mathew stepped backward, avoiding a scythe-like axe swing from one of the painted Orlocks. When his eyes met those of the creature, he could almost feel the rage and hatred flowing from them. Before it could make another stroke, he lunged, piercing it through the heart. To his right he saw Father Thomas moving swiftly and with incredible precision. Two Orlocks fell before his blade. As a third ran at him, the priest ducked down and drove his shoulder into the creature's body, then straightened up and tossed the Orlock over his head. The priest turned, pivoted, and beheaded it with a swinging backstroke.

Mathew knew that Collin was fighting somewhere behind him, but he had no time to look around as another Orlock charged at him and leveled a pike at his chest. Its lips were pulled back, baring its teeth. Mathew braced himself and parried in the opposite direction, deflecting the weapon to his outside, then stepped in and cut diagonally upward, using both hands. A bright line of red appeared across the creature's throat and its eyes bulged. The Orlock raised its hands to clutch the wound before toppling over.

Near one of the shops, he saw a man desperately trying to get another arrow off before he was overrun. There was nothing he could do to help. Two more men went down, one from an axe, another from a pike in his stomach. He couldn't say how long the fighting went on. Exhaustion was beginning to close in, and with each stroke his blade seemed a little heavier than before.

Then, to his surprise, he realized there were less Orlocks. The defenders of Tremont waded in and cut down the remaining few still alive on their side. While the barricade continued to burn, archers on the rooftops fired down on the Orlocks trapped on the opposite side until they too began to fall back.

A cheer went up from all those who were left, but Mathew's breath almost left him when he saw the number of men and women they had lost. There were only fifteen or so left.

"Back! Everyone back!" Father Thomas yelled.

Mathew turned with the rest of the men and began running down the street, only to stop abruptly. The smoke-blackened face of Akin Gibb grinned back at him.

"My God, Akin!" he exclaimed. "That was you under the wagon?"

Akin shrugged. "I'm considering switching to a Church where the priests are somewhat less demanding."

"And I'm considering acquiring some new congregants who don't complain as much," Father Thomas replied, falling into place alongside them.

Akin clapped Mathew on the shoulder and they resumed their pace down the street. It was fully dark by the time they reached the North Gate, save for the red-orange glow of the fires still burning throughout the town.

"I've been hearing the most interesting things about your trips into the country," Akin remarked. "Something about stealing horses, Orlocks . . . and collapsing hills, if I got it correctly."

For the second time that evening Mathew recounted what had happened, quickly and without embellishment. Several men stopped to listen but said nothing. He knew they were looking at him oddly.

When he finished, all Akin said was, "Hmm."

"Modesty is virtuous, or hadn't you Elgarians heard?" a deep voice boomed out from their left.

"Gawl!" Father Thomas burst out, rushing forward to embrace the giant. "Well met, man. Well met."

Father Thomas barely came up to Gawl's chin.

"I said it before, Siward, and I say it again, you keep some very interesting company. I leave you to watch this little town in my absence, and I return to find it filled with Orlocks and Bajani generals."

"Where is everyone else?" Father Thomas asked, looking around for the defenders.

"We've been taking your people out for the last hour. Another ten minutes and we should have everybody. It seems our new friend General Val is unusually well-informed about the layout of not only the town, but also the old abbey."

Darias Val stepped out of the shadows to join then, making a small bow to Gawl, who returned it.

"It appears," Gawl continued, "the monks who built the abbey felt some necessity to provide means of exiting it quickly, though for what reasons, I wouldn't care to speculate. The general was kind enough to show us the passage out. There's a long tunnel that comes up about three hundred yards on the other side of the forest. We're camped about four miles from here."

"What news of the battle?"

"Some good. As Val has said, with the death of their leader, the Bajani, being God-fearing people, are in a period of mourning. They won't fight, and Duren can't risk an internal war by provoking them. We're holding, but just barely. Even with Bajan out of the battle, Delain is still badly outnumbered. Hopefully, the Mirdites can level the situation a bit more when they arrive."

Father Thomas blew out a long breath. "How many men did you bring with you?" he asked.

"Two full companies, but they'll do well enough," Gawl replied with a broad smile. In the dim light, Mathew thought he looked even more feral than usual.

"Two companies?" Father Thomas said, looking around, puzzled.

"Up there at the castle, Siward," he said, inclining his head in that direction. "Actually, it was the general's idea. If the Orlocks want Tremont so badly, we're going to let them have it."

"I've stationed your men in the buildings and on the roofs around the courtyard of the castle," Val said, speaking for the first time. "The Orlocks will enter . . . but they will not emerge."

"How do we get them in there?" Collin asked.

"We must offer a sufficient inducement," Val replied noncommittally.

Twenty minutes later Collin, Akin, and ten other men, including Val, who insisted on remaining with them, stood just on the other side of the smoldering embers of the last barricade. They watched the Orlocks cautiously advancing down the street.

"Remind me not to ask any more questions," Collin said under his breath.

Akin gave him a sour look and mumbled something about finding another Church again.

Darias Val stood in the middle of the street, feet widely planted, holding a curved sword in one hand, with a fist resting on the opposite hip, his belted black robe moving slightly with the evening breeze.

"Be gone from this town, eaters of filth! You are an abomination to the sight of men. Be gone, and we shall let you live," he called out.

Confused by the show of bravado, the Orlocks stopped and looked at one another, then at the stores and rooftops. No more than fifty yards separated the two groups.

Finally, one of them stepped forward and spoke, "Send us the boy and we will let *you* live, human."

"What boy do you speak of, creature of the night?"

Emboldened, the Orlock took another step forward.

"Move no closer, monster," Val snapped. "You expect us to take the word of an Orlock?"

"You expect us to take the word of a human?" it mimicked back with surprising accuracy.

"Why do you want the boy? Why not just take the ring?" Akin called out.

There was a pause before the Orlock answered. "The ring would have sufficed before. But now we would like the boy to be . . . our *guest*. Thousands of my people are dead. So tell me, human, which of us is the monster?"

"Well, at least they don't want me too," Akin said to Collin, pitching his voice loud enough to carry. "I'm the one who set fire to his people earlier."

The words had the intended effect. With a roar, the Orlocks rushed forward. The remaining twelve men spun about and fled up the street. Close on their heels, the enraged Orlocks pursued them past the North Gate and up the hill into the castle.

By Gawl's count, over two hundred of the snarling creatures flooded into the courtyard, only to find it empty.

When he gave the order to fire, both companies of archers, previously hidden, stood as one, releasing a storm of arrows down on the Orlocks as the gates were sealed.

It was over in five minutes.

37

Elgaria, Ardon Field

MATHEW AWOKE IN THE PREDAWN LIGHT FEELING tired and sore. His sleep had been fitful and gave him little rest. Orlocks or not, the fact that he had killed thousands of living beings weighed heavily on his mind—so heavily that his sleep was racked by terrible dreams. The creature's question about which of them was a monster bothered him more than he was able to say. He made another attempt to use the ring, but it proved just as futile as those the previous day. He gave up, splashed some water on his face from the basin, grabbed his sword and began to walk back toward the town of Tremont. Solitude and time to think were what he needed at that moment.

At the edge of the forest, a short distance from the path leading to camp, were the remains of three ancient buildings. Gawl had pointed them out to him on their way in the night before. Two of the buildings had crumbled, leaving cement foundations and portions of granite walls still standing. The third still contained a complete first floor and part of a second.

Mathew stood there, imagining how huge it must have once been. There were no doors or windows anymore and whole sections of the walls were broken, revealing a battered metal frame. An entrance in the center of the building led to the largest single room he had ever seen. It consisted of marble that extended all the way to the ceiling, which had to be at least fifty feet above his head. At either end of the room were the oddest-looking staircases. Each rose up at a steep angle to the second floor of the building. They were made of glass and a light, shiny metal Mathew didn't recognize. The steps had lines or grooves running across them, and above the glass enclosure, a handrail made of a soft black material extended from the top of the staircase to the bottom and disappeared into the floor at the base. Mathew wondered whether the Ancients might have designed the staircase to move. It certainly seemed possible. The steps at the very bottom were not the same height as the other steps. They got smaller and smaller, eventually becoming flat at the bottom, and, like the handrail, they seemed to collapse and disappear into the floor. He stared at the structure in fascination. It was both beyond his comprehension and sad how the Ancients could create such things and then destroy themselves.

Mathew glanced down at his ring. There was little question now his ancestors had created it. Perhaps like the staircase, it had finally failed, never to work again.

The previous night, before they reached the camp, he had watched an Elgarian patrol engage the Alor Satar in a late-evening skirmish. Try as he might, he was unable to do anything to save them. All ability to make contact with the ring seemed to have simply vanished, and what little support he was able to lend was with his sword. Thankfully, the enemy broke off the engagement when Delain's reinforcements arrived. Now Mathew slipped the ring off his finger and stared at the strange lettering on the inside of the band. He wanted desperately to believe the power was still there, but if it was, for some reason he could no longer reach it.

His mind considered and reconsidered the possibilities, searching to come up with an explanation for what had happened, but each time his own ignorance mocked him. It was like a blind man trying to understand color. He desperately needed to do something to save his people—but what?

He wandered around the colossal wreck for the next

hour before finally giving up in frustration and heading back to camp. The numbers arrayed against them were too great, and it was going to take a miracle for Elgaria to withstand Duren for more than a few days. It seemed that the madman was going to win after all.

The camp Delain had chosen was on the south side of a place called Kolb's Farm. Duren and his army were camped across a broad green field at the north end of it. Too tired and depressed to talk to anyone, Mathew listened to bits and pieces of conversations. The fighting had gone on throughout the day, coming to an end only because of darkness. Both sides sustained heavy losses. The Elgarians had managed to hold, but just barely. At that hour of the morning, a few people were up and about. As he walked along, Mathew noted that Delain had posted sentries every hundred feet or so around the camp's perimeter, in the event of a surprise attack during the night. None came. Apparently, Duren didn't think there was any need for one.

A light mist hung over the field between the two armies, covering the ground. Mathew stopped next to a campfire, allowing the heat to warm his back. Although Duren and his people were camped three or four hundred yards from them, there didn't seem to be much activity there. Well to the west, the rugged mountain range marking the border between his country and Sennia was showing highlights of golds and yellows. Though winter was long gone, some of the peaks were still capped in white. Gawl had told him that at the higher elevations snow could be found on many of the mountains the whole year round.

After a few inquiries, he found Daniel and Collin sitting outside Daniel's tent, talking. They waved as they saw him walk up. Daniel was resting on a cot, his left leg heavily bandaged.

"You're up early," Mathew said to them.

"So are you," Collin replied, handing him a cup of hot tea.

"Where's, uh . . ."

"She's with the other women, two tents down," Daniel said.

"Did she say anything last night?" Mathew asked.

"Nothing you'd want to hear," Daniel said. "She was . . . well, a little, ah . . . oh heck, you know Lara."

Mathew winced. "Great." He sat on the edge of Daniel's cot and leaned forward, holding his cup of tea in his hands. "Duren's out there trying to kill me, and she's probably willing to help him. What are you both doing up at this hour?"

"We were watching old Duren through Daniel's farsighter."

"Really? Where?" Mathew asked, looking across the field.

"Over there on that little hill," Daniel said, pointing. He offered Mathew the brass tube.

Mathew put his teacup on the ground and took the instruments. Closing one eye, he squinted through the tube with the other. Duren was under an awning of some sort, sitting in a high-backed chair, his sword resting against the side of it. He was dressed all in black again. Mathew pulled the tube away from his eye, blinked, and put it back. There was something unnatural about Duren's posture. With the small field of vision the lens provided, it was difficult to tell for certain, but Duren actually looked to be under strain. His whole entire body appeared stiff and tense, and his arms tightly gripped the sides of his chair.

"How long has he been like that?" Mathew asked, taking the tube away from his eye.

"Ever since last night when Lara and I got here," Daniel said. "He was the same way this morning. I don't think he's moved all night."

"Strange," Mathew said under his breath.

"What is?" Daniel asked.

"Look," Collin said, "before you get another idea into your head and go running off again, how about telling your friends? I'm in enough trouble with Lara as is."

He was about to respond when he saw Jerrel Rozon's lean form walking by. He was talking with two men. The short iron-gray hair and rigid shoulders hadn't changed much since Devondale.

"Jerrel, may I speak with you a moment?" he called out, standing up.

Rozon stopped, and his hard blue eyes fixed on Mathew. "Ah, Mathew, there you are. I've been meaning to speak to you as well. In all the commotion yesterday, I didn't have an opportunity to tell you how sorry I was to hear about your father. He was a fine man and a good soldier."

"Yes, sir. Thank you very much," Mathew replied.

"What was it you wanted, son? I'm in something of a hurry this morning. It seems the enemy is already stirring."

Mathew looked across the field and saw what Rozon was referring to. There was indeed movement now in the enemy camp—a lot of movement.

"You were at Anderon, weren't you?" Mathew asked.

"Yes."

"I was told that Duren used fire and explosions to gain his victory there . . . among other things."

"That is correct. Why do you ask?"

"Did anything like that happen here yesterday?"

Rozon frowned and thought for a moment. "No, there was nothing like that."

The two men with Rozon moved closer to listen. Rozon didn't bother introducing them, though his face grew increasingly serious.

"Mathew," he said patiently. "I have no time to pass the day with idle questions. What is your point? If you are worried, perhaps it would be better—"

When the boy stiffened, Rozon knew he had made a mistake. "I'm sorry, lad," he said quickly. "That was uncalled for. You've more than proven yourself, but part of what I said was true. I *am* quite pressed for time."

The apology had the intended effect. Mathew relaxed. "There *is* a point to my questions," he said. "Is it true that Duren has been sitting there since yesterday?"

"Since the later part of the afternoon when the battle was joined," one of the men with Rozon said. "He was standing at first, but then some of his people brought him that chair he's sitting in now."

"Don't you find that strange?" Mathew asked them.

"To be perfectly candid, I find everything Karas Duren does to be strange," Rozon said, looking across the field. "Now I really must be—"

"Those wooden contraptions in the field—they're catapults aren't they?"

"Correct."

"Could they be trained to lob a rock at Duren from where they are?"

It was only in the last few minutes that Mathew had begun to actually understand what was happening.

"A good idea, lad," said the shorter of the two men with Rozon, "but those catapults are not terribly accurate. The chances of scoring a hit would be quite slim. Besides, the rocks are too heavy to fly that far."

"Not if you increased the elevation and decreased the mass," Daniel said from his cot. Everyone turned to look at him.

"It's simple, really," he explained. "It's just a matter of physics. If you raise the launch angle of the catapult and put a smaller rock on it, I'd bet you could reach him."

Rozon smiled and shook his head. "I appreciate the suggestion, but Karas Duren is only part of the problem. Right now there are a hundred thousand of his soldiers getting ready to come down on us. I suspect they won't just go home if we hit their leader with a rock."

"I'm not interested in hitting him," Mathew said, "only distracting him."

Rozon looked at him as if he'd lost his mind.

"Listen," Mathew continued, speaking rapidly, "I think he's found a way to block me from using the ring, but it's taking all of his concentration to maintain whatever he's doing. I'm almost certain of it. Otherwise he'd have done the same thing to us he did at Anderon."

"The ring," Rozon said, nodding. "The wildest stories

are circulating about you and this ring. I saw what happened on the trail yesterday, or at least I saw the aftermath. It was impressive, but I must tell you that I'm too old and tired to start believing in magic and goblins."

A long blast of a horn from the enemy camp turned Rozon's head in that direction. It was followed by an answering blast from their own camp. Suddenly, people were moving all around them. At the far end of the field it was obvious the enemy was massing for an attack.

"Jerrel, we need to get ready," the second man prompted.

"We'll talk about this later," Rozon said, patting Mathew's arm. "In the meantime—"

"Meantime be damned," Mathew shot back, throwing Rozon's arm off. "How long do you think we'll be able to hold out against their numbers? You've got to listen to me."

Rozon's eyes turned as hard as diamonds, and he repeated, "We'll talk later," then spun on his heel and walked rapidly away.

"I don't believe him," Collin said angrily. He was now on his feet too.

Mathew stood thinking for a moment. He liked Jerrel, but the man was inflexible and he hadn't been there to see what had happened at the cave or to the Nyngary fleet. He almost didn't believe it himself. Rozon was a soldier and thought like one. Show him an enemy and he'd fight, but this was like trying to grab smoke.

"Collin, find Father Thomas and Gawl and meet me at that catapult there on the left as quickly as possible."

"Right," Collin said, and sped off.

Lara was just coming out of the women's tent when she spotted Mathew trotting toward her. Despite some charitable efforts on her part, she was still angry about his bolting off the day before without so much as a word to her. After an entire evening to think about it, she decided to give him a good piece of her mind. As he approached, she folded her arms across her chest and mentally rehearsed her speech. But she never got the chance to give

it. Before she could get a word out, Mathew grabbed her
by the shoulders and kissed her full on the mouth in front
of all the other women there. Then he dashed off again,
calling over his shoulder, "I love you in that gray dress."

A mixture of gasps and titters came from behind her.
Lara heard them but kept looking straight ahead. She
took a moment to calmly smooth the front of her dress
and blow a lock of hair that had fallen across her forehead
out of the way, then turned to her open-mouthed companions, shrugged, and said, "He's in love with me. I can't
seem to do much with him."

She walked off humming to herself.

Mathew reached the catapult in under a minute. A brief
try to use the ring while he ran proved to be as unsuccess-
ful as his previous efforts. The same wall was there between him and the source.

"What news, lad?" the corporal in charge of the catapult asked.

"Rozon wants you to train this on that hill over there
and begin firing at once."

"Rozon? When did he take charge of the catapults? I
thought Delain wanted them to concentrate on the center
today."

"Look, you haven't much time. The enemy is about to
advance."

"Doesn't make any sense," the corporal said, frowning.
"There's no one up there except Duren and a few of his
people, and they're out of range. He turned to the soldier
next to him and said, "Frederick, run back to the camp
and get these orders confirmed. No offense, lad."

"Right," the man replied, and took off across the field.

"But—"

"You just stand out of the way till Frederick gets back,
lad. It shouldn't be just a minute. What's this, now?" he
asked, looking over Mathew's shoulder.

Father Thomas, Collin, and Gawl were running toward
them, along with Akin and Fergus.

"Collin told us what you want to do," Father Thomas

said as soon as he got there. "Are you sure about this, my son?"

"No, I'm not . . . but I think I'm right."

Father Thomas nodded and said to the corporal, "All right, let's get this thing swung around."

"Just a minute. I've sent one of my men back to confirm the order. Delain wanted us to concentrate on the middle, and now the lot of you come running up telling me something different."

Seeing the six men standing in front of them, grimfaced, the remaining two soldiers in the corporal's squad looked distinctly uncomfortable. Their discomfort only increased when Gawl stepped forward.

"I would hate to damage one of Delain's men." Gawl smiled, looking down at the soldier. "But I'm afraid that's what I'll have to do if you don't get out of our way in the next ten seconds."

The corporal, who was slightly below middle height, swallowed and took a step back. "All right," he said, "but this better be under orders."

At that moment the quiet of the early morning was shattered as the two armies met a little more than two hundred yards from where they were. It took only a glance for Mathew to see how overwhelmingly outnumbered the Elgarians were, even without the Bajani army on Duren's side.

"Hurry," Mathew yelled as everyone got behind the massive catapult.

They lifted as one and slowly began to turn it.

"It's not going to work, whatever you've got in mind," the corporal said when they were through repositioning the wooden machine.

When no one responded, he shook his head, then nodded to his companion. They reached for the levers and began to raise the base.

From the opposite side of the catapult the soldier said, "This is as high as it goes. I'm telling you, you can't reach them from here."

A blaring of trumpets in the distance caused Gawl and

Father Thomas to look up. Seconds later a cheer went up
from the hill where Prince Delain's tent was located.

"The Mirdites," they both said together.

"Uh-oh," Collin said. "Looks like Duren's just gotten
to his feet."

"Quickly," Mathew said, piling seven or eight stones
into the basket of the catapult's twenty-foot arm, some
not much bigger than good-size pebbles. "Let's try to find
the range."

The corporal climbed up on to the machine, made a
few more adjustments with another lever, then jumped to
the ground and came around to the rear.

"Everyone back," he said, grasping hold of the release
lever. Satisfied, he pulled sharply back on it. The arm
sprang out and upward in an arc, hurling its contents
skyward.

"Short by thirty yards," Collin yelled, having had the
good sense to bring along Daniel's farsighter.

"How can we raise it any higher?" Akin asked.

"You can't," the corporal said. "Like I told you, this is
as high as it goes."

"Excuse me," Gawl said. In three long strides he
stepped to the front of the catapult and grasped its frame.

The men assembled there watched in amazement as
the front wheels came off the ground.

The muscles in Gawl's arms and back stood out as he
lifted again, and the machine moved higher.

"May I suggest you hurry?" he said. "I'm not as young
as I used to be."

The soldiers rushed still wide-eyed to the pulleys to
reposition the throwing arm once more.

"All right, here we go," Mathew said, dumping a
handful of small rocks and pebbles in to the basket one
more time.

"Clear!" the corporal yelled, and pulled the lever.

There was a loud twang as the arm shot forward, hurl-
ing its cargo toward the hill where Duren stood standing.
Collin tracked the flight all the way with the farsighter.
Through the lens, he saw Duren look to his right. The

chair he had been sitting in only a moment before was hit in rapid succession by three of the stones, the last of which shattered its back.

"Yes!" Mathew cried out, pumping his fist in the air. He felt the release in his mind almost immediately.

Then Duren's head swiveled in their direction.

"Damn," Collin said, pulling the farsighter away from his eye. "It looked like he was looking right at me."

The next moment, there was a loud boom, and the earth around them heaved itself up, knocking everyone to the ground. Gawl managed to let go of the catapult and jump clear of it in time. A second bolt of white light struck the main body of the machine, smashing it to pieces.

Mathew's ears were still ringing from the blast as he pushed himself up onto his knees, trying to clear his head. Just as he had on the hill the previous day, he formed a picture in his mind of an impenetrable shield and raised it, protecting himself and those around him. Almost immediately two more bolts, louder and more powerful than the first, tore into the ground near them, sending a shower of dirt into the air. Mathew looked around to make sure the shield was holding. Desperately, he sought to recall what he had done in Elberton when the explosion occurred, but with all the chaos, it was impossible to concentrate. The most he could do at that moment was defend himself and his companions.

Far up the field, the Elgarians continued to fight, but they were steadily losing ground. Trumpets were blowing and screams seemed to be coming from everywhere at the same time. Mathew knew he needed time to collect himself, and Duren wasn't giving him any. Behind him, he heard Gawl's deep voice bellow for everyone to run. Collin grabbed him by the arm and pointed frantically at the hill where Duren stood. A cold shiver of fear ran down Mathew's back and his breath caught in his throat.

Rolling inexorably down the field at them was a wall of orange fire nearly sixty feet high and over eighty yards wide, obliterating everything in its path. Paralyzed, still on his knees, Mathew could do no more than stare at it. Then in the back of his mind Duren spoke to him, his voice scarcely more than a dry whisper, like the breath of a grave.

"Too late, fool. You are too late. It is done. Your father is dead for your weakness. You could not save your friend from death, and now you will watch as your people die."

Thousands of miles away, far beneath the earth, a giant crystal in a long-forgotten cavern began to pulse and glow red, waking from three thousand years of dormancy as Mathew drew more and more power into himself. At the same time, a series of gauges in a laboratory came to life, and alarms went off in the darkness. Mathew Lewin slowly got to his feet, focusing all of his concentration on the thing before him. The fire itself seemed not like fire at all but like a shimmering liquid. Even through the shield he could feel the heat of its approach.

Meanwhile, Duren's voice continued to whisper in his ear.

"A trail of death follows wherever you go, boy . . . How many more must die for you? . . . Oliver Donal . . . Zachariah Ward . . . Pryor Coleman . . . his poor young brother Jaim . . . all dead . . . just like your father. And for what? A coward who cannot keep his hands from shaking . . . coward . . . coward," the voice echoed. *"Yes, I know you for what you are . . . I have touched your mind, boy . . . hide it from others, but you can't hide it from me. Murderer . . . killer of innocent Cincar sailors . . . of women . . . of my sister . . ."*

It went on and on until Mathew could no longer stand it. He recoiled from the relentless onslaught of Duren's words, staggering backward as the wave of heat approached.

For the second time in his life, a hatred so palpable he could taste it enveloped Mathew. It was fueled by the images of thousands of innocent people hanged and left to die along the cliffs in Tyraine, the faces of women and the innocent children of Anderon, people he had never met or known. They burst into his consciousness with a clarity so great he was astonished by the vividness. His father, Giles Naismith, Captain Donal, all stood there watching him with solemn eyes.

Then, from deep within the core of his own being, a scream, primal and elemental burst forth from his lungs and he struck back. It was born of rage at the monster on the opposite side of the field, rage at everything he had done to his people and to his country—rage for the children.

When he thought about it later, much later, the vision still vivid in his mind, it was the faint smile that played across Duren's face that caused him to pull back from what he was about to do. Only at the very last second did he manage to draw back from that precipice, or everyone and everything within twenty miles would have been destroyed.

To those watching from both hills, and to the armies in the field, it appeared that a second wall of blue fire sprang up out of nowhere, directly in front of where the catapult had been. Both firewalls sped toward each other and collided, shooting straight up and spreading across the sky, blotting out the light. A terrible thunderclap shook the ground, knocking many off their feet, leaving a crater nearly fifty feet deep and over seventy-five yards wide in the earth.

Duren fought back with all of his considerable strength, hammering Mathew with blow after blow. The walls of fire joined as he and Mathew fought. The battle between them went on and on as the battle on the ground continued to take place around them. The commanders of the Alor Satar army redoubled their efforts, now settling on the boy fighting their leader as their objective.

Rozon countered by swinging the second Elgarian army from the flank to meet them. As hard as the Elgarians fought, they continued to give way to the superior numbers pressing them backward. The end of the Elgarian line was now a scant hundred yards from where

Mathew stood before the walls of fire. Sweat beaded on
his face and his fists were clenched. The muscles in his
back and neck knotted with the effort. All the while,
Duren continued to whisper to him.

Delain watched the unfolding battle from his vantage
point on the hill. The Elgarians were being forced back.
Men were dying everywhere. In his heart, the cold realization of the inevitable outcome began to shape itself.
There were not enough of them to stem the tide. The
country—his country—was lost. History would record
him as the man who allowed the destruction of a nation.
Tears streamed down his face, and the men nearest to him
looked away, unable to bear their prince's pain.

Two things happened then that kept Delain from order-
ing a retreat in the hope of saving as many of his people
as he could. At the farthest end of the field the white
cloaks of the Mirdite army appeared, having broken
through the Alor Satar rear guard; and the Sennian cavalry arrived at the western end of the field. The Mirdites,
whose capital city of Toland had been destroyed by
Duren, attacked like men possessed.

Gawl saw the arrival of his countrymen and immediately sprang to his horse. He tore off across the field, crying, "Sennians to me!"

Moments after he reached them, the fabled Sennian
wedge formed. And with their king at its head, they began their charge directly at the enemy flank. The horses
started down the slope of the hill slowly. After fifty yards
the walk became a canter and the Sennian spears came
down as one.

Twenty lines deep, five thousand of the finest mountain
fighters in the world, their ranks never wavering, maintained the bizzare wedge formation, seeming to flow over
the rolling terrain like water as they bore down on the enemy. Above the din of the battlefield, a sonorous voice
roared out, "Charge!"

The Sennians broke into a full gallop no more than a
hundred yards from the Alor Satar. At the very point of

the attack, sunlight flashed off Gawl's massive broadsword swinging in circles around his head.

When Delain saw the Sennian phalanx strike the enemy's flank like a thunderbolt, splitting their ranks, he spun around to Jerrel Rozon and screamed, *"Now!"*

Rozon stood upright in his saddle and relayed the signal to Colonel Targil. The Elgarian light cavalry, under his command, had been kept in reserve throughout the day.

"Well, *Father*," Targil said to the man seated next to him astride a black stallion, "I hope you remembered to put in a good word for us today."

"There is an old expression about the Lord helping those who help themselves," Father Thomas replied. "Perhaps you've heard it?"

Targil chuckled. "Let's hope you're as good at your new profession as you were at your old one," he replied.

"We'll know in a moment, my friend."

The one-eyed colonel turned in his saddle and yelled out, "Elgaria will advance!"

The trumpeter blew the charge as the Elgarians burst from cover at the eastern end of the field.

Mathew could tell when Father Thomas and a small group of soldiers reached him. The priest, fighting like a madman, moved through the enemy like the proverbial angel with a flaming sword. He was also aware that Duren had stopped whispering to him. For the first time in his mind's eye he looked at the malevolent face of his enemy. The hooded eyes stared back at him, merciless and filled with hate. There was no longer any trace of a smile on the man's lips. By degrees, Mathew's blue firewall was advancing. And Duren knew it too. Sweat was streaming down the King of Alor Satar's face and he was breathing heavily.

Suddenly, a cry of exultation burst from Duren's lips. He threw his arms up in victory, tilted his head back and began to laugh hysterically. A second later a ball of liquid fire materialized out of the sky and roared directly at the hill where Delain and Lara were standing.

It took the last reserves of Mathew's strength to deflect
it from its course, turning it back, back—back at Duren
himself, who, still laughing, never saw it coming until
the end.

Delain looked across the field and saw Karas Duren collapse to his knees. The Lewin boy was also down. He
couldn't tell if he was dead or alive. *Alive,* he thought.
Beldon Targil's regiment, with Siward Thomas, had finally fought their way through to Mathew and were trying to hold back the Alor Satar soldiers driving toward
them. Whatever Mathew had done, the prince prayed to
God that it would not be in vain. Despite the valiant efforts of the Mirdites and Sennians, Delain knew it would
not be enough to stem the tide. There were still too many
arrayed against them. Elgaria was doomed.

Seconds later a ball of fire appeared in the sky out of
nowhere, hurtling down upon him at a frightening speed.
The rational part of Delain's mind acknowledged he had
only a moment to live. He was frozen in place, unable to
move. But then, miraculously, the fireball veered sharply
away. It rose into the air and streaked directly back at
Duren. The resulting explosion leveled the hill where
Duren was, and from clear across the field the concussion
was strong enough to knock Delain down, as it did almost
everyone around him. The noise was deafening. The billowing smoke made it impossible to see.

Minutes passed until the field gradually began to clear.
Delain got to his feet, expecting the fighting would resume. Instead he heard the Alor Satar trumpeters blowing a
recall for their army. It took a moment before he realized
what it meant. The prince was dumbfounded. He looked
around at the officers nearest to him and saw similar expressions on their faces.

Across the field there was a crater where Duren's command tent had stood only moments before. Delain stared
at it in disbelief. He cupped his hands to the side of his
head and squinted. Through the drifting smoke he saw

the figure of a woman looking back at him. There was something familiar about her, but she turned and walked back into the haze before he could place it.

What the hell is a woman doing on a battlefield? he asked himself. The sound of shouting abruptly pulled his attention away—some type of commotion was going on where the catapults had been. A moment later a lone rider broke away from the other soldiers and came galloping back across the field directly toward him. It was Colonel Targil. He rode up and jumped off his horse.

"What news?" Delain asked.

"The boy is gone."

"Dead?"

"Disappeared, your highness—vanished."

"What? But how . . ."

"I don't know," Targil said. "We had just broken through the Alor Satar flank to defend him as you ordered. At least ten men saw it happen. Siward Thomas is beside himself. Gawl is there with him, but I think you ought to come."

Delain felt the color drain out of his face and glanced quickly at Lara, who was standing with Akin Gibb and one of his officers, fifty feet way.

"Do you think he's dead, Targil?" he asked, lowering his voice.

"Your majesty, I don't know," the colonel replied, making a helpless gesture with his hands. "I was not fifteen feet from the boy. There was a flash of green light and suddenly he was gone—disappeared. No fire, no noise, it was just like that," Targil said, snapping his fingers.

Delain looked at the man for a second. "I'll come," he said. "Stay with the girl."

henderson

MATHEW'S HEAD BEGAN TO CLEAR. HE BLINKED AND looked around him. He had no idea where he was. It seemed he was in the middle of a town, but one like no town he had ever seen before. Far above him the stars were out, twinkling in the night sky, but there was something unusual about them. The grass he was lying on also felt odd. He ran his hand over the surface, then abruptly pulled it away. It was perfectly green, but it felt stiff and lifeless.

Maybe I'm dead, he thought.

He got up, looked around, and saw that he was standing in the middle of a square. A street ran along one side of it that reminded him of the ancient roads he'd seen in Tyraine. He turned, slowly taking in his surroundings. There were several streets running off the square in different directions. The lit street lamps were unusual too, emitting a bright orange glow different from anything he'd ever seen. Near him, a large clock sat atop a lamp post. It read ten minutes past ten.

There was a large rectangular white sign in front of a building directly across from him. The words NOW PLAYING stood out in black letters.

Playing? Playing what? he thought.

At the far corner of the square the largest crystal he'd ever seen rose prominently out of a low one-story building. It was more than twenty feet thick. He followed the octagonal-shaped column up until it eventually disappeared into the night sky. Once again the feeling that something was wrong came over him again. It wasn't just that he was in a strange place. Things *felt* wrong. The last thing he remembered was turning the fireball back at Duren. He'd blacked out after that and woken up here. The question was, where was he?

Mathew stared up at the crystal to where it disappeared into the sky and realized with a shock that what he was looking at wasn't a sky at all. It was a dome of some sort. Gargantuan in proportion, but a dome nevertheless. His hands began to tremble.

Where in God's name am I?

He looked up and down the street. There were no people anywhere. No horses. No wagons. Nothing. On the opposite side of the square there was a row of shops with large glass windows. Two mannequins dressed in the oddest clothing looked back at him from one of the windows. The name CAROLYN'S FASHIONS was painted above the door in gold letters. Curious, Mathew walked toward it. For some reason, he remembered that Margaret Grimly had a mannequin in her store in Devondale to display the dresses she made. These mannequins were different. The dresses the women wore were so short they almost made him blush. In the middle of the street a few tables and chairs had been set out on the sidewalk. Each of the tables had a brightly colored umbrella.

Well, I'm obviously not dead, he decided. *There has to be an explanation.* The question is how do I get out of here?

He scratched his head and looked around again. His stomach felt queasy.

Where is everybody? Surely, there has to be someone here who can help me.

He noticed a number of houses along one of the side streets running away from the square. They were quite different from the kind he was familiar with. After a moment's reflection, he decided they would be his best chance. He started off in that direction when something made him stop and turn around.

There was a woman seated at one of the tables he had

just looked at. He was positive she hadn't been there a moment ago. She saw him as well, but made no move to get up. She just sat there watching him.

Mathew walked toward her. When he got closer, he could see that she was wearing a silver dress with long sleeves that came to a point at her wrist. Her figure was trim and elegant, complimented by a startlingly beautiful face. She had large, blue eyes and a mass of black hair that fell loosely about her shoulders. There was something strangely familiar about her, but at that moment he couldn't say what it was. Then he noticed two glasses of wine on the table.

They weren't there before either.

"Excuse me, do you live here?" he asked,

The woman tilted her head slightly and looked up at him. "No."

"I'm sorry. I'm a stranger here. My name is—"

"Mathew Lewin. I know."

His hand reflexively reached for the hilt of his sword.

The woman only responded by raising her eyebrows.

"Do you honestly think you're going to need that?"

"What? Look . . . I'm sorry. I'm a bit confused. I don't know how I got here, and I don't know where I am."

"Why don't you sit down?" she said pleasantly. "We can talk. Would you like some wine? It's an excellent vintage."

Mathew made no move to sit. "Maybe you should first tell me how you know who I am, and who you are."

"My name is Teanna. I know a great deal about you, Mathew."

Teanna? He'd heard that name before but couldn't quite place it.

"Please don't be tedious," she said. "I promise I won't bite, and I'm sure you've noticed I'm unarmed."

She didn't appear to be carrying a weapon, and Mathew was beginning to feel foolish, standing there in front of a woman with his hand on his sword. So he took a deep breath to relax himself and sat down.

"Do you know what place this is?" he asked.

"Mm-hmm. I believe it's called Henderson."

"Henderson?"

"Mm-hmm."

"I've never heard of it."

"Well, I should think not. It's several thousand miles under the surface of the world. The Ancients built it. It's really quite interesting."

"Several thousand miles! But how—"

Teanna held up her hand to calm him. "I brought you here so we could talk privately."

"You brought me . . ."

Then it came to him. *Teanna!*

"You're Teanna d'Elso."

He stood up so abruptly, he knocked over his chair.

Teanna remained where she was, completely unruffled. "Please," she said, motioning for him to be seated again.

"But—"

"You do look so silly standing there, Mathew. If I wanted to harm you, I could have done so already."

Mathew felt his face go red, and he slowly sat down again. "I'm sorry. It's just that—"

"I'm Karas Duren's niece," she said, finishing the sentence for him. "He's quite insane, you know."

Mathew nodded in agreement.

"My mother can be equally excessive. You don't have to say anything," Teanna said, holding up her hand. "I'm aware of what happened to her. You didn't have a choice."

Mathew looked back somberly at the woman in front of him but didn't speak. After a few seconds he decided she was probably closer to his age than he had first thought.

"I'm sorry," he said. "Truly, I am. If there were some way—"

"Mathew," she said, putting her hand on his. "I understand. I know how much pain this has caused you. It wasn't as if either of them left you any choice."

A warm smile appeared on her face and she looked into his eyes. That was when he noticed the ring she was wearing.

Teanna saw his reaction. "That's right. This is one of the other rings. We're unique, you and I. I'm sure you've already guessed the Ancients created this place . . . just as they created these rings. But there's so much you don't know. You were right when you told Delain that my uncle hated for hatred's sake alone."

"How could you possibly know that?" Mathew whispered.

"As I said, there's a great deal you don't know yet—so much to learn. There's power here, Mathew. You can only begin to imagine it."

He sat back and looked at her more closely. Her smile seemed warm and genuine. What she'd said earlier was also true: Had she wanted to harm him, she could have done so while he was unconscious.

"Teanna, you said you brought me here. I don't remember anything. The last thing I recall was Duren—your uncle—creating a fireball and sending it at my people."

His body instinctively began to tighten as the memory flooded back into his mind.

"Shh," she said, squeezing his hand. "Delain is fine and so are your friends."

"But the battle—"

"Is over. I had a word with my cousin, Armand. Alor Satar has withdrawn its soldiers. There's no more need for the fighting to go on. My uncle is dead."

Mathew looked at her beautiful face and could find no deception.

"Why are we here?" he asked. "You said you brought me. I don't understand."

"I was about to tell you that. We're unique, you and I. Two of a kind. Although you don't know it yet, we have the ability to do anything the Ancients could do, and more. We shouldn't be fighting each other. If we work together, we could rebuild the world. People would follow us without question. We could do things—wonderful things. We could lead and bring order—"

"Order? I don't understand," he said slowly. "I don't want to be anybody's leader."

"Really? What *do* you want, Mathew?"

"I don't want anything. I guess I'd like things to be the same."

Teanna laughed. It was a warm rich sound, like perfectly struck crystal chimes.

"I'm afraid that's impossible. The world has changed. People will hear stories about the ring. They'll seek you out. They'll tell the stories to other people and they'll do the same. No," she said, squeezing his hand again. "It's too late for that. You and I must work together to help restore things."

"But what can we do?" Mathew asked.

Teanna reached forward and brushed the lock of hair off his forehead.

The fragrance of her perfume drifted across the table to him; her touch was warm and intoxicating.

"A man who's not afraid of his destiny can hold greatness in his hand, Mathew. We have the ability to lead— together. Nothing and no one can stand against us." Teanna's fingertips gently touched his cheek.

"What?" Mathew said, pulling away.

Teanna frowned. "Oh, dear, I'm afraid I've upset you."

"I don't want to be great, and I'm not interested in leading anybody. People's lives are their own."

Teanna took a deep breath and made a small clicking sound behind her teeth with her tongue.

"I knew this would be too much for you all at once. Father is right. I do need to be more patient. Oh, well . . . I suppose we can talk about it another time. There's really no rush. Now close your eyes and I'll bring us back. Sometimes it makes the stomach a little sensitive."

"But . . ."

Before Mathew could say anything else, the deserted town faded. A green light enveloped him and a sound like rushing water filled his ears. It felt like he was being pulled into a giant black funnel.

Seconds later he was standing on a hill at the far end of Ardon Field. There was no sign of Teanna. The fighting had ended, just as she said. In the west, the sun was just above the treetops. Mathew looked toward Delain's tents and could see that campfires had been lit. His friends were there too. Though his head was still swimming, he took a deep breath to clear his thoughts. After a moment, he began walking across the field toward the flickering orange glow of the fires, Teanna's words still fresh in his mind.

Sennia, The Abbey at Bacora

MATHEW LEWIN STOOD ON THE RAMPARTS HIGH ATOP
the sanctuary of Barcora, looking out across the plain at
four riders who were moving steadily closer. Lara put an
arm around his shoulders and pulled her cloak tighter
against the late autumn chill. It was almost six months
since the battle at Ardon Field. Akin and Fergus had left
to return to Devondale, taking Daniel with them to recu-
perate. Before they went, they promised to stop in Elberton and deliver Father Thomas's letter to Ceta Woodall.
Lara had helped the priest compose it, but refused to say
anything about its contents. Somewhere below in the
main courtyard, Mathew could hear the sound of blades
striking each other. Collin was taking a fencing lesson
from Father Thomas.

With official duties to perform and a country to run,
Gawl had returned to his palace in Barcora. Though he
came to visit several times in the past few months to see
how they were getting on, he only remained a short
while. The king was not on the best of terms with the
clergy.

For their part, the priests were content to leave Mathew
alone to study in their library. He passed the majority of
his days poring through the books they had preserved
down through the centuries. Most ancient texts were

dust-covered and musty, almost illegible. Fortunately, there were copies and translations available. After weeks and weeks of work, he began to make sense of what he was reading. It often required consulting several versions of the same book. Learning the old language was a painstaking and laborious process. Wherever possible, he avoided translations as well as the copies, electing to read the original version because what had been reproduced often contained the interpretations of others, which colored the facts.

He knew for a certainty now that his was one of the last of the eight rose gold rings the Ancients had created, confirming what Teanna had told him. He read of the terrible war his ancestors had fought, virtually destroying all of mankind. Several of the texts contained references to something called the "*horror*." And he knew that toward the end there had been a desperate search to find and destroy all of the rose gold rings, with the exception of the last eight. Though Mathew had been unable to learn exactly what the books spoke of, a vague suspicion had begun to form in his mind. In recent months he had stopped wearing the ring altogether. It was back on the leather cord around his neck. The answers were out there.

Somewhere beneath the earth in a vast underground cavern was a town called Henderson. He didn't know where it was or how to get there. He had found several references to an entrance located a thousand miles to the west across the wasted lands, but for now that would have to wait.

In the speech to his men after the battle, Delain promised to rebuild their country, making it a nation of just and honorable laws. Mathew hoped with all his heart that would be so as he watched Constable Quinn ride up to the gate.

GLOSSARY

al Mouli, Ra'id	Kalifar or leader of the Bajan Nation.
Alman, Silas	Member of Devondale council.
Alidar	God of Coribar.
Alor Satar	Duren's country, located to the northeast of Elgaria.
Anderon	Capital of Elgaria.
Ashford	A town in Elgaria mentioned by Lara and Akin while they visit Elberton.
Ashots	A religious sect in Elgaria. Their priests don't marry and they celebrate the Lord's Day on the seventh day of the week.
Barcora	Capital of Sennia and home of the famous religious sanctuary.
Bajan	Country to the east of Elgaria.
Berne, the	Name of the southern province in Elgaria where Elberton is located.
Blue Goose	Tavern in Elberton.
Broken Hill	A town some distance from Devondale where Lara's mother rode from by herself.
Bruhier, Asad Arif	Sultan of Cincar.
Bruhier, Tarif Ja'far	Alias used by Father Thomas in Tyraine.
Calthorpe, Thom	Coach of the Mechlen team.

Cincar	Country located northeast of Elgaria; ally of Karas Duren.
Coast Road	Road running along the Elgarian coast near Tyraine.
Coribar	Large island nation to the south of Elgaria.
d'Elso, Marsa Duren	Karas Duren's sister. Queen of Nyngary.
d'Elso, Teanna	Marsa d'Elso's daughter, Karas Duren's niece.
Danus, Abenard	Commander of Tyraine occupation force from Vargorth.
Darcy, Stefn	Devondale boy killed by Orlocks with Thad Layton's son.
d'Lorien, Cormac	The man who Father Thomas killed years before he became a priest.
Donal, Oliver	Captain of the *Wave Dancer*.
Douhalia	Ship that Daniel and Akin sail on from Elberton to Tyraine.
Duren, Karas	King of Alor Satar.
Duren, Kyne	Grand Duke, Karas Duren's brother.
Elberton	Town in Elgaria.
Elgaria	Mathew's country.
Elgars	The currency used in Elgaria.
Emson, Lucas	Village smith of Devondale.
Enders, Beckie	Devondale girl who flirted with Collin.
Farolain, Lee	Mathew's teammate and Marla Farolain's son; went after the Darcy boy.
Farsighter	Name of Daniel's invention.
Fenton, Ben	Devondale resident, killed by Orlocks.
Galwin River	Located near Sturga to the east of Devondale.
Gawl	Also known as Baegawl Atherny.

A sculptor by choice, the King of Sennia.

Gibb, Akin	Silversmith. Fergus Gibb's brother.
Gibb, Fergus	Silversmith. Akin Gibb's brother.
Gravenhage	A town near Devondale; participated in a fencing meet.
Grimly, Margaret	Owner of a dress shop in Devondale.
Henderson	A town one thousand miles below earth.
Herne, Lt. Darnel	A soldier who came to Devondale for the first fencing meet.
Idaeus, Gerard	Commander of northern army charged with the defense of Anderon.
Kesherit	A board game.
Kyat, Naydim	Prince of Cincar and commander of their army.
Lang, Garon	A friend and teammate of Mathew. Killed by Orlocks.
Lewin, Bran	Mathew's father. Killed by Berke Ramsey.
Lewin, Janel	Mathew's mother.
Lewin, Mathew	Devondale resident.
Kalifar	Title for leader of Bajani held by Ra'id al Mouli.
Kraelin, Aeneas	Duke of Queen's Province of northern Elgaria. Commander of Anderon defense forces.
Layton, Thad	Devondale farmer whose son was killed. Believed to have been murdered by the Orlocks.
Levad	A religious sect to which Father Thomas belongs. They celebrate the Lord's Day on the sixth day of the week; allowed to marry.
Luzon Valley	Site of the last battle in the Sibuyan War.

Malach, Delain   Prince of Elgaria.

Malach, King   King of Elgaria.

Marshall, Ilona   Devondale resident. Danced with Collin.

Mastrich   A town Mathew once visited.

Mechlen   A town near Devondale; participated in the fencing meet.

Melfort   A town in Elgaria.

Miller, Askel   Devondale resident. Collin's father.

Miller, Collin   Devondale resident.

Mirdan   A country to the northeast of Elgaria. Capital is Toland.

Naismith, Giles   Gravenhage resident.

Naismith, Terren   Giles's brother and a soldier with Lieutenant Herne.

Nobody's Inn   Name of the inn located in Elberton. See also Ceta Woodall.

Nyngary   Country situated east of Elgaria. See also Marsa d'Elso.

Orlocks   Creatures that fought with Alor Satar during the Sibuyan War. Questionable eating habits.

Quinn, Jeram   Constable from Anderon.

Queen's Province   Northernmost province of Elgaria, where Anderon is located.

Palmer, Lara   Devondale resident. Also known by alias as Lina Palmeri Batul Asad.

Palmer, Truemen   Mayor of Devondale.

Ramsey, Berke   Gravenhage resident. Member of the fencing team. Killed by Mathew Lewin after the death of Mathew's father.

Roeselar   The longest river in Elgaria.

Rozon, Jerrel   Coach of the Gravenhage team. Former general in Elgarian army.

Rocoi   Capital of Alor Satar.

Royd   Name of commander of regiment sent to Senecal with Father Thomas.

Senecal	Peninsula to southern end of Sennia. Mentioned by Father Thomas on board the *Wave Dancer*.
Sennia	A country to the southwest of Elgaria.
Seth, King	King of Vargoth.
Sibuyan	A people who fought the western nations along with Orlocks in a war twenty years before Mathew's birth.
Sindri, Evert	Member of Gravenhage team whom Collin hits with his quarterstaff.
Southern Sea	Ocean that *Wave Dancer* sails on from Elberton to Tyraine.
Stermark	A city in northern Elgaria, Queen's Province, attacked by Duren.
Stone Pheasant	Name of the tavern in Tyraine where Father Thomas told Mathew and Collin to meet him.
Sturga	A large trading town on the Galwin River. Visited by Harol Longworth.
Tanner, Cyril	Innkeeper and proprietor of the Rose and Crown in Devondale.
Thomas, Siward	Devondale resident. Priest. Also goes by the names Miles Vernon and Tarif Ja'far Bruhier.
Toland	Northernmost city in Mirdan.
Tilda	Mathew's horse.
Tavish, Will	Worked for Ceta Woodall; attacked Mathew in streets of Elberton.
Tyraine	Port city in southern Elgaria.
Tyron Fel	A town near Devondale. Had team fencing competition with the Devondale team.
Vance, Jaim	Apprentice aboard the *Wave Dancer*. Younger brother to Pryor.
Vance, Pryor	Apprentice aboard the *Wave Dancer*. Older brother to Jaim.

Vargoth	Country to the southeast of Elgaria; hires its soldiers out as mercenaries. See also King Seth.
Vanko, Notas	Colonel of Vargoth mercenaries. Second in command to Abenard Danus.
Wain, Randal	Owner of a shop of armaments in Devondale.
Ward, Zachariah	First mate aboard *Wave Dancer*.
Warren, Daniel	Devondale resident. Mathew's friend. Inventor.
Wave Dancer	Name of the ship Mathew sailed on from Elberton to Tyraine. See also Oliver Donal.
Werth Province	The province where Devondale is located.
Westrey's stream	Landmark near Devondale.
Woodall, Ceta	Innkeeper of the Nobody's Inn in Elberton.
Wycroft, Lucien	Doctor in Elberton. Discussed the role of the subconscious mind with Mathew.